MW01611750

AN ORPHAN OF SCOTLAND

A totally heartbreaking and unputdownable page-turner

GWEN KIRKWOOD

The Maxwell Family Quartet Book 1

Originally published as
The Laird of Lochandee

Revised edition 2023
Joffe Books, London
www.joffebooks.com

First published by Accent Press Ltd. in 2013
as The Laird of Lochandee

This paperback edition was first published
in Great Britain in 2023

Cover art by Jarmila Takač

ISBN: 978-1-80405-804-6

CHAPTER ONE

'Well!' Gertrude Maxwell gasped. 'I can't believe Connor O'Brian would write after all this time. And such a letter.'

'He must be desperate,' Cameron agreed. Since the seizure he was not the energetic, decisive man he had once been, but his mind still functioned clearly — except when his wife administered more of the medicine than the doctor had recommended. He had a way of considering his words now, but once uttered there was no mistaking his opinion.

The letter had been addressed only to him but he knew Gertrude longed to snatch the single page and read it for herself. He and Connor were old friends; they had attended the same village school, all those years ago.

'He must feel his end is near.' Cameron sighed with regret for a youth long past. 'I'll . . .' 'We'll ignore the letter.'

'Gertie! You canna mean that. He needs reassurance that his lassie will have a roof over her head.'

'I do mean it.' Her mouth tightened into a thin line.

'Where's the Christian spirit you're always preaching, woman?'

'I've told you, Cameron . . .'

'Oh aye? Well, I'm not finished yet. I'll have my way over this, Gertie. We can't see Connor's bairn without a home, and neither kith nor kin to help her.'

1

She stared at him. Her mouth opened, then shut with a snap. Even in the early days, when he was fit and strong, Cameron had rarely argued, but he had always got his own way when something mattered to him.

Those days were gone. Cameron needed her to care for him now. He was dependant on her to keep the farm going, along with Meg and Willie. It was harder since the war — the Great War that had taken away her beloved Josh to fight, and to die, in the trenches. Only this week, Lloyd George had announced that Germany would have to pay for the devastation in France, but that would not bring Josh back, or the thousands of other young men.

'The lassie can bide with us for as long as she needs a home.' Cameron's tone was still firm, but gentler. 'You're always saying you need more help now that I'm not fit to work. She will help you.'

'I have a daughter of my own to help.'

'Aye, you have that. And fine you know Meg would be happier married to Peter Sedgeman and looking after his wee bairnies. You can give her your blessing and stop making her feel she'd be deserting us if you'll only give Connor's lassie a home.'

'I will not see my only daughter waste her life slaving after another woman's family!'

'She loves bairns. You've told her often enough she'll never have any of her own.'

'Don't change the subject. When I need a maid I'll find my own. There's folk everywhere looking for work. I don't want a brat of Connor O'Brian's in my home.'

'Gertie!' Cameron fixed her with his steady gaze. She turned away. He didn't understand. How could he? He didn't know the memories Connor O'Brian's letter was awakening. She felt the old panic rising, tightening her chest. The past came flooding back. She could not bear to have the daughter of Mhairi MacLean and Connor O'Brian under her roof — a constant reminder of her rejection, her humiliation — and the horror of it.

They had all attended the same school, and later the same village dances. Gertrude had been an only child. Her mother had borne two boys before her. They had died in infancy. There had been another baby after her, but he too, had died at birth. So she had been doubly cherished and shamefully indulged.

'My ain lassie, ye're a survivor,' her father had told her often. He had doted on her, buying her the smartest wee pony he could afford and teaching her to ride at an early age. When she was bossy at school it was because she was used to having her own way.

Mhairi MacLean was the daughter of a shepherd and walked three miles or more to school, and back in the afternoon. She had rarely mixed with other children and had never seen so many faces until she started school. She was dark and pretty and very shy and Cameron Maxwell and Connor O'Brian had taken her under their wing with youthful chivalry. Gertrude had been envious, until she realised that Mhairi gave everyone that same shy smile, including herself.

As the years passed Mhairi's gentle manner made her popular with all the children, especially the younger ones. When they were thirteen, Cameron's sister, Cathie, started school. In spite of the eight years difference in their ages she adored Mhairi and they had much in common. They smiled and helped, and rarely criticised, so they were liked by everyone from the stern Dominie to the youngest pupil. Gertrude resented such effortless popularity while she strived to gain attention.

Cameron had inherited the Maxwell family's musical skill. He could entertain pleasingly with his harmonica by the time he was ten. As they grew older and attended the local dances Cameron was frequently invited to take a turn with the fiddle. Reluctantly he left Connor to partner both Gertrude and Mhairi in the reels and jigs. Gertrude always had the prettiest dresses, no hand-me-downs or makeovers. Whatever her heart craved her father bought for her and she revelled in the attention of the charming Connor, but he was not to be bought.

Connor O'Brian had a smile which could charm the birds from the trees, but he had a mind of his own — except when it was fuddled with alcohol.

When a letter arrived from his uncle, Connor travelled the fifteen miles with eager anticipation. Uncle Sean had no children of his own, but he did have a thriving blacksmith's business and he wanted to train his nephew in the smiddy. Connor would take over when he grew too old to do the work himself, especially shoeing the big Clydesdale horses.

Connor was delighted at the prospect, but he loved Mhairi MacLean with all his heart. He could not bear the thought of being separated from her so he asked her to marry him and go with him, swearing he would decline his uncle's offer if she refused.

Even now, standing in her own kitchen at Windlebrae, gazing back down the years, Gertrude could not suppress a shudder. She remembered the shock when she learned Connor was to marry Mhairi.

She couldn't believe it. She wouldn't believe it. How could Connor choose the meek, mild mannered Mhairi for his bride? Gertrude would not accept it. Connor was hers. She wanted him. She needed him. She couldn't bear to see him with Mhairi. She made plans.

She underestimated the strength of true love — Connor's love for the gentle Mhairi.

Oh, he had fallen into her trap all right. He had taken all that Gertrude had offered so freely — but only because he was too drunk to resist.

In the cold light of the following day he had come near to hating both himself, and her. Worse, his dismay and remorse were not because he had taken away her own virginity, but because he had betrayed the trust of Mhairi, his dearest love. Even now Gertrude felt the chagrin, the disbelief, the humiliation — and then the anger.

Nothing would sway Connor from his chosen path.

Gertrude shivered as events she had thought forgotten, memories she had swept into the past, came rushing back.

Nothing had prepared her for the horror which resulted from her night's lusting. The shame burned afresh in her mind as though it had been yesterday. The disgrace to her family. The prospect had been unbearable. She had considered drowning herself in the river. She would hang herself from the beam in her father's barn. She had been half-crazed with worry and shame.

Cameron had been quietly devastated by Connor's marriage to Mhairi. He was bereft, but they were dear friends and he summoned all the control and generosity of spirit he could muster. He wished them well and played the fiddle as they danced on a cloud of happiness. Only Gertrude guessed his true feelings and another plan came to her mind. Life was precious and Cameron would be an easy prey while his own heart was sore.

In desperation she resorted to another trap, more of the raw whisky from her father's secret still.

Her hasty marriage to Cameron Maxwell had saved her from the ultimate shame and disgrace and in return she had vowed to be a good wife, but when Josh was born, a fine boy to be premature, Cameron had eyed her keenly, expectantly. She had seen the questions in his eyes but she had offered no explanation, uttered no confession. In silence he had turned away from her, but as he looked down at the sleeping infant she saw his expression soften. He was kindly, like his sister, Cathy, but Cameron could speak with his eyes, without a word passing his lips and she saw the doubts, the questions. She pursed her lips and no words were spoken, and so she had convinced herself the secret was hers alone.

She did her duty to Cameron, working hard in the house and dairy at Windlebrae, the Ayrshire farm they had rented, with help from their respective families. Two years later Meg had been born. They had lost a baby the following year causing Cameron concern for her health and drawing them closer. The following year Willie had been safely delivered and Gertrude felt she had repaid Cameron for her past deceit. She had given him a daughter and a son, while she had her beloved Josh.

Several years passed before the calm was shattered by the news of another birth, another child to be given a home at Windlebrae. Gertrude did not want another baby to feed and clothe and care for, least of all a bastard who would bring shame to her own children. She hurled every possible argument at Cameron. He listened in silence, but he remained adamant and tension mounted.

Secretly Gertrude was afraid the gossips would awaken old rumours and tongues would be set wagging. She was obsessed with her love for Josh and she could not bear anything which might destroy his respect for her. She wanted the best for all her children, but especially for Josh.

Cameron considered himself responsible for the baby — bastard or not.

'He will be brought up the same as Josh and Meg and Will,' he had insisted. 'His name will be Ross and he will be just as much a Maxwell as they are.' He had given her one of those steady stares of his. Although he had refrained from mentioning Josh's birth, Gertrude had known it was in his mind as clearly as if he had shouted it from the rooftops. Josh did not resemble either of them and as he grew older his black hair and dimpling smile bore unmistakable resemblance to Connor O'Brian.

In the end she had gone away from Windlebrae and returned with the baby, passing him off as her own, forestalling questions and wagging tongues. The four young Maxwells had grown up believing themselves to be brothers and sister.

There was no future to be considered now for Josh. There was nothing to make her obey Cameron this time and she would never take Mhairi MacLean's brat into her home.

As though he had read her thoughts Cameron's mouth tightened.

'You liked Connor well when we were all young. I've always known how things were. I never held it against you

6

— or young Josh. So now you will not hold a spite against Mhairi's bairn, or so help me, the whole parish will hear about it.'

Gertrude stared at him. After all these years he had finally uttered the words she had dreaded. Guilty colour stained her sallow skin, even to the hollows at her scrawny neck. Still his gaze held hers. Her heart hammered and her eyes fell. Cameron nodded, knowing she valued her reputation, her standing in the eyes of the minister, the kirk, the congregation. Her character would be worth nothing if she turned an innocent, homeless lassie out into the road.

A sudden clatter of buckets came from the adjoining dairy. Relief surged through Gertrude at the interruption.

'The milking must be finished. I must boil up the porridge. They'll be hungry.' She hurried to the gleaming black range. The fire had settled to a steady glow but she poked it agitatedly, striving for composure.

'Tam was early with the post,' Meg said, coming to stand at the door which led from the dairy into the kitchen. She was drying her hands on a piece of rough, well-washed towel, which had once been a meal sack.

'Aye, he's going to Duncan Watson's funeral.' Cameron grimaced. 'That's another one away. Probably be my turn next.'

'Please don't say that,' Meg pleaded. She loved her father deeply.

'Well it's true lassie, and for all the good I am here I'd be as well in my box.'

'Not yet you wouldn't, Father!' Ross Maxwell called cheerfully, moving to stand at Meg's side, sharing the rough towel. He towered head and shoulders above her, his blue eyes sparkling with laughter. 'You haven't taught me to play all your jigs and reels on the fiddle. How can I take your place at the dancing if I don't know the tunes?'

'You're doing fine from what Tam was telling me,' Cameron told him with a glow of pride. He surveyed the tall, straight figure of the youngest Maxwell. Why had Gertie never been able to love him, he wondered, shaking his head. She had done her best to knock the laughter out of him.

He wondered if he had ever really understood the woman who had taken his name and borne his children. Sometimes he had blamed himself for the hardness in her. When Mhairi MacLean had married Connor, he had known that anyone else would always be second best for him. It had seemed natural that he and Gertie should find solace with each other. Theirs had been a marriage of convenience, but Gertie had wanted it and she had planned for it. Too late, he had guessed the reason.

She was capable, hard-working, thrifty and clean, God-fearing — but he had often wished there had been more laughter in her. Since Josh's death, in the Flanders mud, there had been little but bitterness and bigotry. She had barely shown kindness, even to Meg, her own flesh and blood and the best of daughters. Meg reminded him of his sister Cathy — too caring, too gentle for her own good.

It was three years since the end of the war. Ships were bringing in huge cargoes of cheap corn, yet men were unable to afford bread and milk. They haunted street corners, desperate for work. Discontent was rife. So far his own family had been fortunate in comparison, in spite of his illness.

Meg and Ross drew in their chairs, hungry for the steaming plates of porridge.

'Did Tam bring any letters?' Meg asked, her dark brows raised quizzically.

'Aye, he did. He brought a letter from an old friend. His name is Connor O'Brian.'

'O'Brian?' Ross frowned, and rubbed his temple thoughtfully. 'The name seems familiar . . . Surely that was the name of the blacksmith who helped me out when my horse cast a shoe? It was the first time I took your place at the fiddling.'

'That's right . . . the MacEwan wedding, over at Bonnybrae. You met O'Brian's lassie, I believe?'

Ross supped several spoonfuls of porridge as his mind moved back to the evening two years ago. His father had already suffered a seizure and he was to take his place entertaining at a wedding feast. He had been seventeen and nervous. His tension had increased unbearably when his horse cast a shoe, threatening to make him late.

'What was she like?' Cameron prompted.

'Who? Oh, the O'Brian child. She was about thirteen I suppose. Not very tall, but she was a spirited young imp.' He frowned, remembering how she had told him he would need to go to the next village to get his horse shod. It was a three mile detour and he suspected she was misleading him. Tension had made him angry but she would have let him make the journey if her father had not appeared and asked what business he had with his daughter. They had been very close — very protective of each other — father and daughter.

Ross remembered feeling a pang of envy at the bond they shared. She had not wanted her father to blow up the bellows to shoe any more horses that night. Later she explained that O'Brian had suffered pains in his chest and the doctor had warned him to take care.

'Was she like her father?' Cameron persisted.

'Not really. She moved so lightly it was almost as though she danced along on her bare feet. Her father was dark and thick set.'

'Aye, that's Connor all right. Tell me more about his lassie?'

'There's nothing to tell, except she made me angry. She was sitting on a wee humpback bridge at the entrance to the village so I stopped to ask directions. She seemed to want me out of the village almost before I had even entered it.' He remembered the way she had swung her legs to dry them after paddling in the burn. Her hair was in a long thick pleat down her back but it curled in damp tendrils around her face. He had not been sure whether she was laughing at him or angry with him. Her greenish blue eyes had sparkled as brightly as the ripples of water glinting in the sunlight.

'O'Brian attended to my horse, in spite of his daughter's protests. He instructed her to bring me a glass of buttermilk and a scone. He would have detained me longer when he knew who I was. I remember telling you he seemed eager for news of you. Why has he written after all this time?'

He sensed the tension in the air and glanced to the other end of the table. His mother's eyes were fixed on her porridge, the thin line of her mouth making her lips invisible. His heart sank. What had he done now? He always seemed to be the cause of their mother's displeasure. As a child he had often been hurt and bewildered by her caustic tongue but she had never shown him tenderness. Sometimes he had considered running away.

Meg, nearly ten years older than himself, had been more of a mother to him, offering comfort, cuddling him when he was frightened, calming his temper when he grew into a rebellious teenager. As he grew older he had learned to hide his feelings. Some people thought him arrogant but Meg understood it was only a shell for his own protection.

He longed to make a life of his own. He dreamed of renting a farm, of proving that he was just as good as any other son, but he had no money and no hope of earning any. Their mother handled everything now and she believed food and clothes were more than sufficient payment no matter how hard he worked. Someday he would go off to the hiring fairs to find work with some other farmer if things did not improve. Only the thought of leaving his father held him back.

'Why did Mr O'Brian write you a letter, Father?' Meg repeated Ross's question.

'He's dying.' Cameron's reply was stark. 'He's worried about his daughter, Rachel. He wants us to give her a home.'

Gertie gave a snort of contempt.

'Ah, now I see . . .' Ross nodded.

'Her mother died when the lassie would be about eight or nine,' Cameron Maxwell mused. 'Connor had no relations this side o' the water.'

'What about her mother's family?' Ross asked.

'A bunch of weaklings.' Gertie spoke derisively.

'Her two brothers were fine men,' Cameron Maxwell protested. 'The younger one was killed in France at the end of the war. The older one died with consumption. Neither of them married so O'Brian's bairn will be scarce o' relations.'

'Then of course she must come here . . .' Meg jumped as her mother thumped her fist upon the scrubbed table.

'No one asked your opinion my girl!' Meg clenched her fingers. She had a tender heart, but she hated arguments.

'But surely if the child has nowhere to live . . .'

'She's not a child. She's nearly sixteen, and if she takes after her father she'll be a born philanderer already.'

'That's not fair, Gertie,' Cameron protested. 'Connor was true to Mhairi. Even after she died he never married again. Anyway, the lassie will be coming here. She will help with the dairy and the hens. Connor writes that she's a good hand at the baking and she can churn butter to match the best.'

'Typical of him to boast.' Gertie snapped. Cameron ignored her.

'When you've finished in the dairy, Meg, come and write a reply for me.' Meg glanced at her mother. There were few letters written at Windlebrae and it was usually her mother who wrote them since her father had suffered the seizure.

Both Ross and Meg were glad to escape to the warmth and peace of the byre where their brother, Willie, was already feeding the cows with chopped turnips.

Willie lived in a neat house just a quarter of a mile from Windlebrae Farm road end. He, too, had been glad to escape from their mother's bitter tongue. He had a wife called Ruth and a three- year-old daughter, Annie. Ruth had recently given birth to a son. They planned to christen him Donald Joseph, but already Gertie called him her 'wee Josh'.

Fortunately Ruth had a placid temperament, though Willie declared she had an iron will underneath. He insisted she was the only woman he knew who was a match for his mother.

'I wouldn't like to be in the lassie's shoes if she's coming here against mother's will,' Willie remarked now.

'Father says she has nowhere else to go.' Meg's eyes were troubled.

'Do you think she will help with the work if she comes?'

'I expect so.' Ross's face broke into a grin. 'We shall have to unite. It will make a change to have someone else to share the sharp end of Mother's tongue.'

'You're a hard-hearted wretch!' Willie laughed, punching him playfully. 'You can stick up for yourself, but it's different for a young lassie alone in the world.'

'I think we should all be extra kind to her. It will be lovely to have someone young in the house, but I hope mother will soon get used to her.' Meg said.

Willie and Ross raised sceptical eyebrows but even they could not have guessed the repercussions Gertrude's actions would have on their lives, and the generation to come.

* * *

Two weeks later the black-edged envelope arrived with news of Connor O'Brian's death.

'I wish I had been able to attend his funeral,' Cameron sighed, 'for old times' sake. Don't you remember, Gertie, the grand fun we had when we were all at the village school? It was a pity we lost touch when Connor moved away. He always had a great way with animals, especially horses.'

'Well you're not fit to go anywhere. That's the end of it so stop your foolish reminiscing.'

'I made a promise to a dying man. Ross has met Rachel O'Brian. He can take my place at the funeral. He must bring the lassie back with him.'

'No! I told you, I will not have her here . . .'

'A promise is a promise.'

Gertie stared at him tight lipped. He really meant it. She had always been a little in awe of that resolute gleam in Cameron's eyes. He had rarely raised his voice, or his hand, to any of his family, but they respected him and they all knew better than to defy that look.

'I don't want Mhairi MacLean's brat under my roof.'

'Windlebrae is still mine, Gertie. While I live, I am master in my own house. If the lassie needs a home Ross must bring her back.' Gertie glared at him, then turned on her heel and left the kitchen.

She did not return until it was time for the midday meal. Long before then Cameron felt a desperate need to relieve himself. He realised this was Gertie's way of punishing him. She had not even left his two sticks near his chair. They were propped in a corner by the door.

It was a supreme effort of will to struggle outside and down to the privy. In spite of the smells which pervaded the earth closet when the wooden lid was lifted, Cameron sat for a long time, leaning forward on his sticks, his eyes closed. His lean buttocks felt as though they had been welded to the hole in the long wooden bench. He hauled himself up with a sigh of resignation. Far better if the good Lord had taken me and left Connor O'Brian to care for his own lassie, he thought.

Eventually he regained his wooden armchair beside the kitchen fire. He was exhausted and Meg and Ross found him sleeping uncomfortably when they came in for their meal.

The sleep had refreshed Cameron, even though he had wakened with a crick in his neck. His resolve hardened and he gave them the news about the funeral.

'I want you to go in my place, Ross. Drop the milk off at the station then you can take the pony and trap. If the lassie wants to bide a while with us at Windlebrae you must bring her back with you.'

'But surely Willie should take your place, Father?' Ross did not relish the task of hauling a weeping child all the way back to Windlebrae.

'You have met her, and her father. It will be better if you go. Treat her kindly.'

Meg and Ross glanced to the other end of the table. Gertrude's face seemed carved in stone and Meg's heart went out to Rachel O'Brian.

CHAPTER TWO

It was a cold day at the end of February, but even allowing for the chill wind, and the ravages of sorrow, Ross was shocked by the frail appearance of Rachel O'Brian. Only two years ago she had sparkled with youth and joy, her smile that of a mischievous child, her eyes glowing with challenge. The ashen-faced young woman he saw now looked as though a puff of wind might blow her away. She was clad from head to toe in black, her bright hair hidden beneath her hat.

The whole of the village, indeed most of the parish, seemed to have turned out to pay their last respects to the blithe and obliging blacksmith who had tended their horses, mended ploughs and fashioned fire irons. Apparently the son of a neighbouring blacksmith had taken over his trade. Ross listened silently to the whispered comments of the men who overflowed from the house into the garden, waiting to hear the minister's last blessing. He learned that O'Brian's successor was hard and unyielding. If a man did not have the money in his hand his horse was turned away unshod.

'Connor couldna bear to see a horse neglected for want o' a copper or two.'

'That's true enough, but he was too trusting for his own good. There's some who could have afforded his fee twice over but still pleaded poverty. I'll wager they'll walk away from his lassie today like the hypocrites they are.'

'Aye, ye're right there, John! And there's one o' them!' The man gave a nod and a knowing glance. Ross followed his eyes to the undertaker and the gleaming hearse pulled by a black horse.

On the way back from the graveside a man fell into step beside Ross.

'Would I be right in thinking ye're a Maxwell from Windlebrae?'

'Why, yes. Yes, I am.' Ross smiled down at the middle-aged man beside him. The man nodded.

'I'd know that smile anywhere,' he said softly, almost to himself. 'My name is Jim MacDonald. I'm a distant relative of Gertrude's. I live down in Dumfriesshire now, not far frae the Border. I came up for my aunt's funeral. She was ninety-one. It's a good age, eh? I'm doing a bit o' visiting while I'm here. Looking up old friends, and a few remaining relations. Maybe I'll call in at Windlebrae . . .' He chatted on about the trains he had to catch until someone else came and interrupted. Ross did not see the man again.

Towards the end of the day a crippled old woman laid a gnarled hand on Ross's arm. He had noticed she had scarcely left Rachel O'Brian's side all day. She bid him accompany her to her cottage a few yards down the village street. Rachel herself had not yet spoken to him but he had been struck by her quiet dignity as she talked briefly with each one who had turned out to see her father on his last journey. Now, seeing the old woman take his arm, she came towards them. When she raised her face to his he saw that her eyes were red-rimmed and she looked weary enough to drop where she stood.

'This is Mrs Ferguson, Mr Maxwell. Nearly everyone calls her Granny Ferguson. If you will go with her I will follow in a few minutes.' She looked around the nearly deserted living room and her thin face crumpled. She swallowed convulsively, striving for control. 'I just have to make sure everything is tidy, then pay Mr Steele for the use of the hearse before I leave. I shall not keep you waiting long.'

Ross nodded. 'Take your time,' he said gruffly, a little overawed by her youthful dignity and competence.

'My box is packed. It's at Granny's cottage.'

'You come with us now, lassie,' Minnie Ferguson hissed softly through the gaps in her teeth. She tugged at Rachel's sleeve. 'You can leave Jake Steele to me. Rumour has it he owed your father more than you're ever likely to owe him.'

'Granny Ferguson's right, lass.' Another woman, who was flicking away imaginary specks, paused beside them. 'I'll see that everything's tidy here for Mistress Black — not that the besom deserves it!' she muttered angrily. She looked at Ross curiously, then explained. 'Her man took over the smiddy last year, but the Laird promised Connor that he and Miss Rachel could keep the house for as long as they needed it. Master Black and his wife could scarcely wait for the poor man to draw his last breath before they were on the doorstep asking how soon this wee lass would be out. I ken, because I live next door, and there's not much I miss.' Again Ross found himself nodding but a gentle tug on his arm prompted him.

'I must go. I'm sure Miss O'Brian is grateful for your help.'

'Aye, I ken fine she is. Just you see your folks take good care o' her. She's needing a kindly body to care after all she's been through.' The woman gave Rachel an unexpected hug. 'Ye were always a good-natured wee lassie,' she added huskily. Ross watched helplessly as tears filled Rachel's eyes. Minnie Ferguson saw too and ushered her firmly towards the door.

'Come on now, lassie. My old legs will not hold me up much longer this day.' She glanced back at the empty living room and shook her white head wonderingly. 'I don't know where all the food went.'

It was true, Ross reflected. The table had been laden with bannocks and oatcakes, scones, butter and jam, a cheese, as well as gingerbread and apple pies.

'Everyone has been kind,' Rachel murmured wearily. 'Almost every woman in the village brought something.'

'It was no more than you deserved, lassie — you and your father. There'll be many a one wishes they could do more to help now.' The old woman sighed. 'If only I could have . . .'

'I know, Granny, I know.' Rachel squeezed the old woman's arm as she helped her hobble with painful slowness across the village street to her own tiny one-roomed cottage.

The early darkness of the February day was almost upon them as Ross and Rachel set out on the journey back to Windlebrae. Unknown to her mother, Meg had stowed a blanket beneath the seat of the trap. Ross remembered her instructions and tucked it round Rachel as if she was the child he remembered. He buttoned up his cape collar and pulled his father's hat more closely onto his head against the rising wind. Soon he would stop to light the two lanterns which would guide them homeward, but for the time being he was intent on making the best speed the pony could manage in the remaining light.

It was dark and bitterly cold by the time Ross drove the trap up the final stretch. They had talked little on the journey. He had sensed the deepening sadness settling over his young companion now that the day's events were past, but eventually exhaustion claimed her. After several jerky attempts to stay awake fatigue overcame her. When her head fell against his shoulder Ross leaned closer so that she might rest more comfortably.

A single lamp burned in the kitchen at Windlebrae, and even it was turned low. Ross frowned. Surely they had not all gone to bed? His parents slept in the box bed at one side of the fire. Surely mother could have waited for us, he thought wearily. He was tired, cold and hungry. He needed to attend to the pony, but how could he leave an exhausted young stranger alone in a dark and silent house?

Meg must have been listening for them. Seconds later she appeared in her flannel nightgown with a large knitted shawl pulled around her shoulders.

'I told you to get to your bed, girl!' Her mother's stern voice came from the dark depths of the alcove. So! His mother had not been asleep, he thought indignantly, but she had not uttered a word of welcome.

'They must be cold and hungry, Mother,' Meg protested and for once she turned her back defiantly. 'You must be Rachel.' She gave an encouraging smile and drew the forlorn figure towards the rag rug in front of the hearth. 'I made some gruel earlier,' she added looking at Ross. 'Or there is broth left in the pot. I'll poke up the fire and hook it on the sway to heat. It will be ready by the time you have bedded the pony.'

'I'm ready for it, and I'm sure Miss O'Brian must need something to warm her. Thank you, Meg.' Ross's eyes met hers, expressing his gratitude. She gave him a wry smile. They both knew their mother was going to need a great deal of humouring. Even so they were taken aback when Gertie hauled herself up on her elbow and spoke with the icy tones Ross knew so well.

'You girl! Your room is through there.' She pointed to a darkened corner of the kitchen, next to the larder. Meg gasped, but her mother went on remorselessly. 'Be out at the byre by five o'clock tomorrow morning. Don't be late for the milking.'

'Mother! She canna sleep in there! My bed is plenty big enough for two . . .' Meg protested.

'That's where she'll sleep if she stays here.'

'Th-thank you ma'am,' Rachel stammered, but she could not suppress a shudder. Where was the kindly welcome her father had assured her she would receive?

'I shall be all right,' she whispered in a choked voice as her eyes met Meg's. She looked and sounded so young and dejected that Meg almost wept. The room her mother had prepared had once been a larder for storing salt meat because it was the coldest corner in the house. It had a single pane of glass, no more than nine inches square. It was bare and damp.

'Let . . . lassie sleep with . . . Meg.' Cameron's voice, slurred with drug induced sleep, rumbled from somewhere behind his wife.

'I've told her where she's to sleep.'

'Tomorrow . . . soon enough . . .' Cameron muttered with a great effort. Ross, on his way to the door to see to the pony, turned, remembering.

'I met a man named Jim MacDonald at the funeral. He reckons he's a distant relation.' He was astonished when such a trivial bit of news effectively diverted their mother's attention.

'Jim MacDonald?' Gertie stared. 'What was he doing at Connor O'Brian's funeral?'

Ross moved back to the alcove, jerking his head towards the stairs. Meg needed no further prompting. She took Rachel's hand and led her up to her own attic bedroom above the kitchen.

'I will bring you something hot on a tray,' she whispered. 'You climb into bed and get yourself warm.'

Downstairs Gertie had not even noticed as Ross went on,

'He plans to call on us.'

'What was Jim MacDonald doing up here?' she repeated. 'His parents moved to a farm near Lockerbie in Dumfriesshire.'

'He came up to Ayrshire to attend another funeral — his aunt, or great-aunt, I believe.' Ross frowned, trying to recall the brief meeting, little realising the importance it would play in his own life.

'My father and Jim MacDonald's father were cousins,' Gertrude mused aloud, her mind concentrating on the family connections.

'The old lady was ninety-two.' Ross supplied obligingly. 'He's staying with friends on the other side of the glen, so that he can catch the milk train to Kilmarnock on Friday morning. There's a train south from there.' Ross stifled a yawn. 'I must see to the pony now.'

Rachel trembled as she climbed into Meg's large bed. The prospect of living with Mistress Maxwell was daunting. She was not afraid to work, but she sensed Mistress Maxwell did not want her at Windlebrae. Yet what alternative did she have? She remembered the dismay she had felt when she discovered her father had no money to pay the doctor's fee. She had already killed the pig. When the hens stopped laying she had made them into soup, praying that nourishing food would restore him back to health, or at least keep him alive. At the thought of her beloved father, the scalding tears spilled once more. She wished she could join him. Surely the grave could be no less welcoming than this house?

Granny Ferguson would have given her a home, but she had no space and little money. Her cottage belonged to the Laird and would return to him when she died. She could not inflict herself on an old woman of ninety, even if she could have found work. Doctor Gall said there were a million unemployed men in the country and work was hard to find even for men in desperate need of it.

Well, she was young and strong and she would work hard and prove that she was worthy of her keep. A hazy memory of her mother floated into her mind. She remembered the soft voice telling her always to say her prayers each night, and to think of pleasant things before she settled down to sleep. Wearily she scrambled out of bed and knelt down to pray. This was the way Meg found her when she returned with hot milk and bread and butter.

It would take a great many prayers to win her mother round, Meg thought, in spite of her assertions that she was a God-fearing Christian. Even Meg did not suspect the depth of her mother's bitterness, much less its cause and a growing obsession for revenge.

CHAPTER THREE

Gertrude Maxwell made no effort to hide her resentment and Rachel realised she would extract her pound of flesh at every opportunity. She was young, she was innocent of the ways of the world, but she was intelligent. She sensed that Mistress Maxwell bore her a grievance, though they had never met until now.

She had not come to Windlebrae expecting charity. She was used to work. Minnie Ferguson had taken her under her wing from the day her mother died when she was eight years old. She had been a stern tutor.

'It's for your ain' good, my lassie,' she wagged her white head, whenever she made Rachel repeat a task. She had a wealth of experience gleaned in her long years of service in the household of Lord and Lady Danbury. She had started as an under-maid at twelve years old and finished as housekeeper. In return for her labour and loyalty she had been granted the use of her tiny cottage for the remainder of her life.

Rachel was grateful for her training now but nothing had prepared her for a house so lacking in warmth and laughter as Windlebrae.

On that first dark February morning Gertrude Maxwell marched her across to the byre as though she was a prisoner.

Rachel soon guessed she was to be given the worst of the cows to milk — a flighty young heifer who was bent on kicking, a dejected looking old cow with long tough teats who seemed to grudge parting with every drop of milk, and a fidgety blue-grey young cow with a wild gleam in her eye. Meg gasped a protest. She was silenced with a quelling scowl. Ross was more outspoken.

'You canna expect the lassie to milk Bluey!' he objected. 'I'll milk her.'

'You'll get on with your own work and mind your business,' Gertrude snapped. She stood with her hands on her hips watching Rachel settle herself on her stool. She tucked her head firmly against the cow's flank as her father had taught her to do. She felt drained and deadly tired. It was the morning after his funeral, her first morning in her new home. Home? The memory of her father brought tears to her eyes. She turned her head away from Gertrude's gimlet glare only to encounter the wild eyes of Bluey. Instinctively she murmured in the soothing way she had with animals. Her hands were gentle, almost caressing on the swollen udder. After a few uneasy movements the cow stood quietly and let her milk flow.

At breakfast Ross and Meg praised her success with Bluey.

'Aye, lassie, your father always had a way with animals, especially horses,' Cameron told her. 'There was no one like him for gentling a spirited young colt. You must have inherited his skill.'

His wife sniffed, but before she could comment they were interrupted by the cheerful whistle of Tam McGill with his mail bag.

'I see ye'll be having a visitor?' he remarked curiously, handing Gertrude a postcard.

'Is that any business of yours?' she snapped, snatching it from him.

'Och, I just wondered if it was one o' the MacDonalds who used to bide across in the Lang Glen. They had a laddie called Jim. His family went to a farm in England I believe.'

'They went to a farm down in Dumfriesshire — near the Border.'

'Ah, so it is the same MacDonald then?' Tam grinned and winked across at Meg and Ross. Then he caught sight of Rachel. 'Well, well, a new face at Windlebrae! And who might you be, lassie?'

'This is Connor O'Brian's bairn,' Cameron enlightened him swiftly, before Gertie could make any more acid remarks. 'You'll remember him, Tam?'

The two men fell to reminiscing about old acquaintances while Meg poured Tam a cup of tea.

* * *

Gertrude made a surprising fuss over Jim MacDonald's brief visit. The flagged stone floor was scrubbed regularly but it had to be scrubbed again from corner to corner, and the outdoor steps edged with scouring stone. The china tea service was taken from the corner cupboard and washed. She baked shortbread and a fruit cake, although these were usually reserved for Christmas.

Outside the yard had to be swept, the byre and stable given an extra clean and the dairy, which Meg kept spotless at any time, had another scrub.

'What is all the fuss about?' Cameron grumbled irritably when he and his wooden armchair were pushed aside and a cold east wind blew through the wide open door to dry the floor and freshen the air. 'Jim and you were never great friends as far as I remember, Gertie. He spent more time at our house when he first left school.' He added reminiscently. 'Mother used to think he was sweet on our Cathie . . .'

'Stop your foolish talk! He was only a lad.' Gertrude cut his meandering.

'Aye, Cathie was his childhood sweetheart.' Cameron sighed. 'It was a pity the MacDonalds moved away. They've done well by all accounts.'

'I'll show Jim we are as good as he is . . .' she broke off.

23

'Aye? What were you going to say? I can tell you have some bee in your bonnet. I know the signs after all these years — but I can't think what business ye can have with Jim.' He frowned thoughtfully. 'He isn't even a close relation.'

After all the preparations Meg and Ross were disappointed not to meet this long-lost relation. Meg was dispatched to town on the bus which ran once a week from Five Lane Ends. Usually Gertrude went herself to sell her butter and eggs and buy essential groceries. In spite of the two mile walk from Windlebrae, Meg considered the outing a rare treat.

Ross was less pleased with his task of loading the cart with oats to take to the local mill. He had only spoken briefly to Jim MacDonald at O'Brian's funeral but he had quite liked the man and he would have enjoyed hearing about his farm in the Borders.

Rachel was left to carry out the daily tasks. As soon as Gertrude heard the pony and trap, which Jim MacDonald had hired, she gave Rachel a thick crust of bread and told her to eat it in the dairy and get on with her work.

'So how is the farming in your area, Jim?' Cameron asked. 'Is it as bad as it is up here?'

'Much the same everywhere, I reckon, but we're still managing to make a living. I've got both of my laddies into farms on the same estate so we're not grumbling. Mind you there's a few tenants giving up. The Factor was telling me he has had one farm vacant for more than a year. He's offering it rent-free for twelve months if he can get a tenant who would take it on and improve it.'

'That may not be easy with prices the way they are and all the food coming into the country,' Cameron said.

'You're right there. None of the tenants can afford to do repairs, or fencing and draining. One of the best farms on our estate is called The Glens of Lochandee. It has been in the same family for generations — almost gentry themselves. There is just a widow left now and the Factor was saying he has never seen a farm deteriorate so fast in his life.'

'Aye, it's the same on this estate. Our neighbour is giving up his tenancy. If I had been in good health I'd have taken it on for Ross. He's keen to have a farm of his own. He and Willie would have helped each other with the hay and the shearing if they were neighbours.'

'Well you're not fit. It's out of the question,' Gertrude snapped. 'Can I give you another cup of tea, Jim?' The subject of a farm for Ross was dismissed. Rachel celebrated her sixteenth birthday on the third day of March, 1902 — eighteen days after her father's funeral.

'Mother's not coming to the milking regularly from now on,' Meg announced that morning. 'She says she has plenty to do attending to Father and cooking the breakfast for us.'

'If you ask me she has seen that young Rachel is just as good at milking as she is — maybe even better,' Ross grinned, 'but she would never admit it.'

'Mother does not believe in giving much praise,' Meg admitted reluctantly and was rewarded by Rachel's shy smile, her nod of acceptance. It was the lack of tenderness and affection which she had missed since coming to Windlebrae, the absence of laughter. Gertrude Maxwell's presence was like a cold dark shadow, forbidding merriment. Her absence from the milking was the best gift Rachel could have wished for.

The warmth and friendliness which now filled the byre, even on the coldest March mornings, began to dispel some of the chill and grief from her young heart. Ross teased her as though she was his young sister and Meg was always ready with a kind word of appreciation or encouragement. Willie looked after the horses and fed the cattle and sheep so he was rarely in the byre at milking time, but he included Rachel in the conversation when he came to feed the cows.

'You must come to the cottage and meet Annie and the children,' he suggested one afternoon when she was helping him sweep the byre and prepare the cows for the evening milking.

'Oh, I would love that.' Rachel was delighted at the prospect of seeing the children. 'But . . .' she looked at him doubtfully.

'Even Mother can't keep you working all the time,' he said dryly. 'She's strict about keeping the Sabbath but after you have been to the kirk you could walk down to see us, maybe?' Rachel nodded eagerly, feeling a surge of optimism. Maybe life would not be so bad at Windlebrae after all. In any case she had no money and nowhere else to go so she must make the best of her situation. She had no way of knowing that youthful optimism and innocence could prove a hazardous combination for a pretty girl with no one to guide her.

When Rachel accompanied the family to church the following Sunday she sat at the end of the Maxwell pew next to Meg so she could not help noticing the frequent glances which passed between Meg and the man in one of the pews across the aisle. There was something strangely sad, almost wistful in the man's smile as they filed out of church after the service. It was Willie's wife, Ruth, who told her his name was Peter Sedgeman, a widower with three young children.

'According to Willie, he and Meg loved each other even before he married. They still do if you ask me,' Ruth declared.

'Then why didn't he marry her?' Rachel asked innocently.

'It was all before I knew Willie,' Ruth shrugged. 'Willie says Meg can't have children and their mother convinced her it was wrong to marry, knowing she couldn't give a man a family. Meg would make a wonderful mother though. I reckon Peter would marry her tomorrow if he got any encouragement. He feels he has nothing to offer her except the burden of his children now.'

'But if Meg still loves him . . . ?'

'She scarcely gets chance to see him. Peter has a grocer's shop in the village of Ardmill about four miles away. He delivers round all the farms in the area, but Mistress Maxwell will not have him near Windlebrae. Did you notice he didna get speaking to Meg on her own after church?'

'How awful.' Rachel frowned.

'She is selfish. My father summed up Mistress Maxwell the first time they met. That's why he insisted we should have a cottage of our own. Willie is loyal but he's not blind to his mother's faults. She worshipped Josh apparently so Willie and Meg and Ross are all used to playing second fiddle. Now that Willie's father needs so much care she will never let Meg out of her clutches and Meg is too gentle to defy her. She hates quarrels and Willie says she has always been close to their father.'

Rachel enjoyed playing with Ruth's little girl, Annie, and nursing the baby. She felt she had made a new friend and enjoyed Ruth's cheery company. She returned to the farmhouse in time to change her best black dress ready for the milking, her pale cheeks glowing. Cameron Maxwell noticed the lifting of her spirits and was relieved. He was grateful to Ruth and Willie for making the lassie welcome. Gertrude also noticed the little smile and the tender light in Rachel's eyes and remembered Mhairi MacLean. She looked just like her mother.

'You should be mourning your father, girl instead of gallivanting around the countryside on the Sabbath.'

'B-but . . .' Rachel stared at her. 'I was visiting your grandchildren, Mistress Maxwell.'

'My grandchildren do not need the likes o' you. Your time would be better spent reading the Bible and showing respect for the dead.'

'Oh, come on Gertie,' Cameron protested. 'Connor would never have expected his lassie to mope. It's good for her visit Ruth and the bairnies.'

'I'll thank you not to interfere with the way I discipline my maids, Cameron Maxwell. Get into the dairy and remember what I've told you. I'll have a word with Willie.'

So the brief pleasure of getting to know Ruth and the children ended before it had begun.

CHAPTER FOUR

Rachel was surprised when Tam the postie delivered a letter for her. She sensed that Gertrude Maxwell would have snatched it from him if she could, but he arrived while they were having breakfast. She fancied there was a devilish gleam in his eye as he deliberately stretched across the table to hand it to her personally. Certainly there was no doubt about the wink he gave her. She turned the letter over and over, puzzled by the unfamiliar, rather shaky, writing.

'Well don't stare at it all day, girl. Get it opened and then we can all get on with our work.'

'Oh no!' Rachel gasped and the colour ebbed from her face. Meg placed an arm around her thin shoulders.

'Surely it can't be bad news for you, Rachel?' she prompted gently, wondering what could upset her so much when she had already lost both her parents and she had no other close family.

'It's Minnie.' She looked across at Ross, her mouth trembling. She bit her lip. 'You remember Minnie Ferguson, Ross?' she pleaded.

'Of course I do,' he agreed recalling the old woman who had befriended Rachel. 'Is she ill?'

'She has died. Two weeks ago,' she added in a whisper, 'and I never knew.' She scanned the careful sentences. 'This letter is from our neighbour. She lived next door to the smiddy. The minister gave her my address. Minnie has left a vase for me as a wee minding. It belonged to her parents.'

'Much good an old thing like that will do you,' Gertrude sniffed. 'A few sovereigns would have been more use.'

'Minnie did not have much money,' Rachel defended her old friend. 'The vase was the thing she loved more than anything else in her little cottage. It was a wedding gift to her parents. It was very pretty. Mistress Chalmers says she will keep it safe for me until I can collect it.'

'Aye, weel I reckon it's real nice of the old lady to leave the lassie something to remind her of an old friend,' Tam nodded vigorously. He looked shrewdly at Rachel. 'You canna have too many friends, lassie.'

'Tam's right. If I'm invited over that way to play the fiddle I will collect it for you, Rachel.'

'Oh, would you, Ross? Really?'

'A-ah,' Tam gave a knowing wink at Ross, 'I reckon you'll be collecting it before long then if Widow Fawcett has anything to do with arranging the entertainment over there.' Ross scowled silently at Tam, but Cameron saw the guilty flush which coloured his fair skin. He felt a twinge of uneasiness. He knew only too well the temptations which could fall into the path of entertainers after a good evening of merriment.

Gertrude sniffed impatiently and made a noisy clatter of collecting the porridge plates, a pointed hint that Tam should get on his way.

Memories were awakened by the letter and Rachel could not dispel the brooding melancholy which descended on her during the days which followed. The last true and trusted friend from her old life had gone and she felt deserted and alone in an alien world. Cameron Maxwell noticed her pre-occupation and the haunting sadness which filled her eyes.

'A-ah, lassie you're like your mother, and no mistake. I remember how upset she was when one o' the girls in our school died with scarlet fever. You need a bit of a change.' He scratched his head thoughtfully. 'Gertie will be going to market tomorrow to sell her butter and eggs. If you can finish your tasks you might enjoy a wee visit to Ruth's cottage to see the bairns.' He frowned. 'No, on second thoughts you'd better not do that. Wee Annie might tell tales now she's beginning to chatter. It's real bonnie up the burn at this time of the year.'

'You're very kind,' Rachel smiled at the old man. She knew he was doing his best to make up for his wife's constant criticism. 'But I must not idle my time away.'

'What's that about idling time away?' Ross asked, coming to stand at the dairy door, grinning down at them.

'I was just telling Rachel to take herself for a walk by the burn. It's a lovely spot where the two burns meet — on the far side of the top meadow.' He sighed heavily. 'What I'd give to be able to walk up there now. I've spent many an hour guddling for trout, and helping you laddies collect frogspawn. The wild roses will be out and the air . . .' he drew in a long breath as though he could smell it still, 'it will be filled with the scent of the honeysuckle.'

'Father is right. It is beautiful, especially on a summer's day,' Ross agreed. 'We'll hurry up with the work and take a basket of food. Meg will help us. We shall be back long before the bus brings mother home.'

'Aye, you and Meg go with her,' Cameron nodded. 'You'll see great golden King Cups, and dainty Milkmaids, and Cowslips. There's a little wood a bit further up the hill. There's always something of interest there, even in winter.'

Meg decided to stay with her father, despite his protests, but Rachel knew she would remember the tranquil beauty of that day for as long as she lived. The peace seemed to fill her heart and help her set aside the pangs of loneliness and loss.

'Mistress Ferguson must have been a very good friend?' Ross remarked as they walked side by side across the low meadow.

'Oh, she was, she was my one true friend in all the world.'

'But you have us now — Meg, Willie, and me — and I know my father is pleased you came to Windlebrae. You seem to bring back memories of his youth.'

'Thank you,' she said simply, but she was frowning at some inner thought.

'What are you thinking about?' Ross asked curiously.

'My father always said you could never be certain people would not let you down — even your closest friends. But I knew in my heart that Minnie would never let me down. Even though I was no kin to her, I knew she loved me as though I had been hers. I said that to Father once . . .' She frowned again.

'Didn't he agree?'

'Oh yes. He believed Minnie was a rare person with a truly honest heart. But he said even a parent could sometimes let down his own flesh and blood.'

'I'd say he was right about that,' Ross muttered glumly. Rachel glanced up at him. She knew he was thinking of his own mother.

'Father said even parents are human beings with weaknesses, the same as everyone else.'

'But surely he didn't mean you could not trust him?'

'When he was dying he felt he was letting me down. I expect it was because he could not protect me anymore, or leave me any money. But I didn't feel he had let me down. He was a wonderful father.' Her blue-green eyes were luminous with remembered affection. 'He seemed troubled towards the end, though. He kept saying he had betrayed someone's trust.' She rubbed her brow as though the matter still perplexed her. 'Yet he said he would still have made the same choice. I hate to think he may have died with a troubled conscience. Minnie said he was just trying to warn me not to be too trusting.'

'I suppose we are all human,' Ross reflected. 'There's a bit of bad in the best of people. No one is perfect.' He grimaced. 'I think Mother would have gone through fire and flood for Josh, but I know she would not do much for me if I needed help. She has always regarded me as the black sheep, even when I tried my best to please her.' Rachel caught a fleeting glimpse of pain and bewilderment in his blue eyes, before he lowered his lids and flicked impatiently at a clump of grass with a hazel wand he had taken from the hedge earlier.

'I don't believe any mother could really favour one of her own children more than another.' She had intended the words to comfort him but they seemed to make him angry.

'Well, my mother must be unique then, because she has always made me feel like a cuckoo in the nest.'

'I-I'm sorry. I didn't mean . . .'

'Och, let's forget the rest of the world. The day is too beautiful for dark and serious thoughts.'

'All right.' She knew Minnie would not have wanted her to grieve. She smiled as she remembered the old lady's dry humour. Seeing the tiny smile lifting the corners of her mouth Ross knew his father was right to get her out of the dreary atmosphere at Windlebrae. He clasped her hand in his.

'Come on, we'll run to the top of the brae.' Without waiting for her consent he loped away, pulling her with him. She bunched up her skirts with her free hand and did her best to keep up with his long legs.

She was light and fleet of foot but she was gasping for breath, her cheeks flushed as they breasted the hill and sank down together onto the soft turf. Just below them there was the tinkle of running water where a silver spangled cascade tumbled over some rocks. It swirled into a pool where two burns met, before flowing onward, a little deeper, a little wider than before. They were sheltered from the north by the gentle rise of the hill behind them. In front, beyond the meandering burn, a green patch of fields and hedges stretched away to meet the sky. At their feet wild flowers spread their petals and a little further up the burn she could see the edge of the wood.

'It's just as pretty as your father promised.' She laughed with delight. She had scarcely seen anything except the farm-yard and the kirk since she arrived at Windlebrae. Today she felt free and light as the summer air.

'It is good to see you smile, Rachel.' Ross was fascinated by the tiny dimple which came and went at the corner of her mouth. 'You were meant for laughter. No wonder my father is pleased to have you at Windlebrae. Somehow I can't imagine my mother ever being young and truly happy. Even Meg does not sing to herself and laugh aloud as she used to do. It is as though there is a dark cloud over the whole house. It was different when Josh was alive.' He turned onto his stomach, propping himself up on an elbow, his eyes studying her intently. 'It's strange, but you remind me of Josh in a way. He had a little dimple at the corner of his mouth that seemed to flicker in and out.' His finger traced the contour of her cheek wonderingly, coming to rest on the spot where the dimple was hidden. He looked down at her, shaking his head. 'Josh was meant for laughter too. He could charm the birds off the trees. Even when he was up to mischief, he never roused mother's anger. She was not always as grim as she is now.' He sounded almost apologetic.

'It must have been dreadful to lose a son. It was kind of your parents to give me a home. I don't know what I would have done if they had refused my father's request.'

'Well they didn't refuse,' Ross grinned. 'And Meg and Willie and I are all thankful for that. When a little more time has passed and your heart is less sore, I think you will be a ray of sunshine in all our lives. Now shall we eat the food Meg packed for us?'

'Mmm, I'm ravenous!' Rachel agreed. 'Meg is so kind to me. I feel in my heart that she is just as trustworthy as Minnie.'

'Then follow your instincts. Meg is one of the best. She deserves more happiness herself.' As they ate his eyes wondered to the distant fields. Eventually he turned his head and stared morosely up at the hill behind them.

'Are you worried about something, Ross?' Rachel ventured as the silence lengthened between them.

'What?' He seemed startled, almost as though he had forgotten she was there. 'No, no I'm not worried — just dreaming impossible dreams.'

'Are your dreams impossible? Tell me about them?' She lay back on the grass, shielding her eyes, her appetite assuaged, her skin caressed by the dappled sunlight filtering through the leaves of an ash tree.

'The farm just over the hill will be vacant at the term. Mr Willis is giving up. He says prices are so bad he can't pay the rent. He is probably right but I wish someone would just give me the chance to rent a farm of my own. If only I had enough money to buy a couple of cows and a few hens and a horse.' He sighed. 'I'm young. I'm strong. I work hard. If only . . .' He shrugged. 'There's no point in dreaming. Mother will never let go of the purse strings now that Father is an invalid. She'll keep Meg and me tied to Windlebrae as long as she lives. Speaking of Mother!' He jumped to his feet. 'Come on young Rachel. We had better hurry back and pretend we have both been slaving hard all day.

'Ah, the fresh air has put a real glow in your cheeks, lassie,' Cameron Maxwell remarked as soon as they entered the house. 'You'll need to get your work done in good time every Wednesday and have a bit of time to yourself.'

'Father is right,' Meg smiled. 'And if Mother asks, you can tell her the bottom hen house has been cleaned out.'

'But I couldn't tell a lie! Or claim to have done the work you have done, dear Meg.'

'No-o,' Meg smiled conspiratorially, 'I'm not suggesting you tell a lie, but there are ways and ways of saying things . . .' Her dark brows rose humorously.

'You are so good to me,' Rachel chuckled in response. 'One day I hope I can repay your kindness, Meg.'

When Gertrude Maxwell returned home she was too tired and anxious to notice the glow of happiness which seemed to cloak Rachel like a mantle. It had been almost impossible to sell the butter. In the end she had had to let it go to Taffy for six pence a pound, and the eggs had not been much better. She had barely made enough to purchase the week's flour and oatmeal and the other few essentials for her household. Taffy's comments on her butter had not helped either.

She had known the little Welshman since he moved to the town twenty years ago. His real name was David Lloyd but from the beginning he had been known as Taffy. Consequently he had put the name above the grocer's and general store he had opened. Like herself he was getting older. Life was getting harder for him too. People wanted to buy food but many of them had no work, and therefore no money. He was a staunch Methodist and on that account alone he and Gertrude had always had a love-hate relation-ship, or maybe it was more of a cut and thrust. Despite her wariness Gertrude knew he was basically a fair trader and she respected his opinion, though she would never have admitted it.

'It is a just man, I am, Mistress Maxwell,' he would chant in his sing-song voice, and cocking his head on one side and with his forefinger wagging, he always added, 'Not a generous man, maybe, but a just one.' It was true too. Even Gertrude had to admit that. Why should he pay more for her butter and eggs when he could get them cheaper from a dozen other farmers' wives, eager to sell their week's produce.

Apart from the poor price she had been forced to accept, Gertrude Maxwell was still reflecting on Taffy's shrewd observation about the high quality of the butter she had sold to him two weeks ago.

'You never grumbled about the quality before,' she told him.

'A-ah, no, but then you never let me have your best butter before — at least not recently. A mistake was it? Taffy got the wrong batch, eh? I expect you sell your best butter to the fellow Sedgeman? Fancies your daughter, does he? That's what I hear . . .'

'I sell nothing to Peter Sedgeman!' Gertrude bristled. 'I would not have him and his grocer's cart near my house.'

'So, a fluke it was then, a fortnight ago? Beautiful butter it was. Churned to a grain and worked just enough — neither greasy nor still holding the water. Two pounds of it I was keeping for me and my girls.'

Gertrude knew the butter had been good. She had been surprised by its quality. She had set Rachel to churn and work the butter, fully expecting to take over herself and give the girl a thorough tongue-lashing. She had kept a watchful eye on the dairy and been surprised at the easy rhythm with which the girl churned, and the songs she hummed as she worked. She had even gone down to the burn to get the coldest water she could obtain to keep the perfect grain of the butter. She had worked it as deftly and lightly as a woman twice her age. It was clear that she enjoyed the dairy work too, and Rachel O'Brian's enjoyment of life at Windlebrae had no part in Gertrude's scheme. She dispatched her to the fields to hoe turnips and made the butter herself after that. The galling thing was that Taffy had noted the difference.

CHAPTER FIVE

'You'll have to move out, girl.' Gertrude issued the order abruptly as soon as supper was over. 'We need the coldest room for setting the cream.' Rachel met her fierce glare with startled eyes. Guilty colour flooded her cheeks. Had Mistress Maxwell discovered she had spent her afternoon idling with Ross in the sunshine? Where would she go? What would she do? Panic gripped her.

'What do you mean, Gertie?' Cameron asked sharply.

'What I said. We need to keep the cream cooler. The butter must be the best we can make. And the milk cows need the clover pastures to get the best flavour.'

'But you have never set the creaming pans in that wee room before.'

'The market for butter has never been as bad before,' Gertrude retorted. 'People can't afford to buy it. Besides there's stuff called margarine in the Co-operative store. Taffy says some of his customers are buying it instead of butter because it keeps longer.'

'So that's it!' Cameron exclaimed. 'I wondered why you've been looking so grim since you came home.'

'Grim!' Gertrude's eyes flashed, her mouth opened . . .

'All right! All right, m'dear,' Cameron soothed, holding up a placating hand. 'Though I can't see what difference it will make setting the cream in that wee room where Rachel sleeps. It's no cooler than the dairy in summer. If that's what you want I expect Rachel will soon clear out her bed and her box.'

'It is what I want. If she wants to go on staying here she'll have to sleep in the loft above the byre. It's hard enough to keep our own family.' She spoke as though Rachel was invisible.

'Mother! She can't sleep there!' Meg and Ross protested in unison. Cameron's eyes narrowed. There was something irritating Gertrude. He knew the signs, but why did she vent her spleen on a bit of a lassie who more than earned her keep?

Rachel flushed unhappily. She knew Gertrude did not like her, or want her here, but where else could she go?

Ross had told her the farmers round about barely made enough to keep their families. He said the ground above the neighbouring farm rose steeply and their neighbour's was the last farm up the glen which was suitable for keeping dairy cattle. He had explained that Windlebrae was better situated because it was on a south-facing slope and it had more fertile land beside the burn which ran right through the farm.

'Perhaps I should look for other work?' she said uncertainly.

'Indeed you will not, lassie,' Cameron objected strongly. 'We made a promise to your father. This is your home for as long as you want it.' He glared at his wife. Her thin mouth grew even thinner.

'The May term was the time to look for work if you'd wanted it,' she snapped. 'The twenty- eighth of November will be the next hiring day. You'll need to get a bus into the town to get there.'

'She will not be getting there. You will go to no hiring fair, lassie, not while I have breath in my body.'

'Rachel can easily sleep in my room.' Meg wondered how her mother could be so cold and unfeeling towards a girl who had no family of her own. The cream would not keep any better in Rachel's tiny room, cheerless though it was.

Why did she make her so unwelcome? Why did she want to get rid of her? Why did she dislike her so?

* * *

Meg and Ross were especially kind and sympathetic in the weeks which followed. Cameron Maxwell did his best to liven up the atmosphere with his gentle humour. She was growing fond of the old man and she looked forward to Wednesdays when his wife went to market. Since that first afternoon in the High Meadow she and Ross had spent any brief spell of leisure together, finding contentment and an easy companionship.

Sometimes they walked hand in hand wandering aimlessly, chattering like school children, then rushing back when Gertrude Maxwell's return from market loomed perilously near. Often they had no more than half an hour together because the tasks she had set claimed all their time. They were happy just sitting in harmony on a grassy knoll, or racing breathlessly against a stiff breeze to find a blessed calm in the shelter of the ancient beech tree. They were kindred spirits, filling an unacknowledged loneliness in each other. They found pleasure in small things, like the simple perfection of a dainty flower, or the heady perfume of a hedgerow. The exquisite song of a bird above their heads hushed them instantly to silence. The simple delights of nature took on a new meaning when they were together.

One afternoon, after a strenuous race up the hill behind the farm, Ross laughingly caught her in his arms and kissed her. It was a gentle, fleeting kiss, almost childlike in its butterfly caress, but it had been enough to awaken the age-old awareness of a man and a woman. The ready blush coloured Rachel's skin.

'I do believe that is the first time you have been kissed,' Ross said. 'Tell me I am right, dear Rachel.' He brushed a gentle finger across her mouth, wonderingly. 'Am I the first to take such a privilege?'

She nodded shyly. Ross seized her slight figure and swung her round in joyous glee.

'You are as light as a feather, yet I often forget you are so young. You are as skilled as any woman in the house and in the dairy, and you have borne so many troubles already. We all forget you are scarcely more than a child.'

Rachel's head jerked up.

'Is that how you see me, Ross? As a child?' He looked at her then, intently, his eyes moving over her small neat features, her thick burnished hair escaping from beneath the ridiculous cap his mother insisted she should wear. He thought there was a shadow of anxiety in her blue eyes, but her lips were red and faintly mutinous. One day she would be beautiful and she would have spirit. His heartbeat quickened. One day she would be his. His eyes widened as the thought came to him.

'No,' he said huskily, 'No, I do not think of you as a child.' Without warning he cupped her face in his work roughened hands and kissed her lips, lingering this time, feeling a yearning within him which he knew could swiftly turn to passion. He lifted his head and heard the soft lingering sigh as he released her. For a moment he was silent, his heart filled with an impossible desire. Then he smiled.

'You see,' he whispered softly, 'Kissing gets even better with practice.'

* * *

Willie and his horses were mowing down the grass ready to make the hay. Everyone prayed earnestly for fine weather. A good crop could make all the difference to the survival through another winter. Hands were blistered and sore, tempers were short as they turned and re-turned the rows of grass to make the most of the summer sun.

'I'll have to get my own field of hay in as soon as this is finished,' Willie said. He turned to look at Meg and Rachel.

'I hope you will come down with Ross and help us in the evenings, if you are not too weary.' He winked at Meg.

'I think you will enjoy it this year.' Meg flushed and Rachel looked at her curiously, wondering what Willie's unspoken message conveyed.

It did not take Rachel long to interpret Willie's meaning the first evening she went with Meg to the small paddock behind Willie's cottage. Peter Sedgeman, the grocer, was already there, wielding his long two-pronged fork. He greeted Meg warmly and as they worked he was never far from her side, talking quietly as they moved along the rows. The air was fragrant with the scent of newly mown hay and the atmosphere was happy.

Ruth brought a jug of her freshly made lemonade to refresh them and for a little while they sat together on the warm grass enjoying the peace and the evensong of the birds. The weather was calm and settled but it could change without warning. They all worked steadily until the purple shadows of evening crept over the sky. When Willie called a halt Ross beckoned Rachel and they strolled together over the field towards the Windlebrae boundary, leaving Meg and Peter Sedgeman deep in conversation.

'We'll walk slowly to give Meg time to catch us up. If Mother suspects she's talking to Peter there will be trouble.' Rachel nodded agreement. It suited her to walk slowly, and not just for Meg's sake.

'Mr Sedgeman seems a pleasant man, but he has such a wistful look. He makes me feel sad.'

'His wife died soon after the twins were born so he has his hands full. She was an orphan and had been brought up by Peter's parents. I think it was probably a marriage of convenience after Peter's parents died. Anyway she is dead now and Peter employs a housekeeper to care for the children. Ruth saw her once and thinks she is a slovenly creature.'

'No wonder he looks so unhappy.'

They reached the boundary wall and Ross turned to lift her over, but before he let her go he held her close and kissed her until she gasped for breath. Only then did he set her on her feet again. He vaulted easily over the wall himself and pulled her back into the circle of his arm.

'We'll wait here for Meg.'

It took two more evenings at Willie's hay. They finished earlier than they had expected on the last evening. All day the weather had been sultry and the air seemed to hang heavily, pressing their clothes against sweating bodies.

'It looks like we shall have thunder before morning,' Willie remarked. 'Ruth and I can't thank you all enough for helping us get the crop in safely.'

'I'm going across to the burn to cool my feet,' Ross said. 'Anyone else fancy a paddle?' He looked at Rachel but she looked at Meg for guidance. It was Peter Sedgeman who answered.

'Meg and I will meet you at the boundary wall in about an hour.' He took Meg's elbow and squeezed it gently. 'That all right, Meg? I want to hear what your mother said last night. It would give us a chance to talk properly?' There was pleading in his brown eyes. Meg nodded.

'I'll leave the paddling to you two youngsters,' Willie laughed, glancing at Ross and Rachel. 'I'll go and wash myself at the pump.'

So Rachel and Ross wandered over a small meadow and down a slope to where the burn looped onto Windlebrae land and back again.

'All of this semicircle of land floods when we have the winter storms,' Ross told her. 'It's as though the water is in such a hurry it is trying to find a short cut to the river. It will be fairly low just now but there is a decent pool in the hollow down there by the trees.'

'If it is wet and cool it will be wonderful,' Rachel sighed, glancing down at her boots and feeling the heat in her woollen stockings. She wondered how Meg and Mrs Maxwell managed to work at all in the heavy corsets they both wore. Meg had told her only the other day it would soon be time for her to wear them too, now that she was growing into a woman and her figure was developing. They had been preparing for bed. Rachel blushed when Meg eyed her narrow waist, her slender buttocks and small firm breasts, comparing them with her own rounded curves.

'I didn't mean to embarrass you, dearest Rachel,' Meg chuckled. 'As a matter of fact I'm glad Mother decided she wanted to use your tiny room for setting the cream. It's lovely having you share my bedroom — almost like having a young sister. Mind you it can be so hot up here under the eaves in the summer. Sometimes I throw off my nightgown and the bedclothes to try to keep cool. I expect Mother would be shocked if she knew.'

'I never had anyone to talk to before — n-not about girl's th-things,' Rachel stammered shyly.

'Well you have now so if ever you are worried about anything just tell me and I will help if I can.'

'I thought I was going to die,' Rachel confided, 'the first time there w-was blood. I ran to Minnie's house.'

'Did she explain that it was a natural part of being a woman?' Meg asked curiously, remembering her own alarm and how grim and abrupt her own mother had been, how brief and unsatisfactory her explanation.

'She said it was only a sign I was a woman grown and nothing to worry about. She said I must keep myself clean and behave like a young lady and I would come to no harm.'

'Mmm . . .' Meg murmured doubtfully. 'I suppose that's sound advice.' She was hardly qualified to offer any better herself, she thought ruefully.

Rachel's attention came back to Ross as he threw himself down on the springy turf beside the burn. He unlaced his boots, peeling off his thick socks, and wiggling his toes with relief.

'Come on Rachel, surely you are longing to cool your feet? The first time we met you had been paddling in the burn.'

He edged nearer the water and dangled his feet in the flowing stream. Rachel bit her lip. His back was towards her. Swiftly she pulled up her long grey skirt and unlaced her boots. Guiltily she pulled down her stockings and laid them on the grass.

The running water was deliciously cool on their hot skin and Rachel soon forgot any pretensions to hide her ankles and act like a lady. She laughed with delight as her toes slipped on the smooth pebbles. Ross bent to roll his trouser legs up as far as they would go, revealing his long muscular calves. She watched him enviously, wishing she could do the same.

'I would have had them off altogether if you had not been here,' he grinned.

'Do you want me to leave then?'

'Indeed I do not!' He seized her hands. 'You know how much I like your company, dearest Rachel.' Then the merry sparkle left his blue eyes and he stared down into her face intently.

'I've never been very sure what this thing called love is, but I'm beginning to think it must be what I feel for you.' He watched the delicate colour rise in her cheeks and she lowered her eyes shyly. He released one hand and gently touched the golden crescent of her lashes where they rested on her cheek. Then his hand slid behind her back and he drew her closer, holding her tenderly as he bent to kiss her lips. Around them the clear water of the burn rippled on its way.

Rachel was growing more familiar with Ross's kisses now and her natural shyness was disappearing as her ability to please him grew. Tentatively she slipped her arms around him and felt the beating of his heart against her own. His kisses deepened with passion as he felt the soft yielding curves of her body against his own. His foot slipped on a large pebble and he almost lost his balance. Rachel had not noticed until then how wet the hem of her dress had become. She lifted her skirt a little and hastened out of the water. Ross followed, flinging himself on the grass and waving his feet in the air to dry them.

'Come on, sit beside me, Rachel. You will soon dry in this heat.' He reached up and tugged her hand, pulling her onto the grass. She wrinkled her nose at the feel of the wet material under her thighs. Propping herself on one elbow she struggled to spread her skirt more comfortably but Ross pulled her off balance. She landed breathlessly across his chest. He chuckled and cupped her face in his hands, savouring each kiss as he covered her features one by one.

'I love this wee dimple best of all,' he murmured huskily as his lips settled at the corner of her mouth. Gently, he eased her onto her back and looked down into her face. His eyes moved to her bare toes, still glistening with water. 'Every bit of you is perfect.' He reached down to cup one foot in his hand, rubbing it dry, then moving to the other one.

It was a natural progression to wipe away the droplets from her legs but as his fingers moved to her knee and back again, up and down, he was aware of the smooth white skin, the firmness of her limbs. Involuntarily his hands moved to the softness of her thigh, the pad of his thumb automatically massaging its silken skin. He heard her sharp intake of breath and looked down into her face, seeing her parted lips, the twin patches burning in her cheeks, her blue-green eyes fixed on his face, as trusting as a child's. But the swift rise and fall of her breasts told him she had all the feelings of a woman, all the passion he himself had been striving to control each time he held her in his arms. He buried his face against her neck, feeling the pulse in the soft hollow of her throat. Her cap had fallen off and he longed to loosen her hair from the confines its braids. Instead he kissed her again, and again, over and over.

His hands sought the places he had barely dared to dream of. Rachel had neither the strength nor the will to stop him. In the dim recesses of her mind she knew she should, but the desire to please Ross, the longings he had aroused in her, were beyond reason.

They were waiting at the boundary when Meg joined them. She seemed too preoccupied to notice Rachel's creased dress with the patches of damp. She was vaguely aware of the aura of happiness which seemed to surround both Ross and Rachel, but it only added to her own misery.

None of them wanted supper. Gertrude assumed they had eaten with Ruth and Willie. In the dim light of the kitchen she did not notice anything amiss and the girls hastened to their attic room, neither of them ready for an inquisition.

Rachel soon feigned sleep wanting only to relive the moments of ecstasy she and Ross had shared. Mentally she hugged herself with joy, hearing again the words Ross had breathed against her warm skin — over and over.

'I love you, I love you. Now you are mine. I love you, my own Rachel.'

Her half-waking, half-sleeping reverie was disturbed by Meg's trembling body. Gradually she became aware Meg was trying to stifle her sobs. Rachel lay still, afraid to move. She sensed Meg did not want to share her troubles but her sorrow dimmed her own happiness a little. Meg was so kind and caring, surely she deserved to be happy too.

Meg knew she could be happy with Peter and his little family, but her mother was so vehemently opposed to the idea. She was wise enough not to criticise Peter outright but instead she reminded Meg of the burden of having an invalid in the house, of the extra work, of her own aging body. Her father never grumbled, rarely asked for attention and he had never lost his whimsical smile. His eyes still crinkled with humour and Meg wondered how a man could ever be a burden if you loved him. Did her mother love her father? Did she love any of them, Meg pondered with a bitterness which was alien to her nature. In her heart she knew her mother was trading on the love and loyalty she had always shown towards her father. He had always been a kindly, caring parent and she would never neglect him now that he was the one who needed care. Meg felt torn between loyalty to her parents and her love for Peter but as she sobbed into her pillow she knew she was reaching the limit of her endurance.

CHAPTER SIX

Willie's father-in-law, John Landell, often brought a bundle of newspapers and magazines when he came down from the city. Cameron Maxwell and Ross liked to read them, even though the news was often old. Towards the end of July Ross looked up from one of the papers. There was a challenge and defiance in his blue eyes.

'It's fifty years since the first Bank Holiday. I think we ought to have a holiday too.'

'Holiday?' Gertrude exclaimed, 'I never heard of such a thing!'

'Mr Landell's hiring a charabanc. He's taking Ruth and the children and two of his friends to the coast.'

'Is he?' Cameron looked up with interest. 'What about Willie?'

'Mr Landell wants him to go too, but Willie didn't think he could leave us to do the work. Of course he wouldn't feel guilty if he thought we were having an afternoon at the fair.'

'John Landell might have bought himself a bit of land but he doesn't understand anything about farming,' Gertrude muttered. 'There's always work to do.'

'Well I think it would be good for Willie,' Ross insisted. 'I told him we could manage the milking. But it would be a pleasant change if Meg and Rachel and I could go to the Bank Holiday Fair. We could take the pony and trap. We would be back for milking.'

'I shall be at the butter churn while you are idle. And who would look after the hens and pigs, and take care of *him*?' She glowered at her husband. Meg winced at her disparaging tone. How could her mother talk about her father and the hens and pigs in the same breath?

'I will stay at home and look after father.'

'Eh, lassie I don't need a nursemaid. Just leave me a bite to eat and pull the table a bit nearer. A change would do you more good. You look pale and wan these days. Are you well enough, Meg?'

'I'm well, Father,' Meg assured him but her smile was forced. Rachel knew Meg was often restless at nights and she looked pale and weary in the mornings.

'You would like to go to the Fair, wouldn't you Rachel?' Ross asked anxiously. 'You're very quiet.'

'I don't think my best black dress would be very suitable for the Fair,' she said diffidently, unwilling to disappoint him. 'And it is much too soon to wear my muslin dress. Besides . . .' she hesitated, reluctant to say she had no pennies to spend on the rides and coconut stalls and all the other pleasure of the fairground.

'You can wear my grey silk dress,' Meg offered at once. 'It was always a little tight and it does not fit at all now. In fact you may keep it.' Gertrude scowled. Meg pretended not to see. The grey silk dress was the one her mother had insisted she should wear after they came out of mourning for Josh. If Gertrude had had her way they would all have worn black for the rest of their lives.

So, despite clouds of disapproval, Ross and Rachel took the pony and trap and set out for the annual Bank Holiday Fair promising to be back for milking. Meg had no heart for celebrations but her mother was not placated by her presence.

The sky was overcast but nothing could dampen their spirits, just being alone together was enough. Ross did not have much money to spend either and for the first time he understood why Willie and Ruth kept their own cow and a few hens and a pig, why John Landell had insisted his daughter should have her own cottage and a bit of land. It was just as well that Ruth's father had enough money to be generous to his daughter and his grandchildren. They would have had few pleasures otherwise.

No one had much money these days but the holiday atmosphere and the music would have cheered all but the most melancholy hearts. After a couple of rides on the gaily coloured horses, Ross won two ribbons for Rachel's hair. Eventually they came to a stall selling sticky buns and one next to it with large savoury pasties.

'Shall we buy something to eat and find a quiet place to ourselves?' Ross asked. His eyes met hers and Rachel saw the desire in them. Her colour deepened. Twice more he had loved her and each time was better than before. Her stomach seemed to turn upside down as her own desire quickened. She nodded, her eyes bright, her colour high.

It was a day to remember and they sang softly together as they jogged along the narrow leafy lanes back to Windlebrae. It was the first time Rachel had been away from the farm, other than the walk to the kirk. She was completely lost as the narrow roads turned and twisted and crossed over but Dolly, the pony, seemed to know instinctively which way to go and Ross claimed Rachel's attention as they jogged along with his arm around her waist.

* * *

All too soon the corn was ripe and the field of oats was cut and stooked. It was vital that it had wind and sun to dry it out and harden the grain so that it would keep until it was thrashed in winter. Several times in the next fortnight the rain came down in torrents. All the carefully erected stooks had to be moved to dry ground like so many Indian wigwams. Rachel felt lethargic. Her limbs seemed leaden. It was an awful effort to gather up the cows from the meadow and bring them in for milking, but at last the corn was safely gathered into two round stacks.

Two days after the harvest was finished Rachel suffered a bout of sickness. Meg rose before anyone else in the mornings to gather in the cows ready for morning milking. On this particular morning at the beginning of October she had just left the bedroom when Rachel swung her legs over the bed. The wave of nausea came as a shock and she reached for the chamber pot. She soon felt better. She was not one to make a fuss.

The next few mornings she felt slightly dizzy but she decided the mild illness had passed so it was a shock the following morning when a sudden wave of sickness came over her. She ran to the midden. She was thankful no one had witnessed such indignity — or so she believed. The same thing occurred the next morning but this time she managed to gain the privacy of the closet. It took her a little while to recover. Ross and Meg had almost finished milking their second cow when she returned to the byre. Ross grinned.

'Hello, sleepyhead. Did you curl up and go back to sleep?' he teased. Rachel gave him a wan smile and got on with the milking. She felt much better by breakfast time, though her stomach was still doing minor somersaults. She ate her porridge slowly unaware of Gertrude's watchful stare.

Later in the day Gertrude harnessed the pony and yoked it into the trap, her mouth pursed into grim satisfaction.

'I expect she has gone to the Manse to see the minister,' Cameron said in reply to Meg's query. It was rare for Gertie to leave the farm except on market day. That evening, when Ross and Meg and Rachel had gone to bed, Gertrude reached for the stand which held her pen and ink bottle and drew out two thick sheets of writing paper. She seated herself at the kitchen table and drew the oil lamp close.

'Why are you writing letters at this time of night?' Cameron asked sleepily. His voice was more slurred than usual. Gertie did not answer. She had given him twice the usual amount of medicine which Doctor Jardine had prescribed. She knew he would sleep soundly until morning, and he would probably be drowsy well into the day. She proceeded to write two letters, stopping every now and then to consider. One was for Ross, though she had no intention of letting him read it until he was many miles from Windlebrae. The other was to her half-cousin, Jim MacDonald, a further explanation of the telegram she had sent him that afternoon.

Since the first morning she had heard Rachel vomiting in the room above, her mind had been in a ferment of speculation, her eyes sharp, her ears alert. Cameron had foisted two unwanted people on her. Now they had both played into her hands. Her brain schemed furiously in preparation for one final step to banish them from her life forever.

Gertrude was up early. As soon as Ross and Meg had gone to the byre she hurried up the narrow stairs to the attic room. She tapped on Rachel's door but she did not wait for a reply. Rachel was startled at her entrance. Her stomach was churning with the dreadful nausea. She was beginning to dread wakening. She could not understand it. All her life she had been healthy.

'A-am I late for the milking?' she gasped in alarm.

'No, no.' Gertrude crossed to the other side of the bed. The autumn morning was still dark and the tiny window shed little light. She held up the lamp and looked down at Rachel, hiding her malice behind a sympathetic tone.

'I've noticed you have been a bit pale lately, lass. Maybe you are too young for so much work . . .'

'Oh no,' Rachel protested. 'I am used to working.'

'Then maybe it's something else that ails you? I've noticed you're a mite sickly, especially in the mornings.' Rachel stared at her in amazement. The soft voice was so unfamiliar.

'I hope I did not offend you, if you saw . . .'

'I've seen bairns o' my own being sick before. I've come to tell you to take a rest. I will go to the milking this morning in your place.'

'Oh, but I couldn't possibly do that!' Rachel made to swing her legs over the bed. The awful nausea made her head swim. It was a relief when Mistress Maxwell's hand on her shoulder pressed her back against the pillows.

'Now you stay there until I come and tell you to get up. We don't want you falling sick with the winter coming on, do we?'

'N-no,' Rachel stammered in bewilderment, but she was thankful to sink back against her pillows. Gertrude nodded.

'Remember, you stay here until I tell you to get up.'

Gertrude closed the door firmly behind her. Rachel did not hear the key turn in the lock. She felt exhausted enough to sleep for a week. Gertrude crossed the narrow space to Ross's door and reached for the leather case from the back of the cupboard. She packed a night shirt and a change of clothes from Ross's chest. She took his tweed suit and a clean shirt over her arm and carried them all to the kitchen, then she added the letters and locked the case. She hurried out to help with the milking.

'Where's Rachel?' Ross asked immediately.

'I'm taking her place today. The poor lassie is not very well.' Ross was surprised at her apparent sympathy. He smiled warmly.

'She was a bit pale and quiet yesterday morning.'

'Yes, she has not been her usual self,' Meg agreed. 'Perhaps she has been working too hard with the harvest taking so long to bring in.'

'We had better get on with the milking,' Gertrude said briskly. 'I have a lot to do today. Meg, I want you to take a basket of eggs over to Mrs McNaught straight after breakfast. She's going to send me a sitting of duck eggs in exchange.'

'But I thought you were getting them ready for next week.'

'No, you must go today. They are all ready. Go straight after breakfast.' Meg nodded resignedly. It was no use arguing with her mother, but she knew for certain that the exchange of eggs had been planned for next week.

There were still three more cows to milk when Gertrude followed Ross to the dairy. She watched him empty his pail of milk over the ridged water cooler.

'I've a surprise for you, Ross — a telegram. You remember Jim MacDonald, my second cousin, who farms near the Border?'

'Yes, I remember him,' Ross frowned, 'Is he coming back to visit?'

'No. There's a farm on his estate to rent. He wants you to go and have a look at it. It's a fine opportunity for a fit young man. It's being offered rent-free for the first year.' She hoped it was still vacant. 'He will meet you at Lockerbie station today.'

'Today?' Ross echoed in dismay. 'I can't go today.'

'Yes, you can. If you take the milk to the station instead of Willie you can travel on the milk train to Kilmarnock. Jim travelled from there down to Dumfries, and then to Lockerbie.'

'But who will bring back the pony and trap from the station?'

'Ach, you know as well as I do that Dolly could find her way home from the station blindfold.'

'We-ell that's true, I suppose,' Ross agreed slowly.

'I have not said anything to your father. You know Doctor Jardine said he should not get upset or too excited. Time enough for that when you have seen the place and had time to consider. Jim will give you lodgings. I've packed the suitcase with a few things for you. Your suit is in the kitchen. You can change in the wee back room as soon as you've had your porridge. That way you will not disturb your father or waken poor Rachel.'

'Rachel. I must talk to her . . .'

'You can talk when you return. She will be better by then. Don't dally or you'll be late.' Gertrude reverted to her usual abrupt manner. She was tense with the effort of planning.

Ross was astonished by her encouragement. He had believed she would thwart any opportunity he might ever have to farm on his own. Excitement rose in him but he wished he could tell Rachel. She was too young to marry yet, but if he could establish himself as a tenant farmer he could take a wife sooner than he had dreamed possible. He wanted her at his side more than anyone else in the world. She had dispelled the isolation he had often felt, even within his family. They laughed together and talked together, they were friends as well as lovers. All his thoughts were on Rachel and their future as he blindly followed the plans Gertrude had made for him.

Cameron was still sound asleep when Meg came for her breakfast.

'Is Father ill too?' she asked in concern.

'Just a bad night,' Gertrude mumbled. 'If you've finished eating you can get away with the eggs. It's a long walk across the fields and you will have to go carefully and not chip any.'

Meg shook her head, her mother talked as though she was still a little girl of three instead of a grown woman. She sighed. She was getting old. Her thoughts were melancholy as she set out across the fields, pulling her shawl closer against the October chill. There was a damp mist in the air. She was certain it would turn to rain long before she returned.

As soon as Meg had left the house Gertrude shook her husband awake.

'Cameron! 'tis time you were waken. If you sleep much longer you'll be wetting the bed again.' Cameron Maxwell was only vaguely aware that his wife was speaking, much less that she was addressing him as though he was a child. He grunted and closed his heavy eyelids but Gertie pulled the blanket back and shook him with grim determination.

'Come on I'll help you on with your breeches and across to the closet.'

'I'm not ready to go to the closet,' Cameron mumbled, slurring his words even more than usual.

'Well I've work to do. Rachel isna well. She's staying in bed. I'll take you now before I start churning the butter. I've hung up some fresh squares of newspaper behind the door. You can read some of them until I come back for you.'

Cameron felt too groggy to argue. He allowed himself to be helped into his boots. His head was swimming and he would have lost his balance in spite of his two sticks if Gertrude had not grasped him under the arm.

She settled him onto the wooden seat and placed a few of the paper sheets near at hand, then she removed his walking sticks and closed the door behind her.

There was little time to waste if she was to get the girl well away from Windlebrae before Meg returned. She whisked into the house, snatching the long horsewhip from the stand behind the door as she went. Dolly never needed a whip so it was rarely used. Its leather thong was sharp. She paused only to unlock the bedroom door. She was beside the bed, the whip raised. Rachel was sleeping like a child, on her stomach, her face cradled in her hand and she was the image of her mother. Gertrude's teeth clenched at the sight of her. The lash of the whip scorched through her thin nightgown, instantly drawing a raw weal across her shoulders. Rachel yelped with pain but before she could gather her senses the thong descended again, and again. Rachel tried to shield herself. She managed to pull a blanket over her head. Gertrude was breathing hard. She flung the whip aside and pulled the blankets off the bed.

'Get up! Get out of my house! You wicked, ungrateful wretch,' she hissed. She tugged at Rachel's slight figure. 'Get dressed!' Her voice rose shrilly as she pushed and pulled, scarcely giving the bewildered Rachel chance to put on her petticoat and dress. 'I took you in. I gave you a home. How do you repay me? You sin! You sin!' She was almost screaming now. 'Fornication is a sin! A sin, do you hear me?'

In her mind she was reliving her own sin, and the penalty she had paid. At that moment Gertrude was scarcely sane as she sought to take her revenge. This girl was the daughter of the man who had used her. He had cast her aside for another. Rejected her! The anguish. The terror. Memories rose in her like bile. She forgot the part she had played. The scheming to steal Connor from the girl he loved, Mhairi MacLean.

'Please, please do not hit me again,' Rachel pleaded, shielding her face with an upraised arm, trying to pull on her boot with the other. 'Ross!' she called, 'Ross, please help me!'

It was her shout, and Ross's name, which brought Gertrude back to the present. There was no time to lose. She grabbed the cover from the pillow and bundled Rachel's few belongings into it, almost flinging it at her.

'Now get out of my house! Don't ever come back!' Gertrude's words were a hiss of venom as she hustled the helpless girl down the stairs and out of the house. Rachel barely had time to cast a hopeful glance towards Cameron Maxwell's chair, then the box bed beside the fire. He was not there. Where was Meg? Where was Ross? Surely he would save her. But Gertrude had raised the dreaded horsewhip again. Rachel hurried out into the chill October drizzle.

'Ross . . . ?' she faltered when she was several paces away from her persecutor.

'He's gone,' Gertrude gave a nasty laugh. 'Just like your father. He's let you down.' Rachel turned then and stared at her.

'M-my father?'

'Your father was no saint, whatever your mother believed.'

'M-my father was a good man. Ross . . .'

'Ross won you over with his silver tongue. He's just like your father. He's had his way with you. Now he's gone. Taken the pony and trap and gone off on the train. Away from here. A long way away.'

'I-I don't believe you . . .' Rachel gasped, feeling the blood drain from her face. Gertrude shrugged. 'Please yourself. He will never be back in these parts again.' She turned on her heel and closed the door firmly. Rachel stared at the unyielding dark brown wood.

Then she turned and walked slowly out of the farmyard, down the road, away from Windlebrae. What could she to do? Surely Ross had not gone away? Where would he go? As she walked she listened, praying he would call her name, come running after her. Surely she would waken and discover this was a bad dream?

The pangs of hunger were no dream, nor the faintness which accompanied them. She had no money, no food. She had nowhere to go. She did not even know which road to take to the nearest village or to the station. The whole world was a vast grey blanket of mist and rain. She shivered but she plodded on. She dare not go back.

CHAPTER SEVEN

Rachel walked wearily, lost and alone, on roads which appeared to have no ending, but which must surely take her away from Mistress Maxwell and her wild eyes and the dreaded whip.

Meanwhile Ross was experiencing a jumble of emotions as he climbed aboard the train which would take him to Dumfries. He had never been further than Kilmarnock before. He could not control the fluttering in his stomach. Feelings of apprehension and foreboding mingled with excitement. The whole adventure was a surprise, and a shock. There had been no time to think, to ask questions, to consider. No time to talk to Rachel, or even to Meg.

It had all been such a rush. Why hadn't his mother told them yesterday? When had the telegram arrived? Could that be the reason for her trip with the pony and trap?

Her help, her encouragement, astonished him. She had never shown any interest in his future before. Yet today she had organised everything, even thrusting a packet of sandwiches into his hand and wedging his suitcase between the milk churns.

'Your ticket is in your waistcoat pocket and there's half-a-crown in the other and the key for the case. There's a letter for Jim MacDonald. Er — there's a package for you as well. Find them before you go to bed.' Maybe she thought they would not feed him, he thought with a grin.

It had all been such a bustle, loading the milk onto the platform, turning the trap and heading the pony for home with a slap on the rump. He had felt a pang of regret, a sinking in his stomach, as he watched the empty trap disappear. Sternly he reminded himself that he would be back at Windlebrae by tomorrow night.

As the train gathered speed, with great huffs and puffs of black smoke, his anticipation mounted. He watched the fields flying by and wished Rachel could have come with him. He grinned wryly to himself. His mother would never allow that — two of them away. He still couldn't believe she had made all these arrangements for him. He would have liked to tell Rachel though. She must have felt very ill to miss the milking.

The green fields gave way to bleak hills and moor where rocks seemed more plentiful than sheep and cascades of water sprang from nowhere to fall down the sides of the hills. He felt his spirits sink but the train puffed ever onward away from Ayrshire, away from Windlebrae, away from Rachel. Why did he have this awful feeling of dread when he thought of her and of his home?

As the train headed south the drizzle gave way to patches of blue sky and the hill and moorland became greener and more kindly again. Little whitewashed farmsteads nestled into the lea of green slopes, sheltered here and there with the darker green of woodland. Ross began to daydream. Maybe by next year he would have established himself with a few cows and a couple of pigs, some hens and a pair of good Clydesdales horses for the ploughing and carting.

He sat up straight, frowning. His mother had not mentioned how he would stock a farm of his own, even if Jim MacDonald could get him one for a year without rent, as she believed. They ought to have discussed it with his father. Surely it would be easier to have a farm nearer to Windlebrae so that he and Willie could share some of the tools and implements? His mind raced, but his thoughts kept returning to Rachel. He felt vaguely troubled without knowing why.

Could she be seriously ill? His life had taken on a new light since she came to Windlebrae. She had become his friend and confidante — and more. His cheeks flushed and he felt his insides clench at the thought of her in his arms, held close to his heart.

Ross changed trains at Dumfries without trouble. So far, so good. The see-saw of his spirits rose again. There were a number of people waiting at Lockerbie station when the train lurched to a halt but Ross and Jim MacDonald recognised each other at once.

'You're just like your mother. I thought that when I saw you at Connor O'Brian's funeral. That's what made me speak to you.' Jim nodded. 'Aye, I'd recognise you anywhere.'

'Like my mother?' Ross was surprised. 'Most people say I am a Maxwell. Maybe that's because I'm the only one who plays the fiddle.'

'Aye, that's what I . . .' Jim MacDonald floundered. He stared intently at Ross. Then he gave an exasperated sort of sigh. 'Anyway, there's a neighbour of mine over there. He would like us to give him a hand to get some Ayrshire stirks out of the railway wagon and turned onto the road for home. Throw your case into the trap — the big one over there with the red and green wheel boards.' Ross quickly obeyed as Jim MacDonald shouted, 'Here they come!'

The stirks trotted briskly onto the wide main street, guided by an eager collie dog and Bill Murdoch's teenage son. Ross sprinted after the animals. He caught up just in time to prevent them turning onto the wrong road. He learned later it went south towards Annan, the Solway Firth and on to Carlisle.

Jim MacDonald drove over the railway and up a steep road out of the town. According to his mother the MacDonald family had prospered since they moved south. It seemed incredible that she was encouraging him to improve his own prospects after all the years of repressing every idea or suggestion he ever made.

At first Jim MacDonald was silent, apparently deep in thought, as the trap jogged along narrow country roads, bright hued with the autumn leaves, some still clinging to the branches, others strewn in a russet carpet on the road beneath. They passed over a bridge and Ross saw the river below.

'The land seems fertile,' he remarked.

'Aye, there's some of the best, and some of the worst, on the estate.'

'Do you live in this direction?'

'No. Our land is down the road Bill Murdoch took. We are about two miles from him. The farm we are going to see has been without a tenant for some time. The Factor, Mr Shaw, will be meeting us there. He's offering the farm for a year rent-free. He says it needs a young man, a strong one, who is not afraid of hard work. I have not seen it myself, but . . .' He broke off frowning and Ross felt he had something on his mind.

After a short silence he flicked the horse's reins. His name was Flash and he was a strong young gelding with a hint of Clydesdale in his breeding. He broke into a smart trot, although the road was beginning to rise and bend first one way and then the other like a giant corkscrew. The land on either side rose with it. Patches of rushes and heather began to appear. The fields were less green. Jim MacDonald turned to look at Ross, his eyes shrewd and thoughtful.

'Look, laddie, what did Gertie say exactly? I mean to bring you here today?'

'Why, just that you knew of a suitable farm for me,' Ross shrugged, puzzled. 'And that it was an opportunity I must seize if I wanted to farm on my own.' Jim MacDonald seemed to be waiting for more. 'That's all,' Ross told him. 'Is there something else? Something more she should have told me?'

'I'd say there was a lot more,' Jim muttered darkly, 'A whole lot more — but then I never did understand how Gertie's mind worked.' They both fell silent but as the road curved round one bend after another with the land rising ever more steeply in front and on either side, Ross sat up stiffly.

'I think, Mr MacDonald, I am beginning to understand why she wanted me to come so far away.' His lean jaw clenched, his eyes were bleak with disillusion. He felt sickened. 'I think you should turn around and get me back to the station. I will take the next train back to Kilmarnock. This land is worse than anything around Windlebrae. Our neighbour's farm will be vacant soon but she would not even consider letting me tender for that. I would not move so far away to rent this kind of land if it was rent-free for ten years!'

'Ah, don't be too hasty, laddie,' Jim MacDonald soothed. 'It's good enough sheep land, even if it is a bit steep in places.'

'There's even less money in sheep than there is in milk! We can scarcely give them away!' Ross tried not to shout. 'Surely you know they are bringing in mutton from the other side of the world now?' He felt angry and let down. His mother did not wish him well at all he thought bitterly. Was she trying to make a fool of him? Sending him on such a journey? Or did she just want rid of him? Anywhere, at any price? 'I do not want a farm in this area. I will not stay! Turn around, please Mr MacDonald. I'm sorry you have been put to so much trouble.'

'We've come this far. We might as well take a look now. It's not much further and the Factor will be waiting for us. We canna leave him in the lurch. I would not like to offend him.'

'I suppose,' Ross took a deep breath, 'that's the real reason I am here — because you want to help the Factor find a tenant. You and your family want to keep on the right side of him?' He knew he sounded blunt, arrogant even, but he was bitterly disappointed. Jim MacDonald's eyes flashed and an instinctive jerk on the reins brought the horse to a sudden halt. He turned to glare at Ross.

'I have no need to keep in with the Factor. He knows well enough how I farm my land. No, young man, I have no need to curry favour with anyone.'

'Then why did you insist I came today — not yester-day, or tomorrow, or next week. You wanted me here today. Why?'

'I . . . ? I wanted you here?' Jim stared at him in disbelief. 'Look here, laddie, I reckon we have got things wrong some-where. I got a telegram from Gertie yesterday, asking — no, telling me — to meet you off the train today. As a matter of fact it was not very convenient. I had promised to help Bill Murdoch get his stirks from the station. It's quite a walk for frisky young cattle. I didn't have any option but to meet you with so little warning. You are lucky the Factor could see us at such short notice. I had to go down to the village and ask Doctor Lawson to contact him on his new contraption. A telephone, he calls it. Amazing thing it is. He talked just as though Mr Shaw was in the same room. They made arrange-ments for us to meet.' He rubbed his temple. 'Where were we? Oh, yes, I told Gertie about the farm being vacant when I was up there. I was just agreeing with Cameron that farming was in a bad way and poorer farms were falling derelict for want of tenants in every area. It was not in my mind to set you up here. I'd say you were a bit young to be considering taking on a farm of your own yet. You must be . . .' He paused while he did some mental arithmetic. 'Aye, you must be about twenty.'

Ross nodded absently. He was still puzzled and angry. Jim MacDonald seemed to sense his mood and his expression grew less stern.

'Gee-up, Flash,' he urged the horse forward. 'Put this down to experience, laddie. It will be good for you to meet the Factor and talk with him. Don't be too critical. It's not his fault if you have come on a wild-goose chase. There's a lot of farmers struggling to keep going. I've heard of a couple who are emigrating to Canada.'

'Maybe that's what I should do,' Ross muttered disconsolately.

'In the telegram Gertie said she would write me a letter. Maybe I'll know better what is in her mind when I get it.'

'She put a letter in my case,' Ross remembered. 'Do you want it now?'

'No. When you get to my house will be time enough. My wife's looking forward to meeting you. I have two laddies of my own. They rent farms just a few miles away. I wouldn't be surprised if they come over to meet you too.' Ross felt a little comforted by the idea that someone welcomed him.

He was silent as he walked beside the Factor and Jim MacDonald over the boundaries of the farm. It had certainly been neglected. There were pools where the drains should have been repaired and vast patches of rushes, whins and bracken. Huge gaps yawned in the stone walls which bordered many of the fields.

'It looks to me as though the sheep must have run wild,' he commented at last.

The Factor and Jim MacDonald came to a halt.

'Well I'm glad you have not lost your powers of speech altogether,' Jim grunted.

'I get the feeling you are not very impressed, young man?' Mr Shaw raised his bushy eyebrows questioningly.

'No, Sir, I am not.' Ross was civil but firm. 'I expected the land would be a great improvement on our own, but this is much steeper and wetter. I would dearly like a farm of my own, but not just any farm.'

'You mean you want to start with the best,' Mr Shaw commented wryly. Ross flushed.

'No. If a farm had room for improvement I would not mind hard work. I'm used to that. I can do most things — hedging, ditching, ploughing, sheep shearing, milking. Father insisted we learned to do everything, but I like dairy cattle best.'

'And you think this place cannot be improved?'

'Even I could improve it!' Ross exclaimed, 'but I could never make it fit for milk cows. We must be fairly high above sea level up here?'

'We are and I can't say I blame you, especially if you have set your heart on milking cows.'

'I'm more familiar with cows. I'm sorry if I have wasted your time.'

'That's all right. There was always a chance I might have found a tenant.'

'Well I must say it's even worse than I had expected,' Jim MacDonald admitted. 'We may as well be getting back. Ross is staying with us tonight and taking the train back to Ayrshire tomorrow,' Jim explained.

The two men chatted amiably as they walked back to the farm steading where the horses were enjoying a nosebag of oats to revive them both for their homeward journeys. Ross felt too deflated to join in the conversation. He wished he could have gone straight back to Windlebrae and shared his disappointment with Rachel. She was always gentle and understanding.

* * *

Ginny MacDonald was a plump motherly woman who welcomed Ross with genuine warmth and plied him with food until he thought he would burst. Her two sons were blithe and cheerful. They told him about their own farms. Both wanted to breed pedigree Ayrshire cattle but agreed with their father that in the present farming doldrums they would be happy just to pay their way and survive.

They plied him with questions about Windlebrae and any of their distant relations with whom he might be acquainted. Eventually they rose reluctantly, pushed their chairs back from the large kitchen table and declared they must make their way back to their own homes and beds if they were to be up in time for the milking.

'I enjoyed meeting your family,' Ross told Jim MacDonald. 'It has made the journey seem almost worthwhile after all.'

'I'll show you your bedroom,' Ginny MacDonald beamed. 'I've aired the bed so I hope you sleep well, son.'

'I feel tired enough to sleep for a week,' Ross smiled down at her.

'My, but you're a handsome laddie when you forget your troubles!' she chuckled.

'You'll not forget to bring me Gertie's letter, Ross?' her husband reminded, puffing hard on his pipe to get it to draw.

Ross found the letters in his case. Disappointment and anger made him rip open the one for him.

He was astonished to find five large ten pound notes inside. Fifty pounds! It did not make sense. Could it be that his mother had genuinely thought the farm would be suitable for him? There was a letter beside the packet and he began to read.

The first sentence was like a punch in the stomach. He slumped onto the side of the bed. He read the sentence again. He read it a third time. It was brief. It was stark. He was stunned.

'It can't be true!' he muttered. The colour drained from his face as he read on.

To Ross, It is time you learned the truth and made your own way in the world. You are no kin to me. You were born out of wedlock. I have treated you as a brother to my children. Knowledge of your true parentage would have brought shame to their good name. The evil shadow of your birth would have cast itself upon them. I am a God-fearing Christian. I tried to bring you up the same. I have failed in that. I fear you will bring more shame to me and mine. Now you must go your own way.

I am not without charity even in these hard times. I enclose money but in return I insist that you never return to Windlebrae, or to this area. Cameron's health is uncertain. Another scandal could kill him and you would be responsible.

Meg and Willie are in ignorance of the disgrace your birth brought upon us. I trust they will remain so.

* * *

Ross read and re-read the letter. It was stiff, like its writer. There were no words of tenderness. Could he ever have expected any?

Should he have guessed? His mind was in turmoil. The woman he had believed was his mother was no kin at all. He had no right to the love he had craved, no right to anything . . . food . . . clothes, not even the roof he had shared. Nothing. Certainly not the fifty pounds to buy his absence, and his silence.

Oh yes, it was clear to him now why she had given him the money. She never wanted to see him again. He was nothing. He was nobody. He was like a plant without roots.

"*Your true parentage*". The words echoed and re-echoed around his brain. Who was he? Why had the Maxwells taken him in?

As through a thick fog he heard Jim MacDonald calling up the stairs.

'Did you find Gertie's letter for me? Ross?'

He rose stiffly from the edge of the bed. He had no idea how long he had sat there, hunched, his thoughts milling round and round. His brain felt numb. He picked up the letter addressed to Jim MacDonald and descended the narrow stairs like one in a nightmare.

'Mercy me, laddie!' Ginny MacDonald greeted him. 'Are you ill? Is it something you've eaten?'

'I'm fine.' His voice was no more than a croak and he cleared his throat with an effort. 'I am all right, thank you.'

'You dinna look it,' Jim frowned. 'Sit down in that chair while I see what Gertrude has to say.' His eyes met his wife's concerned stare and he jerked his head towards the corner of the room. Ginny scuttled to an oak cupboard fixed to the wall and reached down a bottle of whisky and two glasses. It was her husband's cure for all ills. She poured two stiff measures and carried them back towards the fire.

Ross hesitated when she proffered one to him, then he reached out a shaking hand and grasped the glass.

'Thank you, Mrs MacDonald. Thank you.' He lifted the glass, tilted back his head and drained the lot. Jim MacDonald raised his eyebrows.

'Well, well,' he mused. 'That was not the first time you've tasted whisky.'

'No.' Ross acknowledged grimly. He breathed deeply, desperately trying to control his quivering nerves. The amber liquid warmed him. Gradually his hand steadied. He became aware of Jim MacDonald eyeing him shrewdly. 'I am not a drunkard, if that's what you are thinking,' he said stiffly.

'No?'

'No! I was offered it often enough after a night's fiddling. Once only I accepted all that I was offered. That was lesson enough.'

'I'm pleased to hear it. Whisky has its uses. I'd say you have had a shock?' His eyes moved from the letter in his own hand to the page still grasped tightly in Ross's fist. He had been unaware that he was still clutching the single sheet. He glanced down at it.

'A shock?' He gave a harsh laugh, but to his dismay there was almost a sob in it. 'You could say that.' His mouth tightened and his square jaw jutted, but a pulse beat visibly in his temple as he strove for control. He felt as though he had been beaten inside out, then back again, but the pain was not in his body.

'The cure for shock is a cup of hot sweet tea,' Ginny insisted, bustling to shove the big kettle back onto the fire to boil the water.

'Please, don't bother for me,' Ross protested.

'It's no bother, son,' Ginny smiled kindly down at him. 'I couldn't rest if I let you go to bed in your present state.'

Son. Her words, her gentle smile, the comforting pat on his shoulder were almost Ross's undoing. He was alarmed to find himself on the verge of tears. He was a grown man. He couldn't remember shedding tears since the day he fell out of a tree when he was five years old, and here he was swallowing a huge knot in his throat like some stricken maiden. He coughed huskily. When he looked up he saw Jim MacDonald's blue eyes were blazing and his face was ruddy with rage.

'That's just typical of Gertrude McQuaid. Just like her old grandmother! My father used to say the old woman could cause trouble in an empty field.' He looked across the hearth at Ross. 'She didn't have the courage to tell you to your face! Did she? That's the trouble, isn't it? You've just found out? Is that what's in your letter?'

'That I'm a — a bastard?' Ross's tone was bitter. 'That she is not my mother?' He nodded. His mouth twisted but whether in pain or scorn it was hard to tell.

'When you get over the shock, I reckon you might be grateful for that,' Jim muttered. 'Does she say she doesn't want you back at Windlebrae? You would bring shame to her family?' He mimicked his half-cousin's waspish tones. 'For God's sake they are grown men and women!' He muttered an oath which made his wife raise an eyebrow.

'Gertrude's father ruined her when she was a girl. Since she grew older she's always been a bit unbalanced whenever things didn't go her way. Holier than the saints one minute and supping with the devil the next. Cameron must have been a saint to put up with her all these years.'

'Do calm down, Jim,' his wife said quietly. 'It isna good for you to get so upset.'

'Maybe you'll be upset, Ginny, when you read this letter.'

Ross sipped the tea gratefully. Right now he did not want to think — not even about Meg or Rachel, or anyone at Windlebrae.

'Gertrude certainly makes it clear she is expecting me to keep you down here,' Jim MacDonald stated dryly. 'How I am supposed to do that if you don't want to take on the farm we saw, I don't know.'

'This will not make me take a farm like that. And I would not go back to Windlebrae now if it was the last place on earth. I can work. I shall look for a job.'

'Surely we can find work for Ross here, can't we Jim?' Ginny pleaded.

'We can find work all right. There's always plenty of that, as you'll know, laddie.' Jim MacDonald frowned, measuring his words carefully. Ross respected him for that. He felt he would not make a promise he could not fulfil. 'While prices are as poor I could not hire another man, but you are welcome to earn your keep here for as long as you like. Ginny misses not having her own lads to feed and care for and worry over.'

'That's all we ever had anyway — our food and clothes — in return for our labour,' Ross said flatly. 'Moth . . .' He cut his words short. 'She has controlled everything these last few years. I promise not to be a burden to you any longer than I can help, but I appreciate your offer. I shall be glad to accept it while I look for a job.'

Ross had been with Jim MacDonald and his wife over a week. They treated him with warmth and friendliness. Jim and his men appreciated an extra pair of willing hands, especially now the days were growing shorter, but Ross was well aware Jim MacDonald was giving him work to ease his pride and earn his keep. He was glad to throw himself into hard physical labour so that exhaustion might bring him sleep and blessed oblivion from the confusion of his tortured thoughts.

'Don't get discouraged, Ross,' Ginny MacDonald said at breakfast. It was nearly the end of his second week with them and she had noticed his downcast expression as he watched Jim opening a letter. Ross did not realise she was watching him. 'There will be work available at the end of November. Not many men move before the term and it's only a few weeks away.'

'Just another account to pay. It's for the stallion fees,' Jim announced, setting aside the letter. He glanced at Ross. 'Ginny is right, laddie. There will be more work available at the hiring fairs, but I've put word around the neighbours to say you are available. We are all keeping our ears open in case any of the farms round here are expecting a change of men. Meanwhile you are doing a good job. If prices showed any sign of getting better I would be glad to keep you.'

Ross nodded and ate his breakfast but his heart was heavy. He had no desire to return to familiar haunts now but he couldn't get Rachel out of his thoughts. He had gone over and over his situation, his ignorance of his roots. He felt he had no identity. He was like a boat adrift on an endless sea — no anchor to hold him fast, no sails to propel him forward. Was he the son of a whore? Why had Cameron Maxwell taken him in? "*We are not your parents*," the letter had said. Was she telling the truth? Was it possible Cameron Maxwell had sired him after a night of revelry?

Again and again his thoughts returned to Rachel. He ached for the feel of her in his arms, the warmth of her body against his own, her sweet smile and sparkling eyes. He yearned for the comfort she could give him. He had written her a letter, pouring out his heart, his dismay at finding he had no roots, the sick feeling of isolation, and lastly his love for her. He had promised to write again when he found work. He had given the letter to the postman who called most days at Briarbush, the MacDonalds' home.

Each morning he longed for Rachel's reply. He was desperate to know she still loved him for himself. He needed her reassurance but there were no letters for him. Ross grew despondent, he began to question himself. Was Rachel ashamed of him? He could only interpret her silence as one thing — rejection. She no longer wanted to be his friend, or even acquainted with him.

CHAPTER EIGHT

Gertrude Maxwell would not have admitted that Rachel's arrival had brought the past vividly alive again, and with it an overwhelming and bitter desire for revenge. Rachel was the only living link to Connor O'Brian and Mhairi and her happiness was linked with Ross. Getting rid of him too suited her well.

The drizzle which Ross had left behind on the morning of his departure had turned to a persistent rain as Rachel made her way along unfamiliar roads and tracks. She could scarcely bear the touch of her garments against the raw and bleeding lacerations on her back and shoulders. She was completely lost and shivering from shock and cold and the ever-present nausea. Her stomach churned from lack of food.

The narrow twisting roads all looked the same. There were tracks but whether they lead to fields, or to isolated farms, she could not tell. The mist creeping down from the hills obliterated everything more than twenty yards in front of her. The very silence seemed ghostly, not even the forlorn bleating of an ewe or the cry of a curlew.

Rachel shivered and huddled beneath her shawl but it was already damp. Droplets of rain clung to the woollen fibres. She plodded on doggedly.

Her legs began to tremble with weakness. Her bundle was pitifully small but it seemed to weigh more with every step. Rachel had no idea how far she had trudged but she had to be several miles from Windlebrae by now. She was half-afraid she had been walking in circles.

When a small stone building loomed out of the mist some way up the hill to her left she knew she must take the chance to rest. She leaned against the bank of earth at the base of the hedge, gathering strength to climb the slope. She stared at the building, willing it to show some form of life. There was nothing, not even a lone sheep or cow. The rain was falling faster now. Even the animals would be seeking shelter.

Wearily she dragged her leaden limbs up towards the barn, slithering on the wet grass. The door was partly open and she shoved at it tentatively. It was dark inside but as her eyes became more accustomed to the gloom she could see it had been used to store hay, probably for winter feed for sheep. There were remains from a small truss of hay against one wall, bristly where it had been cut from the stack. She bent to feel it. At least it was dry. Her stomach churned with hunger. She wished she had thought to find a spring and have a drink of water.

The more she thought of it the more she craved a drink. She shuddered as she recalled a newspaper cutting she had read about Russian children dying of starvation and people eating twigs and mixing clay with their corn. The thought made her stomach heave. She took off her shawl and shook it, then spread it out to dry on some of the hay. Even that small effort made her feel faint. She plumped up a mound of hay and lay down pulling the hay round her to keep herself warm.

Her mind was buzzing with the worry of what to do when the mist cleared. She must find her way to a house or farm and plead for shelter. How she would find work she did not know. The little money she had was in her box at Windlebrae.

Inevitably the memory of Gertrude Maxwell's fury returned. What had she done to deserve such a cruel beating?

She had worked and tried hard to please. What was the sin she had committed? Forni . . . Forni . . . Her brow creased in an effort to recall Gertrude Maxwell's accusations, but she had not understood and could not remember. Why had Meg not come to her aid? Had Ross really run away? Rachel trembled. She had believed Meg and Ross and Willie were true friends. "Friends for ever," Ross had pledged.

She must have fallen into a light sleep because she suddenly sat up with a start. She felt disorientated but the pain across her shoulders from the whipping was intense. Memory flooded back and she began to shake.

The sound which had wakened her was growing louder. It took her some seconds to recognise it was a horse and cart. She jumped to her feet, wincing at the pain, but she grabbed her shawl and threw it round her shoulders as she slithered down the slope towards the road, clasping the pillowcase which contained everything in the world she possessed.

She was sure it must be Ross with the pony and trap. Or perhaps Willie, with his favourite Clydesdale, Lucy? They were coming to take her back.

Yet could she ever live in the same house as Gertrude Maxwell again? The thought brought her to a halt almost at the side of the narrow road. A cart was coming round the bend towards her. It was much larger than the trap, higher and covered in. The driver sat up at the front under a small overhanging shelter and the chestnut horse looked plump and well-groomed. Rachel shrank back with a feeling of despondency. The wind had risen, driving the rain away and improving the visibility but the cold penetrated her thin dress and she shivered miserably, tugging at her shawl to hold it closer. She was certain she must look like a vagrant woman and wished she had tidied herself. She wanted to hide but there was nowhere to go. The driver of the vehicle had already seen her and was drawing the horse to a halt.

'Can I help y . . . ?' The driver of the horse-drawn van broke off with a startled frown, then uncertainly, 'It is Miss O'Brian — isn't it? Rachel O'Brian?' Rachel nodded mutely.

She stared up at the man but her head swam. She sank down onto the wet grass, fighting against the waves of dizziness which threatened to overwhelm her. She recognised Peter Sedgeman as the driver of the cart, and felt deeply ashamed of her appearance. Her hands and face were grubby, her hair straggling and unkempt. He had jumped down and was speaking to her again, his voice low and full of concern.

'You are miles from Windlebrae, lassie. Why are you heading into the hills? Are you hurt? Are you lost?' The kindness in his voice was her undoing. Her control snapped and she was sobbing into her shawl like a frightened child. At length she managed to calm herself. She felt Peter Sedgeman's hand on her shoulder. He tried to help her to her feet but she cried out as the pressure of his arm reopened the wounds on her back.

'Are you hurt? Look lassie, tell me what ails you. I will help if I can, but I have groceries to deliver and the daylight will soon be gone.' He eyed her keenly, seeing the way she held her shoulders as though afraid to move. Her face was deathly pale, stained with mud and tears. Her hair was blowing wildly where it had escaped from its braids.

She bit her lip hard, striving for control. Haltingly she tried to tell him that she had lost her employment at Windlebrae. Peter listened in silence, his brow growing darker as he filled in the gaps which Rachel would not, or could not, put into words. At last he moved to her side again and put a gentle arm about her shoulders. She winced sharply.

'You're hurt. Surely . . . have you been beaten?' She nodded miserably, her head bowed.

'Who?'

'M-Mistress M-Maxwell,'

'Surely even she . . . but where was Ross?'

'She says he has gone away. She — she says h-he is not c-coming back.' Rachel bit back a despairing sob. She stared at him, her eyes wide and pleading. Wanting him to tell her it was not true. Indeed Peter Sedgeman could not believe Mrs Maxwell would allow Ross to go anywhere. What Gertie had, Gertie kept, he thought bitterly.

'I must find work and shelter,' she told him urgently. 'I must earn money — for food.'

'Have you eaten since breakfast?'

'I did not have any breakfast.'

'No breakfast? Nothing all day! No wonder you can scarcely stand.' He left her side and opened the double doors at the back of the van. He returned with a small loaf of bread. 'I'm afraid I've no butter to go with it,' he apologised.

'It's wonderful!' Rachel's eyes shone with tears of gratitude. Then she put her hands behind her back. 'But I c-cannot accept it. I have no money to pay for it.' Suddenly the tears flooded her eyes again and ran down her cheeks. 'She would not let me bring my box — the wee carved box Dada made for me. It has a secret drawer. I had a shilling and a gold sovereign from Minnie, and M-Mama's necklet and ring. Wh-what am I to do?'

'For a start, lassie, you can take this wee loaf. Eat it now, if you can eat it dry?'

'Oh, I can, I can.' Rachel assured him fervently. 'I c-can't thank you enough, Mr Sedgeman.' It was all she could do not to cram the bread in her mouth. She had eaten nothing since the previous afternoon and the sickness had drained her strength. She turned away from him, to return to the shelter of the barn, out of the rising wind. Peter watched her.

'It's no use, I can't leave you here.' Peter frowned, pushing back his cap. He rubbed his head. 'No, I can't leave you here alone,' he repeated firmly, making up his mind. 'It's usually after seven before I finish my deliveries, but if you can squeeze up onto the seat beside me I will turn for home at the next crossroads. My housekeeper will make you a bed for tonight. In the morning we will decide what can be done.'

'If — if you give me shelter Mrs Maxwell will be displeased with you.'

'Ugh!' Peter uttered a harsh sound. 'Mrs Maxwell and I are old enemies, didn't you know?' Rachel was too busy chewing on the crusty bread to answer. 'She banned me from Windlebrae long ago. So that just makes me more willing to help you, Miss O'Brian.' He smiled suddenly and Rachel noticed what a pleasant face he had when he was not looking harassed and unhappy. 'Let me help you up onto the seat.'

She gasped at his touch.

'Sorry,' Peter said apologetically. 'She must have beaten you badly to make you wince like that.'

'She used the horsewhip . . .' Her voice faded as the horror returned. 'Her eyes . . . they were so wild.' She shuddered.

'I must make one more delivery to an old woman who is crippled with rheumatism. I can't let her down but after that we shall return to my house. It will be a surprise for the children to see me home so early. I will deliver the rest of the groceries tomorrow.'

'I am sorry to be a trouble,' Rachel mumbled unhappily.

'Don't worry, there's plenty of room. My premises used to be three small shops. I have a paddock at the back for my horse, and we have a large garden.' He was trying to put her at her ease but he had the feeling nothing he could say would comfort her. 'I have a housekeeper to look after my three young daughters,' he went on speaking quietly. 'Her name is Eliza. She came to live with her elderly aunt in the village about three months ago — just when I was desperate for help.'

'Ruth told me you had lost your wife. I am so sorry.'

'Yes. We had an elderly neighbour who looked after us but she became ill. Eliza MacDougal is a poor substitute.' His mouth tightened. 'She comes in daily to care for the children. They are usually in bed before I return home, except on Saturdays. I don't go out with groceries after three on Saturdays.'

Rachel made no response. When he glanced at her he saw she had fallen into an exhausted doze, the remaining bit of loaf clutched tightly in her hand, her head propped against the side of the wagon. He fell silent, deep in his own troubled thoughts. Surely Meg could not have known how cruelly her mother was treating Rachel. Where had she been?

* * *

Rachel woke with a jerk when Peter pulled the horse to a halt. He had not stopped directly outside his shop. Rachel could see the long stone building with one larger window and two sash windows, then a tiny window in a low steeply roofed lean-to at the end. It was at this building that Peter set her down, leading her along a narrow path away from the street to a side door with peeling green paint.

'This is the scullery, Rachel. The wash-house adjoins it through that door and the closet is just down the garden.' He pointed to another green door. 'I thought you might like to wash your face and tidy yourself a bit before you meet Eliza and the children?'

'Yes please!' Rachel agreed gratefully.

'There is cold water.' He indicated the long stone sink with a single brass tap high above it. There were dirty dishes which looked like the breakfast dishes and a porridge pan with a little cold stiff porridge still in the bottom. There was an enamel bowl and a tall jug at the other side. Neither looked very clean but Rachel was longing to wash her face and brush out her hair and re-braid it. She looked at Peter Sedgeman with troubled eyes.

'Everything I have now is in the pillowcase,' she said apologetically.

'Ah yes,' Peter smiled suddenly. 'I had forgotten I had it.' He set down the small bundle. 'Your clothes will be very creased.'

'Yes, but at least I have a clean apron and my hair brush.'

'When you are ready just come through here,' he opened a door at the far side of the scullery and Rachel saw an L-shaped stone flagged passage. 'The kitchen is straight across. The other two doors lead to store rooms and through to the front shop. The stairs are at the end of the passage. We have a front room upstairs. It looks out over the village — but we seldom use it now.' Rachel heard the wistful note in his voice. 'I shall go and surprise the children,' he smiled with real pleasure this time, 'and I will ask Eliza to make a little extra dinner.'

He closed the scullery door behind him and crossed the passage to the kitchen. He was surprised to find the door locked and the key on the outside. He frowned, puzzled. He turned it and entered the large room. One small head turned fearfully towards him. At the sight of her father, four-year-old Polly stared incredulously, then with an expression of intense relief, gave a squeal of joy and hurled herself into his arms.

'Daddy! Daddy!'

'Well, well, my wee lassie. What a welcome! Maybe I should come home early more often.' The last he had muttered regretfully to himself but Polly clutched him tightly.

'Oh, Daddy, could you?' Her soft mouth trembled. The twins did not even look up. They were huddled side by side, on their stomachs on the rag rug which their mother had made shortly before they were born. It was dull now with dust and spills. Both toddlers were sucking at their thumbs as though life depended on it and whimpering miserably to themselves.

There was little heat from the banked down embers in the bottom of the grate. As Peter knelt before the grate he realised the smell in the room was coming from the twins.

'Where is Eliza?' he asked sharply. 'Is she ill?' Polly shook her head, still clinging to her father as though afraid he would disappear.

'Is her aunt ill? Has she been called away?' Again the silent shake of Polly's head. 'Where is she then, my wee lamb?'

'In the shop.' Polly looked anxiously into his face, then she put her mouth close to his ear. 'Eliza goes to talk to Mr Johnson in the shop. Every day.' She drew back and stared at him with fear in her eyes. 'It's a secret. She will hit me with the rolling pin if I tell.'

'I see . . .' Peter only half-believed his four-year-old daughter, but as his eyes moved round the untidy, dirty room, he recalled other incidents, work not done, meals not made. 'Indeed I do see,' he repeated slowly, his eyes narrowing. He felt anger rising in him but he controlled it when he saw the terror in his small daughter's eyes. 'Don't worry,

Polly, Eliza will not harm you. I came home earlier than she expected today so she cannot blame you.'

Polly still clung tightly. Her eyes looked doubtfully into his. It was clear that his child was more certain of retribution from Eliza than she was of his own ability to protect her. His first inclination was to stride along the passage and confront her with Johnson. He had thought his young manager was a trustworthy fellow with a wife and a family of his own. He felt thoroughly disillusioned and despondent. He needed someone to care for his children, and someone to help with the business. His father had started with a small grocer's shop but together they had built it up into a thriving delivery business as well as the shop. He had concentrated all his energies on it, but I have neglected my children, he thought with self-disgust. He was just as much to blame as Eliza MacDougall.

He bent to the fire and began to blow some life into it with the large bellows which stood beside the fender stool. There was a basket of logs which he had filled himself before he left that morning. It was untouched. When he thought about it the pile of logs in the shed had scarcely gone down at all, but the bags of dross, which he bought with his good coal, had almost disappeared. Did Eliza do this every day? How could she leave his children cold and alone?

'Have you had tea?' he asked. Polly shook her head, her eyes on the door. She was still apprehensive. He drew her to him with one arm while adding logs to the fire with the other. 'We shall soon have a nice warm fire and we'll make the kettle sing and have some tea and toast, shall we?' Polly nodded and offered a tentative smile.

'What did you have for dinner?'

'Haven't had any.'

'What? No soup and bread?' A shake of her head was Polly's only response. 'Did Eliza make potatoes and gravy today? Or pudding?'

'No.' Polly hung her head and looked guilty. 'We drank the milk,' she added in a frightened whisper. 'Jane and Mary cried. They always cry. We were hungry.'

'Then you were a clever girl to give them some milk,' Peter reassured her and was rewarded by a relieved smile. 'When did Eliza go out?'

'She goes when we hear you drive Tommy out of the yard.' 'And when does she come back?' Peter asked tensely.

'When Mr Johnson shuts the shop. She unlocks the door and runs everywhere and shouts at us.'

There was a tentative knock on the door. Peter had been so engrossed in his problems he had almost forgotten he had left Rachel out in the scullery. As she entered the dingy kitchen he marvelled at the difference in her appearance. Her face was clean and shining, her hair brushed and neatly braided around her head but there was a red mark down one cheek where the end of the whip lash had caught her. Her white pinafore was creased but it was clean and only the muddy hem of her skirt bore evidence of her ordeal.

'Come in. The fire's beginning to blaze and the kettle will soon boil to make a hot drink for all of us. Polly, this is Rachel.'

'Hello, Polly,' Rachel smiled and held out her hand but Polly hung her head and clung to her father's leg. Peter bit his lip. He felt thoroughly ashamed of his home and the condition of his children. He was seeing everything through new eyes — ones which till now had been clouded by his own despair and his obsession with work.

'Eliza MacDougal, my housekeeper, has been neglecting her duties. She will be surprised to see me home so early today.'

Rachel nodded. She could not help wrinkling her nose at the smell from the two toddlers still lying lethargically on the rug together. It dawned on Peter they were barely aware he was their father. His heart was heavy as he looked down at them.

'I'm afraid they need cleaned up before I do anything else,' he apologised.

'I will attend to them,' Rachel offered.

'You will? You can?' Peter asked in surprised relief.

'I loved to help when we had a new baby in the village where we lived,' Rachel gave him a wan smile and he guessed she was wishing she was back there. Peter wondered again how Gertrude Maxwell could have treated her so cruelly. 'Will you help me, Polly?' she asked, holding out her hand again. This time Polly slipped her own small hand shyly into Rachel's and they smiled at each other. 'We shall need two clean napkins and something to wash them. A clean rag will do?'

Polly bit her lip and looked anxious. 'I don't think we've got any clean nappies. Eliza has not done any washing for ages.'

Rachel looked questioningly at Peter Sedgeman. He rolled his eyes heavenward.

'It's probably true. I'm beginning to think Polly knows more about my household than I do. I don't know what I can do about it, but I must not neglect my children any longer, whatever happens.' He rubbed a tired hand over his brow.

'I will bring water from the scullery and perhaps we could have a little from the kettle to take away the chill for the poor mites.' Rachel winced at her own pain as she knelt beside the twins. Gently she removed the filthy napkins. She gasped in horror at the sight of the raw and bleeding buttocks. Their whimpering had grown louder as soon as she touched them and now she knew why. Polly brought her a piece of soft flannel and a towel which Peter had found for her. As gently as she could she cleaned up the children but their restrained sobs tore at her heart. She looked up at Peter Sedgeman with troubled eyes.

'They really need a warm bath. Perhaps we could use the kettle and have some tea later?'

'Oh, I would like a bath too!' Polly declared excitedly. 'Eliza never lets us bath. She says it's too much trouble emptying the water after.'

Peter's eyes widened, then narrowed angrily.

'I am sorry I have brought you to such a house, Rachel.'

'I shall feel happier if I can do something to repay your kindness. Can you show me where you keep the bath, Polly?'

'I'll bring it.' Peter offered. 'We fill the bath from this tap beside the fire.' He indicated a brass tap at the side of the big black range. 'This is a side boiler. The fire was very low but the water should be warm enough for the small bath which the children use.'

'You can be first, Polly,' Rachel told the little girl, then the twins can go in together and soak their little bottoms. A handful of salt would help. It will sting but they will feel much better afterwards.'

'I'll go through to the shop and get some while Polly has her bath,' Peter offered. 'And I will bring some towels from the store. Perhaps we could cut one to make napkins for the twins.'

He was through the first store room when Cyril Johnson's voice brought him to a halt. He had not meant to eavesdrop on his shop manager but he could not help but catch the drift of the conversation and it sickened him.

He turned on his heel and moved silently away. He must make changes but he needed time. He ran a worried hand through his hair. He made his way back to the kitchen.

Polly was chuckling happily as Rachel helped her from the bath and wrapped her in the grubby towel. The fire was glowing cheerfully now.

'I will get salt from the larder,' he said briefly.

'But, Daddy, you didna bring towels for the twins either.'

'How silly, I forgot!' Peter summoned a smile for Polly. Rachel said nothing but she saw how troubled he looked. She guessed something had distracted him.

The twins screamed when Rachel lowered them into the warm water but she persuaded them to sit in the bath and gradually the initial sting eased a little and the water soothed them.

'I really will bring towels this time,' Peter said as he headed for the door again.

'And Vaseline too, if you sell that in your shop?' Rachel suggested. 'It would ease the soreness.'

'Aye, I'll bring a jar. Maybe you should use some of it yourself, lassie.'

This time he went out through the scullery and entered the shop from the street. Eliza and Cyril Johnson could not have looked more startled if a ghost had entered. Eliza was immediately on the defensive but he sent her for milk from the farm at the other end of the village, deaf to her protests, blind to her sullen scowl.

'I will speak to you later, Johnson, after you have closed the shop for the night. Open the new bale of towels in the upstairs store, if you please. Bring me three, quickly now. My children have been neglected enough already. I will get a jar of Vaseline and attend to the shop until you come down.'

Rachel deftly cut a towel into napkins and dealt with the twins. They were chortling happily now. Peter heard Eliza returning with the milk. He met her in the scullery and took it from her.

'I will see the children to bed myself.' His voice was cold. 'I will talk with you in the morning.' He closed the door, silencing her arguments. He had no intention of allowing her to upset Polly tonight and he was glad he had made that decision when he saw her relief.

Rachel boiled milk and made bread saps for the twins. They ate them hungrily and went willingly to their grubby cots. Eliza had made no preparations for an evening meal. Polly enjoyed holding the long toasting-fork to help her father make toast in front of the fire. Rachel felt too sore and weary and anxious to care what she ate. Peter went back to the shop and returned with butter and cheese and four eggs, as well as a jar of honey. She made a concoction of scrambled eggs with cheese and bread crumbs and they finished the meal with toast and honey and tea. When she had finished Polly got down from her chair and hugged Rachel.

'You made the bestest tea I ever had. I am glad you came to live at our house.'

Rachel gave her a startled glance but before she could contradict her a tap at the door heralded Cyril Johnson. He withdrew quickly at the sight of Rachel sitting at the table. Peter got up and accompanied him back to the shop where everything was clean and tidy, as usual.

'I shall have to make changes around here,' Peter announced grimly.

'Please, Mr Sedgeman, please don't dispense with my services. I need the work. We need the money.'

'I have not decided what the changes will be yet but I have been neglecting my children, I can see that now.' He looked directly into Cyril Johnson's unhappy eyes. 'You are a family man with children of your own. Why did you not tell me Eliza MacDougall was neglecting mine?'

'I-I tried to tell her. I wanted to tell you b-but . . .' he looked down at the floor shamefacedly. 'I c-could not.'

'Threatening you, was she?' Peter suggested dryly. 'Threatening to tell your wife you had been unfaithful?'

'But I have not! Indeed I have not, Mr Sedgeman.' His voice trailed away and again he stared down at the floor. 'I-I did kiss her once. She almost begged me to do it. It was when she first came. She said she was lonely in a strange village. She had tears in her eyes.'

'Yes. She tried that with me.'

'She did?' Cyril Johnson's head jerked up in astonishment. 'She is a — a . . .'

'So it would seem.' Peter muttered wearily. 'I am not sure what other arrangements I can make yet, but I intend to put my children first from now on, even if that means taking care of the shop myself.'

'You — you mean you will cut my hours?' Cyril asked hoarsely. He looked such a picture of dejection Peter felt sorry for him. He was a good shopkeeper, clean and honest, and civil to the customers.

'Well, we shall see. I don't suppose you can think of a good woman in the village who might be willing to help with my children?'

Cyril Johnson scratched his head thoughtfully.

'Not that I can think of. Mistress Jenkins might be willing to do some washing and cleaning. You'll recall Mr Jenkins died three weeks ago?'

'Ah, yes, so he did. Mistress Jenkins was always a kindly soul, but she must be nearly seventy?'

'Sixty-six, and short of money. She's thinking of going to stay with her son and his wife in Ayr, but she doesna want to leave her own wee cottage, or her friends in the village.'

'Would you call in on your way home and ask her if she would come to see me, please?'

'Will do.' Cyril smiled for the first time. 'And thank you, Mr Sedgeman. I love my wife and children. I don't wish ill to anybody, but I hope Eliza MacDougall goes back to the city as she keeps threatening to do.'

'Maybe she will. I doubt if her aunt has been any better for her company.'

'Indeed she has not. She told Miss Witney, she would be pleased to see the back of her niece.'

Rachel and the three children were asleep upstairs when Peter answered a knock at his door. It was Mrs Jenkins.

'Mr Johnson said you wished to see me,' she said diffidently.

'I do, but I did not expect you to come so soon.' Peter ushered her into the dusty kitchen. 'The fire's low. I was just making my way to bed,' he explained apologetically.

'That's all right. Mr Johnson said you might have work for me. I couldn't have gone to sleep without coming to see you first.'

'Strike while the iron is hot, eh? Is that your motto, Mrs Jenkins?' Peter gave her a wry, if weary smile.

'Well, I don't mind telling you, Mr Sedgeman, it would be a lifeline for me if I could have a few hours' work to earn some extra coppers.' She sighed. 'It's not only the money either. Time hangs heavily now I'm on my own. Well, you'll know all about that. You've had your own sorrows.' Her tone was matter-of-fact and Peter was relieved she was not going to ramble on in a maudlin fashion.

'I have three young children,' he reminded her. 'They are my greatest concern at present. I had not realised until today how badly I have been neglecting them.' He looked round the dirty room. 'And our home,' he added with a grimace.

'Well, I like children,' Mrs Jenkins said slowly, 'But I'm not as young as I used to be.' She slumped dejectedly. 'Children are a big responsibility. I wouldn't have minded cooking for the wee mites. As for cleaning and washing, I've done that all my life. Enjoyed it, I did.' She sighed. 'I'd welcome that occupation two or three days each week, but I couldn't look after three wee lassies every day. I'm sorry, Mr Sedgeman.'

'I wouldn't expect you to do everything, Mrs Jenkins,' Peter assured her quickly. 'It would be a relief to me to know the children were fed and clean, at least until I can find a better solution.'

'Well I could certainly help a bit,' Mrs Jenkins offered, casting a swift glance around the grubby room. 'I could come tomorrow? See how we get on?'

'Very well. We shall take each day as it comes.'

'Aye, that's what the minister keeps telling me. "Take one day at a time and the Lord will provide." I've found his advice a bit hard to accept these past three weeks, I can tell you,' she wagged her head grimly, 'But maybe He has answered my prayers after all.'

Peter found it difficult to sleep that night. He had not known Polly was so frightened of Eliza MacDougall until today. He was convinced the bruises on her arms had not been caused by a fall. He resolved to keep the woman away from his family in future. But where was he to find someone reliable, and able to cope with three lively children? He could not neglect his customers entirely. They depended on him, and he needed them for his living. He could not afford to pay a full-time delivery man as well as paying Cyril.

His mind went round and round. He heard the grandfather clock strike midnight and hoped it would not disturb Rachel O'Brian. The poor child had been exhausted. Suddenly he sat bolt upright. That was it! The obvious solution! Rachel O'Brian had been wonderful with the children tonight. She seemed to know instinctively what they needed. She was kind and patient. She needed work. Why hadn't he thought of that before? It was true she was very young, but surely his family would be safe and cared for with Mrs Jenkins and Rachel together?

At last he settled down to sleep. His mind was easier than he had believed possible a few hours earlier. He could not have guessed the further shocks awaiting him.

CHAPTER NINE

Rachel wakened early as was her habit. As soon as she moved and felt the pain, the events of the previous day came crowding back, filling her with apprehension. Why had Ross not come to look for her? Had he really gone away? She must find work, a place to stay, and money for food. Should she go back to her own village? Tears threatened when she remembered there would be no Granny Ferguson to offer comfort or advice.

She rose and washed in the cold water from the ewer she had carried to her chamber the previous night. The least she could do was go down and light the fire and prepare breakfast for Peter Sedgeman and his children before she set out. She knew he must rise early to load his van with groceries. Today he had to make up the deliveries he had missed because of her.

The fire was blazing merrily, the hearth swept and the kettle was beginning to sing on the hob, but Rachel could not find oatmeal for the porridge. Indeed there seemed to be little food in the larder at all. Disconsolately she wandered through to the scullery and from there into the wash-house. The tin washtub and the wicker basket were both piled high with dirty washing and there was a heap of soiled baby napkins on the flagged floor. She suspected some of them had been there for several days. The smell was overpowering.

She set about lighting the little fire under the brick-built boiler and filling it up with water. Some of the clothes would need more than a boiling and a good rubbing if they were ever to come clean. She bent to pick up the pile of nappies. She stood up sharply, holding her throat, trying to control her heaving stomach — but it was no use. She dashed outside, down the short path to the closet, unaware of the woman observing her from the scullery doorway.

Eliza MacDougall had arrived earlier than usual, intending to wheedle her way back into favour with Peter Sedgeman. She had had no doubts about her success. He needed her to look after his brats.

Eventually Rachel felt recovered enough to make her way back up the garden path but as soon as she entered the wash-house she heard angry voices in the scullery.

'Now, I know why you came back early yesterday! You wanted to trap me!' Several oaths followed. Rachel winced. She had heard men swear often enough at the smiddy, but even they had not used words such as this woman was using — and to her employer. She stood frozen to the spot, but the tirade which followed shocked her even more.

'I will not be quiet! Every day you pretended to be working late, saying you had deliveries to make. Liar! Leaving me to look after your brats. Pretending you didna want a woman in your bed. A real Holy Willie you've turned out to be!' Eliza gave a harsh laugh. 'All the time you were taking your pleasure with a bit of a trollop. And she's young enough to be your daughter by the looks of her!'

'Be quiet I say!' Peter Sedgeman commanded angrily. 'The girl you saw has nothing to do with me, I tell you. She . . .'

'No? Then what is she doing here? Why is she staying here? No wonder you didna let me into the house when I brought the milk! She slept here last night, didn't she? She must have done. You wouldn't let me sleep in the same house. Not fitting you said!' She spat the words at him. 'And there she is, spewing her heart out. I know morning sickness when I see it. If she's not expecting your bairn, why bring her here? You are planning to keep her here, aren't you? That's why you want rid o' me!'

'You've got it all wrong . . .'

'Liar! You're a liar, *Mister* Sedgeman! And you supposed to be a pillar of the kirk,' she jeered.

Rachel could not believe the words she was hearing. As their implication registered she gasped aloud. She would have fallen had she not grasped at the mangle. She leaned against it, striving to combat the waves of faintness. Both Eliza and Peter heard her, saw her cling to the heavy iron frame.

'Are you all right, lassie?' Peter Sedgeman moved to her side. Eliza watched, her lip curling. She was filled with a jealous rage.

'Now tell me she's not expecting a bairn! Why, she can barely stand without fainting. And it doesna look to me as though there's much else wrong wi' her . . .'

'Take that money and get out!'

'Why should I?' Eliza stood, hands on hips, her eyes hard.

'Take that packet and think yourself lucky you are getting a week's wages after the way you have neglected my children.' Peter's voice was like ice.

'You can't get rid of me that easily!'

'Get out of my house!'

'You'll pay for this! She's little more than a bairn. You've used her. Your customers will soon take their trade to the new Co-op Store when they hear what you've been up to. As for the kirk, you'll not dare to show your face at the door when the rest of your puritan Elders and *oh, so proper* wives hear what I have to say.' She slammed the door so hard the whole house shook.

Peter's face was white. He knew how easily gossip spread. It grew with the telling, especially in country districts. He knew the sort of malicious gossip Eliza MacDougall would spread. However untrue it was it would be bad for his business. Trade was already poor enough with so many out of work.

'We both need a cup of tea,' he muttered. 'I'll help you through to the kitchen.' Rachel's fingers were clasped so tightly around the frame of the mangle she seemed incapable of letting go.

Her mind was filled with nightmarish pictures. A young woman from her village — a pretty laughing woman. "Flaunts herself in front of the men". "Harlot". "Deserves all she gets." The women had muttered darkly. Even Minnie, who was always fair, had considered her wicked. They had shunned her. The Elders of the kirk had condemned her. One evening just before dark Rachel had seen her, head bowed, huddled in her shawl, hurrying from the village. A few weeks later she had heard the horrified whispers. Someone had found her. She had hanged herself from a tree in a wood. Her shame and misery had been too much to bear, or so Mrs Chalmers had told Granny Ferguson.

'She thinks I'm going to have a baby!' Rachel stared at Peter. Her eyes were dark with horror. 'That's what she said. She meant me, didn't she?'

'Aye, I'm afraid she did.'

'It's not true!' Rachel's voice was rising as panic filled her whole being. 'It can't be true! It can't! It can't!'

'Hush, lassie. Hush now. Calm yourself. Come through and have a cup of tea.'

Rachel allowed him to lead her into the kitchen like someone in a trance. All three children were sitting on the rug in front of the fire. Peter made tea and added a generous measure of sugar to Rachel's. He could see she was in a state of shock. She was shivering and staring unblinkingly into space. After much prompting she drank the hot tea while Peter went into the shop for oatmeal.

'Listen to me, lassie,' he said urgently, taking her by the shoulders and staring intently into her face. 'Was it reaction made you sick?' Rachel stared at him dumbly.

'Have you been sick other mornings?'

She nodded. 'But I was better after. I did my work. I'm not ill. I'm not . . .'

'No, I'm sure you're not ill.' Peter sighed heavily and rubbed his temple. What a mess. He came to a decision.

'I have a lot of work to get through today, Rachel. I need your help. Do you understand? I have sent Eliza away. I need you to look after the children.' He shook her arm. 'Rachel? Will you do that for me? Will you look after my children today?'

'Oh, yes please!' Polly cried joyously, moving eagerly to Rachel's knee and peering earnestly into her face. 'You will look after us, won't you? Please, please, oh please?' She tugged at Rachel's arm. Rachel looked at her in bewilderment for a moment. Then Peter's voice, very quiet, very firm, penetrated her numbed brain.

'Rachel, I need you to stay here today, to look after my children. I am depending on you. Do you understand?'

'Yes.' Rachel's voice was no more than a whisper, but she nodded. 'Yes, I will look after the children until you return.' Her face crumpled. 'What if she is right? Where shall I sleep? Where shall I go? What can I do?' Peter thought she sounded like a frightened child. Indeed she was little more than that, in her ignorance of life. She must know where calves came from, but it had probably never occurred to her to question how they got there. Anger surged in him. Ross must be responsible for this. As for Mistress Maxwell . . .

'You'll stay here for now,' he said briskly. 'Mrs Jenkins is coming to help with the washing and cleaning. Now, lassie, will you make the porridge? I must load the van and get on my way.' He knew the best thing for Rachel was to keep her busy. The children would certainly demand her attention for much of the day and Mrs Jenkins seemed a sensible woman. He pushed a harassed hand through his thinning hair. He could only hope and pray nothing else would go wrong.

Some of Peter's deliveries were to isolated farms up in the hills and catching up on the previous day's deliveries had delayed him. Just before midday he found himself less than a mile and a half away from Willie Maxwell's cottage. A detour would delay him even more but he needed to find out whether Ross really had left Windlebrae.

Ruth was pegging out the baby's nappies when she saw his cart. She went down the path to the little wicker gate.

'Hello, Peter! This is a surprise. I suppose you must have heard the Windlebrae gossip?' She was smiling merrily. Peter stared at her. Ruth was not the kind of woman who took pleasure in the misfortunes of others.

'What gossip?' he ventured warily.

'About the elopement of course. Ross and Rachel. They have run away together.' She gave an exaggerated sigh. 'Oh, to be young and so much in love. They have gone off on the train together. Isn't it romantic?'

'It might be, if it were true,' Peter said. 'In my experience it's easier to believe the course of true love never runs smoothly.'

'Oh, you old cynic!' Ruth teased, opening the gate wide. 'Are you coming in for a bowl of soup and a cup of tea? I'll do my best to cheer you up.' Her face sobered and her eyes were sympathetic. 'Though I know there is only one person who could make you truly happy, Peter.'

'I came to see if Ross really has gone away?'

'Oh, it's true all right. He took the milk to the train yesterday morning, set the pony on the road for home by herself, then away they went. My father is staying here again. He rode over to the station to make sure Ross had not had an accident and been thrown out of the trap on the way home. The station master said he had gone on the milk train to Kilmarnock.' She frowned thoughtfully. 'The funny thing is he never mentioned Rachel getting on the train with Ross. But Willie's Ma is convinced they have eloped together.'

'Did she say that?' Peter asked sharply.

'Why, yes . . . at least she must have done. Willie would never have thought of it himself.'

'And what does Meg say?'

'Poor Meg. She's hurt because neither of them confided in her. She had grown very fond of Rachel. She thought they were good friends even though Rachel is so young.'

'Where was she yesterday?'

'Meg? She took a sitting of eggs to one of the neighbours in exchange for duck eggs. Rachel was in bed. She had been unwell. She had gone by the time Meg came back . . .' Ruth broke off at the blazing anger in Peter's eyes. She had never seen him look so grim before.

'Now I will give you my version,' he muttered through clenched teeth, 'The truth.' He gave Ruth a brief account of finding Rachel. 'I would never have believed Ross would shirk his responsibilities. If I could lay my hands on him right now I would flay the skin off him.' Ruth stared at him aghast, her face pale.

'Rachel had been whipped, you say?' she asked in a hoarse whisper.

'Yes. I have not seen the wounds, but I know a victim of whipping when I see one. I have no doubt she is telling the truth, poor lassie. It was in my mind to give her a home with us, helping to look after the children. I can't do that now. Eliza MacDougall's accusations will make her reputation worse. I darena' think what she will have done to my trade already.' He grimaced and proceeded to give Ruth an edited account of Eliza's vile accusations. 'The problem is, Rachel seems so innocent,' he frowned. 'The possibility that she might be expecting a child didn't seem to have entered her mind until she heard Eliza.'

'She has no mother, nor anyone else, who would warn her about such things.' Ruth frowned. Meg might have warned her but in Ruth's opinion her sister-in-law seemed almost as innocent and gullible as any sixteen-year-old herself, in spite of her age.

'She really needs a woman to advise her,' Peter frowned. 'but she appears to be quite alone in the world. Do you really think Ross has no intention of coming back?'

'I don't know.' Ruth shook her head. 'I thought he was very fond of Rachel. I think we should tell Meg what has happened. She deserves to know the truth.'

Their conversation was interrupted by the appearance of Ruth's father, dressed for riding. When he heard of the two outlying deliveries which Peter had still to make he offered to take them for him.

'That would help me enormously.' Peter accepted the offer gratefully.

'You will have time for some soup now. Willie will be in for his soon.'

'All right,' Peter agreed. 'but I must not delay too long. Rachel seemed so distraught.'

'This is market day. Willie's mother will be away. It would be a good chance to tell Meg about Rachel. I'll go while you and Willie have some soup. He'll keep an eye on the children until I come back.'

Meg was preparing the midday meal when Ruth reached the farmhouse. She smiled a welcome, then saw Ruth's serious expression. 'Are you alone? What's wrong? The children . . . ?'

'They are with Willie. Peter Sedgeman is there too. He came to see if Ross had really gone away.'

'Why? I mean why does he want to know?'

'Did your mother actually say Ross and Rachel had eloped?'

'Yes.' Meg frowned. 'Well, maybe she didn't say so exactly. But that is what she seems to believe.'

'There's no easy way to tell you this, Meg.' Ruth said quietly. 'Rachel did not go with Ross on the train. Peter found her last night. She was miles from here. She must have taken the road leading to up to Ben Gowan at the crossroads. She wouldn't know where any of the roads led come to think of it. She had been beaten and . . .'

'Beaten! Ross would never harm Rachel! How could Peter think such a thing?'

'Not Ross. It was . . . it was your mother. She used the whip.' They both turned to where the whip was kept behind the door. Meg stared at Ruth incredulously, her eyes widening in horror.

'No! I can't believe it. Surely Mother would never . . . ?'

'Peter thinks Rachel may be expecting a child.'

'Expecting a . . . Oh no!' Meg slumped onto a chair.

'He thinks your mother guessed.'

'I-I can't believe Mother would whip her! Especially if that's true.' Meg covered her face. 'Poor Rachel. She will need help more than ever. She needs Ross. Surely he cannot mean to desert her, can he . . . ?'

'I should have known!' Both women turned to look at Cameron Maxwell, sitting upright in his wooden armchair. 'I should have guessed Gertie was up to something!'

'Father! Don't upset yourself, please,' Meg pleaded urgently.

'Upset myself? I promised Connor O'Brian I would take care of his bairn. Oh my God! What have we done to the poor lass.'

'She is safe for now,' Ruth reassured him quickly. 'She's at Peter Sedgeman's. But I don't think she can stay there.' She told them about Eliza MacDougall and her threats to make a scandal and ruin Peter's reputation and his business.

'How could Mother treat her so?' Meg was near to tears herself. 'I must have been away with the eggs.'

'Aye, and I must have been half-asleep in the closet. I remember Gertie insisted I should go. I must have dozed off because I nearly fell off the seat. It wakened me up.'

If the situation had not been so serious Ruth would have gone into peals of laughter.

'We must bring her back,' Cameron insisted.

'She wouldn't want to return, Father. Or at least I wouldn't if I was in Rachel's shoes.' Meg loved her father dearly. She couldn't tell him how often she had considered running away from Windlebrae. It was for his sake she had stayed and now she felt even more torn between her loyalty to him and her love for Peter. 'Rachel may be young and innocent, she may have been foolish too, but she is proud.

She has done her best to earn her keep but Mother made her unwelcome from the day she arrived. But I never thought she could she be so cruel.' Her voice shook with anger. 'I cannot forgive her for this . . .'

'I should have guessed Gertie was up to something,' Cameron said again.

'I am thankful it was Peter who found Rachel.' Meg shuddered at the possibilities. 'He is the kindest man I know, but he was right about Mother. He says she can't bear to see other people happy, especially since Josh died. Ross has been happier since Rachel came. I think they were falling in love.'

'Then why has Ross gone away?' Ruth ventured.

'I don't know.' Meg frowned thoughtfully. 'Maybe this is his way of standing up to Mother. It seems I shall have to do the same.' Ruth had never seen Meg look so angry, or so determined.

'But Meg, you're her own daughter. Surely . . .' Ruth broke off at Meg's bitter laugh.

'That makes it worse. She thinks it's my duty to stay here and help her, especially . . .' She broke off. She hated making her father feel a burden. She looked Ruth in the eye. 'Peter asked me to marry him the night before we finished Willie's hay. He understands how I feel about neglecting father. He promised to bring me back to help Mother two days every week. He's so good, and so willing to compromise. I thought when Rachel was here too it would be a good solution. Mother would not even listen. As soon as I mentioned marriage to Peter she flew into a rage. She — she looked . . .' Meg lowered her voice for Ruth's ear alone. 'Almost insane.'

'Oh Meg, I am sorry. What did Peter say?'

'He will probably never ask me to marry him again. Half of him agrees with Mother because he thinks he has only burdens to offer me with three small children. But the only life I ever wanted was with Peter.'

'Why didn't you tell me he had asked you to marry him, lassie?' Cameron Maxwell asked with some distress. 'He is a good man.'

'Oh, Father, I don't really want to leave you. Mother said she would not let me in the door to see you if I marry Peter . . .'

'Eh lassie, as long as I'm here the door will never be locked against you, whatever Gertie might threaten. Now you listen to me, I'm not going to be here forever, and I may not be any use for work now but I don't need nursing, as your mother makes out. In fact, I often think I'd be a lot better still without Doctor Jardine's medicine. Now if you really love Peter, you go to him. Go now. Tell him so.'

'Oh, I do love him, Father, I do, but I can't desert you . . .'

'Think about it lass. I appreciate you considering me, I really do, but it's your life you have to think about. Now, not when I'm gone. Besides I'd like to see you happily wed, before I die. But it's your decision.

'Oh Father,' Meg whispered hoarsely. 'Don't talk of dying.'

'Dinna fret so, lassie. I've done my best to live a decent life. I've no fear of death. Just do what's right for you. We'll manage all right here. Maybe I should have done a bit more plain speaking years ago.' He nodded to himself. 'I never did like quarrels. You take after me, Meg, but this time you need to think about yourself. If you love Peter, go and tell him.'

'Yes, go on, Meg,' Ruth urged. 'I will wait here until you return.' Meg hesitated for only a moment, looking from one to the other, then she turned on her heel and sped out of the house, down the track to the cottage, her skirts bunched high above her flying feet. Peter was just climbing up onto his wagon to drive away when Meg came in sight of the cottage.

'Peter! Peter, oh please wait!' she called breathlessly. He turned in surprise.

'Meg?'

'You were right about Mother, Peter,' she panted. 'Even Father agrees. Can I . . . ? Do you . . . ?' She looked down at her feet. What if Peter no longer wanted her for his wife? 'If you still want me . . . ?'

'Want you?' Peter stared at her. Suddenly he grasped her shoulders so hard it hurt but Meg didn't care. The light in Peter's eyes told her all she needed to know, even before he repeated gruffly 'Want you? Meg Maxwell! I want you more than anything in the world. I've wanted you for as long as I can remember.' She smiled tremulously then. He seized her in his arms and swung her off her feet in his joy. When he set her down again he kissed her with tenderness, but Meg could feel the passion in him and her heart sang.

'Hey, what's all this then?' Willie chuckled from the cottage door.

'Meg is going to marry me,' Peter told him triumphantly. 'You are going to marry me?' he asked in sudden consternation. Meg nodded. Her smile was radiant.

'Well, I don't know what's brought this on, but it is about time. Congratulations! When's the happy day?'

'Soon. I'm sorry, Willie, it will make you terribly busy until Ross returns.'

'If he returns,' Willie corrected glumly.

'I can't believe Ross would run away,' Meg frowned.

'Even if it is true Rachel is expecting his baby, he probably doesn't know yet.'

'Mother must have been fairly certain.'

'You will not let her change your mind, Meg, will you?' Peter asked urgently, his arm tightening around her shoulders. 'Come with me now . . .'

'I shall not change my mind.' Meg's tone was calm and firm. 'I just wish I had talked things over with Father, instead of telling Mother.' She smiled up at Peter. 'I think he's really pleased you will be his son-in-law.'

'But you will still have to face your mother. Shall I come?'

'No. Now that I know we have Father's blessing, and that he does not mind me leaving Windlebrae, I can deal with Mother. I hate quarrels but I'm not a coward. I must tell her to her face. I will pack my clothes though and maybe you will bring them down to your cottage, Willie?' She grinned at

Peter. She was the old mischievous Meg Willie remembered. 'I don't want to be coming to you without any clothes to wear.'

'O-oh, I wouldn't mind that.' Peter winked at Willie and they both chuckled at Meg's ready blush.

'Rachel told me she had a carved wooden box. Can you bring that for her? I will collect you as soon as I finish my rounds,' Peter promised, his smile broadening by the second. 'Rachel will be pleased to see you too. She needs help to bathe her wounds, as well as a friend to give her comfort and advice.'

* * *

Much later that evening Meg felt exhausted by the events and emotional upheavals of the day. Peter sat beside her on the horsehair sofa at the side of the fire. It was time to go to bed but they were both reluctant to part.

'You will not be sharing a bed with anyone else for long, my love,' Peter said softly. 'I saw the minister tonight. He had heard some of the rumours Eliza MacDougall has been spreading already. He has agreed to call the banns on Sunday — just once instead of thrice.'

'Can he do that?'

'Oh yes. It costs a pound instead of four shillings and sixpence. Three times the price for a third of the work.' Peter grinned. 'What do we care, if it means we can marry sooner?'

'Thank you, Peter. You are a good man,' Meg murmured against his shoulder. Then she sat up with a shudder. 'Even though you had warned me, I could not believe how cruelly Mother had wielded the whip until I saw Rachel's back and shoulders.' Her voice shook as she struggled to hold back her tears. 'I think Mother has been a bit unbalanced ever since Josh died but she seems to have been worse since Rachel came. She flew into a terrible rage. She said if I left Windlebrae tonight I would never be allowed through her door again. Father was so calm about it all. She turned her

101

fury on him then, but Willie intervened. In fact Willie was more stern and in command than I have ever seen him.'

'Perhaps that is what your mother has needed since your father was ill,' Peter reflected without criticism. 'I suppose it became a habit to take charge.'

'You're making excuses? After the way my mother has treated you? And Rachel?'

'Her treatment of that poor girl is unforgivable,' Peter agreed. 'As for us, she will have to get over her disappointment. Maybe you will be able to visit your father on market days, while she's away from home.'

'I never thought of that.' Meg smiled happily. 'I'm just sorry I didn't talk to Father before. You are so good, Peter.'

'I don't feel good.' His voice was muffled against the warm hollow at her neck and his arms tightened around her. 'In fact I feel decidedly wicked — and happier than I ever believed possible. You blush so delightfully, my darling girl.'

CHAPTER TEN

Ross knew nothing of the changes that had taken place at Windlebrae so soon after his departure. As the days passed into weeks he despaired of hearing from Rachel and the thought of not seeing her again depressed him terribly.

He was on his way to the turnip field when he saw the Factor riding up the track to Briarbush on his big chestnut gelding. Jim MacDonald was surprised to see him.

'Good morning, Jim. I heard your young relative was still with you?'

'Good morning, Mr Shaw. Yes, Ross has decided to settle in the area. I have been putting word around that he's looking for work.'

'So I believe. I still think he's a bit young to take on a farm of his own. I have another proposition to put to him, but I'm not sure whether he has enough experience.'

'He is a hard worker, I can say that for him, and tidy too. Ross has been well-trained.'

'Good, I'm pleased to hear that, as you'll appreciate when you hear what I have in mind.'

'Will you come in then and take a cup of tea? I expect Ginny will be in a bit of a fluster. We were not expecting you.'

'I would welcome a hot drink. It's a raw morning with the autumn mist so slow to clear. Tell your wife I insist on drinking it at the kitchen table today, and one of her girdle scones would be a treat.'

A little while later, the Factor looked quite at ease in the MacDonalds' cosy kitchen. It made Ross feel less in awe than he might have done when Jim called him in.

'You do know Alice Beattie, Jim? She farms at The Glens of Lochandee?'

'I know her slightly. How is she keeping?'

'In good health, but struggling to pay her way like the rest. Worse than that, in fact. She thinks she may have to give up the tenancy. It will break her heart to leave Lochandee. Her family have been there for generations.' He turned to Ross. 'I have a proposition to put to you, young man, and I want you to consider it very carefully. It would be a big mistake to let Alice Beattie down if you changed your mind, or found the responsibility too much. There would be no place for you on this estate, or any other in this area.'

'I understand,' Ross nodded. Privately he felt he had nothing to lose. He would welcome any challenge which would take his mind off Rachel. He had to make a new life and learn to face the future without her.

'Alice Beattie is the last member of a family called McAllister, except for some cousins in Canada and they were really her mother's side. She married Thomas Beattie late in life. They had no family. Tom died eight months ago. He was a sick man for five years or more, before that. Alice gave him all her attention and devotion. It meant she had to leave the farm to hired men. They were good men. Most of them had been at The Glens of Lochandee for years, but they were all getting old. One died and another lost his wife and moved away to stay with his sister near Annan. Nathan Wright and his wife are still in their cottage but they will not go near the farm since Mrs Beattie hired a new fellow — or at least one of her neighbours hired him for her. I expect McNish was half drunk before he even reached the hiring fair. He would probably have hired a monkey if he had seen one.' Mr Shaw gave an exasperated sigh.

'Anyway since then the whole farm has deteriorated at an unbelievable rate. Really unbelievable. The Glens of Lochandee was one of the best farms on the estate at one time. The McAllisters were highly respected tenants. At Mrs Beattie's request we let some of the Lochandee land to two of the neighbouring farmers when her husband became ill. Neither of them is doing as well as Alice did on her own.'

'I see. How many acres is it now?' Ross asked, his interest awakened.

'A hundred and fifty acres. It's good land. It will be about seven miles from Briarbush wouldn't you say, Jim?'

'About that. It's a bit further south, nearer the Solway Firth.'

'The land is all south-facing, well-watered fields — a real dairy farm.' Mr Shaw quirked an eyebrow at Ross, recalling his previous comments.

'Sounds too good to be true,' Jim frowned. 'Where does Ross come in?'

'Alice would like to end her days where she was born. I'm certain she could manage with the help of a good reliable man, someone trustworthy in every respect. She has discovered the man she has been depending on during her husband's last illness is bone idle. But I've made a few enquiries myself and I have good reason to believe he's a cheat, and a liar. I just wish she had asked me to find her someone earlier instead of relying on McNish. She also has a young fellow. He's a sort of half-wit, but he is intensely loyal to Alice. He's as strong as a horse, and willing with it, but he needs constant supervision. His family were at Lochandee before Alice was born. He has nowhere else to go if she gives up.' Mr Shaw looked up at Ross and held his gaze.

'Are you offering me the job?' Ross asked.

'Not even that exactly.' Mr Shaw hesitated, then he went on, 'Mrs Beattie has the stock. She can just about afford the rent. If she had a man she could rely on I'm convinced she could pay her way.' He grimaced. 'The truth is she can't afford to pay much in the way of wages. She needs someone who would farm the place as though it were his own. You would be well-fed, that I can guarantee, and clothed. If there is any profit at the end of the year, after the rent and all the expenses have been met, then Alice would be willing to share it instead of wages.' He met Ross's eyes steadily. 'It's a challenge but I feel there would be some reward for the right man, even in these days of poor prices.'

'There's not much profit in any farming at present,' Jim MacDonald, demurred, 'but it sounds a fair proposition to me. Certainly it would be less risk than being a tenant on your own, lad. Tell me, Mr Shaw, what does Mrs Beattie hope to get out of it?'

'No more than I have told you already — just to keep her beloved Glens of Lochandee to the end of her days. Of course she keeps hoping the Government will honour the promises made after the war when the nation was starving. If that happens she could afford to pay decent wages and employ good men again, as her father did. Before you make your mind up, young man, you will need to meet her. You can see Lochandee for yourself. Are you interested?'

'If I managed to keep the farm going,' Ross said, choosing his words, 'for as long as Mrs Beattie needed it, what chance would I have of taking it on as a tenant in my own name?'

'Well, well!' Mr Shaw threw back his head and laughed. 'I'm pleased to see you consider all aspects, my boy. You are looking ahead. I'd say you would have every chance of becoming the next tenant, if you prove yourself worthy with Alice Beattie. I should warn you, though, she may not be fit enough to carry on alone, but she is still a healthy, energetic woman. She's in her late fifties I think.'

'I would like to meet her and to see the farm. Would you mind if Mr MacDonald came too, to give me his opinion.'

'That would be in order. What do you say, Jim?'

'I should be pleased to see The Glens of Lochandee. I've heard a lot about it. They used to sell some fine Ayrshire cattle. But I'm convinced Mistress Beattie and young Ross here will make up their own minds.'

'I have nothing to lose,' Ross said bitterly to Ginny MacDonald, when her husband had escorted the Factor back to his horse.

'Maybe not,' Ginny agreed, 'but you might have a lot to gain, if you are patient. Never underestimate a woman, Ross. Alice Beattie was brought up to farming. She will know as much about it as most men, even if she does not have the physical strength to do all the things she would like. I've lived in this area all my life and her father and grandfather McAllister were well-respected as breeders of Clydesdale horses and Ayrshire cattle. Her grandfather was more than just the largest tenant farmer on the estate, he was a close friend of the present Laird's father. His wife was a distant relation, I believe. I can scarcely credit that Alice Beattie has fallen on such hard times. A sick husband needing her attention would make life difficult, of course, but I'm sure there must be some other reason for it.'

* * *

The following morning Jim MacDonald harnessed Flash into the trap. He knew most of the country roads around Briarbush and Mr Shaw had given him detailed directions once they reached the village of Lochandee.

'We'll cut across country and skirt around Lockerbie heading south,' he told Ross. It will save Flash a couple of miles or so both ways and you will see a bit of the countryside as we go.'

Almost as soon as they reached the village of Lochandee Jim turned the trap on a narrow road to their right.

'Two miles along here before we turn onto the road into The Glens of Lochandee,' he told Ross. 'It's not so far as the crow flies but Flash hasn't grown his wings yet.' He grinned at Ross. 'When we get a bit higher you will see the village if you look back.'

Ross followed his advice. He liked the lay of the country as they jogged along. More than that, he had the strangest feeling of belonging, of being a part of the gently sloping fields, the wooded banks and meandering burns. In spite of the misty autumn morning he could see the glint of a loch through a fold in the hills, with the village spread out along one side. Clusters of low whitewashed cottages hugged the side of a wide street, at the end of which the red sandstone of the church spire glowed warmly against a blue-grey sky, with the shining arm of the loch curling round the back of it. Here and there large sandstone villas dotted the land behind the cottages.

The farm itself was another mile off the road. The buildings were arranged on three sides of a good square yard. The house, with its garden and a small orchard, was set a little distance apart making up the fourth side. It was much larger than the MacDonalds' neat whitewashed farmhouse, and more than twice the size of Windlebrae. Moreover it was built in red sandstone with pillars on either side of the wide front door.

'The house looks big, almost . . . grand!'

'Aye, The Glens of Lochandee was known to be a fine place,' Jim reflected. 'The sandstone is quarried locally and most of the farmhouses round about the Laird's mansion are built with it. It's not the look of the house that pays the rent though,' he added warningly.

'No,' Ross nodded solemnly, 'I know that, but it does give a warm, welcoming sort of feel to the whole place. I feel I could belong here.'

Jim MacDonald gave him a startled look, then he laughed. 'It's funny you should say so. That's exactly how Ginny and I felt about Briarbush when we first saw it, and I've never wanted to leave it. Like Alice Beattie, I hope I can stay there until they carry me out feet first.'

'Briarbush was not where you lived with your parents then?' Ross asked in surprise.

'Oh no. My elder brother took over the farm where we lived. We looked at a number of farms before I got Briarbush, and I was impatient to be married. I have never regretted either step,' he grinned. 'Though I did believe there was no lassie as gentle and pretty as your own mother when I was a bit of a laddie.'

Ross stared at him open-mouthed.

'You knew my mother?' he whispered hoarsely.

'Of course I knew her. Half the lads in the village worshipped her.' He smiled reminiscently. 'We would have run miles just to have her smile at us. The old folks in the village all thought Cathie Maxwell was one of the kindest, gentlest young women God ever made.

'Maxwell? Did you say Cathie Maxwell?'

'Well Catherine if you used her full name I suppose. Cameron always referred to her as his "wee sister, Cathie". They were a talented pair — him with his fiddle and her with a voice as clear as a nightingale.'

'Well!' Ross was dumfounded. 'Why didn't they tell me?' he muttered to himself. Jim MacDonald looked at him curiously.

'Tell you what, Ross?'

'That Cathie Maxwell was my mother, of course!'

'You mean you didn't know? Gertrude didn't even tell you that?' Jim was astounded.

'Not a word,' Ross breathed, shaking his head in disbelief. 'I had no idea my mother was a Maxwell . . .'

'It was a tragedy that your father was killed only a few days before their wedding.'

'You knew my father too?' Ross was incredulous. 'They were going to be married?'

'I didn't know your father, but I know they were going to be married. The Ross's had a hill farm. It was very isolated. Cathie was staying there. Mrs Ross was in poor health and your mother was good at nursing people. She seemed to have a gift for caring.'

'I see . . .' Suddenly Ross felt as though a huge weight had been lifted from his shoulders. It was true he was still illegitimate. Nothing could alter that fact, but it was a relief

109

to know he was not the son of a whore. 'How was my father killed? Do you know?'

'Everybody knew. It was in all the papers. There were twenty people killed. Didn't Gertrude tell you anything about your parents?'

'No.' Ross's voice was grim. 'I didn't even know my name was my father's surname. There was nothing in the letter about them.'

'Cameron should have told you! Gertrude and her morals and religion! She's just a hypocrite. If the truth be known she might have caused a bigger slur on the Maxwell name than anyone if some of the rumours were true,' Jim muttered angrily.

'My father . . . ?'

'Your father had gone to a football match in Glasgow with some of his friends. According to gossip at the time, he hadn't really wanted to go, his mother being so ill and the wedding only a few days away. They persuaded him to join them as a last fling before he settled down.'

'When was it — the football match I mean?'

'As far as I remember it was about March or April. The year was 1902, I remember that.'

'I see . . .' Ross's eyes were narrowed thoughtfully. Jim cast him a sideways glance, 'and I was born on the twenty-fifth of November . . .' he muttered under his breath.

Ross's mind was racing. He felt his spirits rise for the first time since he had opened the letter and learned he was a bastard. He knew who his mother had been. She sounded just like Meg. And she had been going to get married. His father had not been someone she had met at a dance. His own face burned as he recalled the one occasion he had been persuaded to drink enough to fuddle his senses and be led astray by a woman nearly old enough to be his mother. He had feared he might be the result of just such a fleeting union. He had even wondered if Cameron Maxwell really was his father and if that was the reason for Gertrude Maxwell's resentment.

He was startled out of his reverie by the Factor's greeting.

'So what are your first impressions of The Glens of Lochandee, young man?' he asked pleasantly.

'They're the very opposite to the last farm you showed me. I knew I could never live there. But here . . .' he lifted an arm in a wide arc, embracing the sweep of fields spread out before them, the gentle folds of the low hills, the silvery ribbon of the burn meandering in and out of view, and beyond them the sheltering peaks of higher hills. Suddenly the lines of a poem he had learned at school sprang to his mind:

Land of brown earth and shaggy wood,
Land of the mountain and the flood,
Land of my sires! What mortal hand
Can e'er untie the filial band,
That knits me to thy rugged strand!

He breathed in deeply. He was overwhelmed by the intensity of his feelings for a place he had never seen before. He smiled, the slow wide smile which had not lit his face since he set out from Windlebrae.

'This is as near to perfect as I can imagine.'

'Ah, now you're a laddie after my own heart!' A middle-aged woman chuckled at his elbow. He had not heard Alice Beattie approach. She was plump and rosy-cheeked with hair that still had more brown than grey. It was drawn into a bun but it was thick and wavy at the front. Ross guessed she had once been very pretty. Her smile was warm, her brown eyes dancing. She reminded him of an older edition of Meg. At the thought of Meg his face softened.

'Come away in, all of you. You'll be ready for a cup of tea, I'm sure.'

'If you don't mind, we would like to take a look around the farm first,' Mr Shaw suggested. 'Ross may have some questions he would like to ask you when he has had a chance to see everything.'

Alice nodded agreeably and the three men moved away to the buildings. The dairy was adjacent to the house and there was a large empty room next to it.

'This was the cheese dairy,' Mr Shaw told them. 'Alice has not made cheese since Tom fell ill. The milk has to be taken three and a half miles to the station early every morning. It goes by train to a buyer in the city.'

They moved from the dairy to the stone-built byre with its wooden stalls. There was a passage in front of them to make it easier to feed the cows in winter, and a hay-loft above.

'Stalls for thirty milking cows,' Jim MacDonald whistled. 'Six more than we have at Briarbush.'

'Milk is the main income,' Mr Shaw nodded. 'Unfortunately they seem to have lost a lot of the cows since the man Kerr has been in charge. Nathan Wright and his wife have spent most of their married life in the cottage here. They were sickened and disgusted by Kerr's neglect. I believe they might come back to help a bit when he gets out of the way.'

At the far end of the byre a door led outside. Ross walked ahead, leaving the two men discussing the buildings. As he had anticipated he found himself in the stack-yard. He was dismayed to see how badly thatched the round straw stacks were. They would never keep out the winter rains. Adjacent to the byre an open-fronted shed ran to his right. It was piled high with dung and Ross drew to an abrupt halt at the sound of a man's voice uttering obscenities, apparently haranguing someone.

He peered through the slatted enclosure of the pens and saw a gangly limbed man loading mammoth forks of manure onto a cart. A little distance away another man was lounging on a low wall, smoking a pipe, one leg propped on the other. Between puffs at his pipe he continued his crude insults, exhorting the other man to impossible feats although his labours were already causing him to sweat profusely. Ross felt sickened by the bully. Mr Shaw approached.

'Who is that lazy ruffian?' Ross asked. The Factor's face tightened with anger. He stepped forward.

112

'Good afternoon, Alfie,' he addressed the gangly young man. A wide grin split his thin irregular features. He lifted his arm in a wobbly salute.

'G-g-'fte'n, M-M-M.' He cackled with delight. The other man had jumped to his feet, stuffing his lighted pipe into his trouser pocket.

'I should put that pipe out, if I were you, Kerr,' Mr Shaw commented coldly, 'Though a flame or two around your backside might get you moving enough to dirty your own fork.'

'I-I was just . . .'

'Just watching Alfie do the work, as usual,' Mr Shaw nodded contemptuously. 'That manure should have been out in the spring.'

'I'm the only man around here. I can't be expected to do everything myself!' he argued sullenly.

'That's the trouble, you don't do anything yourself — at least only when Mrs Beattie is there to watch over you. Let me tell you, my man, you will not get another hiring on any of the farms on this estate, I shall see to that. You are not worth the salt for your porridge.' The man's eyes narrowed angrily.

'That old bitch has been complaining again, has she?'

'If you mean Mrs Beattie, then you are wrong. I know you . . .'

'You know nothing about me! What can you know? Riding around on your fine horse, acting like the Laird himself.'

'If I were the Laird you would have been away from here months ago. If he hears how you have cheated Mrs Beattie you might find yourself without a place before the hiring fairs,' Mr Shaw told him icily. 'Oh, don't deny it. I heard how you had sold half a dozen sheep to a dealer and another four to one of your cronies. You told Mrs Beattie they had died. Word of such treachery travels swiftly around an estate like this. Don't you forget it.'

Watching the encounter, Ross realised that Mr Shaw might be a good friend to Alice Beattie, and to the MacDonalds, people with an integrity to match his own, but

113

he would make an implacable enemy. It was evident he kept his eyes and ears open too. Not that he could feel sorry for the man called Kerr. He was a typical bully to the poor young fellow who had been trying so desperately hard to please.

'You can act all high and mighty if you like, but she can't manage without me. This stupid idiot,' he glanced malevolently at Alfie's grinning face, 'he doesn't know whether to pull a cow's tail or its tits to get it milked.'

Mr Shaw simply turned on his heel with a look of contempt. Jim MacDonald raised his eyebrows at Ross and they followed on the Factor's heels in silence.

Except for the unpleasant encounter with Watt Kerr, Ross thoroughly enjoyed looking around the rest of the farm, though he could see many jobs which had been neglected. Both he and Jim MacDonald commented on some of these as they passed, especially the breaks in the boundary fences and hedges which clearly allowed the cattle to stray onto their neighbours' pastures, and vice versa. They paused at the highest point of the farm and turned to scan the panorama of fields below them.

'It's a beautiful stretch of countryside,' Ross sighed. 'Much kinder than Windlebrae.' He turned to Jim MacDonald.

'A great improvement,' he agreed. 'If I were you I'd put Windlebrae and Ayrshire into the past from now on, laddie.' Ross sensed he was referring to more than farming. 'Look you can just see the glint of the Solway Firth in the distance, to the left of that line of trees. The tide must be in. They are the Galloway hills beyond. If you look further round towards the south-east you will see the peaks of the Cumberland Fells.'

'Yes, I see the Solway now. I didn't appreciate we were so near the shore!' Ross's surprise was evident and both the men smiled.

'We don't often get snowed in here,' Mr Shaw said.

'It does happen sometimes though,' Jim MacDonald cautioned. 'Then you have to cart the milk across the fields to get it to the station if you want to sell it. Of course we get more than our fair share of rain. The westerly winds bring it. There is no such thing as an easy haymaking — you'll have to remember that if you and Mrs Beattie come to an arrangement. It will be up to you to organise that side of things and make a good job of it.' There was a grave note in Jim MacDonald's voice now.

'Yes,' Ross nodded. 'I may need to come to you for advice.'

'You'll be more than welcome, Ross,' Jim agreed warmly. Glancing up he met Mr Shaw's eyes, and saw a faint nod of approval. A display of over-confidence would not have gained the Factor's recommendation for his young protégé, he realised.

Mr Shaw made few comments until they returned to the house. He waited until Alice Beattie had carried the tea tray into the large square dining room. The mahogany table was already set for a hearty afternoon tea.

As they discussed their walk around the farm and steading Alice was pleased to note Ross's deference to the opinion of the older men but his own comments regarding the poor thatching of the corn stacks were valid, she acknowledged ruefully.

'That is one task Alfie cannot attempt,' she told them. 'The poor boy cannot climb a ladder. His legs seem to go in the opposite direction to the rungs. In fact he's not very good with heights of any kind. Watt Kerr had to do the thatching but he made a poor job of it. I shall be glad to be rid of him — even if it means having to give up my home,' she concluded wistfully.

'I don't think it will come to that,' Mr Shaw assured her. 'Ross knows you can't offer him much more than his keep. Anything extra will be what he has earned for you and for himself. Fair dealing all round.' Ross thought there was a note of warning in the Factor's voice. He remembered Kerr's dishonesty.

'For my part I would not want it any other way.' He lifted his head proudly.

'In that case it's up to you and Mrs Beattie. What do you think Alice?'

She looked at Ross, her eyes kindly but shrewd, her head on one side as she considered him. He felt his colour rise in embarrassment. Suddenly she gave a chuckle.

'I think we shall do very well together. We both have a lot to gain. I shall be content if we can work in harmony and keep The Glens of Lochandee as his Lordship expects his farms to be kept.'

Ross smiled widely in his relief.

'And I shall be glad to accept the challenge of helping you do it.' He looked at Jim MacDonald and gave an unexpectedly mischievous grin. 'We shall aim to make Lochandee the best farm on the estate — even better than Briarbush!'

'Well, you young rascal!' Jim MacDonald chuckled. His heart had given a tiny flip. The glint in Ross's eyes, his irresistible smile, reminded him of his youth and Cathie Maxwell. 'I'll take you up on that. Five years from now and Mr Shaw can be the judge, God willing.'

Five years! The light died from Ross's eyes. Would Rachel still be free? Would she be married? She had never written. He had to put her out of his mind. It was clear she did not want him. He must start a new life without her.

* * *

'Take one day at a time, and do your best with it, laddie,' Alice Beattie advised, seeing the shadows in his eyes, the pulse beating tensely in his jaw. 'No one can do more than that.' She had a good feeling about this young stranger.

CHAPTER ELEVEN

Back at Ardmill, Peter Sedgeman's village, Rachel would have given her life to know Ross had not forgotten her, that he loved her and wanted her. As it was she had no idea where he had gone, or why. She felt deserted and filled with anxiety and dread about the future.

Meg knew little of babies but it seemed likely that Rachel was expecting a child.

'Ross told me he loved me,' she sobbed. 'He said he would always be my friend. He said I could trust him — always.' She had subsided into Meg's arms the second evening they spent together under Peter's roof. Her distress almost brought Meg to tears.

Meg had brought the carved box from Windlebrae and Rachel immediately offered her single gold sovereign to Peter.

'Lassie, I don't want your money!' he exclaimed, and folded her small, work roughened hand around the precious coin. 'You keep it safely.'

'But I owe you so much . . . more than money.'

'You have given me more than you'll ever know,' Peter beamed. 'I'm sorry you had to suffer but it helped Meg to see her mother does not deserve her unswerving loyalty. Anyway, there's plenty of room here, and plenty of work too. You are welcome to stay and help Meg until Ross returns.'

'He will come back, won't he, Mr Sedgeman?' Her eyes were wide and troubled.

'He'll be back one of these days, lassie.' Peter wished he could speak with true conviction. Neither he nor Meg could understand Ross's disappearance, or his silence. Meg thought he might be on a ship bound for a new country.

* * *

Peter and Meg were married quietly in the village church where Peter was an Elder. The whole house seemed alight with their radiance and joy. Rachel tried to be happy for Meg's sake but whenever she went to church with Meg and Peter she saw the women casting her sly looks, and whispering behind their hands. She knew they were gossiping about her.

Once when she went into the shop to take a batch of scones she overheard two of the women discussing her and Peter and her cheeks burned with shame and embarrassment.

'There's no smoke without fire. Maybe Eliza MacDougall had the truth o' it. She was sure the bairn was Mr Sedgeman's.'

'Aye, could be. We've never seen any other man hanging around her.'

Rachel wanted to go and shout at them. She wanted to defend Peter, but she couldn't bring herself to speak to the women.

The winter days grew shorter and darker and the full horror of her predicament preyed on her mind.

'You are working much too hard, dear Rachel,' Meg said anxiously one morning as they finished cleaning the last of the store rooms. Between them they had cleaned every inch of the house and shop, including the old bakery and the oven and griddle plates. Meg planned to bake more scones and bread to help Peter's trade. Rachel shuddered when she considered her own future. How was she to manage? Where

118

else could she find work — the kind where she would have a roof and where her baby would be accepted?

The hurt she felt over Ross's desertion was like a knife twisting in her heart. He had not even bid her a word of farewell. Day after day she had hoped and prayed for a letter. As time passed, her hopes faded. She knew Meg was hurt by his silence too. Neither of them mentioned him anymore.

Yet, in spite everything there was a little fountain of delight which bubbled up inside her every now and then. Rachel loved children. She would have her very own child to love. She would no longer be alone in the world. How she would feed and clothe a helpless mite, without money or employment, she dared not think.

She worked hard to help Meg with the bakery, determined to earn her keep. She was good with pastry and scones and Mrs Jenkins had promised to show her how to make bread.

'I like the company m' dear' she had said to Meg the first week after her marriage to Peter. 'If you don't mind I would like to come and read a story to the wee ones, or help with the ironing and other wee jobs you might find for me. Every little bit ekes out the coppers and I'm managing fine — but I do enjoy the company most of all,' she confided to Meg. 'It was the best thing ever happened to Mr Sedgeman when he married you.' In return Meg made sure she shared a good meal with them at midday. Peter was a kind man; he was also a very happy man now that he had Meg for his wife.

Rachel and Meg used their new skills, with the help of Mrs Jenkins to bake cakes for Christmas, black bun and shortbread for Hogmanay, as well as soda scones and pancakes, oatcakes and potato scones, and loaves of bread. The venture was a huge success. Peter was delighted.

In the cobbler's shop next door to the grocery store Sam Dewar watched the changes with interest. He lived alone. His paddocks adjoined Peter Sedgeman's and he often saw Rachel carrying out the huge wicker baskets full of washing, or tending Peter's two horses and the cow he had bought.

He wondered why a girl who was as young and pretty should look so pensive, even sad. As time passed and he noticed her thickening waist, he guessed her secret and shook his head sadly. Sam did not condemn. His own grandmother had suffered the same fate. She had not been a wicked woman. She had loved the wrong man and he had let her down. There were few people in Ardmill now who would still recall his family history, but Sam never forgot.

He longed to banish the sadness from Rachel's face, to see her smile and offer her reassurance for the future, but Sam was a shy man. He had known Peter Sedgeman all his life but they rarely passed more than the time of day or a vague comment on the weather. Even so an idea gradually formed in his head. It would not go away. As time passed it grew into an embryonic plan — a plan which would give Rachel security, and maybe bring a little comfort to his own life.

At Glens of Lochandee Ross was settling in more easily than he had expected but there were few nights when Rachel did not come unbidden into his thoughts as he settled to sleep. He longed to tell her of the work of the day, changes or improvements he had made. He wanted her to share his hopes and dreams. If she had loved him, as he had believed, surely she would have replied to his letter? His insides twisted with yearning as he recalled the passion she had aroused in him. He thought she had shared it too. But he could not dismiss the shame of discovering he was a bastard. Rachel was so innocent of the world. Could he blame her if she had been shocked by his revelation?

During the day he threw himself into his work. It was a great relief when the surly Watt Kerr took himself off to the Annan Fair to hire himself to some other unsuspecting farmer. Old Nathan Wright came back to help as soon as he heard. He was an old man but he had been at Lochandee all his life and he could supervise Alfie and help with the milking.

'I kenned he was a thief and a liar,' Nathan told Ross. 'He tried tae blame me when the sheep went a-missing but

I kenned he had sold them on the sly. That's why I stayed away. I couldna bear to see him cheating Mistress Beattie so I told the Factor.'

Even Nathan Wright had not known the full extent of Kerr's treachery. The first morning Ross took the milk to the railway station he was waylaid by several women, all holding their milk jugs, waiting for them to be filled from the Lochandee churns.

'O-oh, so we've got a new face today, have we? Didn't that devil Kerr tell you to stop at my gate,' one woman panted, when she caught up with him. She thrust her jug at him before he could reply.

'He didn't mention it,' he said cautiously, curious to find out more.

'But we're all regular customers!' she told him indignantly. 'I get a pint every other morning. There's my money.' She held out a penny. 'We pay as we get it — just like he said. Mrs Perkin gets a gill every day because her man likes fresh milk for his porridge. He charges her a ha'penny a gill and it's poor measure I can tell you.'

'How did he measure it?' Ross enquired, holding her jug uncertainly.

'He dipped the jug in the can of course. Guessed the measure. Cheated if he could.'

Ross made several stops along the way for waiting women and almost missed the milk train as a result.

When he returned to Glens of Lochandee he emptied the coppers he had collected onto the white-scrubbed table.

'Now I know why the dairy company kept complaining about short measure, in spite of the lead seals we used on the milk churns,' he announced triumphantly.

'Was there a reason?' Alice asked, 'and where did you get the money?'

Ross told her about Kerr's regular milk customers.

'He was charging them eight pence a gallon? That's more than we get from the dairy company! And he kept the money to himself . . .' Alice was indignant. 'No wonder things seemed so bad. I had a feeling in my bones that you and I would do well together, Ross. You could easily have kept the milk money, as Kerr did. My instincts told me you were honest.'

'I would never do that!' Ross gasped. 'But I would like to have a proper measure if we continue. Some of the jugs were not very clean, and one woman complained of short measure.'

'Yes,' Alice nodded. 'I can see there might be problems of a different sort. It takes more of your time too, but the price is better. I knew Kerr was dishonest but I never thought to this extent.'

* * *

Ross accompanied Alice Beattie to the kirk in the village each Sunday. It had been a habit Gertrude Maxwell had instilled in him for as long as he could remember but his presence delighted Alice. She insisted he must share her family's pew, for which she paid a yearly rent.

The minister, the Reverend Simms, welcomed him warmly and introduced his wife. Mrs Simms immediately asked if he would like to join the choir.

'I noticed you have a fine tenor voice and we are always looking for more members.' Ross declined with a smile. No one had ever mentioned he had a good voice before. He felt a sudden yearning for his fiddle, which he had left behind that morning at Windlebrae. His heart sank as it always did as he thought of the things and people he had left behind without a word of farewell. He found it hard not to have bitterness in his heart for the way Gertrude Maxwell had tricked him.

Alice also introduced him to Doctor MacEwan and his wife, as well as several of the other people who lived in the village and a few of the farmers who came in their traps from more distant parts of the parish.

'This is our nearest neighbour, Andrew McNish,' Alice told him but he could tell by the stiffness of her manner that she had little respect for the man.

'I am pleased to meet you.' Ross shook hands but before he let go he added, 'I am looking forward to having a new boundary fence between us. We shall be needing all our grass for our own cattle from now on.' The man scowled. He made no effort to keep his cattle from straying.

'You certainly seized your opportunity there, Ross,' Alice chuckled as they made their way back to The Glens of Lochandee. 'I don't think we shall be seeing much of the McNishes. That pleases me because he spends most of his time tipping up a whisky bottle.'

One of the men Ross had met at the kirk was Mr Pearson who kept a cycle repair shop.

A week before Christmas Ross decided to call on him with a view to purchasing a second-hand bicycle for himself so that he could explore the surrounding countryside on Sunday afternoons.

'You are Mrs Beattie's new man,' Mr Pearson greeted him. 'She introduced us at the kirk. What can I do for you?'

'I am looking for a bicycle.'

He eyed Ross's long legs. 'I could make one from parts.'

'How much would that cost?' Ross asked warily.

'About thirty-five shillings,' Mr Pearson answered promptly, too promptly Ross decided shrewdly.

'That's more than I had a mind to pay for a second-hand machine,' he turned away, denying himself the temptation to smile. He guessed the old man liked to bargain, even if he was the Beadle at the kirk.

'Ah, don't be so hasty, now,' Mr Pearson caught his elbow, turning Ross back into the dim store. The walls were adorned with parts of cycles. He saw Ross's gaze travelling over his stock. 'I never throw anything away. I'm sure I can make something to suit your purse and pride. Mind you the cheapest you could buy new would be three pounds, nineteen and sixpence. A good frame and decent wheels and tyres and you would pay five or six guineas, maybe as much as nine guineas.'

'But, I'm not buying a new one,' Ross reminded him. 'That looks a good sturdy frame up there.' He pointed to the far wall.

'It is. It was off Master Patrick's last bike. 'You know, the folks who live in the big house on the other side o' the loch. They're friendly with young Laird Lindsay.' After a few more discussions and much bargaining, Mr Pearson agreed to make up a bicycle for one pound, seven shillings and sixpence.

'I'll tell you what, Mr Maxwell,' he called Ross back again. 'I would include this front lamp, as well as one for the back if you do me a favour. It would cost you four and sixpence to buy a ruby red with a bulb and bracket. You'll need lamps if you're thinking of coming down to the village dances? The new constable's a sharp young fellow.'

'What is the favour?' Ross asked resignedly.

'Ask Mistress Beattie if she could make a place up at The Glens of Lochandee for my granddaughter. She's a grand wee lassie, but she needs to get away from that step mother of hers. She has a tongue as sharp as a razor and she has Beth doing most of the work for her own pair of lazy wretches.'

'How old is she?'

'Beth? She's thirteen. Tell Mistress Beattie she wouldna need much besides her keep and lodgings. I'd like to see the bairn getting a decent training. The Glens was always the best place for a man or maid starting work. Kindly folks the McAllisters. Always treated their men fairly.'

'I must be getting back for the milking, Mr Pearson,' Ross had to cut short his ramblings.

'But you'll remember my wee lass? You'll ask Mistress Beattie?'

'I'll see what she says,' Ross promised. He was astonished when Alice Beattie took the pony and trap to the village the following day and returned with a slight shy girl beside her.

'This is Beth,' said Ross. 'I hope you will be patient with her. I intend to teach her to milk. Maybe we could start to churn again. I need a live-in dairy maid now that Nathan's wife is too old to help in the house.'

Ross decided he would write one more letter to Rachel, and one to Meg. He smiled to himself as he took his first cycle ride down to the village to post them on Christmas Eve. When they opened his letters on Christmas morning they would be full of goodwill. Surely they must reply this time. Optimism bubbled up in him. Life was improving.

* * *

When Tam McGill pushed his red post bicycle up the road to Windlebrae he also believed Christmas might be a time of goodwill and forgiveness.

Gertrude waylaid him in the yard and relieved him of his mail. He was no longer welcomed indoors for a cup of tea and a blether with Cameron, even as an old friend.

As he pedalled away Tam reflected sadly on the changes. Things had deteriorated since Meg and the lassie had gone, and young Ross too. He was almost certain the letters were from Ross and he wondered if the girls would receive them. Whatever the quarrels that had driven them all away he knew Gertrude Maxwell was the most unforgiving of women.

If he had guessed how desperately Ross and Rachel longed to hear from each other, Tam would have walked the four miles to Ardmill in his bare feet.

* * *

As winter turned to spring Peter's cow calved and Rachel milked her each morning. She made butter once a week for the household and Peter sold any surplus. The three little girls followed her around at every opportunity. Despite the heaviness of her own heart their company cheered her and she was always kind and patient with them.

'I think we should buy another cow,' Peter suggested one evening. 'I can't supply all the orders for your butter, Rachel.'

She flushed with pride.

'We must wait until Rachel's baby is born,' Meg warned. 'She's working far too hard already.'

'She must have something new to welcome her into the world,' Mrs Jenkins declared sentimentally, convinced the baby would be a girl. 'I shall knit a jacket and bonnet, with leggings and mittens to match. I shall use up all my wool ends to crochet a blanket. Now Polly, just you sit there and hold the hank of wool while I wind it into a ball.' The little girl held the skein of wool patiently, full of excitement about the new baby.

In fact the baby took them all by surprise, coming into the world swiftly and with the minimum of fuss during the evening of the twenty-second of May. It had been the hottest day for half a century in London but at Ardmill Rachel had ignored the increasing pain in her back and had fed the chickens and milked her cow without complaint. Two hours later her baby son entered the world with a lusty cry.

'Mrs Jenkins will get a surprise when she comes in the morning,' Meg laughed with relief. 'This baby has done everything contrary to her expectations.' Meg's smile was getting broader by the minute as she cradled the newborn infant tenderly in her arms, crooning softly between her chatter. 'He has not taken several days to come into the world as she said first babies do. Dear Rachel, I must leave you to get some rest, but have you thought of a name for him?'

'No,' Rachel shook her head. Tears began to roll down her cheeks. 'If only Ross had come back. He must bear my name now.' She gulped on a sob. 'He will never know his father.' Gently Meg laid the small swathed bundle in her arms.

'He is beautiful,' she crooned softly. 'He will comfort you.'

'Perhaps I should name him Peter? You have both been so kind to me,' Rachel looked up through swimming eyes.

'Think about it tomorrow,' Meg murmured. 'Sleep now, Rachel. Everything will seem better when you are not so exhausted.'

'Thank you, Meg,' Rachel caught her hand and squeezed it. 'Thank you for everything.'

The baby was christened — Connor Cameron Peter O'Brian — after both of his grandfathers and the man who had befriended her in her time of need. Even before the christening the twins had given him their own version, combining Connor and Cameron to Conan — a name which was to stick. Rachel made no further mention of Ross so Meg and Peter tactfully avoided his name.

Willie and Ruth came to visit and brought a perambulator.

'It is such a generous gift!' Rachel said with tears of gratitude.

'It's a Burlington,' Ruth chuckled. 'Don't worry, Rachel. They may cost three guineas new but Father always gets a bargain. He brought it ages ago and we have been keeping it a secret.'

The three little girls, Mrs Jenkins, and most of all, Meg, were thrilled with the pram. They all wanted to take Conan for walks down the village street, but Rachel would not venture near except to attend church.

'This wee fellow is going to be the most spoiled young man in Ardmill,' Peter chuckled, 'With so many women to look after him.'

Peter watched Meg's attachment to her nephew with growing concern. Her love for children was evident in the way she cared for his own young daughters and their love for her could not have been greater had she been their natural mother. It was the wistful look which troubled Peter. He saw it in her eyes as she cradled the baby to her breast, or allowed him to suck the tip of her little finger. On the evening he first smiled at her, Peter's worst fears were realised. 'He's so beautiful,' she breathed softly. 'If only I could have given you a son of your own, Peter. It would have made me the happiest woman on earth to bear your child.'

Peter shuddered with fear at such a thought and hugged her closer.

'Meg, I am the happiest man on earth already, now you are my wife. You are all I ever wanted. I could not bear it if I lost you now.'

'I know, I know how you have suffered, my dearest,' Meg whispered against his chest, but there was a kind of desperation in her response to his loving that night and many more nights when her emotions were aroused. Peter was troubled.

Every second week Meg had returned to Windlebrae while Gertrude was at the market. Since the birth of Rachel's baby she had been torn between her desire to see her father and her reluctance to leave the baby.

'You must visit Windlebrae, Meg,' Peter advised with some concern. 'You know that Rachel is the best of mothers.'

'But she is so young, Peter.'

'She has a natural instinct. She's a wonderful mother and you would be the first to admit it. Anyway Mrs Jenkins is always here the day you are away.'

Cameron Maxwell was also concerned by his daughter's obsession with Rachel's baby son. He alone knew of her secret hope that Peter would allow her to adopt him and rear the boy as their own. He prayed she would not develop her mother's possessive nature. Whatever struggles lay ahead he was convinced Rachel would never agree to give up her child, even to Meg.

'Is there no word of Ross?' he asked one day.

'No. It's strange that he has not written to you, Father, not even at Christmas. Sometimes I feel so angry with Ross, but at other times I do worry about him. Suppose he's ill or had an accident? How should we know?'

'I don't know, lassie, but there's little we can do. He could be working his passage on a ship to Canada to start a new life there. I hear others are trying their fortune over the sea.'

He had asked Gertrude several times if she had any idea where Ross had gone. She evaded his questions. In his heart he was sure she had had something to do with Ross's disappearance.

In August, the death was announced of Mr Alexander Graham Bell. Whether it was coincidence, or whether his death had brought attention to his invention, Peter did not know, but there were several proposed installations of telephones in the towns and villages. Peter decided such a link might prove useful for his business.

The household and shop accounts were showing a small profit in Meg's capable hands and he felt more confident. They had already decided that he should change his horse-drawn van for one with an engine before winter. Meg was concerned for his health when he was out in stormy weather. Peter agreed it would shorten many of the country journeys.

Rachel's skill at making butter was proving a great asset. Peter decided she should be paid a small wage, in addition to her food and lodgings. Rachel was surprised.

'It's no more than you deserve, dear Rachel,' Meg assured her with a warm smile. It's time you had something of your own. When Conan grows too old for wearing dresses he will need breeches and shirts.'

'Yes. It troubles me, wondering how I shall clothe him. Mr Dewar has promised to make him his first pair of clogs as soon as he's able to walk.'

'The clogger is a kind man,' Meg agreed, 'even if he is rather quiet and shy.'

'He's not really shy when he gets to know people.' Rachel bit her lip. The old cobbler was always kind and gentle when he greeted her and they often exchanged a few words together while she attended the cows and chickens. 'He — he offered us the use of his paddocks now that Peter has bought two extra cows. All he asks in return is some butter and a little fresh milk for his porridge each morning. Do you think Peter would agree? We really do need extra grass and Mr Dewar does not even keep a horse to graze.'

'He does not go anywhere to need a horse. Apparently he has no family either. I'm sure Peter will accept his offer.' Meg agreed enthusiastically, little guessing what other plans Sam Dewar had in mind for the wellbeing of Rachel and her baby son. 'Speaking of going out — it's time you went out more, Rachel.'

'There is nowhere I want to go. Conan is my life now.'

'Peter has promised to buy me a Singer sewing machine before winter sets in so that I can make clothes for Polly and the twins. Mrs Jenkins says the new women's association — Women's Rural Institute, I think they call it, is going to give demonstrations in sewing and other crafts in the village. It would be very useful for both of us. Would you come with me to the meetings during the winter?'

'Oh, I couldn't, Meg! You know I couldn't.' Rachel's face had flushed and then paled, even paler than before.

'You must meet people now that the birth is over. You never go near the village, except once a week to the kirk.'

'And that's hard enough,' Rachel admitted with a distinct quaver in her voice. 'You know the women whisper behind their hands. You know they think I am wicked and sinful because I have a baby and no husband.'

'There are always some people eager to make the most of any gossip,' Meg said sadly, 'Once they get to know you they will realise what a fine person you are. They will learn to love you as we do.'

'No,' Rachel shook her head. 'They are not all as generous as you, Meg.' She shuddered at the thought of meeting the women in Ardmill. Her eyes filled with the tears which came so readily since the baby's birth, and caused Meg much concern. Her anger with Ross flared. Rachel did not deserve the shame of bearing his child alone.

CHAPTER TWELVE

As the year of 1922 progressed Ross threw himself into his work. Alfie had become his constant shadow. His had phenomenal strength and an eagerness to please. They were great compensations for his handicap. Between them they fenced and ditched and mended boundary walls, thatched the stacks and cleaned out the sheds. Slowly The Glens of Lochandee was returning to the tidy, well run farm which Alice Beattie remembered.

She blessed the day the Factor had brought Ross to her. She enjoyed his company in the house too and was beginning to look upon him more like a favourite nephew. She sensed there was something overshadowing his happiness and keeping him from being totally content. It troubled her. She knew little of his family or his background. When such matters arose in conversation he seemed to draw a veil between them.

On Sunday afternoons Ross explored the countryside on his bicycle, even when the weather was less than kind. He could not rest. Whenever he was not working his thoughts returned to Rachel and Windlebrae. Although he knew nothing of her changed circumstances and the shame she felt at bearing a child without a husband, he experienced a growing tension within himself, as though some sixth sense mirrored Rachel's need.

Beth Pearson was so thankful to be out of the clutches of her stepmother and would work endlessly to please Mrs Beattie. She had her own small bedroom off the kitchen. It had been the maids' room for as long as Alice could remember and Beth was always up first to clean out the ashes and kindle the fire ready to cook the porridge as soon as milking was finished. In her free time she went to see her grandfather in his cycle shop.

'Grandpa is going to make me a bicycle of my own,' she announced joyfully on her return one afternoon. 'He says if you had been going to sack me, Mistress Beattie, you would have told me to leave at the May term. That was last Sunday, the twenty eighth.'

'So it was. The term day,' Alice Beattie reflected, 'And I did not even think of it. Indeed lassie, I wonder how I got through all the work before you came.' Beth beamed happily. She was not a clever girl, but she was far from stupid and she had blossomed under Alice's guidance.

The month of May had always filled Ross with a joyful exhilaration. The trees and hedgerows burgeoned with buds and unfurling leaves. Lambs danced in the fields and the world seemed refreshed. He remembered last year how Rachel had lifted her head to breathe in the scent of the hawthorn blossoms floating in the breeze like snow in summer. She had loved to watch the birds flying hither and thither in their search for wisps of straw or wool, or bits of dried grass to build their nests. She had clapped her hands like a happy child when she discovered a four-leaf clover.

This was the first spring Ross had ever spent away from Windlebrae and he told himself it accounted for his tension, the vague anxiety, the restlessness which disturbed him whether he was awake or sleeping. He could not get Rachel out of his mind.

Rachel's yearning at this time more than equalled his own. They were separated by many miles, with memories and thoughts their only link. It had never occurred to Ross that she could be carrying a child — his child. He had no way of knowing she had given birth to a son. He simply knew he had the strongest urge to see her again, to hold her in his arms and talk with her.

He was tempted to ask Alice Beattie if he could take time off to journey back to his old home. Only the thought of Gertrude Maxwell held him back. He owed her a debt. She may not have loved him, but she had not abandoned him to an orphanage. She had fed and sheltered him. The price was his silence and his absence. The gift of fifty pounds he could repay but in his heart he knew nothing would make Gertrude Maxwell accept him, even less welcome his return. But Cameron Maxwell was his uncle, his flesh and blood. Had he agreed to his wife's plan? Ross could not believe he had known of it.

The only home he had now was at Glens of Lochandee with Alice Beattie. She showed him more warmth than Gertrude Maxwell had ever done. He was grateful, but if only he could get Rachel out of his mind . . . The memory of her, the scent of her skin, the feel of her body . . . He groaned. However hard he worked, however many plans he made, Rachel's shadow was there.

* * *

At Ardmill Grocery Store Peter had sold the horse and wagon. He was well pleased with his new motor vehicle and had gained one or two extra customers. He still kept the small trap and a pony which Meg used to visit her father, and for local deliveries.

Rachel was determined to prove herself worthy of her wages by supplying the growing demand for her butter. So Peter had bought two more milk cows. They grazed in the adjoining paddocks belonging to Sam Dewar.

'We shall need a shed for them in the winter,' Rachel reminded Peter. 'Mr Dewar says we can use his byre. He has been helping me to clear it out.'

'Then I must call on him and arrange payment for the use of his fields and buildings,' Peter nodded. 'I will go round to see him tonight.'

He need not have worried. It was not part of Sam Dewar's plans to drive a hard bargain. He was enjoying the activity and Rachel's company.

'I am pleased to see Miss Rachel attending her cows each day. Such a lovely smile she has, though still a little sad. The sight of her pretty face cheers a man's heart. As for storing the hay you could use the lean-to shed at the side, there is a door leading into the byre so it is quite convenient. Jock McCabe was in here to collect his clogs yesterday. I took the liberty of asking if he would have hay to sell. He said you could buy all you would need and he would deliver it here if you are interested?'

'That's splendid. Thank you very much.' Peter was delighted by Sam Dewar's co-operation. 'But we must agree on a rent for the use of the paddocks and the buildings. I would rather pay my way,' He waved aside the cobbler's protest. 'You are obliging me greatly. Will the Laird be agreeable if you sub-let your land and buildings to me? I would not like to cause any trouble for you.'

Sam Dewar did not answer immediately. He took his time lighting up his pipe, then he had another sip of whisky.

'Not often I take a second glass these days,' he commented, 'But it's a good blend you've brought.' He frowned and when he spoke his words came slowly. Peter was astonished at the story which unfolded, but he was even more surprised at the careful thought Sam had given to this arrangement. He was even more astonished at the attention Sam had given to Rachel's situation, and to her future.

The August day was well and truly over by the time Peter returned to his own home. Rachel and the children were asleep. Only Meg was waiting for him and she stifled a yawn as he entered.

'Come on to bed, lass,' Peter said apologetically. 'I'll tell you about my talk with Sam Dewar once we are tucked up for the night.' Meg agreed readily but once Peter started to recount the evening's events her weariness disappeared.

'Apparently, when Sam's grandmother was a young girl in the 1830s, she went to work for the family who owned most of the houses and property in Ardmill. The eldest son fell in love with her. He wanted to marry her. That did not suit his parents. They sent him abroad to travel. Unbeknown to them, he had already given the poor girl a child. She returned to her father who was one of the cloggers in Ardmill. When the young Laird inherited the estate he returned with a wife. He realised the misery he must have caused. As a form of recompense and a measure of security for his child he gave her the deeds for the clogger's property, and the two extra paddocks. That's why he has more fields than the rest of us in Ardmill. The child was a boy — Sam's father. He learned his trade from his grandfather and took over from the old man. He passed his skill on to Sam, along with some artistic additions in leather tooling apparently. Sam says there is little call for such things in the village now. The gentry all shop in Edinburgh or London, but he does nicely from making and repairing the clogs and boots.'

'So Sam Dewar owns the house and the land.' Meg smiled in the darkness. 'He is such a shy, modest wee man you wouldna think he owned two matchsticks. Some of the women in the village say he fills his mouth full of nails so that he does not have to talk to them, but he is always very civil to me. I often see him chatting to Rachel.'

'He's a very genuine man. I have lived next door to him all my life and tonight I had the longest conversation I have ever had with him. Anyway he's perfectly willing to rent the land and buildings to us at a very modest price. Apparently Rachel has confided her desire to earn her keep.'

'She's a little more settled now that she's more independent.'

'Yes. Sam is planning . . .' Suddenly, instinct warned Peter that Meg might not accept the cobbler's observations, or his proposals, with quite the same approval as he had done.

Sam Dewar's perception had surprised him. It was clear the old man had noted Meg's devotion to Conan. He approved of her love, but it troubled him too.

'The way I see it,' he had said slowly, choosing his words with great deliberation in case he caused offence, 'The bairn will scarcely know whether his mother is Miss Rachel, or your wife. When he gets older he will cajole one whenever he canna get his way with the other — not good for a boy's character,' he added, puffing thoughtfully on his pipe. 'Not that I have had any o' my own to rear, but I've watched two generations of bairns growing up in the village and I can tell which ones will turn out to be men and women to respect.'

'Well, what else did you and Sam Dewar discuss?' Meg asked with some amusement at Peter's apparent reverie.

'Sam has plans . . . not until next spring. We must not interfere. He will discuss them with Rachel. It must be her decision.'

'What plans?' Meg was suddenly alert. 'What decision?'

'He's going to improve his cottage, install a water closet and a hot water boiler. He's going to paint the windows outside and in. When it is finished he intends to ask Rachel if she will live there, as his housekeeper, with Conan of course . . .'

'Live there! Take Conan? No! no . . .'

'Hush, Meg,' Peter reached out for her, pulling her back beneath the bed clothes, trying to calm her agitation. 'He's not doing anything until the spring. He was asking my opinion . . .'

'Well I hope you told him it's a stupid idea!'

'No-o. As a matter of fact I think it would be a good opportunity for Rachel to have a house of her own to run, and a place to bring up her son.'

'Oh Peter! How could you? How could you send them away? After all the hard work Rachel has done for you?'

'Meg, I'm not sending them away. If Sam Dewar puts his proposition to Rachel it's up to her to accept or refuse. He's getting an old man. He needs someone to look after him. He obviously likes Rachel's quiet manner, and he has

136

seen how capable she is. I suspect her situation reminds him of his grandmother's. He has some sympathy for her predicament and that is a lot better than condemnation, which is all most people offer her.'

'I couldn't bear it, Peter! I don't want Rachel to take Conan away. We have plenty of room here — you said so yourself.'

'Oh come on, Meg! They would not be going away. They would be next door — just a few yards away.'

'But Conan would live in a different house. He would eat there, sleep there. I would not be able to bathe him. He loves his bath already . . .'

'Please, Meg, calm down.' Peter was worried. Meg sounded almost as obsessive as her mother. 'Think about Rachel and her son. Think about Sam Dewar. He has neither kith nor kin.'

'You want rid of Rachel and Conan. I love him, Peter. He is the nearest I shall ever have to a baby of my own. He's so lovely . . .'

'He's Rachel's son, Meg,' Peter insisted sternly. 'And you have to admit it does not look as though Ross is going to help her bring him up. We must encourage her to look to the future for her sake as well as Conan's.'

Meg began to weep. Peter could not bear to see her so upset. He drew her into his arms and comforted her in the only way he knew — loving her with all the warmth which came so naturally to him. As always the desire he had been denied for so long flared into passion. The whisky he had drunk earlier added fire to his veins, sweeping aside his usual control as he gave himself up to Meg's wild passion. The sublime ecstasy of their loving exhausted them both. They slept, arms entwined around each other, harmony restored.

Peter was careful to avoid the subject of Sam Dewar in the following weeks and Meg preferred to put the whole matter out of her mind. Her thoughts were preoccupied with Windlebrae and her father. The signs of neglect were increasing and it was clear her mother had too much work to do in spite of the girl she had hired from one of the neighbouring farms. It hurt and troubled her that her own mother maintained the silence between them.

'Mother must be aware of my visits but Father says she never comments on the baking and groceries I take for them.'

'At least your father appreciates your visits, lass,' Peter comforted. 'There's little more you can do. Willie and Ruth have done their best too.'

'That's true. I would be happier if they had a live-in maid. Father says Carrie is often late in the mornings. They have fewer cows too. That's a sure sign mother is finding the work too much.' Peter murmured soothing noises but he knew Mistress Maxwell's stubborn attitude.

* * *

It was the end of October. Alice Beattie received a letter from Mr Shaw to say the Laird hoped to pay one last visit to The Glens of Lochandee.

'He wants to meet you, Ross. I remember the time when his Lordship used to ride round the estate on his pony with his father. They always visited the tenants at least once every quarter. The present Laird kept up the visits until he became crippled with the rheumatism but his son has never accompanied him. Now that he has two small boys of his own I thought he might have shown more interest in his tenants and the way they farm. After all the estate will be his one day.'

'Is Mr Shaw coming too?'

'Yes, they are coming in a motor car this time.'

Alice and Beth cleaned the house from top to bottom, although the Laird would only see the front hall and the dining room. She took the silver tea service out of its layers of tissue paper. 'This was presented to my grandfather by the old Laird,' she told Ross proudly.

* * *

After the visit Alice seemed well pleased. 'They were both sorry to hear Nathan had died so suddenly,' she said. 'They had called in to offer their condolences to his widow.'

'His Lordship too?' Ross was surprised because he had seen the effort it had taken to get in and out of the motor car. 'Was that the reason for his visit?'

'He has always cared about the people on his estate, but he wanted to meet you. Did you notice him giving a slight nod to Mr Shaw?' 'No.' 'I think it was a nod of approval. It was after that the Factor said he would make improvements to the cottage. He's going to have a wooden floor put in one end to replace the stone flags. It would make it warmer and drier.' 'Are you thinking we should hire a man to replace Nathan?' Ross asked. 'Can we afford one?' 'That depends on you, Ross. Joint profits require a joint decision, but I do think you are working too hard. If we had more labour perhaps you would find time for a little pleasure. Did you ever go to the village dances up in Ayrshire?'

'Oh yes. After my . . . well, when they needed me I sometimes played the fiddle for the dancing.'

'You play the fiddle? Well, well! There's an old fiddle up in the attic. My grandfather used to play sometimes. It will be badly neglected and out of tune but I will ask Beth to look for it. What about the bowling club? Or badminton? Do you fancy going? I have noticed how melancholy you seem sometimes and I want you to be happy. I don't want to lose you, Ross?'

He could not miss the question in her voice. He knew Mistress Beattie meant well, but he could not confide in her about his family. Even less could he tell her about Rachel. Maybe Mistress Beattie was right. Perhaps he ought to go out more, meet other girls. He sighed heavily. There was only one Rachel O'Brian and he was finding it impossible to put her out of his mind.

'Well Ross? Do you think you will attend the hiring fair?'

'I think we should wait until the May term. By then we should be able to afford a few more cows. A man with a wife might bring help with the milking as well as the ploughing and turnip hoeing. We could certainly find plenty of work.'

'All right,' Alice nodded, pleased that Ross was thinking ahead. 'But remember you must make time for a little leisure too. You are too young to stay at home every Saturday night. Surely you would enjoy the dancing?'

'I will think about it,' Ross promised but Alice noticed the shadows did not leave his eyes and the set of his jaw was much too stern for a young man.

CHAPTER THIRTEEN

It was a bitterly cold morning in November and Meg welcomed the cup of hot tea to warm her up.

'Ugh,' she shuddered as she tasted it. 'You must have bought a new blend of tea, Peter? This tastes terrible.'

'It's the usual blend,' Peter said in surprise. 'It's very popular.' A week later Meg still had a dislike for the tea, but Rachel saw her munching her way through her third raw carrot.

'I think you have developed a craving for carrots, Meg,' she laughed. 'I hope you have left enough to make the soup.'

Cyril Johnstone was serving a customer when Meg carried a loaded tray of scones through to the front shop. She waited while he weighed the sugar into the thick blue bag. As the woman closed the door behind her Meg stepped forward, but the floor suddenly came to meet her. Cyril grabbed the tray just in time and Meg managed to steady herself against the solid wooden counter. Her knuckles gleamed white with the effort.

'Here you are, Mistress,' Cyril Johnstone guided her anxiously onto a chair, peering into her pale face with concern. 'Shall I call Miss Rachel?'

'No, no,' Meg whispered. 'Just — a drink — of water, please.' By the time Cyril returned with a cup of water Meg was feeling better. She sipped it gratefully and summoned a smile, feeling rather foolish.

'I don't know what came over me.' she apologised. 'I've never fainted in my life.'

'Maybe you have been overdoing things a bit,' Cyril suggested.

When he got home he told his wife about the little episode.

'If she were not so old I'd say she was the same as me,' she said promptly, patting her swollen stomach. 'But in her case it must be the other thing that women are supposed to get in middle age.' She giggled. 'I don't know anything about that yet.'

'That's obvious!' Cyril grinned.

The same thing happened to Meg during a visit to Windlebrae.

'You must see a doctor,' Cameron said anxiously. 'Maybe you need more red meat, lassie. You're looking pale.'

Doctor Gill had only lived in Ardmill for two years. He was still regarded as a newcomer by the locals, as were Meg and Rachel. He was younger than Meg had expected. She judged him to be in his early forties, about Peter's age.

He asked her many questions and examined her very thoroughly — more thoroughly than Meg thought could be necessary.

'Well, I hope you will be pleased with my diagnosis, Mrs Sedgeman,' Doctor Gill was smiling broadly. 'There's nothing seriously wrong with your health.'

'Then of course I am pleased!' Meg smiled back and jumped up from the couch, only to grasp the side of his table as the room swam around her.

'Please, do sit down. You will have to learn to take things a little easier, a little slower, until your baby is born.'

'Baby . . . ?' Meg gaped at him.

'You mean you did not know? You did not guess . . . ?'

'Well . . .' Meg frowned as she made some mental calculations. 'I suppose I have been a bit irregular. But you must have got it wrong, Doctor. I-I can't have a baby.'

142

'Who told you that? And for what reason?'

'My mother. I had some sort of illness when I was twelve. She said I nearly died. It was mumps, but there were complications, or so I understood.'

'I see. Well, you are most definitely having a baby.'

'I can't believe it. I just can't believe it!' Meg began to cry.

'You don't want a child of your own?' Doctor Gill asked with concern.

'Want a child? O-oh . . . it's what I want more than anything in the world!' Meg stood up and hugged the astonished doctor in a most uncharacteristic display of emotion. Between laughter and tears she apologised. 'You just don't know how happy you have made me.'

'I think it's your husband you must thank, Mrs Sedgeman.' Doctor Gill bit back a smile. 'I trust he will be as delighted as you are yourself?'

'Peter?' Meg's smile faded. She stared at the doctor in consternation. 'No. No, Peter will not be at all happy. You see he . . . His first wife died, after the birth of the twins.'

'I understand . . .' The Doctor nodded thoughtfully. 'There is no reason why such a thing should happen to you, even though you are not so young to be having your first child. I shall do my best to reassure your husband. If he can afford to pay, I could arrange for you to be admitted to the cottage hospital for the actual birth. They have more . . . er . . . more facilities if there are any problems. I can attend you myself, as well as the midwife. But there is plenty of time to think about that.'

'I will mention it to Peter. It might reassure him.'

Meg could scarcely contain her elation, but she was not without some trepidation at the thought of telling Peter.

Predictably he was dismayed but Meg's joy was so great he tried hard to hide his fear. Secretly he vowed he would do everything in his power to provide the necessary fees for the cottage hospital and the doctor's attendance. He would spare nothing that might help his beloved Meg.

Rachel was delighted by Meg's news.

'Conan will be one year old at the end of May. There will be a year between them. I do hope they will be the best of friends.' Rachel's own experiences had made her more mature than her years. Now she felt older and wiser than Meg.

When Peter voiced his concerns Rachel promised him she would do her best to watch over Meg, see that she rested and spare her any extra work.

'You are a good lass, Rachel. I often bless the day it was me who found you by the roadside. Will you — will you stay with Meg, even if you are made a better offer?' he asked, thinking of Sam Dewar's plans for her.

'A better offer!' Rachel scoffed with rare bitterness. 'That's not likely. Anyway nothing would persuade me to leave Meg until her baby is born. I give you my word.'

Cameron Maxwell could scarcely believe Meg's news. Gertrude had always been so certain she would never bear a child after the illness she had suffered. He was a little concerned, but Meg was radiantly happy.

'Meg is positively blooming,' Ruth told Willie. 'I'm sure everything will go well for her and Peter.'

'They deserve it,' Willie agreed with feeling. 'I could never understand what Mother had against Peter, except that he was not a farmer.'

There was great excitement at Christmas with Peter's three small daughters each hanging up their stockings. Apart from the usual apple and orange and nuts, Peter had saved a small box of jelly sweets for each of them. Rachel had made three little dolls out of calico and sewn on faces and woollen plaits for hair — one in brown, one in black and one in bright yellow. Mrs Jenkins knitted three tiny outfits for each of the dolls. Meg had sewn red velvet dresses with lace collars for the girls. They were to wear them to church and then for a party in the village which had been organised by the Sunday school superintendent.

Conan was still too young to understand but Polly, ever a little mother to him, had insisted on hanging one of her own stockings. So Rachel, Mrs Jenkins and Meg made socks and bootees, a tiny velvet jacket and some knitted leggings so that the girls would not be disappointed.

Mrs Jenkins had already agreed to share their Christmas dinner and Peter was dispatched to persuade Sam Dewar to join them.

Rachel was almost in tears when he presented her with a pair of tiny boots for Conan. They were made of the softest green leather and the tiny stitches were exquisite.

'I know he is a bit young for them just now,' Sam Dewar said apologetically, 'but soon . . . ?'

'Yes, he will need them before long,' Rachel laughed and gave the old man a warm hug.

'When he learns to walk I shall make his first pair of clogs,' the old man promised. 'And for the three little girls . . .' He drew a large paper bag from behind his back and held it up mysteriously. In fact Sam Dewar was enjoying himself immensely. He had never minded spending Christmas alone — but then he had never experienced a family Christmas like this before. Out of the bag came three little boxes, each tied up with a red leather lace. Each box held a tiny leather bag with a draw string top. Inside was a bright new penny and a little sugar pig. The children were ecstatic. Polly gave the old man a spontaneous wet kiss on his wrinkled cheek. Shyly the twins gave him a combined, if rather tentative hug — all of which gave Sam Dewar the greatest pleasure.

In the middle of February Meg awoke from a deep sleep. It was still dark. Then she understood what had wakened her.

'Peter, Peter wake up! The bell is ringing. The bell for your telephone.'

'Who could want me at this hour?' he mumbled sleepily. Meg struck a match and lit the candle.

'It's nearly half past five.' When Peter came back upstairs, he was shivering in his night shirt. It was a bitterly cold morning and the stone flagged floor downstairs struck a chill right through his bare feet to his head.

'Meg,' he took both of his wife's hands in his and squeezed them tightly. 'Please try to keep calm, for the sake of our babe.'

'What is it, Peter? Who was calling?' she demanded urgently, sitting up straight now. 'Father? Is he?'

'It was Willie. He was calling from that new telephone kiosk they put at the cross roads. It — it is your mother. She has had a nasty fall. She is asking for you.'

'Asking for me?' Meg stared at her husband. 'After all this time?' she whispered.

'Aye, lass. Get dressed. I will take you in the van. Dress warmly. The weather is bitter. We may have to walk part of the way.' His voice was quiet and controlled, but Peter did not feel calm. Willie had sounded upset. He had telephoned for the doctor. Knowing Mistress Maxwell's views on illness, that was a bad sign.

'How good you are, Peter. You think I should go to her? You are willing to come with me?'

'I would not let you go alone, lass. And I would never keep you from your own mother, whatever she might have done.'

Meg nodded and began to dress. Peter wanted to hurry her but he dare not. He scrambled into his own clothes.

'I will waken Rachel and tell her where we have gone. She will have much to do.'

'Mrs Jenkins will be here later. She will help.'

'I'll put a note through Sam Dewar's door,' Peter decided. 'I don't know how he can help, but I know he'll try in an emergency.' The word triggered alarm in Meg.

'Emergency? Is mother badly hurt, Peter?'

'I think it must be fairly bad, lass.' He could not bring himself to tell Meg that her mother had lain all night on the cold flagged floor. According to Willie she must have fallen outside, on her way back from the closet. She had dragged herself to the shelter of the dairy door and collapsed there. Willie had found her when he arrived for the milking. He was fairly certain she had broken her leg, or maybe even her hip. She had been extremely cold and barely conscious, muttering incomprehensibly most of the time, but clearly wanting Meg.

146

The roads were treacherous with ice. Peter was intensely aware of the effects a nasty skid could have on Meg and the baby. By the time they arrived at Windlebrae the doctor was already there, as well as Ruth and Willie. Cameron Maxwell was hunched in his chair before a blazing fire and his wife was tucked up in the box bed under a pile of blankets and surrounded by all the stone pigs Willie could find. She looked frail and old, lying there with her ashen face and her eyes closed.

Meg moved close to the bed and took her mother's hand gently in hers. The crepe eyelids fluttered, then opened.

'Meg . . . ?'

'Yes, it's me, Mother. Don't try to talk.' There was silence for a few moments as though Gertrude was gathering her strength.

'Not — much — time,' she said haltingly. 'Get Ross.' The words were clear. Meg was startled. Her grip tightened on her mother's fingers. How thin she was. Amazingly she felt a faint pressure in return. Her eyes opened again, then opened wider, staring incredulously at Meg pressed against the frame of the bed. 'You're carrying a bairn? Isn't possible?' The eyelids drooped again.

'Yes, mother, I am.' Meg said softly.

'The — Lord — be — praised!' Her voice was weak, but the words sincere. 'Take — care — lassie. Didn't — think — possible . . .' This time her fingers relaxed completely. The doctor came forward.

'She should sleep now. I gave her morphine for the pain.'

'Get Ross,' she repeated fuzzily, but her eyelids seemed too heavy to open. 'Jim MacDonald . . .'

'She's asleep,' Doctor Jardine said quietly. 'She seems disturbed. About your brother perhaps? Ask him to come as quickly as he can.'

'As quickly . . . ?' Meg stared at the doctor. Peter came to her and put his arm around her shoulders. His eyes met the doctor's questioningly.

'She's very ill. The shock of the fall. Lying out on such a cold night. I think she may have broken her hip.' He shook his head. 'I can hold out little hope.'

In his chair Cameron groaned aloud and buried his head in his hands. 'Never heard her go out,' he muttered.

'Just as well, Cameron,' the doctor assured him kindly. 'You could not have helped her.'

'Should we contact Ross, Father?' Meg asked. 'Where does Jim MacDonald live?'

'His address will be in the bureau. Have a look, lass. Willie can send a telegram.' Meg went to the bureau. She felt guilty, rifling through her mother's papers, but she came across a ledger and found Jim MacDonald's name and address without too much searching.

'I want to stay, Peter,' Meg pleaded. 'Willie will have the milking to do. Would you send the telegram to Ross?'

'I will stay too,' Ruth said quickly, casting Peter a reassuring glance. 'Father will look after the children.'

'Well . . .' Peter hesitated. 'Will you eat something before I go, Meg. We had no breakfast. You might faint again.'

'Peter is right,' Ruth said briskly. 'We must all eat — you too Peter, before you drive down that icy road again.'

CHAPTER FOURTEEN

It was almost midday when the telegraph boy cycled up the track to Briarbush. Jim MacDonald saw him as he was crossing the yard and he opened the yellow envelope immediately, his heart thumping. Telegrams rarely meant good news.

'Well!' he gasped. 'Gertie asking for Ross. Wonders never cease.' He rubbed his jaw thoughtfully. 'Send this reply,' he instructed the boy. 'Ross not here. Will contact him.' He frowned. 'Maybe I should send a telegram to Lochandee,' he muttered to himself. 'Have you any idea what the roads are like over there, laddie?'

'They're not good anywhere, Pa says. He's a postman.'

* * *

Meg's heart sank when Willie brought the reply to the telegram. Her mother was drifting in and out of consciousness. Doctor Jardine had warned them what to expect. Willie wanted to take his father down to the cottage in the cart but Cameron refused.

'I can't leave her now, laddie — not after all the years we've been together. I'll be all right with Meg and Ruth. You do what you have to do. Your mother wouldna have wanted you to neglect the animals.'

It was mid-afternoon when Alice got the message which the Factor had phoned through to the village post office. How frustrating it was receiving cryptic messages via several people, she thought irritably. One thing was clear — Ross was wanted by his family, and urgently. It would soon be dark. How would he get to the station? Would there be a train tonight? Would there be anyone to meet him at the other end?

She went to search for him and found him and Alfie just finishing loading the cart with turnips from the pit.

Alice gave him the message and watched his face grow pale, and then flush — but with pleasure, anger or indignation she could not tell. He looked up and met her gaze.

'I cannot go.'

'You must.'

'I'll think about it.'

'It's urgent.'

'Well, I can't go today. I don't even know whether there will be a train by the time I can get to the station. We must . . .'

'Beth and I will manage the milking,' Alice said automatically, though she knew it would take them until bedtime without Ross. She realised how much she had come to depend on him. Never once had he let her down, or neglected his duties. An awful thought occurred. What if he went home to his own people and decided to stay there?'

'It's too much for you, especially at this time of year. We will start early and get the milking finished. After supper I will cycle down to the village and see if I can get someone to help with the milking and feeding the cows while I am away. We really need someone who could take the milk to the station in the morning too.'

'I'm sure my Dad would help,' Beth suggested eagerly. 'He used to work on a farm before Mother died. He only stopped because *she* didn't like him milking cows and getting smelly clothes.' Beth always referred to her stepmother as "she".

Ross looked at Alice Beattie. She shrugged.

'We can always ask. Even if Beth's father can't help he may know someone else. How will you get to the train, Ross?'

'I will cycle. I could go straight to Dumfries from here. That would save time with a connection. In fact I could take my cycle with me. It would be useful at the other end. I will send a telegram from the village straight after milking.'

* * *

When Peter returned to Windlebrae that evening he found Meg torn between staying with her mother and her duty to the children.

'Rachel is coping,' he assured her, 'and Mrs Jenkins has offered to stay the night. You'll never believe this, but Sam Dewar milked the cows and fed them for Rachel. She says he has been a great help.'

'I am glad. I really would like to stay here. Do you understand, Peter?'

'I have already put a warming pan in the bed,' Ruth told him. 'I guessed Meg would not want to leave. I will do my best to see she gets some rest. I don't think she would sleep much even if you took her home.'

'You're probably right,' Peter agreed, looking down sadly at the shrunken figure in the bed. Gertrude Maxwell had never been a friend to him and he had little to thank her for — but she was Meg's mother. 'I will get back home to the children, but I will come again first thing in the morning.' Meg walked with him to the door. He took her in his arms and kissed her tenderly.

'Take care, Meg. It would break my heart if anything happened to you,' he whispered softly.

It was Peter's parting words which persuaded Meg to go to bed later that night. Her father refused to leave his wife's side. Doctor Jardine had returned late in the afternoon.

'I've given her something to ease the pain. I'll be back in the morning. Any word of Ross's return?' he asked as he moved to the door.

'No,' Meg answered, unable to hide her own disappointment, 'Only a telegram from Mr MacDonald promising to contact him.'

'Pity,' the doctor commented cryptically. Sleep claimed Meg almost immediately in spite of her anxiety. It was still very dark when she awoke but the February days were so short the nights seemed to last for ever. She lay listening to the creaks of the old house where she had been born, where she had lived most of her life. Her mind moved back to her childhood, but her thoughts were interrupted. She had left her bedroom door open in case her father called for her. Had she heard voices? She listened intently. Yes, at least it was her father's voice apparently making a response now and then. Had Ross arrived? Meg reached for the matches and lit her candle. She had not undressed properly the night before and she pulled on her wool dress, shivering in the cold night air. She lifted a blanket from the bed and crept down to the kitchen. She had not been mistaken.

She paused in the doorway but there was no sign of Ross. In the glow from the fire she could see her father's chair close beside the bed as he had requested. Her mother seemed to be speaking more coherently. Her voice was low and weak, and there were long pauses, with her father supplying a word of encouragement or comfort. Meg listened, then moved forward soundlessly. Cameron saw the flicker of her candle on the wall. He turned his head stiffly, lifting his one good arm he put a trembling finger to his lips, willing her not to speak. He pointed to a chair near the fire and Meg crept towards it.

Her mother seemed to be recalling events from the past. A shudder passed through Meg. Her father was listening intently to the low, halting voice. The mention of Josh's name caught her attention, but what could her mother mean?

'I cheated you, Cameron . . . I should have told you. You loved Josh like your own son?'

'Aye. Everybody loved Josh. Dinna worry, Gertie.'

'The good Lord took him . . . to pay for my sins. I loved him too well. I'm a wicked woman, Cameron.'

'No, no lass . . .'

'Ross?' she whispered fretfully. 'Must speak to him,' She tried to rise up in her agitation and subsided with a long low moan.

'Hush, hush, Gertie. He'll be here when it's light.'

'Not — much — time — left for me. I sent him away. The money his grandfather left . . . only gave him fifty pounds. Didn't tell him . . . it was . . . his inheritance.'

'He'll get the rest soon enough,' Cameron comforted.

'No. I-I gave fifty pounds to Josh. Shouldn't have . . . not my money. He — he spent it . . . on pleasure . . .' Her voice wavered and for a while there was silence. Again Cameron looked towards Meg but he put his finger to his lips when she would have spoken.

At length her mother began to speak again.

'I was jealous of Cathie. Always happy, smiling. Everybody loved her . . .'

'Aye,' Cameron agreed sadly.

'She never knew her bairn lived, Cameron . . . I hated Ross after . . . my Josh was taken,' Her voice seemed stronger and her hand fluttered agitatedly. 'I let her down . . . your own sister.'

'It's past. Rest now, Gertie. Dinna worry, lass.'

'I do . . . I do. Wicked . . . to be jealous . . .' She shivered. Cameron clasped her hand more closely but words seemed to burst from her colourless lips. 'Terrible sin . . . sent Ross away . . . tricked him. His . . . birth right had to use it. Can't go on . . .'

'Hush, Gertrude. Dinna trouble your head about the farm. We'll survive, never fear.'

'Fear . . . Cameron . . . much to repent . . .'

'Hush, rest now.'

'Ross doesn't know . . . a bairn.' She was silent gathering strength. 'Mhairi's flesh . . . and Connor's — made her

153

suffer. She is . . .' There was a strange guttural noise in her throat. Meg half rose, thinking she was choking. Afterwards she wondered if it was a sob. She had never seen her mother cry, not even when Josh died. Then more whispered, faltering words.

'Beat her. Turned her out.' Suddenly her voice seemed stronger. 'The Lord sought His revenge. He can't forgive my sins. So many . . .'

'Don't distress yourself, Gertie,' Cameron urged anxiously, clasping her restless fingers in his good hand. 'Remember what it says in your Bible, lass? "Joy shall be in heaven over one sinner that repented, more than over ninety and nine just persons, which need no repentance." There's not many in this world without something to be forgiven.' He sighed heavily. Meg realised he was very weary. She knew now that her mother had needed to talk. He had understood that. Would her mother die in peace now? Tears stung her eyes.

So many secrets hidden from them all. She thought her mother had gone to sleep at last but she uttered one last request, her voice weak. 'Tell Connor's lassie . . . sorry . . . Please forgive . . .'

Meg must have dozed in her chair. Her father's words made her wake with a start.

'I think she's gone.' His voice trembled. 'Your mother is at peace at last, Meg.'

The next few hours passed in a blur for Meg. There was much to be done and she performed each task automatically. Ruth and Willie came together.

'If Ruth will stay with Father and make the breakfast, I'll help you with the milking, Willie,' Meg said. 'I'd like to.' She waved away his protest. 'It has to be done. The cows don't stop milking however we feel. The girl can carry the pails to the dairy for me. I shall just be sitting. Come on . . .'

In the warmth of the byre Meg talked quietly to her brother as the milk thrummed steadily and frothed up the sides of the piggin. She had always enjoyed the satisfaction and the soothing routine of milking.

'So,' Willie said slowly, unable, or unwilling to take in Meg's revelations. 'You are telling me that Rachel's father must have been Josh's father also?'

'It seemed so. After all Mother's grudge against Rachel was unnatural from the beginning. She must have reminded her of the past. I don't think I was meant to hear. Father may tell us more, but I don't think he will. He is very loyal.'

'Poor Ross,' Willie sighed.

'Now that I know the truth I can easily believe that Ross was Aunt Cathie's baby. I remember Mother going away to stay. When she returned she had this tiny baby. Even then I thought it was strange. She had never grown fat or prepared baby clothes and the crib. You just accept whatever your parents tell you when you are young — or at least I did.'

'No wonder Ross always felt Mother resented him.'

'She seemed to think Ross was a blot on the Maxwell name because Aunt Cathie was not married. I suppose she pretended he was our brother to prevent us, and other people, asking questions.'

'I wonder when he found out? It must have been a shock.'

'Yes.' Meg frowned. 'He's in for another shock if he comes back. Mother said he did not know Rachel was expecting a child.'

'He will know nothing of young Conan then? I suppose we cannot blame him if he does not return at all.'

'It's all such a muddle! Mother wanted his forgiveness — and Rachel's.'

It was just after midday when Ross cycled up the road to Windlebrae. His feelings were a mixture of excitement and apprehension. Everything was the same — and yet different. He was dismayed at the signs of neglect.

When he entered the familiar kitchen Willie and Ruth were seated on one side of the table, Meg and Peter Sedgeman on the other, with his father — no, his uncle — at the head. The seat opposite him was empty. His eyes briefly skimmed over the circle of upturned faces, with their varying expressions of amazement, welcome and pleasure — but where was Rachel?

'Ah, laddie, but I'm pleased to see you!' Cameron Maxwell tried to rise but Ross gently pushed him back and clasped the gnarled old hand in both of his.

'It's good to see you too,' he said huskily, striving to control a sudden flood of emotions. He looked to the far end of the table, his eyes speaking the question he could not voice.

'Mother died during the night,' Willie said gently. 'Father and Meg were with her.'

'I see.' Ross's voice was tight as he struggled with an unexpected knot in his throat. 'I'm sorry. I could not get here any earlier.'

'We are all pleased you have come now, Ross,' Meg said warmly. 'Come and have a seat.' She stood up. 'You must be tired as well as cold and hungry. Did you get a lift from the station? Peter says the roads are still treacherous, although it is thawing.' At last Meg stopped chattering to catch her breath.

'I've bought a bicycle. I brought it with me. I . . . Meg!' He was staring at her rounded stomach now that she had risen and moved around the table. Meg's pale face flushed a little but she smiled up at him.

'I am married — to Peter. There's so much to tell you, but now is not the time.'

'Married! Well I'm glad for you, Meg. But where is Rachel? I wrote to her. She never replied. I wrote to you too, at Christmas.'

'Rachel is living with us at Ardmill,' Peter told him quietly. His eyes sought Meg's and by mutual consent they left the rest of the news until later.

'Have some soup and some bread,' Meg urged. 'You must be famished and Mother would not have wanted us all to starve.'

'No, she wouldn't. Eat up Ross,' Cameron urged. Ruth served him a dish of soup and Meg brought more scones and butter and cheese.

'I thought I was hungry.' Ross shook his head in bewilderment, 'but I don't think I can eat anything.'

'Oh you must!' Meg exclaimed. 'Afterwards we will leave you with Father. He has much to tell you and it will give me time to go home with Peter to see the children.'

'Aye, lassie, you get back to Ardmill. You have been away long enough.'

'But you will think over what we were saying, before Ross arrived, Father?' Meg asked anxiously.

'Yes, please do,' Peter urged. 'We have plenty of rooms and you are very welcome to come and live with us.'

'Aye, I have thought about it already,' Cameron said hastily. 'And I thank ye kindly for your offer, Peter.' He turned to look at Willie and Ruth. 'But this is Willie's place now, and Ruth says she's willing to move in here, and look after me. This is where I would like to stay for the rest of my time.'

Meg met Ruth's eyes anxiously.

'I am sure, Meg.' Ruth assured her quietly. 'I've spent a lot of time with your father since you left Windlebrae. We get along fine together, and it's better for Willie to be where the cattle are. Besides, my own father has been spending more and more time down here. I reckon he will be pleased to take over the cottage. I know he will always keep some of his interests in the city, because he is a city man. He will always want to go back there now and then, but he does enjoy the country, and seeing more of his grandchildren.'

Meg nodded, and swallowed the lump in her throat. Peter took her arm.

'Come on home, Meg. The children and Rachel will be longing to see you. We'll come back tomorrow,' he promised.

When they were alone together Cameron and Ross had a long talk. Ross asked all the questions he had been longing to ask about his parents. Cameron answered patiently and truthfully.

'Your Grandfather Ross left you all he had — two hundred pounds. I tried to keep it for you,' Cameron told him.

He was reluctant to admit Gertrude had given some of it to Josh.'

'I have had fifty pounds already. I have scarcely spent any of it. I would like to buy a few cows of my own if Mrs Beattie will agree.'

'Have a look in the bottom drawer of the bureau. There's a false bottom in it. Press the raised bit. It releases the spring.'

'I ought to send a telegram to Mrs Beattie, to let her know I am staying for the funeral. Maybe this is the time to write a letter and tell her the truth about myself.' He shrugged dejectedly. 'If she rejects me as well then there will be no point in returning.'

As he said that he realised how much Lochandee had come to mean to him. It would be a terrible blow if Alice Beattie rebuffed him. In his heart he did not believe she would. He felt he had earned her trust and respect. She was not a hypocrite about religion, though her standards were high and she was a staunch supporter of the Kirk.

'What do you mean — if she rejects you? As well?' Cameron was frowning at him. 'Why should anyone reject you? Cathie was a good girl. It was fate prevented her getting married before you were born,' he said defensively. 'Fate.' He stared wistfully into space 'Take whatever life has to offer. Make the best out of it that you can. It's what I tried to do,' he added almost to himself, then he looked Ross in the eye. 'Now open that cash box and see what there is left. There should be a bit put by for our funerals as well.'

'Very well,' Ross nodded. 'But Rachel rejected me you know — and Meg. I wrote to both of them. They never replied.'

As he talked he fumbled around in the drawer of the bureau amongst the papers, but suddenly a small flap opened and in the cavity he saw a cash box and a few letters. He drew them out and carried them to the table beside Cameron Maxwell.

It was Cameron who opened the box. While he was doing so Ross thumbed idly through the papers. He gasped aloud.

'These are the letters I sent to Rachel, and here's the one to Meg. They have never been opened!'

Cameron glanced up. He groaned and buried his head in his hands. Eventually he raised his eyes to Ross's.

'I didn't know, laddie. They must have come after Meg and Rachel had moved to Ardmill. Gertrude was very . . . bitter then. She must have put them away and forgotten.'

They both knew she had not forgotten, but there was little to be gained now that Gertrude Maxwell was dead. What had Rachel thought of his silence all this time? Had she forgotten him? He had an overwhelming desire to see her.

'There's only seventy five pounds left . . . Take it, Ross, and keep it safe.'

'You fed and clothed me all those years,' Ross said quietly. 'I cannot . . .'

'And you worked long before you left school. No, laddie this money is yours.'

'Where is the money for your funerals then?' Cameron frowned. Slowly he pushed two envelopes across the table, each marked in thick black ink. One, still sealed, bore the name Cameron Maxwell. The other, Gertrude Maxwell, had been opened and emptied.

'She said things were bad. We've been paying a neighbour's lassie to help since Meg left. Gertrude must have used the money to pay the debts. She would think she could replace it when things got better . . .' He sighed and bowed his head wearily. Ross put his hand on the old man's shoulder.

'I wish I had known the truth, then I'd have understood . . . things. But you could have put me in an orphanage and I'm grateful you didn't do that. What money should I have had then? None. So you use some of this money to pay for the funeral, and whatever you need.'

Reluctantly Cameron accepted some of the money. He kept shaking his head.

'Let me help you to lie down,' Ross said. 'You must be exhausted. A sleep would do you good. I saw a new red telephone kiosk at the crossroads. I will cycle down there and send a telegram to Mrs Beattie.'

'Aye, you do that, Ross. I am more tired than I thought.'

When Alice Beattie received the telegram from Ross her heart sank.

'He has arrived safely,' she told Beth and her father who were clearly waiting for news as the telegraph boy cycled away. 'He was too late but he is staying to the funeral. Will you be able to help with the milking for a few more days, Andy?' she asked anxiously.

'Indeed I can, Mrs Beattie. I am enjoying being back on the farm again.' Alice Beattie made no comment. Her mind was on Ross. The telegram had said, "*Letter following.*" Why did he need to write her a letter if he was coming back in a couple of days? Did his mother's death mean other changes? Would he be needed there?' Her heart pounded. She liked Ross Maxwell and Lochandee needed him. She needed him.

CHAPTER FIFTEEN

After Ross had sent the telegram he looked around him as he came out of the telephone kiosk. The greyness of the February day was relieved by a glimmer of golden-edged light on the horizon. It would be a keen frost again when darkness fell. He knew he ought to return to Windlebrae without delay but he longed to see Rachel again.

He peddled along the snow rutted roads, scrunching the remaining icy pockets as he went. It was a good three miles further to Ardmill from the crossroads but he had reached the village almost before he was aware of it. He scanned the row of shops and cottages on either side of the deserted street. He saw the shoemaker sitting in the window, making the most of the remaining daylight.

Sam Dewar glanced up, aware of movement outside. He saw the tall young man peddling slowly, so slowly that he almost wobbled off balance. Suddenly he put both feet on the ground, waving an arm and calling excitedly to someone.

Rachel had been gathering in the washing. It had never dried all day. She carried the heavy basket on one hip as she made her way over the icy puddles at the end of the short track between Sam's premises and Peter's. She looked up at the sound of her name. She nearly dropped the washing basket at the sight of Ross.

He ran across the road, almost tripping as his leg knocked against the pedals. He always treated his bicycle with the greatest of care but now he abandoned it and ran with open arms.

He caught Rachel ecstatically, swinging her round as effortlessly as if she were a child. Sam, watching unashamedly, saw the radiance which lit Rachel's face momentarily, before she had time to consider or compose herself. He understood now what had been missing from her gentle smile. Always serene, always pleasant, ever ready with a helping hand — yet there had been a cloud dimming the light. There was no doubt in Sam's mind that this must be the father of her child. He wondered what had kept them apart for so long. He sighed, rejoicing in the happiness of the girl he had come to regard as an exemplar for the daughter he had never had.

Ross set Rachel on her feet and took her face gently between his hands, wiping away two stray tears with the pads of his thumbs, smiling down at her.

'I thought I would never see you again, Ross.'

'I did write. Did Meg tell you?' he asked urgently.

'Yes.' He saw the pain in her eyes and understood that the silence and separation had hurt her as badly as it had hurt him.

'I found the letters in the bureau. She had hidden them.'

'I see.'

'Do you Rachel? Did Meg . . . did she tell you I am not — I am not the son of Cameron and Gertrude Maxwell?' He stared down at her anxiously.

'She told me. In a way I am glad.' She shivered remembering again Gertrude Maxwell's insane outburst.

'Glad? Rachel, do you understand? I am a — a bastard?'

'I understand very well,' she said sadly.

'You do not condemn me then? For my parents' indiscretion?'

'Who am I to condemn anyone?' Her tone was bitter.

'Who are you? You are the girl I love. The most important person in my world. Does it matter to you that I am illegitimate? Born in sin?'

'Did you think my feelings for you so shallow that the circumstances of your birth would change them?' Rachel asked. The hurt and doubts and fears were evident in her trembling voice.

'I couldn't help but doubt when I received no reply to my letters.' He glanced briefly up the empty street then bent his head, kissing her mouth in a lingering kiss. All the love and desire flooded through her veins like fire but there were more important matters than her own heart's yearning.

'Come and meet Conan.' She slipped from Ross's embrace and grasped his hand, pulling him towards the back door.

'Who is Conan? I have not much time, Rachel. I left Father alone and I promised to help Willie with the milking.' Rachel stared at him.

'Meg did not tell you?' she asked hoarsely, her face suddenly pale.

'Tell me what?' But Rachel was tugging him urgently now, through a wash-house, across a passage, into a large cheery kitchen. Three small girls sat on a bright rag rug before the fire. A baby chortled happily, waving chubby arms at them, as though eager to join in. Rachel crossed to the pram and lifted him.

'This is Conan.' She held the baby towards him. 'Your son.'

'My what?' Ross stepped backwards as though he had been struck.

'Your son. Our son, Ross . . .'

'He can't be . . .' Ross muttered faintly, staring at Rachel. Was she teasing him? Or was he was dreaming.

'He's your son.' Rachel heard the note of consternation in her voice.

'Are you sure?' Ross had not meant to blurt out such a stupid question. Later he knew it must have been there, in his subconscious. He could not believe he had fathered a child.

He would have given anything to recall his words. He could have bitten off his tongue. Even so he did not realise how cruelly, how deeply he had hurt Rachel. He saw the horror in her eyes. He watched her face turn pale, her mouth tighten. She squared her shoulders and hugged the baby close. Tears had sprung to her eyes but she turned away. She would never let him see.

Watching, Ross felt she and the child were one. He was shut out — again. Jealousy flared in him. Rachel was his. She belonged to him. He could not believe the child, that tiny stranger was part of her — even less a part of himself. He was too numb for it to register that his reasoning was irrational.

Mrs Jenkins returned to the kitchen with a loaf and a jug of milk she had just collected from Meg in the bake house. She paused in the doorway, sensing the tension in the air. She looked at the tall young man, all six feet of him. His legs looked extremely long with his trousers still held at the ankles by his bicycle clips. She set the provisions on the table and came forward. 'There's no doubting who you are,' she smiled cheerily. 'Conan's hair is going to be just like yours — can't decide whether it wants to wave, curl or just lie straight — so up it turns at the front and won't lie down no matter how we try.' Ross stared from the old woman to the child. It was true the baby's hair was sticking up at the front. When he was a schoolboy Meg had tried many times to brush his own hair flat. She had called his peculiar front quiff a calf's lick. Mrs Jenkins, head on one side, studied Ross intently. He felt his colour rising at such scrutiny.

'His eyes have more green than yours, more like his mother's,' she nodded. 'Rachel has a good bit of red in her hair as well.' Ross wondered whether he had imagined a warning in the old woman's last remark. Rachel had always had spirit he remembered. He looked at her set mouth. He felt a surge of fear. He must not lose her again. She had managed without him so far. She was proud. She would never plead with him. Conan was her son. He guessed the child had become the most important person in her life during the

164

time they had been apart. Ross looked at Mrs Jenkins. He might face some opposition, but Rachel was his. This time he would fight for her.

'The wee fellow has his mother's mouth and nose,' Mrs Jenkins went on in the way of old ladies. 'He has her dimple too when he laughs, but he has your jaw. He can be stubborn, young as he is and he'll be a strong laddie boy when he's a bit older.' She surveyed Ross critically.

'Er . . . yes, well I shall look forward to — to getting to know him,' Ross stammered uncertainly. 'Where's Meg?'

'She's busy in the bakehouse. She was supposed to be resting but there were things she wanted to do for her mother's funeral.'

'Of course,' Ross nodded. 'I shall see her tomorrow. I must get back now, Rachel. I left Father resting but he will wonder where I am.' His eyes met hers, pleading with her to accompany him outside. He reached out a hand. She did not take it but she followed him into the passage, still hugging Conan close to her breast, almost as though he afforded her protection.

'We must talk, Rachel,' he said urgently as soon as the door had closed behind them. 'It was such a shock, seeing him — Conan.' The name was not yet familiar to him. 'How did you choose his name?'

'The twins shortened his names to Conan. He is christened Connor Cameron Peter,' She swallowed hard, trying and failing to keep the hurt and bitterness out of her voice as she added. 'O'Brian, of course. He's born out of wedlock too,' Her voice was little more than a whisper. Ross flushed. He could only guess at the shame she had felt, the stigma of bearing her child without a husband. He knew well enough how the village folk talked, gossiped, condemned. The thought of just such talk had haunted him ever since he had discovered his own roots — or lack of them. Would the shadow of this child's birth always lay between them? He looked into her eyes. 'I love you Rachel. If only I had known . . . We must be married without delay. We must make plans. I will see you at the funeral . . .'

'No!' Then less sharply. 'No, I cannot attend Mistress Maxwell's funeral. I shall be needed to care for the children while Meg is away.' It was true, and she could not bring herself to tell him how she had been whipped out of Windlebrae. The last thing she wanted was to attend Gertrude Maxwell's funeral and hear everyone saying sweet and pleasant things about her now she was dead. She shuddered. 'You may call on me here when the funeral is over.'

Ross was taken aback by her new maturity, the gravity and decisiveness she had acquired. She had been a pretty young girl when he went away. The capricious years of teenage seemed to have passed her by almost overnight. As he looked down into her face he noticed the more finely chiselled features of her cheek bones, firmer curve of her jaw, the fullness of her lips.

'You have grown even more lovely,' he said softly.

Later, as he helped with the milking, Willie asked,

'Do you intend to marry Rachel? Better late than not at all. Conan would soon be accepted as a Maxwell. I don't think you will be able to change his birth certificate officially though.'

'I want Rachel more than anyone else in the world. I don't know what my future holds now though.' He told Willie of the arrangement with Alice Beattie, how he was working for his keep, how she had promised to share some of the profits.

'I don't know how she will feel about keeping me on when I have a wife to keep as well.'

'A wife and son.' Willie grinned. 'No, I suppose that will make a difference. Can you trust her? This Mistress Beattie?'

'Yes, I am sure I can. I feel I belong there. We get on well together.'

'Well, you can always come back here, Ross, if your Mistress Beattie does not approve of you taking a wife. We would manage somehow.'

'Thanks, Willie,' Ross said quietly 'You're one of the best — just like Fath . . . just like your father.'

'You may as well go on calling him Father,' Willie said wryly. 'He's the only one you've ever known and he looks upon you as a son. He was always proud of the way you play the fiddle — the only musical Maxwell left, he used to say.'

'Tonight I will write a letter to Mrs Beattie. I had intended to tell her about myself and my own family anyway — or lack of family. I just can't believe I have a son.' 'A wife and a son. The people down there need not know when you married.'

'No, I suppose not.' Ross frowned thoughtfully. 'It would be better for Rachel to be Mrs Maxwell before she arrives in a new village amongst strangers.'

As soon as Cameron Maxwell had settled to sleep Ross found the pen and ink and began a letter to Alice Beattie. He knew the brief sentences were stilted but he did not realise his own hurt showed through, or that the letter would explain so much that had puzzled Alice Beattie. "*I shall understand if you do not wish me to return*," he concluded, but his heart was heavy at the thought of leaving the farm he had already grown to love.

As he sealed the letter it did not occur to Ross that Rachel might refuse to accompany him. His main concern was whether Mistress Beattie would want a man with a family. If he posted the letter in the morning she would receive it the following day — the day of the funeral. He wondered how long it would take her to consider and write back to him.

Alice Beattie's response came far quicker than Ross could have anticipated. A telegram was delivered to Windlebrae as the last of the mourners were leaving. When he read the contents he felt more like cheering than mourning, but he had to maintain a modicum of respect. He read and re-read the flimsy yellow page. "*Lochandee needs you. Look forward to your return. A.B.*" It was only when he had read the telegram for about the fourth time that Ross discovered what a great relief it was to know he could return to The Glens of Lochandee. Already it felt like home. Meg and Peter were staying at Windlebrae until evening to make sure everything was clean and tidy in readiness for Ruth and Willie to move in. Rachel would be alone with the children. Ross decided to cycle to Ardmill and tell her his good news. There was no time to lose. He must arrange their marriage and their return to Lochandee.

In his excitement he announced his plans to Rachel after only a brief greeting.

'I will make arrangements for our marriage. Then we shall travel to The Glens of Lochandee together. There's a cottage on the farm where we can live, if Mrs Beattie is agreeable and . . .'

'Ross! Please wait!'

'Wait? What do you mean? I must return as . . .'

'You have not even asked me if I want to be your wife,' Rachel reminded him coolly.

'But you said you loved me . . .' Ross frowned. 'Have you changed your mind now that you know I am illegitimate . . . ?' His tone was accusing and defensive.

'Oh Ross! Forget about yourself! And your parents — or lack of parents. I do love you — or at least I did love you. I am beginning to wonder whether you have changed while you have been away. Our own wee son carries the stigma of being illegitimate. You condemned him to the same fate as you are suffering.'

'But we shall change that when we are married,' Ross protested.

'Nothing can change the facts,' Rachel declared, remembering the weeks and months she had hoped and prayed for Ross's return — always in vain.

'He will have my name of course.'

'Of course,' Rachel repeated. She was shrewd enough to understand Ross was still finding it difficult to accept that he had fathered a child. She had found it difficult to accept that babies were made so easily too, but she sensed his lingering doubt and she was hurt.

'You will be Mrs Maxwell before we go to Lochandee. No one will know the circumstances of our marriage and the child's birth.'

'Not even your wonderful Mrs Beattie?'

'Least of all Mrs Beattie,' Ross said more sharply than he had intended. 'You will like her Rachel, I promise you,' he added more gently.

'Maybe I shall, maybe not. The truth is Ross, I cannot go with you.'

CHAPTER SIXTEEN

Ross returned to Lochandee the morning after the funeral, filled with disappointment. He was also anxious as he recalled the lines from a poem.

Oh! what a tangled web we weave,
When first we practise to deceive!

He had not intended to deceive Alice Beattie but he knew she would be wondering about Rachel, and now he was returning without the wife he had claimed to have. He bit his lip in frustration.

He had missed Rachel so much during their months apart. He could not accept any obstacle to their union now. He longed to have her at his side again. In his mind he went over and over their conversation. He knew his voice had risen with anger and dismay as he repeated her words.

'Cannot go! Why can't you go with me? Why?'

'I made a promise to Peter, and to Meg. I cannot leave them until after Meg's baby is born. You know she's not so young for a first baby and there is so much work to do with the children and the shop, the bakery. We have four cows . . I make the butter to sell. Don't you see? They need me.'

'I need you!'

'You have managed very well without me for more than a year,' Rachel reminded him.

'I thought you didn't want to be associated with me. I was shocked, confused, forbidden to return.' Even he felt his excuses were feeble now. 'Meg will find someone else to help.'

'The children are used to me. I know the routine of the bakery and the household. Meg needs to rest more. The doctor has warned her and Peter is terrified in case anything happens to her. I promised I would not leave her and I owe them both a debt I can never repay. They gave me a home when I was alone.' Her gaze held his steadily. He flushed with guilt and anger.

'This is different, Rachel. I am asking you to be my wife and you have to think about our future — and your son's future.'

'Our son! He's your son too, Ross whether you like him or not.'

'Our son then but surely you want to be married now?'

'Yes, I suppose I do . . .' Rachel said doubtfully.

'Either you want to marry me or you don't!'

'There was nothing I wanted more when I knew I was to have your child,' Rachel told him bleakly. 'But you were not there. Everyone in Ardmill knows he was born out of wedlock,' she added bitterly, 'A few more months will make little difference.'

'A few months? Months!'

'We can be married whenever you arrange it, but I shall not leave Meg until she has had her baby and recovered.' Rachel's mouth set. 'I owe my life to Peter Sedgeman — and possibly Conan's life too. I shall keep my promise to him.'

* * *

It was a relief to be back at Lochandee and find Alice Beattie accepted him as before.

171

'I feel as though I have come home,' he told her later that evening while they sat in front of the blazing fire drinking the bedtime cocoa she had brought on a tray.

'That pleases me more than I can say, Ross,' she smiled warmly. 'I confess it was a surprise to hear you have a wife and son though. I pray they will feel as much a part of Lochandee as you do.' She was cautious, stifling the questions she longed to ask, the doubts and fears she had experienced when she received Ross's letter. He was so young to be married. He had been away more than a year. When had the child been born? Had Ross been trapped into marriage by some cheating hussy? Was the child really his?

'I hope Rachel will be happy here too,' Ross agreed fervently. 'I tried hard to persuade her to come back with me but she is determined to keep her promise to Meg and Peter to stay until their baby is born.'

'I can understand your disappointment, laddie, but perhaps if Rachel forgot her promises easily she would not have earned your respect or your love? In the Bible I believe Jacob waited seven years before he could make his Rachel his wife. If you truly love your Rachel, and if she truly loves you, it will be worth waiting surely?'

'Yes,' Ross sighed heavily, 'you're right. It just seems such a long time until May.'

Alice realised there were still many things she did not know, things which did not add up and which she did not understand. She was relieved to have Ross back and she slept more soundly, but she could not banish her doubts about this unknown wife. Ross's future as joint tenant of The Glens of Lochandee would depend on more than his own ability now. If she did not like the girl, worse, if she did not trust her?

Alice would have been surprised to know that Rachel's doubts and fears equalled her own. Ross had been sparing with details and Rachel had no idea whether the Mistress of Lochandee was a pretty young widow, or another vindictive woman like Gertrude Maxwell. She felt unable to cope with either and half of her wanted to stay in the shelter of her present existence.

Meg felt guilty knowing that Rachel had refused to go with Ross on her account.

'If I can repay a little of your kindness I shall be happy,' Rachel assured her. 'Besides . . . it will give Ross time to get used to the idea of having a son. I don't want him to marry me because of Conan, but because he loves him as a father should.'

'Oh, but he will! Conan is a lovely boy . . .' Meg sighed. 'I shall miss him terribly. I wish you did not have to go so far away.'

* * *

Ross had been back at Lochandee nearly three weeks. It had become a ritual to write a little every evening for Rachel, then post her a long letter each week.

'I want her to understand — really understand — how much The Glens of Lochandee and the work and the cattle mean to me,' he told Alice. 'I want her to share my dreams of the future . . .' He broke off, staring into the burning embers of the fire. 'We shared everything before . . . before I left her alone . . .' he finished in a hoarse whisper.

Alice watched his troubled expression then she voiced the suggestion she had been mulling over since Ross's return.

'I think Beth's father would be willing to help with the work again if you would like to spend another weekend with your family, Ross.' There was no mistaking the flare of longing in his eyes when he looked up from the page, his pen poised in mid-air.

'Do you think he would?' he asked eagerly, 'And you? Would you mind me going away so soon?'

'Not if it would make you happy, laddie. As a matter of fact I think it would be a good idea if Rachel came back with you for a night or two. I should like to meet her and

I'm sure she will be keen to know what we are like and where she will live?'

'Bring her here, to stay?' Ross was surprised.

'Of course. Where else would your wife stay?' Alice asked. She regarded Ross's sudden flush and wondered what other secrets had he hidden away.

Ross was filled with exhilaration at the prospect of seeing Rachel so soon. He wondered whether Peter would be able to help him arrange their wedding. Rachel would feel easier if she was truly his wife — indeed he knew neither of them would be able to deceive Alice Beattie if they were not truly married, and she would certainly expect them to sleep together.

He wrote without delay and waited in a frenzy of impatience for replies from both Meg and Rachel.

Rachel looked forward to Ross's weekly letters but it troubled her that he wrote so enthusiastically about his daily work and Lochandee, yet he barely commented on her own loving descriptions of his young son's achievements.

'He will soon learn to love Conan once you are all together,' Meg reassured her. 'Peter has talked to the minister and the marriage ceremony can be arranged for the evening Ross arrives.'

Rachel felt she was being swept into marriage on a tide of propriety and convenience.

'It's only two months before your baby is due, Meg,' she said desperately. 'I don't think I ought to go away at all.'

'I shall be fine,' Meg promised. 'Mrs Jenkins will be here to help with the children. Peter has made enquiries about a live-in nursemaid when you go to live at Lochandee.'

* * *

So Rachel and Ross were married at the beginning of April shortly after Rachel's eighteenth birthday. It was a quiet, simple ceremony which could not have been a greater contrast to the society wedding of the Duke of York and the Lady

Elizabeth Bowes-Lyon which had been arranged to take place later in the month. However Polly and the twins had new dresses and their excitement was infectious. Even Sam Dewar donned his best suit and top hat and came to the church to act as witness. Afterwards he kissed Rachel's cheek shyly.

'Now remember, Rachel, if ever you need a friend, I am here. There will always be a roof for you and your bairn.'

Ross overheard and frowned. At the first opportunity he asked Meg about Sam Dewar.

'Och, he's a nice old man. He's very shy, but he has taken to Rachel.'

'Oh, has he . . . ?'

'We have all become friends,' Meg amended quickly, 'since Rachel started milking the cows in his byre. If you had not returned he was going to ask Rachel to move into his house as his housekeeper. Of course she doesn't know that because you came back before he got around to suggesting it. He talked it over with Peter last autumn.'

'I see . . .' Ross frowned and his eyes strayed to the toddler who was pulling himself to his feet on the edge of a chair. Meg followed his glance and her eyes softened.

'He's a lovely bairn. We shall all be sorry when he and Rachel go away. I suppose there's no chance of you coming back up here to farm, Ross?' she pleaded.

'No, definitely not. You would love The Glens of Lochandee, Meg.'

'Well, I hope Rachel loves it as much as you seem to do,' she retorted more sharply than she had intended.

Rachel felt shy and embarrassed when Ross accompanied her to the bedroom she shared with Conan. Where else would a husband sleep but with his wife. She had not really considered the implications of being married. Everything had been such a rush.

She need not have worried. As soon as they were alone together Ross drew her into his arms. All the old magic was rekindled. Her fears melted away, indeed her very bones seemed to melt beneath Ross's gentle caresses. There was nothing gentle about the fire which flared between them in an all-enveloping, ever increasing desire, joining them in an ecstasy of perfect union.

They were wakened by Conan's early morning chortling.

'Whatever was that?' Ross demanded, suddenly wide awake at the unfamiliar sounds.

'It's only Conan,' Rachel laughed softly. 'He's letting us know he's ready for a morning cuddle before I go to milk the cows. Come then, my wee love.' She leaned over and lifted the toddler into bed, setting him between them. This did not please either Ross or his son. Ross had forgotten about the baby's presence in the same room and he had been anticipating a repeat of the previous night's delights. Conan, on the other hand, stared unnervingly at the strange man in his mother's bed, then he opened his mouth and howled with unbelievable volume. Rachel was forced to lift him away from Ross and give him all her attention before he would be quiet.

Ross and Rachel had their first argument later that same morning. It was over Conan too. It had not occurred to Ross that Rachel would expect to take the child to Lochandee.

'And where else would he go but with his mother?' she demanded, her eyes flashing more green than blue with indignation.

'I thought . . . I expected he would stay with Meg . . .'

'Don't you think Meg has more than enough to do? Conan is at a very demanding stage and needs a lot of attention. If I go with you to Lochandee, Conan goes too.'

Her tone was firm. Privately she was concerned about Meg's health. She had been easily exhausted since the funeral and Rachel had noticed her ankles were swollen by evening. Ross recognised the stubborn set of her mouth. He was forced to accept her ultimatum.

'It's just that Mistress Beattie did not — she didn't mention inviting your son.'

'Conan is our son — ours, Ross.'

'Umm, yes, I know . . . but where will he sleep?'

'He can sleep in the bed with us if there is nowhere else. Your Mistress Beattie will have to get used to the idea that we have a child. If she does not like him we shall not stay any longer than it takes us to catch the next train home. Perhaps it is just as well we are making this visit. Maybe I should have made it before we married.'

Later that night, in Ross's warm embrace Rachel knew she loved him with all her heart. Even for Conan she could not truly regret her marriage, but she prayed fervently that the two would learn to love each other as she loved them both.

Ross was taken aback by the amount of luggage a baby seemed to require for such a short visit but he was amused and delighted by the wide eyed stare of his wife and child as the railway carriage hurtled them through the fields, or covered them with sooty smuts as they chugged their way through eerie black tunnels.

Rachel was tense with apprehension by the time they reached The Glens of Lochandee, and Ross felt the atmosphere was positively electric as Alice Beattie came forward to greet them.

'I-I know you were not expecting three of us,' he rushed nervously into speech to breach the awkward silence. 'But we had to bring the child because . . .'

'Of course I was expecting your son,' Alice assured him swiftly. 'Beth and I have been busy rescuing my own old crib from the attic. We have washed and polished it. It looks as good as new and it's in your bedroom.'

Rachel could have hugged her for that gesture of welcome to her small son and her smile shone forth in all its warmth. Alice smiled back warily and looked down at Conan. He had slept on the journey from the station and wakened refreshed. He beamed widely up at Alice, captivating her instantly.

'I will show you where everything is before it's time to start the milking,' Alice suggested. 'I am afraid the cows have to be attended whether we have visitors or not.'

'I am used to that,' Rachel nodded, bending to lift Conan on one hip and clutching his bag of baby clothes in her free hand. 'Usually I strap Conan into his perambulator while I am milking. If Ross can find a barrel of hay or some other safe place in the byre to restrain him, I will gladly help you.'

Alice Beattie blinked. The girl was not lazy or unwilling then. She was certainly pretty and her neat russet jacket and skirt accentuated her slender waist and suited the colour of her hair. Alice could not have guessed it was Rachel's one good outfit, bought especially for her wedding. So far so good, Alice decided, unaware that Rachel was assessing herself with equal caution.

It had been a great relief to find that Mistress Beattie was a pleasant faced elderly widow and not the handsome young woman Rachel had envisaged. She did not seem to be short-tempered or vicious either. Indeed she reminded Rachel of a younger edition of Minnie Ferguson — the mentor of her childhood. At the thought of Minnie her own expression softened and her lips curved into a smile. Alice Beattie raised her brows in a silent question.

'You remind me of someone I used to know,' Rachel explained. She looked at Ross. 'You remember Minnie Ferguson — a younger version of course.'

'I remember her,' Ross nodded, then to Alice. 'She was one of Rachel's favourite people.'

'Then I am flattered,' Alice acknowledged, but she remained cautious. She did not know why it was so important to her that she should approve of Ross's wife. She just knew that it was vital to the future of her beloved Glens of Lochandee that they should approve of each other, and get along together. Her experiences with Watt Kerr and his crooked ways had shaken her confidence in human nature.

Rachel was delighted with the large carved oak cot which Alice had prepared for Conan. Ross was amazed at her preparations, even improvising sheets and blankets.

The two days which Rachel spent at Lochandee were filled with new sights and experiences. Conan had taken an instant liking to Beth and crawled after her like a small devoted puppy, much to the girl's delight.

'I was used to playing with my half-brother and sister,' she told Rachel. 'I miss them sometimes, but I like living here with Mistress Beattie. I hate my step mother,' she said with childlike candour. 'I know it's wicked to say so, but I do.' She looked pleadingly at Rachel. 'Will Mistress Beattie send me back when you come to live at Lochandee?'

'Oh, surely not!' Rachel was dismayed. She liked thirteen-year-old Beth and she understood her feelings after her own experience with Gertrude Maxwell. 'Would you like me to ask Mrs Beattie what plans she has?'

'Would you Mrs Maxwell? I'd be ever so grateful.'

Rachel was startled for a moment, scarcely recognising herself as Mrs Maxwell.

It was her last evening and Rachel took the opportunity to tell Mrs Beattie of Beth Pearson's anxiety.

'I had not considered so far ahead,' Alice said truthfully, 'I am glad you told me, Rachel. I would like to keep Beth. She's scarcely more than a child but she's very willing.'

'I wouldn't like to be the cause of her dismissal,' Rachel said with concern, 'but I hope I shall be able to help Ross earn his part of the agreement he made with you.' She looked at Ross. 'We have not discussed how we are to live, or what I am to do when we move to the cottage. Will there be work for me in the dairy? I did not see any butter making?'

'Rachel is especially good at churning,' Ross told Alice Beattie. 'I have been thinking about some changes, especially now there are three of us to keep.'

'What had you in mind, Ross?' Alice Beattie asked curiously, quite unprepared for the suggestions which Ross must have been mulling over, even before he brought Rachel and his son to Lochandee. Perhaps their arrival had precipitated his ideas into plans.

'I have a little money of my own. It was left to me by my grandfather. I would like to use it to buy more cows. I would like to see the byres of Lochandee full again. Rachel is a good milker and perhaps we could sell her butter locally, and set more eggs for hatching so we have more eggs to sell and . . .'

'Are you proposing to be a farmer or a shopkeeper, Ross?' Alice asked.

'A farmer of course, but now that I have a wife I must try to bring more money to our partnership. That's only fair. You know how much I want a farm of my own.'

'I do, but you have taken me by surprise. I need time to think — and so do you.'

'I have thought . . .'

'Not about every aspect,' Alice cautioned. 'For one thing you have not said how the extra money will be divided. You are not a tenant, there'll be additional costs — and some losses no doubt. You may buy in disease with unknown cattle — tuberculosis, foot-and-mouth, abortion for example . . .'

'Don't mention such things!' Ross shuddered.

'But I must. Don't be too hasty. You might lose everything. Now,' Alice Beattie took a deep breath and sat up straighter. 'I have some news for Rachel. Mr Shaw, the Factor for the estate, is coming tomorrow morning with his motor car. He will take you back to the railway station.'

Ross sighed with disappointment, believing she had deliberately changed the subject. In fact Alice was thinking of the Factor. When he had heard Ross was married he was as surprised as she had been and he had asked to meet Rachel at the earliest opportunity. He was a shrewd man. He knew a good wife could do a lot to help a moderate tenant, but a bad wife could ruin the best of men. He knew she wanted Ross to be made a joint tenant with herself because she wanted to make sure he would stay at The Glens of Lochandee, but neither of them had known he had a wife. Mr Shaw had made it plain he would not recommend Ross as a possible tenant if he had made a hasty marriage with an unsuitable wife.

* * *

Naturally Alice could not tell Ross this, and neither would she make any decisions. She knew the Laird would only act upon Mr Shaw's advice concerning the tenancy. On every large estate the Factor's authority and influence were far-reaching. She had a feeling there were changes afoot regarding the estate now that the Laird's health was failing and his son still showed no interest in anything except pleasure. Mr Shaw had told her Lady Lindsay, the young Laird's wife, showed more interest. He felt it was unfortunate that her husband had forbidden her to spend time in the estate office, if only for the sake of her two young sons and their future inheritance.

CHAPTER SEVENTEEN

Rachel could not hide her low spirits when she had to say goodbye to Ross the following morning. She climbed into the car beside Mr Shaw, hugging an excited Conan on her knee while trying to brush aside her tears and wave goodbye, all at the same time.

Mr Shaw gave her a few minutes to compose herself.

'All right now?'

'Y-yes. Th-thank-you,' Rachel stammered nervously. She had noticed Mistress Beattie afforded this man considerable respect and she realised he had influence on matters to do with the estate and its tenants. She gulped and took out a clean white handkerchief to blow her nose and banish the last of her tears. 'You must think me very silly. I did not want to come to Lochandee, and now I do not want to leave.'

'A beautiful place, friendly people with a warm welcome . . . they can have that effect, I'm sure,' Mr Shaw said, surprising himself. 'The Glens of Lochandee is one of the most pleasant places to live.' He gave a wry smile, 'But I'm sure it is not leaving Lochandee which distresses you, so much as leaving your husband?'

Rachel was silent. Lochandee was a lovely place — both the village and the farm above it, but it was true, the thought

182

of another parting with Ross was unbearable. He had loved her so tenderly. He had tried to take an interest in Conan too, but she wondered if there would ever be a bond between them as there was between herself and Conan.

'It-it is very kind of you to take us to the station. We have never been in a motor car before.' She stroked Conan's head with a gentle finger and he cuddled against her breast, though his eyes were wide with curiosity.

'He's a fine boy,' Mr Shaw complimented. 'Ross must be very proud of him.'

Rachel tensed. Had he read her thoughts? He glanced at her delicate profile, noting the slight droop of her mouth.

'How long have you been married?' The question was an innocent one, intended to put Rachel at ease, instead she shot him a startled look. She reminded him of a frightened fawn. He raised his bushy brows in silent question. Rachel bit her lip. Then she sat up straighter, took a deep breath and squared her shoulders.

'Mr Shaw, I am not very good at deceiving people. I know Ross wants to keep our affairs private, but if you asked him a direct question I know he would answer truthfully. We were married last week, when Ross came to stay.'

'Last week!' The Factor was shaken out of his usual equanimity and the car swerved alarmingly. Rachel's heart sank. Mr Shaw set the car back on course. His gaze fell to Conan. 'I see . . .'

'I don't suppose you do,' Rachel sighed. 'It was not Ross's fault. I did not know I was expecting his child. He did not know he had a son until he returned for the funeral. Indeed he scarcely believes it even now.' She stroked the child's hair.

'Well there's little doubt about it,' Mr Shaw commented dryly. 'The wee fellow is the image of Ross, though I suppose he will change several times as he grows up. My own boys resemble my father now they are young men, but they looked like my wife when they were children.' Mr Shaw raised a hand and rubbed his temple. How was he having this kind of conversation with a young woman he was supposed to be vetting as the wife of a possible tenant? Rachel began to feel more at ease. This stern looking man seemed quite human after all.

'It was not Ross's fault,' she repeated slowly. 'I will tell you the whole story, then you can judge for yourself. I know that's what you are supposed to do anyway,' she added with surprising candour. 'My father said the Factor in our own village often had more influence than the Laird. He was responsible for the people on the estate.'

'Your father was right about that,' Mr Shaw agreed wryly. 'Sometimes the decisions are hard to make.'

'You mean when you have to turn people out of their homes because they will not pay their rent?' Rachel asked, recalling once such incident.

'Yes, and when a man dies. Sometimes his widow has to be put out of the farm. It can be difficult. Was your father a farmer?'

'No, he was a blacksmith.' Rachel began to talk, telling him briefly of the circumstances which had led her to Windlebrae, omitting Gertrude Maxwell's insane behaviour, but explaining merely that Meg and Peter had married and offered her a home.

'None of us knew where Ross had gone, or whether he would return. He is very . . . sensitive underneath his stubborn looks. It must have been a shock to discover he was not who he thought he was. I have no parents now but I did know who they were, and that they loved me, as I loved them. Ross has never known that sort of caring. Although Mr Cameron Maxwell is a nice old man and I am sure he regards Ross as another son,' she added warmly. 'And he is his uncle after all.'

'And you are returning to help the couple who befriended you, rather than stay here with Ross?'

'I must! I do not want to leave Ross, now that we have found each other again.' Her cheeks flushed a rosy red at the memory of that finding and uniting. Mr Shaw bit back a smile, but he was in for more surprises as Rachel told him about her cows and churning butter, and the work involved in running the bakery and shop. 'Meg is not in good health. I cannot leave them in the lurch. Do you understand?' she pleaded.

'My word, here we are at the station already,' Mr Shaw exclaimed, 'and your wee son has fallen asleep.'

'He's not used to me talking so much. I am sorry if I . . .'

'Don't be sorry, young woman.' He held up a hand. 'I am glad you told me the truth, and something of your background, and Ross's. I shall respect your confidence, never fear. I usually suspect when people are hiding things. Sometimes perhaps I imagine what they are hiding to be worse than the truth. You have not done Ross a disservice today. Mistress Beattie has great confidence in his ability and in his integrity. I do not think either of you will let her down. Loyalty is a quality I admire.'

He helped her from the car and found a carriage occupied only by a cheery-looking middle-aged couple. Then he lifted her luggage onto the rack and bid her goodbye as the train began to get up steam again, doors slammed and the guard prepared to wave his flag.

Rachel was tired and hungry and Conan was fretful when they arrived back at Ardmill but all thoughts of her own adventure disappeared when she found Meg in bed and the house in turmoil.

'Oh, but I'm pleased to see you back, lassie,' Mrs Jenkins welcomed her thankfully. 'I never knew you got through so much work in a day, all by yourself. What it is to be young.'

'But what's wrong with Meg?' Rachel asked anxiously. 'It's usually such a struggle to get her to sit down in a chair.'

'She collapsed in the bakehouse, barely an hour after you'd gone. Doctor Gill made her promise to stay in bed until he returns. He told her she would damage her baby — and her own health, if she did not follow his advice.'

'I should never have left her,' Rachel said. 'I guessed she was not as well as she pretended.'

'No good blaming yourself, Rachel,' Peter told her, coming into the kitchen and overhearing, 'She wouldn't have listened to anyone except the doctor. But I am thankful to see you back and Meg is asking to see you and hear all your news.'

'I'll take her a drink of tea, but I see there is much to do.'

'Willie has bought the cows. He and Sam Dewar walked them over to Windlebrae. I'm sorry lass, but we couldn't manage everything.'

Rachel nodded. 'They would have had to go anyway. Meg will be busy enough when the baby is born.'

* * *

Concern for Meg grew as the days passed. Even lying in bed her feet and fingers were puffy and swollen. Her face seemed rounder, but it was not a healthy roundness. Rachel thought it looked bloated.

'I think the baby will be due in six or seven weeks,' Doctor Gill confirmed.

'How shall we get Meg to rest for so long!' she wondered aloud.

'It is vital.' His tone was urgent. He lowered his voice. 'It could mean the difference between life and death.'

'Oh no!' Rachel's face paled. 'Peter could not bear that again.'

'I'm sorry. I did not mean to worry you unduly Miss O'Bri . . . Sorry, it's Mrs Maxwell now, is it not? The minister told me Conan's father had returned. I'm so pleased. A boy needs his father. When do you plan to join him?'

'As soon as — as Meg is well again. I pray to God she will be well.' she added vehemently.

'I shall add my prayers to yours,' Doctor Gill said sincerely. 'We must do our best for her. Make her some beef tea and clear chicken soup — keep up her strength without straining her system.'

Even the children seemed subdued. Rachel had taken over the bakery but she was having difficulty fitting everything into the days. It seemed she had no sooner gone to sleep than it was time to get up again.

'I'm thinking of asking the nursemaid to start work immediately, Rachel?' Peter said, after hearing her speak sharply to Conan. 'You look exhausted.' She stared at him blankly. 'She could sleep in the girls' room,' he added quickly. 'She's used to sharing. I don't want you to think I am criticising . . .'

'If only you could get another pair of hands! Any hands. Not to mention a pair of eyes to watch the twins and Conan.' Rachel could almost have wept with relief. She was so tired and so tense with anxiety. 'Is she willing to come so soon?'

'Yes. Her name is Flora and she is 14.'

Flora arrived two days later. She was bright-faced and cheerful and completely unruffled by the busy household.

'It's no worse than home,' she told Rachel laughingly. 'We are all used to work. Work or starve, my Ma says — and sometimes we have to do both when things are bad.'

'Does your father keep cows?' Rachel asked.

'No — only one for the house and a few hens and a pig. The farm's on top of a hill — bleak in summer, snowed up in winter,' she said philosophically. 'Even the sheep struggle to survive. Dad talks about giving up — but what else could he do? There's no work round here. He'd hate living in Glasgow when he's country born and bred.'

Flora's help made a big difference. Even Meg seemed more relaxed, though still lamenting the fact that she was to stay in bed for another five weeks.

Nature interfered with this plan and six nights later Peter knocked urgently on Rachel's bedroom door.

'Meg says can you come!' he called hoarsely. 'She thinks the babe is coming.'

Rachel paused only to light her candle and pull on a woollen dress. She ran to Meg's room.

'Bring the doctor!' she ordered Peter. He obeyed like a child.

Fortunately Doctor Gill was at home in bed and he came at once. His manner was calm, but Rachel sensed his concern.

'We must get your wife to the cottage hospital immediately, Mr Sedgeman.'

'Shall I bring my van round?'

'The back of my car, I think. Perhaps you would follow in your vehicle? Easier for getting home.'

Peter nodded, his face white as the bed sheets. Meg did her best to hide the pain which made her want to scream, but Rachel could see the perspiration already dampening her hair and running down her temple. Her heart was filled with fear. The baby was not due for a month yet. Something was wrong. She packed Meg's night clothes and the sheets and towels they had prepared for the hospital. Then she supported Meg down the stairs with the help of the doctor.

Rachel waited up for the rest of the night hoping Peter would telephone with news, as he had promised to do. Strangely he had forgotten about his new gadget and run to get the doctor in person. It was probably just as quick Rachel reflected wryly. Doris, the local operator, was always curious.

All next day they waited but there was no word from Peter. Rachel's anxiety grew. Apparently Doctor Gill had not returned from the hospital either. The old Doctor had taken the morning surgery. News spread around the village. Cyril Johnson had more customers that day than he usually had in a week. Nearly everyone called in on the pretext of buying a box of matches, a reel of cotton, some linen buttons or four ounces of sugar, a packet of Woodbine cigarettes or two ounces of tea. Without exception they asked for news of Mr Sedgeman's' wife, Cyril reported later.

'Their concern was genuine. Some of them offered prayers.' Rachel could barely speak for the anxiety gnawing at her stomach. She knew she ought to eat but she couldn't. Flora took the children for a long walk. Later they were bathed and fed and put to bed. Mrs Jenkins insisted she could not go home to worry alone. The old house settled down to its usual creaks and groans as darkness fell again. Rachel must have dozed. She wakened with a start. Mrs Jenkins was snoring in the wooden chair on the opposite side of the fire.

The door creaked and Peter, white-faced and exhausted put his head around.

'Peter!' Rachel's voice was no more than a nervous squeak. She ran to his side. 'Oh, Peter, you look exhausted.' She took his arm and led him to a chair. He moved like a sleep walker. 'Meg? Is she . . . ? Is she all right, Peter?'

'Very ill. Doctor thinks she has a . . . a chance . . .' His voice was slurred with weariness and tears began to trickle silently down his cheeks. Rachel turned away and shoved the kettle onto the fire. Mrs Jenkins stirred and stretched stiffly. She opened her eyes, still confused.

'Tea. I'll make you some tea,' Rachel croaked hoarsely. She could not bring herself to ask about the baby. She was sure it must be dead. Peter had not mentioned it. He looked stunned and bewildered.

'They're in a sort of tent . . .' he muttered, half to himself.

'Who? Who, Peter?' Rachel did not know she was gripping his arm. She thought he was hallucinating.

'Boys,' he said, shaking his head. 'Don't think he will live. So small . . . Must get back to her.' He looked up. 'Can't believe Meg could have twins as well.'

'Twins? Two boys?' Rachel stared incredulously.

'So small,' he repeated. 'They say . . . one might survive.' He kept shaking his head. 'My poor Meg.' He shuddered. 'Please God let her be all right.'

'Does she know? About the twins, I mean?' Rachel asked. Peter shook his head. 'It took so long. They seemed to need so many — "things".' He shivered. 'Could only wait outside. They wouldn't let me in. She's sleeping.'

'Sleep is the best cure, Mr Sedgeman,' Mrs Jenkins assured him. 'Now you drink this cup of tea — hot, sweet and strong. It'll put new life into you.'

'The minister is going . . .' Peter sipped the tea, then drank thirstily. 'He's going to the hospital first thing,'

'You've chosen names?' Rachel asked. Peter shook his head and brushed away the tears with a shamefaced glance. 'Don't know. I must get back to Meg . . .'

'Not before you've had an hour or two of sleep,' Mrs Jenkins said firmly.

'I'll make some toast,' Rachel offered, 'For all of us. Mrs Jenkins is right. You must have a rest so that you'll be strong for Meg. I'll waken you as soon as it's dawn.'

CHAPTER EIGHTEEN

Meg was barely conscious when the minister visited her in the little hospital room. Peter had to choose the names alone. He named the stronger twin Maxwell, after Meg's family. The smaller baby he named Ruairidh, after Doctor Gill.

'If he lives long enough to go to school he will not thank you for it,' Doctor Gill grimaced, 'Though I am known as Rory to all except my lawyer now.'

'He will live, and he'll thank you for both your name and your skill, Doctor,' the matron vowed. 'He may be a wee mite, but he's a fighter. Isn't that so, Nurse Laine?'

'Indeed he is. In fact he may be a better feeder than his big brother, who's showing signs of being a sleepy, lazy infant.'

'Is he now? We must watch for signs of jaundice when they are born early.' Doctor Gill frowned, but he summoned a reassuring smile as he turned to Peter. 'I believe your wife was aware of the christening. She seems more at peace now. Her pulse is settling nicely.'

'That's the best news yet, Doctor.' Peter breathed a huge sigh of relief. 'Meg is the most important person in the world to me.'

'I trust you mean that, because she will require a longer spell of nursing than usual after such a difficult birth. Can you afford to keep her here, at the hospital? It would be the best place for her. She will need to rest.'

'We will work out the most favourable terms we can, Mr Sedgeman,' the matron promised. 'My two nurses and I would like to see your little family well on the road to good health after being so near to losing them.'

'Even if it costs me my business and everything I have, Meg must have whatever she needs to make her well,' Peter declared with feeling.

Rachel had written to Ross the day after the birth of Meg's babies. He replied by return. She was dismayed to hear he was expecting her to travel to Lochandee immediately. She thought she had explained Meg's critical condition and the smaller of the two babies was hanging to life by a mere thread. She wished she had not sent him news of the birth so promptly.

It was nearly three weeks before Meg was pronounced well enough to return home. During that time Ross had written several letters, each more impatient and exasperated than the last, demanding to know when Rachel would be at Lochandee.

'An important matter has arisen. Mistress Beattie and the Factor insist you should be consulted,' he wrote. Rachel felt torn in two. She sensed Ross was piqued that she should need to be consulted on anything to do with his work at Lochandee, while she could not think of anything more important than Meg's recovery.

Eventually Alice Beattie wrote to Rachel. The tone was kind and understanding of her dilemma:

> *The matter which has arisen affects you, even more than Ross. I feel you must be free to express an opinion. However there is no necessity to tear yourself away from Mrs Sedgeman until you feel she is well enough to manage without you.*
>
> *Mr Shaw has agreed to my request to make Ross a joint tenant. However the Laird's health is deteriorating more rapidly than we expected and he has advised me to bring forward the agreement. He fears there will be changes in the running of the estate when it passes to the young*

Laird. These may not be to our liking or advantage. Mr Shaw is trustworthy and I respect his opinion, but I am concerned that Ross may not have considered all the implications. The decision affects both of you, and your son.

To become a joint tenant Ross would be required to pay half the valuation of all the stock and equipment at The Glens of Lochandee as well as being responsible for paying half of the rent at the end of each six months term.

Naturally he would receive half of the profits. He is confident, with you to help him, that he will be able to pay off the debt within a few years. Mr Shaw assures me a valuation of one thousand pounds for Ross's half-share is a generous offer — certainly a much better opportunity than he would have if he rented a farm entirely on his own. You may wonder why I am being generous — or you may consider me a selfish woman. The truth is I have grown very fond of Ross and I am sure his happiness here will be complete when he has you at his side.

For my part, my dearest wish is to spend the rest of my life at The Glens of Lochandee. I have begun to hope that may be possible with Ross's help.

I understand both of you will wish to pay off your debt as soon as possible. Mr Shaw has promised to reinstate the original boundaries to The Glens of Lochandee when the lease is up for the present tenants. Ross was already planning to increase the herd but this means we need to hire another man. The Hiring Fair is May the twenty-eighth so time is running out.

The question which really affects you is this: Ross wishes to hire a married man with a wife to assist with the milking and dairy work. This would mean they would live in the cottage, which was to be your home. Would you be content to live here with me and rear your family under my roof? Or would you prefer to furnish the cottage and make it your own home? I should be happy to have you here. I admire and respect the loyalty you have shown to Mr and Mrs Sedgeman. But the decision must be your own.

* * *

There were a few more sentences. Rachel read and re-read the letter and then she showed it to Meg and Peter.

'I can understand how wary you must feel about sharing your home and family, dear Rachel,' Meg said, 'after your experiences with my mother. At least Mistress Beattie is honest enough to tell you what she hopes to gain from such an arrangement. Do you feel you could get along together? Would Conan annoy her, or other children when you get them.'

Rachel blushed at that and Meg chuckled.

'I am sure you and Ross will have lots more babies. I expect they may be irritating to elderly people though.'

'Mistress Beattie has never had children of her own but she seemed very patient with Conan. In fact she appeared to enjoy his visit,' Rachel added remembering the crib.

'It's an excellent opportunity for Ross to get started in a farm,' Peter commented, 'though I think he would require a formal agreement with Mistress Beattie. He should make sure he has the opportunity to buy her share of Lochandee when she no longer needs it — just in case a long-lost relation turns up and claims it when she dies.'

'Yes, that does happen sometimes, if there is money to be gained,' Meg agreed. 'I had not thought of that.'

'I will mention it when I write to Ross,' Rachel nodded.

'It would save you the expense of buying your own furniture,' Peter reflected, 'and it ought to be cheaper if you all live in one house — but as Mistress Beattie says, lassie, it depends how you feel about it. Two women in one house do not often get along without friction.'

'We have got along splendidly,' Meg told him indignantly.

'Yes, my love, but you are exceptional women. Anyway you have both been too busy to quarrel.'

'I expect I shall be busy when I go to Lochandee,' Rachel smiled. 'Ross is hoping I shall make butter to sell in the village. I shall enjoy that. Beth Pearson, the maid, is little more than a child herself and she was wonderful with Conan. He really liked her.'

'Well don't reply in a hurry,' Meg advised. 'Think about it tonight. Make your own decision — not just to please Ross. He always liked to have his own way, even when he was a very small boy,' she recalled with a smile. 'By the way, Rachel, will you go with me to see Father before you leave? I know he would like to see you again, and Conan.'

'Yes, I would like to see him too,' Rachel agreed. 'I expect he wants to see your fine sons?' Rachel teased, glancing down at the two tiny heads in the pram.

'Yes, Peter thought we could make a bed for them in a washing basket and put it in the back of the van. He's going to teach me to drive when I get my strength back.'

'That's a good idea,' Rachel agreed, thinking how well Meg was progressing in spite of the demands of two hungry babies.

Soon she would be able to move to Lochandee and Ross with a clear conscience. She felt the familiar yearning and smiled inwardly. She understood one of the reasons Ross was so impatient.

Cameron Maxwell was almost speechless with emotion when he saw Rachel and Conan, as well as Meg and the two tiny babies, snuggled head to toe in a large, well-padded wicker wash basket.

Ruth and Willie were delighted to see them. Although the babies were very tiny Rory was feeding well and holding his own.

'Doctor Gill is astonished at how well he's progressing,' Meg told them all proudly. 'And Max is wonderfully contented.'

'Well, that's a blessing, lassie,' Cameron Maxwell told his daughter gruffly. 'Though I seem to remember you were always a good-natured wee bairn yourself. Maybe you take after me. I've always thanked the good Lord for a contented soul — even though I was never a great one for attending the kirk.'

'Meg and I certainly have plenty to thank Him for,' Peter said with real sincerity.

'Aye, you're a good lad, Peter,' the old man smiled at him, 'I'm glad things have worked out so happily for the pair o' you.' He reached out a hand towards Rachel and she went closer. He took her hand in his. 'I canna tell you how sorry I am for the way you were treated under my roof, lassie. I promised your father . . .' He shook his white head in distress. 'Can you forgive us?' he pleaded.

'You were always kind to me.' In her heart Rachel knew she would never forget his wife's cruelty. One day she might be able to forgive her, but not yet. She perched on the arm of a chair beside him, bouncing her small son on her knee. 'And see I have Conan. He's called after you and my father but the girls shortened his name to Conan.'

'He's a fine boy. He's just like Ross was at that age. He even has that mischievous twinkle in his eye. I expect he'll lead you a merry dance before he's grown. Ross liked his own way.' Rachel smiled back into his twinkling eyes. 'Ah, but you're a bonnie lassie and no mistake,' he sighed reminiscently and fell silent.

After some consideration Rachel had written to Alice Beattie accepting her offer and Alice Beattie replied by return, briefly but warmly.

'She reminds me of Granny Ferguson,' Rachel told Meg when the reply came. 'She was always fair and kind.' She sighed heavily. 'I do wish I had been able to collect the vase she left for me — just as a reminder. Ross said he would bring it if he ever went in that direction to play the fiddle, but he never got the chance.'

'No, he even left his fiddle behind, but I know he took it with him to Lochandee when he returned after Mother's funeral.'

'He did,' Rachel smiled. 'But he wonders whether he will ever find time to play it again.'

* * *

Peter was very late home from his rounds the night before Rachel and Conan were due to leave for Lochandee. Meg did

196

not seem concerned and Rachel understood the reason when Peter handed her a package containing the vase. Rachel felt tears well into her eyes at the unexpected kindness.

'Mistress Carmichael, your old neighbour, sent this letter for you Rachel, and a "wee minding" to wish you happiness in your marriage.'

* * *

Ross was waiting at the station to meet them with the pony and cart. Conan had been sleeping. He wakened from his nap feeling disgruntled and fretful. Rachel's heart sank. Ross had greeted her so eagerly, but he barely looked at his pouting young son.

'I think the pair of you are more alike than I had imagined,' she said tartly as she tried to soothe Conan while helping Ross get their baggage into the trap.

As they jogged along the leafy lanes bordered by purple rhododendrons and beech hedges with their newly unfurled leaves and golden buds her spirits rose.

'The countryside looks so beautiful at this time of year,' she sighed rapturously.

'It's beautiful at any time of year in this area,' Ross grinned cheerfully. 'I just know you will grow to love it as much as I do . . .' He reached out and squeezed her waist, 'Especially now we are together.' Conan shot out a chubby fist and tried to push his arm away. 'Mama,' he said indignantly 'Mine.'

'Mmm, a possessive wee fellow, isn't he?' Ross remarked with raised brows, but he could not help but laugh when Conan raised his own small brows in perfect imitation. Rachel's heart lightened. More than anything in the world she wanted Ross to love their son as she loved him.

Alice Beattie welcomed them with a warmth which surprised Rachel, considering they scarcely knew each other. She did not know Mr Shaw had confided a little of her story.

'In my opinion she deserves some good fortune in her life. If I am any judge of character I'd say she is the type to repay it many times over,' he had told Alice.

'I respect your judgement, especially when it bears out my own. I should have known Ross would choose wisely, but love can cloud the clearest mind when we are young.'

* * *

Although Rachel missed Meg and the little girls badly it was good to get back into the old routine of milking and butter making. Beth Pearson welcomed both herself and Conan like long-lost friends and Rachel quickly settled into life at The Glens of Lochandee. Conan was not so easily uprooted from his familiar environment. He missed the company. When Rachel wrote to Meg she told her how he had asked several times for "Sam — shoes," and Polly was constantly mentioned.

Gradually he began to settle down but Rachel saw that his presence in their bedroom seemed to irritate and even inhibit Ross.

CHAPTER NINETEEN

Ross had hired a man named Sandy Kidd and his wife, Dolly. They had moved into the cottage at the May term with their two sons. The younger was a year older than Conan and his elder brother was almost four. They accompanied their parents to the byre in the afternoons, but were left in bed, alone in the cottage, during the morning milking. This arrangement troubled Rachel.

'Och, they are used to being left in bed while I'm at the milking,' Dolly said placidly. She loved her boys but she was casual in her care of them — or at least Rachel felt she was. Ross saw nothing wrong in the arrangement and was inclined to think she pampered Conan too much.

'Don't you worry about him,' Alice said quietly one afternoon, after hearing them arguing about Conan's welfare. 'I do not agree with children being left alone in the house either. I will make sure Conan is safe. I confess I am pleased I do not need to go to the milking every morning since you came, Rachel. I shall prepare your breakfasts instead.' Rachel felt reassured to know she had an ally and Conan was happy to have the Kidd boys as his new friends during the days which followed.

During the turnip hoeing the three small boys played together in the shadow of the hedgerows while all available hands strove to make the best of a spell of dry weather before haymaking began. Sandy Kidd was a quiet, rather dour man, but he was patient with Alfie and they were all grateful for that.

The highlight of Rachel's summer was when Ross bought her a bicycle from old Mr Pearson. The old man had fixed a small seat on the back for Conan. As soon as she was competent to ride well enough she cycled down to Lochandee village with him to thank Beth's grandfather. He was delighted to see them.

'Beth told me you had a fine boy,' he chuckled. 'She didna think you would want to leave him behind.'

'We brought you some fresh eggs and a pound of butter for your trouble,' Rachel smiled at him.

'Och, that's verra kind o' ye, but my Beth tells me what a fine woman ye are. She hasna had an easy life, losing her own mother when she was just a wee lassie. She was content up at Lochandee though, and now you and the wee fellow have come she is as happy as a skylark. She loves bairns.'

'She is certainly patient with Conan. He goes with her to feed the chickens and collect the eggs whenever he can — but look at him!'

'Och, the wee rascal,' Mr Pearson chuckled, seizing Conan by the seat of his pants, just in time to prevent him pulling a can of thick black oil from a work bench. It was the first of many visits. Conan always asked to go to the bicycle shop whenever Rachel set out with him. She had no idea of the seeds she was sowing in his young mind when he continually asked the old man to show him how things worked.

Beth's grandfather praised the butter and eggs all around the village and Rachel soon had several regular customers, including the Reverend Simms and his wife, Doctor McEwan's wife, the cobbler, and the blacksmith, as well as some of the people from the cottages. By the end of the summer she was cycling to Lochandee village twice a week with deliveries. Mr Pearson fixed her a wicker basket on the front of her machine.

Rachel decided to get a pair of clogs made for Conan for the winter. He was very disappointed when they called at the cobbler's workshop.

'Not Dewy!' he screamed. 'Not like . . . No go!' When Rachel wrote to Meg she described her small son's reaction.

'I was surprised that he still remembers Mr Dewar so well at his age.' Meg relayed this snippet to her elderly neighbour and his pleasure at being remembered was immense.

'How sad it is that Sam has no family of his own.' She wrote in her reply to Rachel. 'It's such a lonely existence for him, but I am pleased to say he still has long chats with Peter. They are grateful to you for "breaking the ice" between them. It sounds as though you are getting to know lots of people in your new surroundings too. I am so pleased Mrs Beattie treats you more as a friend than as a maid, Rachel. I am sure you will prove to be a very loyal friend to her — just as you are to me.'

Rachel and Meg continued to write regularly and it was the highlight of Rachel's week when the postman brought her a letter.

Ross had built up regular customers for milk deliveries on his way to the station. The better prices helped their income, but attending to their needs took far more time and effort than unloading churns of milk at the station. During harvest he began to take Beth with him, dropping her off with a churn of milk and the measure in the middle of the little hamlet. Several other customers came to buy from her and some of the older women enjoyed a chat and invited her into their homes for a cup of tea. Beth looked forward to these trips in the milk cart.

Just before Christmas an unexpected shadow fell on their lives. Mr Shaw had become a regular caller now that Alice had more time to talk with him. He knew she liked to have news of the Laird, who had been her childhood companion. It was not the Laird's death which cast the shadow, however. Mr Shaw's own wife died in her sleep at the beginning of December. She had enjoyed robust health all her life.

'He is shattered, the poor man,' Alice confided to Ross and Rachel. 'He seems to have aged overnight. And as if losing his wife was not enough to bear, he's having trouble with the young Laird. Apparently he cannot wait to get his hands on his father's money.'

'I heard rumours about him at the market,' Ross said. 'I hoped they were not true or it will not be good for any of us.'

'I fear there may be some truth in them,' Alice nodded. 'Mr Shaw told me — in confidence remember — that the young Laird has already run up debts and is planning to sell some of the farms when his father dies. He and Mr Shaw have had several disagreements already. The young Laird does not even listen to his wife, and Mr Shaw says she is an intelligent young woman who could be a great asset to him. He will not allow her near the estate office. Mr Shaw thinks he may resign when the young Laird inherits the estate. His only daughter is married to a Factor but they live on an estate up north and Mr Shaw owns a house up there. I suppose we cannot blame him for moving nearer to his grandchildren.'

'I shall be truly sorry if he leaves,' Ross said. 'He has treated me very fairly.' Rachel silently echoed his thoughts. She had great respect for Mr Shaw. She felt strangely protected and safe with him in charge.

Early in the new year of 1924 Mr Shaw arrived with a gift for Alice. It was from the Laird. He brought Lady Lindsay and one of her young sons with him.

'They have just come for the ride.'

'Would they like to come in?' Alice asked, feeling a little flustered at the unexpected callers.

'Not today. We ought to be back before her husband gets home. It was his Lordship who suggested they come along to see The Glens of Lochandee. He has told her so much about the farm, and about its Mistress.' Alice blushed but he went on. 'He wanted you to have a wireless set so I am just dropping it off.'

'A wireless? But we have no electricity. It has not come this far up the glens yet. He must have forgotten.'

'No, he remembers well. His mind is very alert. It is his body which is frail. He says you always had a lively and enquiring mind as a girl. He has had great pleasure from his own wireless so he hopes you will enjoy this one. It works from a battery. See, it sits in the back.'

'That square jar full of water?' Alice asked incredulously.

'It's acid. He instructed me to buy two so that you can still use the wireless while the other battery is being topped up.'

Alice and Rachel watched, agog with excitement as Mr Shaw tuned into the station. Suddenly a man's voice filled the room.

'This is the Home Service. It's a very good way of getting news, but you will need to keep it out of reach of young Conan.' Mr Shaw warned.

One of the first pieces of news which Alice heard over the wireless was the announcement of the death of Lenin, the man who had brought about the revolution in Russia. A day later it was followed by the news that King George V had appointed Ramsay MacDonald as the first Labour Prime Minister of Great Britain. Ross and Rachel listened as avidly as Alice.

'Well at least he is a Scotsman,' Ross approved. 'I don't think he will carry out the plans the Red Clydesiders are urging.'

'No. He's in a weak position. His new cabinet is such a mixture. He will not have an easy task whatever policy he pursues.' Alice sighed. 'It's amazing to hear a man who is hundreds of miles away.'

'His voice is so clear,' Rachel marvelled.

'Yes, I will write to his Lordship tonight and send all our thanks for such a thoughtful gift.'

* * *

It was the last gift the Laird would send to anyone. A few weeks later all the tenants on the estate assembled to pay their last respects. Many of the older tenants shared Alice's foreboding.

'There'll be death duties to pay for a start,' Murdoch Rogers muttered gloomily over Alice's shoulder.

'Aye, and some reckon the coffers are nearly empty already.' Henry Mackay joined in. 'Ever since the young Laird had his coming of age celebrations he has been spending money — horses, motor cars, gambling in London and abroad, or so I've heard.'

'Well he'll need a fat purse to go far in his motor cars now,' another tenant muttered. 'Petrol is going up to two shillings a gallon.'

'Don't talk daft, Edward.'

'Just repeating what I've heard.'

'Aye, well I'm more concerned about Mr Shaw leaving. The Factor is the man that matters as far as the tenants are concerned. You can't get anywhere if you can't get on with the Factor. The Laird only watches over the money.'

'Or spends it!'

'Aye, well it seems the young Laird is doing that well enough. I've heard rumours that he and the Factor plan to sell some o' the farms to raise money for the death duties. We are on the edge o' the estate up at Nether Fauchan.'

'Och, even the young Laird would surely have the sense to sell the land to the east if he has to sell any . . .'

'That's not what I heard. My family have been in Nether Fauchan for nearly a hundred years. It's in good heart so it would fetch a better price.'

'It might, if there was anybody daft enough to throw money away on buying a farm!'

Ross listened to the conversations but at the mention of the new Factor he could not help himself.

'Has a new Factor been appointed already then?' he asked.

'Aye, laddie. Have ye not heard? Mr Shaw is moving out as soon as the funeral is over. He'll be on his way north by tomorrow morning. They say he had some fine bits o' furniture. It has all been packed and sent ahead by rail.' The farmer looked keenly at Ross. 'You must be new to these parts, are you? Takes time to hear the gossip . . .'

'Och, this is the young fellow frae The Glens o' Lochandee,' another tenant joined the conversation. 'Geordie Marchbank is the name.' He thrust out a hand and shook Ross's in an iron grip. 'I've seen you putting the milk on the train at the station. You seem to be doing well enough, judging by the number o' milk churns anyway.'

'We are building up the herd again,' Ross nodded.

'Well you should be safe enough. Even a silly young Laird wouldna sell the farms nearest his own doorstep — at least not until he reaches the final fling — and he will if he doesna get himself killed first. You mark my words.'

'Don't talk like that! That would mean another lot o' death duties to raise,' his companion muttered morosely. 'As it is I've heard the new Factor is a ruthless idiot. He'd sell his grandmother's last pair o' drawers if it suited him.'

'Who is he?' Ross asked curiously.

'Bert Elder is his name. I take it you haven't seen him around then?'

'No.' Ross shook his head. 'Never heard of him.'

'It would be better if none of us had,' the man named Edward grimaced ominously. 'He's a big fellow, red-faced, big yellow teeth.' He pulled back his lips in a toothy grin to demonstrate. He used to have red hair but he hasna' much left. He still thinks he's God's gift to women though. I wouldna let him near my old lady, I can tell you — and she's no spring chicken. Anything in skirts and he'll give chase. Put a skirt on an old cow and he'd be after her, if you ask me.'

'Whisht!' His neighbour dug him in the ribs. 'He's over there. He'll hear ye if ye dinna keep your boomer down.'

Ross felt uneasy as he drove Alice Beattie back to Lochandee in the trap after the funeral. She was silent too, saddened by the passing of a well-respected landlord and an old friend. Mr Shaw had made a point of bidding her a final goodbye after the funeral. She knew she would miss his visits and the news he had brought her, as well as his wise advice.

* * *

The weeks passed into months but neither the new Factor nor the Laird came to The Glens of Lochandee.

'You will meet them both if you go to the tenants' dinner when rent day comes round,' Alice told Ross.

'Oh, I'm not anxious to meet either of them from what I've heard so far.'

'I think you and Rachel should attend the dinner. Such gatherings hold no attraction for me anymore. Rachel would enjoy seeing Valantannoch, the laird's house. It's beautiful and in a lovely setting. Yes, it would be good for you both.'

* * *

Long before the Rent Dinner was due at the end of May, Rachel and Ross set out on their bicycles for a rare few hours of pure pleasure. Conan waved his arms excitedly to Alice and Beth as he perched in his bicycle seat behind Rachel. It was a beautiful spring day and Rachel's heart soared as they bowled along the leafy lanes, down to the village and out again on the track bordering the loch. They aimed to reach a small wood on the very far side before they stopped to eat the picnic which Ross was carrying on his back. Some of the wild rhododendrons were beginning to open with splashes of purple amidst shiny dark leaves. Above them a delicate filigree of birch leaves trembled on graceful silver trunks. Here and there an ancient beech tree towered towards the sky and ash trees still held their sooty flattened buds. The sky was a backdrop of clear blue with a few white puffs of cloud sailing slowly before the gentle breeze.

'I don't know when I last felt so happy,' Rachel said as they peddled leisurely along side by side. 'It's such a glorious day.' Ross glanced sideways, returning her smile.

'And a beautiful companion makes it perfect,' he twinkled, and chuckled aloud when he saw the faint blush which still mounted her cheeks when he paid her compliments. Usually it was too dark to see her face when he held her in his arms at night in the big feather bed. Today was theirs.

They found a grassy hollow to eat their picnic and Conan whooped with glee to find so many new places to explore while Rachel set out the food. It did not worry him when his short legs tripped on an unexpected stone or tussock of grass. He simply picked himself up and toddled on again.

Ross stretched his long legs and walked to the side of the loch, peering down into the clear rippling water.

'It seems quite shallow as far as I can see,' he told Rachel, 'but old Mr Pearson told me it's just like a narrow shelf around the edges and then it falls steeply like an underwater ravine. He says it can be a dangerous place, even for strong swimmers, unless they are aware of the structure. Apparently the shallow edges and the pebbles get warm from the sun but the rest of the water is hundreds of feet deep and it's icy cold all year round. Can you swim, Rachel?'

'No, can you?'

'No. I never lived near any water deep enough to swim in at Windlebrae — and as you know,' he grimaced ruefully, 'we didn't get much spare time for walks to the river.'

'I know.' Rachel gave Ross a sympathetic smile before turning her attention to their son. 'Conan! Conan, come and eat your sandwiches.'

He came running as fast as his small legs would bring him, clasping a fat worm in one chubby fist and two small smooth pebbles in the other. He laid his treasure proudly in Rachel's lap. He looked quite hurt when she tossed the worm away.

'Mr Worm wants to go back home,' she explained patiently. 'He lives underneath the earth in a cosy little tunnel.'

'Worm get dirty?' he enquired, 'like Conan?'

'No, never as dirty as Conan,' she laughed, wiping his grubby hands and handing him his favourite, an egg sandwich. He drank thirstily at the home-made lemonade made from a recipe belonging to Alice Beattie's grandmother. It was deliciously refreshing. Afterwards Conan stretched out on his tummy on his own small blanket and began to play with the pebbles, tipping them from one hand into the other and trying to sit one on top of the other. Lulled by the soft intermittent talk of his parents and warmed by the spring sunshine he fell asleep.

Ross pulled Rachel to her feet and lifted their own rug a little distance away out of the hollow and out of Conan's line of vision. He sank down onto it, holding his arms wide, inviting Rachel to join him. The desire in his blue eyes belied his innocent smile. Rachel's heart skipped. It seemed so long since they had been alone together — really alone. She clasped his outstretched hands. He gave a gentle tug, pulling her off balance so that she fell on top of him. He laughed softly as his lips found hers.

They lingered over their loving, savouring each precious moment, each tender caress. They kissed and touched and loved again, rising to the enchanted heights together. At length Rachel dozed dreamily, her head cushioned on Ross's broad chest, his hand cupping the roundness of her breast.

How long they languished in their private heaven neither of them knew. It was the stir of a cooler breeze through the grasses which made Rachel sit up, remembering Conan, thinking it was time to waken him and start on the homeward journey if they were to be back to begin the milking. She stretched luxuriously and dropped a light kiss on Ross's parted lips. He seized her and would have held her close once more.

'Conan,' she murmured. 'He will wake soon.' She stood up and brushed her skirts, rearranging her clothes before she peered over into the grassy hollow. The blanket was there, the dimple where Conan's small head had rested — but of the little boy there was no sign.

'Oh my goodness. Conan has gone! He's gone!' Her voice rose in panic.

'He can't have gone!' Ross jumped to his feet, fastening his braces as he did so, hurrying to her side, his feet hastily stuffed into his boots, laces flying.

'He's not here. He's nowhere around!' Rachel wailed. She stuffed her fist into her mouth. She had to stop the screams before they started. 'Conan! Conan, where are you? Oh please come back to Mama. Please! Conan . . .'

'Conan!' Ross bellowed loudly. 'Answer me!'

'Oh please don't be cross with him, Ross.' Weeping now Rachel clutched his arm. 'He'll never come back if thinks we are angry with him.'

'Conan!' Ross shouted again, less fiercely. And again. There was no reply. He looked down into Rachel's white face, her huge green eyes swamped with tears. 'We'll find him.' He squeezed her shoulder reassuringly but Rachel shrank away.

'If only . . .'

'You search along the path that way,' Ross instructed. 'I will — I will walk along the edge of the — the water . . .'

'The water! Oh dear God, the water. Please don't let him be in the water.' She began to sob.

'Don't Rachel! Control yourself now. Search for him. Keep shouting. Shout his name.' He shook her, none too gently. He was struggling to contain his own panic. 'His name, Rachel. Then listen. Do you understand me?' She nodded dumbly and began to walk along the path, weaving in and out of bushes and small trees and ferns. The day which had seemed so beautiful was now filled with the darkest possible clouds — clouds of misery and guilt. She had forgotten Conan in the sweet ecstasy of Ross's loving.

'Conan!' she called between hiccupping sobs. There was no reply. She began to run. She did not know why. She turned and looked back. Surely a small boy could never have strayed so far? He might have gone in the opposite direction. She turned to retrace her steps, willing herself to go more slowly, to search under every clump and tussock, however unlikely. There was nothing.

She reached Ross, pacing along the edge of the loch, his eyes glued to its rippling surface.

'There's no sign of him,' he whispered hoarsely.

Only now did he appreciate the son he had sired. He had been jealous. Yes, jealous of the child who had caused Rachel to suffer. Jealous of the tiny person who had had her love and care during the long months he had yearned for her. What kind of man was he?

'W-would there be — if he's d-drowned, I mean? Signs?' Rachel was looking up at him, her eyes huge and dark with terror.

'We'll find him. He can't be far away.' We must, he added under his breath. We must. He rubbed his temple, frowning. 'I'll go a bit further away from the loch. He may have wandered further into the trees and lost his way.'

'He's so small . . .' Rachel's voice wobbled.

'You go in that direction this time. I'll go the same way but twenty yards or so further in. We must search thoroughly.' Ross said in desperation. Alice Beattie would wonder where they were when they did not return for the milking. Alice loved Conan too, and Beth adored him. 'Dear God,' he muttered aloud, 'help us.'

They had walked several hundred yards and Rachel was certain Conan would not have come so far without being distracted. He was always stopping to poke or push, to ask questions . . . She bit back a sob. Supposing those big enquiring eyes never gazed up at her again, so full of trust. How could she have let him down so cruelly. She put a hand to her brow and scanned the area. Further back, nearer to their picnic spot, and further into the wood there seemed to be a big dark hump and a sort of path into the trees. She made her way back to it without much hope. She dare not look at the water. She could not bear to think of her beloved child lying in a cold watery grave. She began to shiver, although it was still warm in the sunlight.

As she drew nearer to the hump she realised it was an uprooted tree. It must have been ancient and massive judging by the crater its roots had left. The path she had hoped to follow was no more than the dark shape of the trunk lying across the broken bracken and undergrowth. She made her way disconsolately around the ugly upended root and glanced down into the hole.

'Conan!' she gasped. 'Oh Conan!' His tiny head was wedged against the knot of a smaller root still bound by stones and debris. Most of his small body was covered in loose earth. 'Ross . . . Ross . . . He is here!' she screamed as she scrambled into the earthy pit, slipping and slithering in the loose soil.

'Conan . . .' she breathed tenderly. He did not stir. She knew instinctively he was not sleeping. He was so still. So white . . . Rachel dropped to her knees beside his inert body. She brushed back the earth which had half covered him. Her leaden heart seemed to stop.

CHAPTER TWENTY

Ross ran forward. There was no sign of Rachel. Had he imagined her call?

'Where are you? Rachel?' He stared around the deserted woodland.

'Ross . . . Down here. In the hole. Behind the tree roots. He's dead! Oh, Ross, my baby's dead.' He peered round the side of the huge upended tree. Rachel stared up at him. Her eyes were twin pools, dark with despair.

'He can't be dead,' he breathed incredulously. 'Hold on Rachel. I'm coming round the other side.'

Rachel was cradling Conan's still little body in her arms now, rocking him back and forth, whimpering softly against the bump on his forehead.

Ross knelt beside her and gently took the small body in his arms, brushing back the soft hair. He put his lips to the small tiny rosebud mouth. Rachel watched as Ross bowed his head against Conan's narrow chest.

'I-I think he's still breathing! Rachel . . . ?'

'But he's so still . . .'

'Let's get him out of here. Can you scramble back out of this hellish hole? Look I'll wedge my boot into the edge to give you a foot hold. Hurry now.'

'Oh, don't drop him, Ross.' Breathlessly Rachel scrambled on all fours out of the cavity. Carefully Ross held the child up to her outstretched arms. Then he heaved himself after them, swiftly taking Conan once more, pressing his ear to the little chest.

'Is he breathing, Ross? Is he?' Rachel was in an agony of impatience at his indecision. Conan seemed so lifeless.

'I'm not sure . . . Let me carry him to the side of the loch. Could you wipe his face? Clean the wound on his temple . . .' Rachel ran ahead. She had already dipped her handkerchief into the clear water as Ross laid Conan on the ground. She wiped away the mud and Ross dipped his own handkerchief into the water and helped her.

'Ross!' Rachel's voice was a strangled squeak. 'His eyelid fluttered. I-I'm sure it did . . .' Her voice faltered into silence. Had she imagined it? Ross bent down and carefully wiped Conan's cheeks and hair. He scarcely knew what else to do, yet he could not believe that the child was dead. He had been so full of life and the joy of living . . . As he stared down at the white face the small lips parted slightly and closed again.

'He did move, Rachel! Perhaps we should give him a drink?'

'Yes. No. I mean I don't know . . . He might choke. Let me hold him, Ross. Please.' She cradled Conan tenderly in her arms and pressed her lips against his petal soft cheek.

'Ma-ma,' It was no more than a whisper but Rachel knew she had not imagined it.

'He is alive, Ross! He is, he is . . .' She began to weep, her tears raining down onto her child's face. 'Bring the blanket. We must keep him warm.' Ross obeyed.

'Ma-ma . . .' the little voice was clearer, more plaintive. Ross gave a huge sigh of relief. 'Head hurted.'

'Yes, oh yes, my darling babe, I know. Mama — and Dada — will make it better.'

'We should get him to the doctor?' Ross suggested. 'Could we make a sort of sling for him?' He sounded diffident. 'Use the blanket and the bag we brought for the picnic.

We ought not to shake him about . . . Will you cycle ahead and warn the doctor? We will go back the way we came. It's shorter. You know the doctor's house is the red sandstone one at the fork of the roads?'

It was only when Rachel reached the village and saw people staring at her that she realised what a dirty mess she must look. She did not care. She did not stop, not even to greet Mr Pearson who was enjoying a Sunday afternoon rest outside his cottage door. Fortunately Doctor MacEwan was at home.

Two days later, apart from a dark bruise and a tender cut at his temple, Conan seemed to be none the worse for his adventure. He would forget, but Rachel knew she never would. The shock and horror she had experienced that Sunday afternoon would remain with her. She had to prevent herself from being over-protective in the weeks which followed.

Rachel noticed a change in Ross's attitude too. He did not criticise when she gave Conan her attention and he seemed more patient and attentive. Conan responded with enthusiasm. Ross's attitude to his child had troubled Alice and she was relieved to see him making more effort.

'I never had any doubt that Conan was Ross's son,' she told Rachel one day when they were working together. 'In his heart I don't think he has any doubts either, but he did seem very resentful of Conan, almost jealous.'

'I think the shock of thinking Conan had drowned made both of us appreciate him more,' Rachel agreed. Deep down she knew Ross would always be a little jealous of her love for Conan. Although he was a grown man, and well-respected by those around him, she knew there was a chink in his armour and she blamed Gertrude Maxwell's lack of loving for making him vulnerable.

'How did Conan fall into the hole?' Alice asked.

'He had been playing with a worm. I told him Mr Worm lived in a tunnel underground. He thought he had found Mr Worm's house and he fell in.'

* * *

214

Rachel did not accompany Ross to the Rent Dinner with the other tenants and their wives. She had made herself a dress, with Alice's help, determined that Ross should be proud of her but when the day came she was suffering from a stomach upset and blamed the fish which Ross had brought home after a visit to the market in Annan. Two weeks later, in mid-June, she knew it was not the fish which made her feel so squeamish every morning. This time she knew the cause of the sickness.

She hugged her secret to herself, wanting to be certain before she told Ross. She was delighted they were to have another baby, but she worried whether he would share her happiness.

Although Alice had no children of her own she guessed the reason for Rachel's frequent bouts of sickness. When the haymaking started in July and Rachel had not confided in her she broached the subject herself.

'I don't think you should work so hard at the haymaking this year, Rachel,' she voiced her concern. 'You must consider your health.'

Rachel looked at her sharply, then she smiled.

'You have guessed?'

'Yes. You are usually so brisk and fresh in the mornings. There had to be a reason for the change in you, and for that secret glint of happiness in your eyes in spite of the sickly spasms. What else could do that except a baby?'

'I can't keep my secret very well,' Rachel smiled ruefully. 'I do hope Ross will be pleased. You don't mind another baby to disturb your household?' Rachel asked anxiously as the thought occurred to her.

'No. We all enjoy Conan, but it would be a pity to spoil him. I do think you should tell Ross though. Haymaking is hard work, especially forking hay up into the lofts.'

Rachel took Alice's advice and confided in Ross before they went to sleep that night. He was delighted and concerned and full of questions. Sadly she remembered how much of Conan's birth he had missed. This baby would be

215

like his first born to Ross. Later she had reason to be thankful she had told him before they had an unexpected visitor.

The last two short rows of hay from the low meadow had made up barely half a load.

'The boss says we should start the milking as soon as we get this into the loft,' Sandy Kidd announced. 'He's taking the horse and rake into the next field. We are to start carting in again as soon as milking is finished.'

'I'll fork this to the loft then,' Beth volunteered. 'It's so hot up there now that it's nearly full.'

'All right, lassie, Alfie and me will deal with the loft, if you're sure you can manage.'

'I'll take Bonny from the shafts and water her at the trough before I bring in the cows,' Rachel said. 'They will be ready for milking as soon as you have all finished unloading the cart.'

There were two hay lofts at Lochandee, both with stone stairs leading from the main yard to a full-size door. Each loft had a trapdoor in the floor for pushing the hay to the byre or to the stable below. The backs of these buildings faced into a small stack-yard with fields beyond. In the high unbroken walls were two small half-size doors into which the hay was forked when the carts were brought in from the field.

It was always quiet on this side of the farm. Visitors rarely found their way round about, so Beth was startled out of her wits when a man's voice boomed beside the almost empty cart.

'Surely Maxwell has men to fork up the hay?'

Beth stared down at the portly figure. She had never seen him before.

'It was only half a load. Anyway I offered. Needed a bit of fresh air. If it's Mr Maxwell you are wanting, he's still in the hayfield.'

'I know. I saw him from the road as I was riding by.'

'Mistress Beattie is at the house.' Beth was beginning to feel uncomfortable under the man's close scrutiny. She flung up the last forkful of hay. Alfie caught it and dragged it into the loft. 'That's the last of this load, Alfie,' she called. His only reply was a sort of cackle followed by the shutting of the little door to let her know he had understood. Beth drew a sigh of relief and wished the man would go away. Forking up so high was harder work than she had imagined, in spite of the fresh air.

'Let me help you down.'

'That's all right I can manage.' Beth was reluctant to take the man's hand. It looked white and flabby. His eyes seemed to be boring through her cotton frock.

'Come on. Give me your hand.'

Beth could scarcely avoid him, standing so close to the side of the cart. Frowning, she gave him her hand. He gave her a little jerk forward almost pulling her off balance, but instead of putting his other hand up to support her, he pushed it unerringly up the inside of her skirt. Beth gasped and tried to jump back but the hand gripping hers was stronger than it looked.

'Let me go! Take your hand away from me!' Beth flared, more angry than frightened.

'Come now, that's no way to speak to the Factor. I could make life easy for a pretty lass like you . . .' His eyes narrowed at her glare of contempt. 'Or I could make it difficult for a mere maid.'

'You! The Factor?' Beth was incredulous. She felt his fingers groping for the top of her drawers and kicked out at him furiously. 'I don't care who you are,' she panted. 'Let me go! Stop it! Stop it!'

Elder laughed, an ugly, leering sneer. It made Beth squirm. His red face and big yellow teeth were awful. She tried again to kick at his face but he caught her ankle. He jerked ruthlessly and she fell with a hard thump onto the bottom of the cart. In seconds he was in beside her, his speed belying his hefty body. All the breath had been knocked out of her and Beth could only pant. Elder seized his chance, flinging himself over her. She was too small to push such a heavy weight away. She could feel his fingers groping

217

under her skirt. She screamed. He yanked one hand free and clamped it over her mouth.

'That's better.' He spoke through his teeth, his thick lip curling. 'If you know what's good for you, you'll stay quiet. You'll have had this often enough to know what we're about.'

'No . . .' Beth mumbled against his flabby hand. She tried to shake her head. Tears of frustration, anger and pain welled into her eyes.

'You haven't? A virgin? By all the Gods! Didn't think I'd get another so soon. More fun than I would have got with Maxwell's wife after all.' He lifted his hand. Beth screamed instantly. He clamped her mouth cruelly but his free hand was groping more urgently now and there was a terrible lusting gleam in his eyes. Terrified Beth bit his thumb as hard as she could. He yelped at the unexpected pain. She screamed again and again. There was no one to hear on this side of the farmyard and she struggled desperately.

In the byre Rachel was tying the cows into their stalls. There were ventilation holes in the walls which faced the outer side of the yard. She thought she heard a scream as she was fastening the chains. Then she decided she must have imagined it. When it came again, then again, she dropped the chain and ran down the byre and out of the narrow door at the end.

She could only just see the hump of a man's back, scuffling in the empty cart but she guessed Beth must be there too. She ran towards them. Neither of them heard her. She knew could not drag the man off Beth. She saw the shafts of the cart and lifted them. They were heavy with the weight of two bodies in the cart, but desperation lent her strength.

'What the devil! The cart moved . . .'

Rachel gave one more heave and cart went up on its end, shafts in the air. She knew it would break the extra tailboard which Ross had fixed for carting hay, but Beth's safety was more important.

Fear, and her natural agility, gave Beth an advantage. She rolled to her feet and was sprinting away before the big man could gather himself to his knees. Briefly she glanced over her shoulder to make sure Rachel was following.

'Run, Beth,' Rachel gasped. A painful stitch made her bend double for a moment. Then she also turned to run. Elder threw himself full length along the ground catching her skirts from behind. Seconds later she was lying face down with the stranger panting over her.

He seized her arms and twisted them cruelly up her back. She gasped with pain. That seemed to please him. Holding her wrists up her back with one hand he flung her over, onto her back, pinning her down by her shoulders so that she could not release her arms. The pain was excruciating. Rachel thought she would faint. She could feel the perspiration gathering on her brow. The man seemed to have recovered his breath and was leering down at her. His prominent yellow teeth and thick lips made her feel sick.

'Don't curl your lip at me, you bitch. Jealous of your maid were you? Well you can have it instead.'

'No! Who are you?'

'Bert Elder is the name — your Factor.'

'The Factor! F-for the estate? You c-can't be. Let me go! You're breaking my arms . . .' Cruelly he pressed her shoulders harder. Rachel closed her eyes so that he would not see her pain and fear.

'Now you listen to me, Madam. I could do a lot for your husband if you co-operate . . .'

'Never!' Rachel's eyes flew open.

'Have it your own way.' He shrugged. 'I'd heard you had spirit, as well as looks. Suits me. I like my women with a bit of fight.' He reached down, yanking the hem of her skirt up, groping at her underclothes.

'No! You c-can't do that. I-I'm expecting a child.'

'Are you now? Well maybe I can get rid of it for you, eh.'

'No! No!' Rachel began to scream and scream. She could not stop, even when he slapped her so hard she felt he must have knocked her neck out of joint.

219

It was an unwritten law that the milking never started with cow dung in the channels. Usually the cows were very clean and came eagerly to be milked, though they frequently left dung behind them on their way back to the field. Today one of the cows had been startled when Rachel had flung aside its chain. Nervously she had sent a fountain of dung across the clean path between the two rows of cows waiting to be milked. Alfie cackled and patiently brought his big shovel. He scraped up the mess. He did not need the wheelbarrow for only one cow. He went out of the narrow door at the end of the byre which led to the midden and flung the dung over the side. As he turned he heard Rachel's screams from the back of the wall and went to investigate. He did not understand what was happening but he knew the young mistress was being hurt. He loped up to her and without hesitation he whammed his filthy shovel over the back of Elder's head.

The Factor keeled over without a sound. Rachel could scarcely move for the pain in her arms. She rolled onto her side and held a hand out stiffly. Alfie pulled her to her feet and with one brief glance at the Factor's prone figure sprawled amidst the hay and dust, she clutched Alfie's hand and ran, pulling him with her.

'Stay here. Pretend you saw nothing,' she gasped when they reached the byre. She sped through the opposite door, across the main yard and into the house. She knew the dung had spattered from the shovel onto her face and dress as well as over the Factor's head and down his tweed jacket.

Alice Beattie gaped at the sight of her. Rachel sank onto a stool, clutching her side, gasping for breath. She began to cry and to laugh at the same time.

'Oh, lassie, you're hysterical. Stop it. Rachel, stop that.' Rachel couldn't, her relief was so immense. Alice slapped her none too gently bringing tears to her eyes.

'I'm sorry, lass, but I had to bring you back to your senses. I'll make a cup of tea for you. Then you had better change your dress and wash your face.'

Alice was deeply perturbed. She had found Beth sobbing in the wash-house and had only just calmed her down and persuaded her to drink some tea. She kept shaking her head as she made tea for Rachel. What sort of a man was that to employ? And to employ him as a Factor — with power and authority and influence? She shivered and stroked Rachel's head instinctively, as though she was a little girl.

Rachel was washed and changed and settled down at the milking by the time Ross returned. They had seen Mr Elder riding away on his horse, his dirty jacket rolled into a ball behind him. She decided not to mention his visit to Ross. She was not at all sure what his reaction would be.

She had reckoned without her subconscious. Her last waking thoughts that night were for the safety of her unborn child. Her arms still felt as though they had been pulled from their sockets and she had the muscles across her stomach had strained beneath the weight of the cart as she lifted the shafts. She prayed for the safety of her baby.

Ross was alarmed by Rachel's muffled scream and her cries. She was kicking and pushing him away with all her strength. He grasped her arm and shook her awaken. She groaned aloud and shuddered. Ross leaned over and lit their candle, holding it up to see her face.

'My dearest lassie! Are you fevered? Your brow is wet with sweat and you're as pale as a ghost.'

'I'm sorry. I-I had a dream . . .'

'Dream? I'd say it was a nightmare. You kicked my shins hard. I shall be black and blue tomorrow.' He grinned ruefully.

'I'm sorry,' she mumbled again, but she could not control her shivering. Ross set the candle down and stroked the curling tendrils of hair from her brow.

'Something is troubling you, Rachel. What is it?' Rachel bit her lip. There was always the possibility that Alice might tell him, especially when Beth had been so badly frightened too.

'Blow out the candle and hold me close. Then I'll tell you what happened.' Slowly, haltingly she told him of the Factor's visit. Ross was furious.

'You sure he didn't . . .'

'No, no. He didn't . . .' she shuddered. 'Thank God for Alfie,' she muttered feelingly. 'He really did save me. If it had not been so frightening I suppose we could have laughed at Alfie hitting him with a shitty shovel. I expect he'll find an excuse for his dirty jacket when he gets home to his wife. Does he have a wife, Ross?'

'I don't know. I just know that I would like to break his neck and every bone in his body.'

'Oh no, Ross, please! Don't seek revenge.' She shuddered. 'As it is I'm terribly afraid he will make us all pay if he gets a chance. He — he is that sort of spiteful man I think. I'm so sorry, Ross.'

'Dear Rachel, you have nothing to be sorry about. Anyway I don't think he can do us much harm.' Had it not been so dark Rachel would have seen his troubled frown. He had heard a lot of rumours about the Factor and if only half of them were true he was a man to mistrust.

'What about the tenancy?' she asked.

'Thanks to Mr Shaw the joint tenancy was signed and sealed before the old Laird died. There is nothing he can do about that until the lease is finished — just so long as we stick rigidly to the terms anyway.'

'How long is the lease?'

'Seven more years.'

'I hope we have a new Factor long before then. I don't want to see that man again — not ever.' Mr Shaw was such a kind man — such a gentleman.

In the silence of the night Alice Beattie's thoughts were running along the same lines. She resolved to visit her law-yer without delay. She would do everything in her power to secure the future of her beloved Glens of Lochandee, and the young couple she had come to regard as the next best thing to a family of her own. She had two cousins in Canada but she had not seen them for years. Her future was bound up with Ross and Rachel. She must try to protect them.

She decided she must write a letter of complaint to the Laird. From all accounts he was rarely at home but surely he must attend to such a serious matter. Sandy Kidd's wife had mentioned rumours of the Factor's attack on a young girl on the other side of the glens. Alice had only half-believed the story but Dolly's words came back to her now.

CHAPTER TWENTY-ONE

On the tenth of February, 1925 Ross waited in an agony of impatience and anxiety. The midwife had been well recommended by several women in the village but the birth was long and difficult, quite the opposite of Rachel's experience with Conan. Ross hated being banned from his wife's room. He felt the women were treating him like a child, hiding things from him.

'I want to see my wife,' he demanded when Mrs Semple appeared in the kitchen for yet more hot water.

'Patience!' she commanded brusquely. 'Men were far behind when the good Lord handed out that virtue.'

'But she's my wife . . .'

'Aye, I should hope she is! Ye've certainly given her a packet o' trouble anyway. Now just bide a while and let me get on with setting her right.' She made to bustle past him with the heavy kettle of hot water.

'What sort of trouble?' Ross asked faintly. His face had lost its ruddy colour. The midwife glanced at him. She liked the men to get a bit anxious. They deserved to worry she reckoned, but she relented a little.

'The babe is taking its time. I'd say it will be a good size and Mistress Maxwell is finely made. But she's no one tae complain and scream her head off, poor lass. I'm thankful for that and so should you be, my man.' She nodded her grey head vigorously. 'Now just be patient and I'll bring ye some news in a wee while. Make us all a cup o' tea — if ye ken how.'

'Mrs Semple is clean and efficient,' Alice Beattie tried to reassure Ross when he voiced his concerns to her a short time later. She was growing anxious herself as the hours passed.

As he waited Ross considered how much Rachel must have borne for Conan, waiting alone throughout nine long months, with the ordeal of the birth at the end of it. He had not even been in the same house, had not even known. He buried his head in his hands and groaned. He had felt so sorry for himself, banished from Windlebrae, rejected, with no letters from those he loved. How much worse it must have been for Rachel. He had not been there to offer comfort or support. Thank God, Meg and Peter Sedgeman had taken care of her, he thought belatedly. Even the old cobbler had befriended her. He should have gone back for her. He should have ignored Gertrude Maxwell's wishes. So he berated himself.

His relief was overwhelming when Mrs Semple at last allowed him to see Rachel. He marvelled at the tiny scrap of humanity who was his daughter. Rachel finally managed to reassure him that all she needed was a good sleep.

Tired though he was, he sat down and wrote to Meg.

The waiting seemed to go on for ever. I have sympathy with Peter as never before. I am sorry I was impatient to drag Rachel away from you when you needed her so badly, Meg. I did not understand. I have seen the birth of many a calf and thought it was just a natural thing. Please forgive me? Rachel has chosen the names for our daughter after the two women she values as true friends. She will be christened Margaret Alice.

* * *

Rachel had a fortnight of being pampered by Alice and Beth and spoiled by Ross and Conan. At every opportunity they crept up to her bedroom to sit with her. Conan loved to lie on the bright rag rug in front of the bedroom fire with his feet in the air. He would lay watching the flames dance, or mimicking the shadows on the walls as the short winter days drew to a close. Beth kept the fire alight both day and night to drive away the bleak February chill. She carried up bowls of the chicken soup which the midwife considered the very best restorative for women in Rachel's circumstances.

Alice had prevailed upon Sandy Kidd's wife, Dolly, to help in the house and with the washing. The couple welcomed the extra money and Dolly was a brisk and cheerful worker. Although Alice never complained and never admitted to growing old, Rachel worried about her when she looked tired and drawn.

'The sooner I am up and back to the milking and the butter making, the better,' she said one night to Ross. 'I think Mistress Beattie is doing far too much while I am lying in bed being treated like a lady. She looks pale and tired.'

'We all try to spare her,' Ross said, 'but now we have extra cows the milking takes a long time, especially without you. You seem to have a natural instinct for handling the most nervous animals. Anyway we would never have been able to afford Dolly's help in the house if we had not increased the milk we have to sell.'

'I know,' Rachel sighed. 'I shall soon be back to work.'

'I have heard of one or two farmers installing machines to milk the cows,' Ross told her. Rachel stared at him, then she laughed aloud at such an idea.

'A machine will never be able to milk cows — not properly, like we do.' She chuckled at the thought but Ross looked serious.

'I saw Jim MacDonald's son at Lockerbie market. He said he was having one installed.'

'But how would a machine know if a cow had finished milking? What if one had an infection in her udder? Or if it was sore? How would it know if one teat needed more milking than the rest? No, I don't believe it's possible.'

Ross shrugged. If a machine had been invented which could milk cows properly it would save a lot of time.

* * *

Barely a year later, the subject of a milking machine arose again. Alice was dismayed. She was not as young and fit as she used to be and Rachel was expecting another baby. Margaret would be just sixteen months old by June, when the new baby was due.

Alice loved children but there was no doubt they made a lot of work and frequently a lot of noise and these days she seemed to get so tired. Rachel and Ross had noticed this and once more Ross broached the subject of buying a milking machine.

'Could we afford one,' he asked Alice.

'Would it be any good?' she countered, sharing all Rachel's misgivings about the welfare of their precious cows. One of their neighbours had gone bankrupt and rumour had it that it was due to his new machines and modern ideas. Even so Alice had purchased a motor car at his farm sale so Ross knew she was not entirely against changes.

'I could drive you over to see the MacDonalds' machine. We could see it working,' he suggested. 'To tell you the truth I would like to see one myself before we wasted any money or risked the health of the cows. Did you hear the Factor is proposing to raise all the rents because the estate needs more money?'

'I had not heard that, no,' Alice admitted slowly, 'but it does not surprise me. The Factor never comes round to see the farms now, but I have heard that the young Laird spends most of his time in France and has no idea what his Factor is up to.'

'Ah, but the Factor does inspect our land,' Ross warned darkly. 'He does it slyly. Sandy and I have seen him riding along the road in his motor car, stopping to peer over the hedges. At other times we have seen him ride around the neighbouring farms on his horse and he always rides along our boundary. If he could find fault I fear he would take his revenge.'

He came twice in one week when we were digging drains in the top meadow but he did not venture onto The Glens of Lochandee. I reckon he's afraid of getting another shovel laid around his ears. After all he never knew who had hit him, did he?'

'I had not thought of that,' Alice admitted. 'Dolly told me months ago that he had attacked a young woman on the estate but I couldn't really believe it then. I can't believe the Laird lets him get away with it.'

'He's never here to know what's going on.' Ross's fists clenched and Alice saw the muscle throbbing in his lean jaw, before he muttered, 'He deserves to be hanged.'

'There seems to be no justice for men like that. Anyway, back to business. I can't remember when the estate last paid for any of the repairs, as they agreed to do when we pay our rents on time. It takes all the spare money we can make to keep The Glens of Lochandee in good repair, but I would hate to see it with the gates hanging off and the fences broken, not to mention slates sliding off the roofs.'

'Is that what is troubling you?' Ross asked. 'I know there's something on your mind.'

'It's not money exactly,' Alice sighed again. 'I suppose I'm just getting old and tired. I have a small legacy which my grandmother left me for my own old age. I have never needed it yet, but I worry about the future for you and Rachel. I wonder whether the Factor will renew the lease when it runs out.'

'Surely the Laird cannot sell all the farms on the estate? He must need income from the rents?'

'Maybe he wants the money, but he does not show any other interest. I have been thinking that I ought to show Rachel how to keep the accounts. My concentration is not as good as it used to be and it's better if a wife understands about the money. Rachel is very sensible about such things.'

'She is,' Ross agreed readily. 'Minnie Ferguson taught her to be thrifty and she is good with figures.

'I will suggest it to her then,' Alice nodded. 'We could go through the accounts together and it would take the weight off her feet now she's expecting another child.' Alice was relieved. She had wondered whether Ross would resent his wife taking over the accounts, even though Rachel had kept a careful record of the butter and eggs which she sold in the village. These sales had grown steadily. They paid for the wages of Dolly and Sandy and Beth, as well as their own household expenses and Alfie's food and clothes. In her heart she knew they were better off than most of the other farms round about. It was her own lack of energy, and her anxiety over the Factor, which troubled her.

* * *

A letter arrived from Meg. It was too early for her usual fortnightly news and it bore the ominous black edging around the envelope. It was addressed to Ross. Rachel's heart sank as he slit it open.

'Ah,' he sighed sadly. 'It's my father — I mean my Uncle . . .'

'The man you regarded as a father?' Alice prompted gently.

'Yes. The funeral is the day after tomorrow.'

'Poor Mr Maxwell,' Rachel sighed. 'He was a good man. Meg and Willie will be so sad, and Ruth and the children.'

'I must go to the funeral . . .' Ross frowned, his eyes resting worriedly on Rachel's rounded stomach.

'I shall be all right,' she assured him. 'You will only be gone two days.'

'Perhaps Rachel could drive you to the station after the morning milking?' Alice suggested. 'I will come too. I have some business to attend. We could take Margaret with us. Beth would manage Conan until we get back.'

On the way home Alice held Margaret on her knee and thought how fortunate she was for a woman who had no family of her own. The little girl curled up on her lap, her rosy cheek against her breast. She was such a pretty child Alice thought happily, with her fair curls, her bright blue eyes and rosy cheeks, but it was her contented nature and happy smile which made her so endearing. Alice sighed. Twice the lawyer had asked her if she was sure she was making the right decision.

'I am sure,' she told him firmly. 'I never see, or hear from my cousins in Canada, and I should have had to leave The Glens of Lochandee long before now if Ross and Rachel had not helped me.' She had known Jacob Niven for more years than she cared to remember. He had been her grandfather's lawyer, and then her father's.

'I will have the documents drawn up and send them to you for a last appraisal then,' he promised. 'Before you leave I will introduce you to my son, Jordon. I am retiring gradually. He is taking over any new clients and some of the existing ones. You never seem to get any older, Alice so I expect he will probably be the one to deal with your affairs when the time comes.'

'You always were one to flatter, Jacob,' Alice smiled. 'I just wish you were right. I have felt my age recently. It does not help when there is so much unhappiness in the country either. We thought everyone would live in peace and contentment when the war ended.'

'We did indeed,' Jacob sighed, 'But it has not turned out that way. Who would have believed there would be thousands of men out of work and whole families going to bed hungry. The discontent does not end in Britain either. It's much the same in Europe, especially Germany. I'm told they have built a new battleship. We expected all that would end with the war . . . Ah, here comes Jordon. Let me introduce you to Mistress Alice Beattie from The Glens of Lochandee. This is Jordon my son, and my successor.'

The young man shook hands and greeted Alice politely.

'Glens of Lochandee, you said? Are you having trouble fighting for your tenants' rights as well then?'

'No, no,' his father frowned irritably. 'Mrs Beattie came to make her will. You are not having trouble with the Laird, or his Factor are you, Alice?'

'No . . . not yet anyway,' Alice frowned. 'So it is true then? They are putting some of the tenants out? We had heard rumours, but surely if they are paying their rents and the lease has not expired . . .'

'The Factor makes out a case that they are unsatisfactory tenants. We have fought for two and won. We do know he has put three other tenants out of their farms though, and sold the land with vacant possession.'

'I see . . .' Alice looked anxious.

'I'm sure you have no cause to worry, my dear,' Jacob Niven said reassuringly. 'Your family has been in The Glens of Lochandee for generations and it has always been one of the best run farms on the estate.'

'But it is the best farms they are selling,' Jordon insisted. 'They make the most money. The Laird does not seem to care what happens to his estates. He spends most of his time in France and leaves his wife and children at home.' The young lawyer spoke with contempt.

'It would break my heart if they refused to renew the lease and we had to leave,' Alice said anxiously. 'It would upset Ross and Rachel too. They have grown to love Lochandee almost as much as I do. They work so hard, for little return.'

'Well, you come to me if you need advice on such matters,' Jordon smiled as he held the door open for Alice. 'There's no point in writing to the Laird anymore. Apparently he doesn't even bother to open the letters. He just leaves his Factor to deal with them. There's nothing I enjoy better than a confrontation with that obnoxious Bertrand Elder.'

* * *

The following night Ross stepped down from the train and looked around, thankful to be almost home again. He was disappointed when there was no sign of Rachel with the car.

He managed to get a lift almost to Lochandee village but he still had a good three miles to walk, into the village and then up to the farm. He was tired and hungry, and rather sad.

As he drew nearer he was dismayed to see the cows had not yet been turned back into the fields after milking. It was a fine May evening and the milk yields always increased when the cows ate the fresh spring grass. The milking should have been finished hours ago.

There was so much hustle and bustle in the house that no one seemed to notice he had returned. Then he saw Mrs Semple, the midwife, hurrying up the stairs with a white enamel bowl in her hands. His heart hammered against his ribs. The baby was not due for another three or four weeks. He dumped his bag and hurried upstairs but Alice met him at the top, her face pale.

'What's going on?' he demanded urgently. 'Rachel . . . ?'

'Mrs Semple is with her.' Alice's voice was low and strained. 'Rachel slipped in the dairy while she was reaching up to empty a pail of milk into the D pan above the cooler.'

'But Alfie always does that for her . . .'

'I know, I know . . . He had been delayed. I suppose Rachel felt she could manage.' Alice passed a harassed hand across her brow.

'Are you all right?' Ross asked, frowning.

'Fine, just tired,'

'I'm longing for a drink of tea,' Ross lied. 'Will you have one with me?'

'In a minute,' Alice nodded wearily.

'I'll make it then. I don't suppose that dragon of a midwife will allow me in to see my wife first?'

'No. I-I'm afraid the baby is coming. If anyone can save it Mrs Semple will, but she has sent for Doctor MacEwan to come and she doesn't usually want any men around when she is attending a birth.'

'I see . . .' Ross knew his face had paled. Please God let Rachel be all right, he prayed silently. His first thoughts were always for Rachel.

Two hours later the long shadows of the May evening crept over the landscape. The cows had been milked and were grazing peacefully in the pastures, birds sang their final evening chorus as they settled down for the night. Suddenly a puny cry came from the bedroom. Ross and Alice stared at each other. The thin wail continued. Ross felt he had waited an interminable time. Alice sank onto the window seat to wait but he paced back and forth restlessly and almost collided with Mrs Semple when she appeared at the bedroom door.

'Ah, Mr Maxwell . . . The bairn is alive, but frail. A wee lassie. I am expecting Doctor MacEwan.'

'Rachel? My wife . . . ?'

'Exhausted. She — she's a wee bit emotional. Only to be expected in the circumstances. I . . . I suggest you might want to have the wee one christened? Without delay . . .'

'Oh, Mistress Semple!' Alice hurried to her side. 'Is she . . . ? Is she so weak?'

'She's a mite early and none too robust — but she gave her wee lungs a good exercising. I reckon she's a fighter, like her mother. I'd just feel happier if . . . Ah,' she gave a sigh of relief as they all heard the honking and spluttering of the doctor's car. He was the worst driver in the village. Everyone knew when he was approaching but tonight the noise was a welcome sound.

Half an hour later he assured Mrs Semple she had done all she could for mother and child.

'The rest is in the hands of God, but I will look in again tomorrow. The wee mite has come into a restless world, and no mistake. The strike is to start at midnight tonight — the first General Strike in British history.' He shook his head bewilderedly. 'And yet I canna blame some o' the men.'

The new baby was christened Bridget Mhairi the following day, the third of May 1926. Although small and a slow feeder, Rachel coaxed her daughter with tender patience. As each day passed she held tenaciously to life. By the time the General Strike had been called off nine days later, Doctor MacEwan felt she had a good chance of survival.

Although Bridie Maxwell remained dainty as the months passed she grew in strength and stamina and her happy nature and wide eyed interest more than made up for her lack of size.

CHAPTER TWENTY-TWO

Rachel looked forward to Meg's weekly letters but at the end of July there were two unexpected items of news.

'Willie and Ruth are planning to move to England,' she read aloud. 'They have given notice to the Laird. Their tenancy at Windlebrae ends at the November term.'

'Giving up the tenancy?' Ross was so startled he held his spoonful of porridge poised in mid-air.

'They intend to rent a farm in Yorkshire or Lincolnshire. Ruth's father thinks there will be better opportunities for Willie and his family. Apparently the landlords are welcoming Scottish tenants who are willing to keep cattle, especially dairy cows. They are more able to pay their rents.'

'Well good for Willie,' Ross's slow smile crinkled his blue eyes. 'but I'm more than happy where I am — so long as the Factor leaves us in peace.'

'Mmm . . . me too,' Rachel nodded, turning back to her letter. 'Oh dear, Meg has been looking after Sam Dewar.' She looked up from the closely written pages. 'He's the cobbler who lives next door,' she explained for Alice Beattie's benefit. Her eyes clouded. 'He has been very ill. He was such a shy, kind man,' she sighed. 'Conan adored him. He made his first tiny shoes.'

'Is he recovering?' Alice asked. She always took an interest in family news, possibly because she had none of her own.

'The doctor wanted Sam to go away to convalesce to keep him away from his clogger's bench for a while. Meg says he refuses to go amongst strangers. It is awful for him being so alone when he is ill.'

'Yes,' Alice agreed softly. She could have been like the old cobbler if it had not been for Ross and Rachel. She looked upon them as her family now. She could see how much it troubled Rachel to think of the old man staying alone.

'You could invite Mr Dewar to stay here for a short holiday,' she suggested. 'It may not be the quiet retreat the doctor had in mind but it would be a change for him.'

'How kind you are!' Rachel beamed. 'I wonder if he would be able to travel? I would love to see him again. It is generous of you to offer.'

* * *

Rachel was dismayed to see how Sam Dewar had aged when she met him at the station with Alice's car. He was thin and stooped and his grey hair was almost none existent now. At first Conan was too shy to talk and Sam seemed exhausted as he sat hunched in the front seat beside Rachel.

'I never thought I would ride in a motor car,' He said at length.

'I never thought I would learn to drive one,' Rachel chuckled. 'I was terrified at first.'

'You drive very competently, doesn't she Mr Dewar?' Alice approved.

'She does.' He sighed contentedly. 'I never thought I would see you again, lassie, or visit such a lovely part of the country.'

'Just you wait until you see The Glens of Lochandee,' Rachel told him. 'You will understand why Ross felt so at home here, and why Mistress Beattie loves it so much.'

'And you, lassie? Do you feel you belong now?' Sam asked wistfully. He had forgotten Alice's presence in the back of the car and she waited tensely for Rachel's reply. It was clear to her, even on such short acquaintance that Sam Dewar had a warm affection for Rachel and that it was reciprocated.

'For me, my home is wherever Ross and my children are,' Rachel said simply, 'But I hope and pray we shall never have to leave Lochandee.' Alice expelled a breath she had not been aware she was holding. She relaxed as Rachel described the little village on the side of the Loch, some of its inhabitants, the woodland track where she and Ross sometimes took the children for a picnic, and where they thought they had lost Conan.

At the mention of his own name Conan came to life and chattered eagerly in his high chirruping voice, telling Sam of all the animals he would see and his own secret den where he could hide.

'Margaret and baby Bridie are too wee to find me,' he said triumphantly. 'Bestest of all I like riding with Mama on her bicycle. I'm going to have a bicycle when I'm big. I'm going to make bicycles when I'm ever so old, like Mr Pearson.'

Sam smiled and asked Conan questions. By the time they arrived at The Glens of Lochandee the two were already firm friends.

* * *

Sam had been at Lochandee several days when he saw a man walking wearily up the track towards the farm. It was early evening and the milking had just finished.

'I see you are having a visitor?' He nodded towards a distant figure plodding up the farm road.

Frank Kidd and his wife had just left the byre and were heading home for their evening meal. They recognised the weary figure coming towards them and as one, they hurried back.

237

'That's Bill Carr, Mistress Beattie,' Dolly said urgently. 'D'ye remember I told you his lassie had been . . . Well the Factor got her, and — well she wouldna stand a chance against Elder. Now she has his bairn and nearly died a getting o' it, they say . . .'

'I remember, Dolly,' Alice Beattie nodded. 'But . . .'

'That's her father, that's Bill Carr coming up the road.' Dolly was more concerned than they had ever seen her. 'He — he was sae angry and upset he attacked the Factor . . .'

'And who could blame him! I'd hae done the same if it had been my lassie,' Sandy nodded vehemently.

'Aye, but now the Factor has told the Trains he would evict them frae the farm if they didna get rid o' the Carrs. They have three boys o' their ain and they've been in Marchiemount for four generations. Bill Carr's a guid man, Mistress, and he's been trying up and doon the glens for work but the other tenants are feared to take him on. He must be fair desperate.'

'You think he's coming here to seek work, Dolly?'

'Aye, Mistress Beattie. I reckon so. It's a long walk frae Marchiemount.'

'We were not planning to hire another man, at least not until prices improve, but we always have more work to do than hands to do it, don't we Ross?'

Ross remained silent, frowning.

'We will discuss the situation before Mr Carr reaches us. You go home now Dolly and attend to your family. Beth, will you give the man some bannock and cheese, and a drink of buttermilk, please. Ask him to wait and we will discuss the situation while we eat our own meal.'

'Suppose we did give the man work,' Ross said as soon as they were alone, 'the Factor would seize the first opportunity to terminate our tenancy. Where should we be then? I heard at the market that some o' the tenants got together but Elder was too clever for them, and they couldn't get in touch with the Laird himself.'

'If that happens we shall get a good lawyer to fight for our rights,' Alice said with determination. 'The old Laird must be turning in his grave at the way the estate is going to ruin. I think there is little hope of this Factor allowing us to take back the original boundaries of The Glens of Lochandee, as Mr Shaw intended.'

'None at all, I'd say,' Ross said glumly. 'He's more likely to sell the whole farm.

'Then we have nothing to lose. The man is in dire need. You do see that? Ross?' Alice had an inner conviction that this situation was some sort of test of her own Christian integrity. She had never told anyone of her disgust with a Factor who had used his position to attack both Beth and Rachel in her own yard. She had received no reply to her letter to the Laird, expressing her contempt. She wondered whether the Laird had received her letter and if he had warned the Factor to keep away from Lochandee. Sometimes she was consumed with anxiety in case the letter had fallen into the hands of the Factor himself. Now she felt she was being challenged to prove her own sincerity by extending a helping hand to his victims.

'Supposing we do find the man work, where would he live?' Ross asked. 'We have no more cottages. He and his daughter and her baby can't live in the bothy with Alfie.'

'That's true,' Alice conceded slowly. 'I had not considered that. The shepherd's cottage went with the ground McNish took over. The old calf house at the back of the steading used to be a cottage. It is filthy but the roof is sound and it does have a chimney and a fireplace. It was used as a cottage when I was a girl.'

'If the men moved the hay and straw out Beth and I could scrub it out.' Rachel said. She knew Ross was not in favour of employing another man yet but there was plenty of work to be done, more than enough for one man.'

'I am overruled then,' Ross sighed, 'but don't say I didna warn you if the Factor seeks revenge.'

Rachel dimpled up at him and Ross could not resist that special smile. Tonight, he knew, she would amply repay him, but he could not rid himself of his uneasiness. He had heard the other tenants discussing the Factor's malice and the Laird gave him a free rein.

Bill Carr was almost overcome with relief and gratitude, even when he understood the poor shelter he would have for a home.

'When are you due to move out of your cottage?' Ross asked.

'We were supposed to be out yesterday.' He hung his head. 'Anywhere will be better than sleeping on the road.'

'So soon!' Ross whistled. 'That does not give us much time then. I will send Sandy over with a horse and cart tomorrow morning, straight after milking. Can you be ready?'

'Aye, we're all ready now. We moved the furniture out and covered it with rugs and sacks, in case it rains. The Factor threatened to set fire to the cottage, with us in it, if we didna get out.'

'He couldn't do that!' Alice gasped.

'Mr Train was afraid he might. He reckons the Laird is in France most o' the time so it would be easy enough to say we had caused it, or it was an accident.'

'Well if you are packed and ready you could take the horse and cart home with you tonight,' Ross decided. 'It will save you walking, and the mare would only need one journey tomorrow.'

'Eh, man, I dinna ken how tae thank ye,' The man's eyes glistened and he turned to look at Alice and Rachel. 'May the good Lord bless ye all . . .' He turned away, ashamed to show his emotions.

Long before he reached the bend in the track on the last stretch Bill Carr could see the spiral of smoke curling into the still air of evening.

'Emmie!' he breathed. 'Oh God, please let her be safe.'

* * *

At Glens of Lochandee the milking was barely finished when the horse and cart came up the track. Ross couldn't believe

240

his eyes. There had been no time even to empty the old cottage. Bill Carr must have been up most of the night. As he drew nearer Ross's heart sank even more. The man looked barely fit to stand on his own two feet, much less do a day's manual work.

'We did not expect you so early . . .' He gazed past the two figures to the empty cart. 'You have not brought your furniture, your belongings?'

Dejectedly Bill Carr told him of the three drunken lackeys the Factor had sent to burn everything they possessed.

'Thank God, Mistress Train gave Emmie and the bairn protection.'

Ross's glance moved to the childish figure clutching a whimpering baby. She didn't look woman enough to bear a child, even less to suckle one.

Rachel and Beth had joined Ross in time to hear about the fire.

'He's a swine, that man.' Beth gasped indignantly. Looking at the trembling girl she understood what her own fate would have been had Mistress Maxwell not saved her. 'Somebody should — should knock him on the head like my Da does with the runt o' the litter.' Silently Rachel echoed her sentiments.

'You had better come into the house. I'm sure Mistress Beattie will stretch the porridge for another two until we decide what to do.'

Alice took charge. Rachel envied her calm and supposed it must be the way she had been reared. In fact Alice thrived on challenge and organising.

'Tonight Bill can sleep in the bothy with Alfie,' she said. 'Emmie will share Beth's room and we can make a crib for the baby in one of the large drawers from the bottom of a wardrobe. All right?' They all nodded agreement.

'In that case we had better get on with breakfast or Ross will miss the milk train and your customers will be growing impatient for their milk, Beth. As soon as we have all eaten I will supervise Sandy and Alfie clearing out the hay and sweeping the old cottage. Meanwhile Rachel and I will see what we can find in the way of spare cooking pots and other utensils.' She frowned thoughtfully.

'Grandpa has some pans and mugs and a kettle he doesna use,' Beth volunteered. 'I could ask him if we could get them for Emmie.'

'Very well,' Alice agreed. 'You may call in at the village on your way to the train.'

'We will,' Ross nodded, 'but it is time we set out or we shall be left with the milk still standing on the platform instead of halfway to Glasgow.'

* * *

Bill Carr and his daughter were overcome with gratitude at the kindness of the people around them. Beth's tender heart had been touched by their plight and she told her grandfather their story with a few embellishments of her own.

At the end of the week the old cottage had been cleaned and scrubbed and painted with white lime from top to bottom. Even Alice was astonished at the generosity of the people of Lochandee village although she had lived amongst them all her life. She did not realise it was her own act of human kindness which had set the example. Coupled with Beth's eloquent pleading at the Manse, and her grandfather's coaxing amongst his friends and neighbours, the old cottage looked like a home again. Its blazing fire was sending shadows up the newly whitened walls and a gleaming brass oil lamp from the doctor's wife stood on the well-scrubbed dresser which Alice had unearthed. There was a thick rag rug in front of the hearth and the undertaker had sent his boy to repair the old box bed in the kitchen. Someone else had sent a brass and iron bedstead for Emmie and a cot big enough for three babies had come from one of the big houses on the far side of the loch, along with blankets and a small eiderdown. Several times Emmie was almost in tears as she accepted the gifts which the minister kept bringing with his own pony and cart.

'I know the Reverend MacCreadie slightly. He was extremely concerned when he heard of the Carr's plight and the dilemma of the Train family,' he confided to Alice over one of his inevitable cups of tea and shortbread. 'He tells me Bill Carr and his family are good people. They attended his church regularly. It is a lesson to all of us that you have shown such courage, and a fine example of Christian charity.'

'I only hope we do not pay too dearly for it. The Factor is an evil man.'

'Mr Elder will reap the punishment of his own evil doings one day.'

"*Though the mills of God grind slowly, yet they grind exceeding small.*"' he quoted gravely.

Alice grimaced wryly at the lines from Longfellow's Retribution.

"'*Though with patience He stands waiting, with exactness grinds He all.*" I certainly hope it will prove true in Mr Elder's case,' she said without charity. 'When I witness the plight of Bill Carr and his daughter, I find it hard to see God's justice.'

'He works in mysterious ways,' The minister nodded, 'Sometimes His ways are beyond our understanding.'

* * *

Six weeks later the minister and his parishioners sought a return favour from Ross. It was the occasion of the kirn to celebrate the finish of the harvest. Everyone in the parish was welcome to share the harvest supper in the new village hall. This was always provided by the women of the parish. Many of them jealously guarded their recipes and their reputation for their jams or pies, or some other delicacy and woe betide the minister or his wife if one of them was omitted from the list of helpers.

Much the same applied to the men of the parish who organised the entertainment which followed. There were those who were famous — and sometimes infamous — for their songs and recitations. Equally the musicians jealously guarded their reputations for providing the liveliest jigs and reels. Merrymakers travelled from several parishes, coming on bicycles from as far afield as Lockerbie, to enjoy the Lochandee dancing.

Unfortunately their best fiddler, a man by the name of Henry MacPhail, had fallen off a corn stack while thatching. He had broken his arm. It was the morning of the kirn and by noon a group of gloomy men gathered around the smiddy and pondered the situation.

Seeing them, and guessing their business, Mr Pearson left his bicycle shop and went to join the discussion. It was short notice and fiddlers as good as MacPhail were hard to find.

'Beth told me Mr Maxwell frae The Glens is a fair hand wi' the fiddle,' he offered tentatively, knowing the reputation of Lochandee parish was at stake. Better to have no fiddler at all than a bad one.

After serious deliberation, the Reverend Simms was delegated to Glens of Lochandee to ask Ross to play his fiddle in the village for the first time. Ross had not played in public since he came to Lochandee so he was reluctant to agree. He often played in the kitchen at Glens of Lochandee on winter evenings though and when the Reverend Simms made it clear it was a crisis and the reputation of the men of Lochandee was at stake he agreed to do his best.

'I'm sure they will be obliged to you,' the minister murmured, though he was a trifle uncertain about that, knowing how much the Lochandee men prided themselves on their music.

Beth was excited. She wished Emmie could accompany her to the kirn. The two were becoming good friends and Beth wanted to introduce Emmie to the village people.

'I will look after the bairn,' Bill Carr offered, thinking it would do his wee lass good to have a bit of pleasure for a change. Still Emmie demurred on account of her scanty wardrobe.

'I've a skirt you could borrow,' Beth offered.

'And I have a blouse you can have,' Rachel told them. The blouse was too tight across her chest since she had been feeding Bridget, yet it would probably be too large for Emmie's skinny frame.

Rachel had left her own three children in Alice's care, making sure they were all tucked up in bed before she left, but Conan could wind Alice around his little finger and she had no doubt he would coax at least three extra bed time stories from her.

'Don't worry, Rachel,' Alice smiled as she admonished Conan once more. 'To tell the truth I have felt a great deal better since Bill Carr came to work. I am not so tired.'

'Yes, he is a good worker,' Rachel agreed. 'He looks so frail it's hard to believe he can get through so much, and he's really patient with Alfie.'

'I think we may bless the day he came to Glens of Lochandee — so long as Mr Elder does not find a way of wreaking revenge.'

So Rachel's heart was lighter than usual as she cycled down to the village. Her heart swelled with pride when people praised Ross's skill with the fiddle. She did not lack for partners either when the dancing really got going. During a break for refreshment Ross came to find her, smiling broadly.

'I am glad you are my wife or I think some of these Lochandee men would be claiming you,' he grinned. Rachel blushed at the glint in his eye. She knew that look, knew they would love each other well tonight, however late the hour. She gave him a dimpling smile.

'If I might interrupt a man flirting with his good wife?' a gruff voice interrupted. Ross turned and recognised Andrew McNish. 'We have not seen much of each other to say we are nearly neighbours,' he boomed. 'The bloody Factor warned Jim Douglas and me to keep our distance. He wanted Mistress Beattie out o' The Glens o' Lochandee but the pair o' ye have shown him a thing or two.'

'We manage to keep the place tidy and pay our rent anyway,' Ross agreed warily. McNish flushed, and gave a forced laugh.

245

'A man who can play the fiddle like you wouldna starve, I'll wager.'

'Thank you,' Ross acknowledged mildly. He had little respect for McNish's haphazard farming methods but he knew he had a reputation for being sociable and fond of a dram.

'Aye, ye'll be really part o' Lochandee now so I reckon you deserve to know what's going on. Had you heard Elder is trying to sell our corner o' the estate?'

'Sell?' Ross's face paled.

'He tried to sell my land and Jim Douglas's.'

'But he can't do that, can he?'

McNish reddened and Ross guessed he was probably owing rent.

'Elder says the Laird needs the money. There's rumours he keeps a woman in France as well as his wife in Scotland. Elder says he has authority to raise cash any way he chooses. Glens of Lochandee is one place he's determined to sell. Give him a dram next time he calls on you. That soon softens him up.'

'He never calls on us, and I'm not sorry.'

'He never calls? But how can he make his report and what about repairs?'

'Repairs! We've asked but the estate have not done any since Elder came,' Ross said coolly. 'We do our own.'

'Well, you might get a stay of execution, as they say.' McNish grinned, eyeing Rachel's anxious expression. 'He needs to sell Jim Douglas's farm and mine before he can sell land in the middle o' the estate and he's had no offers so far. I heard two farm sales were cancelled because the tenants hired a clever lawyer frae Lockerbie. Elder couldna prove they were breaking the terms o' their lease. He lost his case so he sold two other farms instead.'

'That's a relief.'

'Temporary I'd say. Anyway the truth o' the matter is, I canna afford to keep paying the rent for the extra land we took over frae Lochandee. Neither can Jim Douglas. We'd be greatly obliged if you and Mistress Beattie would take it back? Restore the old boundaries to Glens o' Lochandee. Maybe ye'd have a better chance o' hanging on to it, so long as the rent's paid.'

'I see . . .' Ross bit back a smile. That was really the crux of the matter, he guessed. 'Well thanks for telling me what's going on. See, they're calling me to start the dancing again.'

* * *

Alice was delighted at the prospect of restoring the former boundaries of Lochandee when Ross told her about McNish and Jim Douglas.

'The problem is I can't see the Factor agreeing to it,' Ross warned. 'It seems he would rather have McNish and Douglases owing rent.'

'According to the Reverend Simms, the Laird will be making one of his fleeting visits to Valantannoch in about ten days. Perhaps we could make an appointment to see him? We may stand a better chance of getting the land back from the Laird himself?'

'That would be a much better idea,' Ross agreed. He had not relished the idea of dealing with Elder.

CHAPTER TWENTY-THREE

Rachel turned off the alarm clock feeling she had never been to sleep. Margaret was the most angelic of children with her happy smile and sunny nature and she rarely cried as she had done most of the night.

'She seems to be sleeping now,' she whispered anxiously, 'but she is very restless. Her cheeks are hot and flushed.'

'She'll be fine,' Ross comforted. 'It's probably the candlelight.' Rachel made no reply. Every instinct told her Margaret was ill. She was coughing and fretful, brushing continuously at her head. Fortunately Bridie slept on undisturbed and Conan was in a room of his own now.

Reluctantly she crept down stairs and followed Ross and Beth out to the byre. Alice was a light sleeper and she had heard Rachel pacing the floor during the night but she assumed it must be Bridie cutting teeth.

Her mind turned to the appointment which she and Ross were to keep with the Laird later that morning, but it was impossible to ignore the fretful whimper from the next bedroom. She lit her candle and carried it through to peer into the two cots. Bridie was sound asleep. It was Margaret who turned and tossed, her little cheeks flushed with fever.

Alice returned to her room to dress, then gathered Margaret in a blanket and carried her down to the kitchen. The fire was burning cheerily in the big black-leaded range but Margaret seemed to be having difficulty getting her breath. She looked up, her blue eyes bright — too bright, Alice thought anxiously. She was relieved to hear Rachel kicking off her clogs at the back door.

'I just had to check if Margaret was all right.' Rachel's anxiety was plain to see. 'I'm so sorry if we disturbed you, especially today of all days.'

'You didn't disturb me, Rachel but I'm concerned for the wee mite myself, and your maternal instincts are the best guide. She is so hot and she doesn't seem able to swallow.'

'I'm afraid,' Rachel whispered, moving closer, her eyes wide and troubled. 'It's so unlike Margaret.' She felt the tiny burning forehead. 'Don't you think her neck seems swollen.'

'I'll take good care of her,' Alice promised. 'If she's no better when you have finished milking we'll telephone for Doctor MacEwan.' Rachel nodded. Alice loved the little girl like a second mother. She never showed favouritism but Rachel knew there was a special bond between the two. Reluctantly she hurried back to the byre and the milking.

Margaret was no better when Rachel sped back to the house after milking her last cow. If anything her breathing seemed to be getting more laboured. To make matters worse, Conan had trailed down to the kitchen dragging a stuffed toy horse and whimpering about his throat.

'I'll get you a drink and tuck you up in bed again,' Rachel promised.

'Don't want in bed.' He sipped a little warm milk. 'It hurts. The milk hurts,' he moaned. Alice met Rachel's eyes.

'Bill says Emmie had a bad night with baby Frances,' Rachel said 'I think there must be something going round. Could it be measles?'

'Telephone Doctor MacEwan,' Alice said. 'He will know best.'

Rachel went to the telephone and called the operator. It was Joan.

'The doctor has been called out three times in the night. You sure you really need him?'

'Was he called out to children?' Rachel asked urgently. Joan was not supposed to listen in but everyone knew she did. She hesitated.

'The Lanes wanted him for one o' their boys. Then the Browns called him for the twins.'

'I must speak to Doctor MacEwan,' Rachel insisted.

'I'm on my way,' he said before Rachel had finished describing Margaret's condition. 'Keep her warm and away from the other two children.' Rachel stared at the silent instrument. The two little girls slept in the same room. Conan was lolling against Alice's knee, right next to Margaret at this very moment. What did the Doctor fear?

'Diphtheria,' Doctor MacEwan pronounced grimly as soon as he saw the choking white membranes rapidly blocking Margaret's tiny throat. The doctor's own face looked white and strained. Dark shadows ringed his eyes, but his manner was calm, his instructions clear and decisive.

All three children were to be taken to the isolation hospital without delay.

'Emmie's baby had a bad night but she has not been in contact,' Rachel remembered tearfully.

'Then I will look at her while I am here. I must wash my hands first.'

Rachel poured hot water from the kettle into an enamel bowl and carried it to the long stone sink. She handed him a tablet of carbolic soap and a white towel.

Doctor MacEwan came back from the Carr's little cottage almost at a run.

'The baby must go to hospital too. She is so frail. She will have little resistance I fear.' He shook his head dejectedly. 'I must be on my way. I have several more calls to make.'

* * *

Neither Ross nor Alice remembered their appointment with the Laird in the torment of preparing the children and getting them to the hospital. Rachel did her best to contain her tears as she cradled Margaret in her arms. Alice nursed a sleeping Bridie in the back of the little car with Conan cowering into her in silent fear. Emmie sobbed uncontrollably as she clung to her baby, her tears falling onto Frances's hot little face.

As soon as they reached the hospital the children were ushered away from them. Rachel bit her lip so hard to stifle her own sobs that she was unaware of the blood until a single scarlet drop fell onto her hand. The matron said she would let them know when they could return to see the children through the window of the hospital ward.

When they returned home the house was silent and forlorn. Beth did her best to comfort Emmie but she was upset herself. She loved the children and they were a part of her daily life.

Rachel felt like a lost soul wondering from room to room, while Alice Beattie looked old and tired. Her heart was filled with dread. She had seen the ravages of diphtheria and scarlet fever several times in her life and she was well aware of the possible consequences, but she had never been so personally involved before. She realised how deeply attached to Ross and Rachel's children she had become.

* * *

When the telephone call came through from the hospital Rachel felt her heart race. An impersonal voice checked that the contact number was correct then briefly announced that Frances Carr had died at 4 a.m.

It was Alice who broke the news to Bill Carr and Emmie. Quietly she told Bill she would pay for the tiny coffin and the funeral. Emmie was inconsolable and Bill Carr left her by the fire and ushered Alice outside so that they might talk.

'I can find the money to pay for the funeral, Mistress Beattie, but I thank ye kindly. Do you think it would be in order to bury the bairn beside my wife? The minister's name was Reverend MacCreadie. He buried my Hannah. He was a fine man.'

'I'm sure he would conduct the service. Would you like me to ask the Reverend Simms to contact him. I know they are acquainted.'

'I'd be grateful, Mistress. Just a short service by the — the grave. There'll only be me and Emmie . . .'

'No, Bill.' Alice patted his arm. 'You are not alone in this. Our hearts ache for you and Emmie. We shall all attend baby Frances's funeral. Only God knows what we may all have to bear before this is over.'

'Thank ye, thank ye, Mistress.' Bill's voice was gruff, his eyes over-bright, but he clearly wanted to get something off his chest and Alice waited patiently. He swallowed hard, then went on. 'Maybe this is God's way of punishing me. I havena entered the kirk since my poor Emmie was brought to such shame and suffering.'

'Oh Bill! The shame was not Emmie's.'

'The Factor told me to knock the babe on the head when it was born but I could never do sic a thing. I prayed to God He'd provide a solution to our troubles but the bairn was born alive and perfect — not even a wee finger, or a toe out o' place. I-I didn't think I could love anything that — that b . . . that man had begotten. But I couldna help but love a helpless, innocent babe . . .' His voice broke. 'And now God is teaching me a lesson. He's taken her away and it will break Emmie's heart. May God forgive me for ever wishing her dead.'

'Don't Bill. You can't blame yourself for this. It's an epidemic and it has taken two of the children in the village already. Doctor MacEwan told me.'

'Ah, but in my ain heart I was feared the bairn might inherit evil frae the man who sired her.' Alice knew Bill was a great believer in traits being inherited in animals. Why should human beings be any different? 'It aye seems to me it's the bad bits that come out. I was feared the bairn would

252

break Emmie's heart if she grew up like her father. Now the Lord has taken her and I'm the one to blame for Emmie's grief.'

'No, Bill. Please do not blame yourself. God works in mysterious ways. I confess they are often beyond my understanding. At least baby Frances will never suffer from the cruel jibes which might have been her lot. The Factor seems to me to be more beast than man.'

Grieved though he was by the death of his first grandchild Bill Carr consoled himself with Alice's words.

* * *

Doctor MacEwan called in on his way home from the fever hospital the following morning. Rachel stared at him fearfully. She could read the message in his tired eyes.

'Bridie?' she breathed, believing her baby to be the frailest of her three children.

'I-I have to tell you . . . Margaret died a few hours ago . . .'

'Dead . . . Margaret . . .' Rachel repeated woodenly. The doctor nodded.

'Not Margaret. Oh no . . .' Alice whispered from the chair where she was rocking beside the fire. It had been her grandfather's chair and she always seemed to find comfort in it when she was distressed.

'I'm afraid so.' Doctor MacEwan looked and sounded deadly tired. 'Your young son is putting up a brave fight. He's a sturdy lad.'

'What about Bridie?' Rachel whispered hoarsely over the knot of tears.

'Bridget? Amazingly she is still resisting the infection.'

'Can't I bring her home then? Oh, please, Doctor MacEwan? Please? She's only a baby?' She rang her hands in despair as he shook his head gravely.

'We have to try to keep the infection from spreading. The baby has been in contact with the others. She may be incubating the disease.'

'What can we do, oh what can we do to help?'

'Pray, my dear. There is little else I can offer by way of comfort.'

* * *

The funeral was arranged for Frances Carr in the grave beside the grandmother she had never known. The Reverend MacCreadie conducted the simple service. No one noticed the lurking figure who prowled in the small copse which bordered the grave yard. Bert Elder gave a nod of satisfaction as the tiny wooden coffin was lowered.

So, my interfering Lady Lindsay, he thought malevolently, you will find no proof for your suspicions now. The business with the Carr girl had caused him more trouble than he had bargained for and he had no idea how her Ladyship had become suspicious. He gave a smirk of satisfaction. If he had his way he would put a stop to the Laird's wife taking so much interest in the estate's affairs. In the early days his Lordship had forbidden her to interfere but he no longer seemed to care if his wife discovered his lavish expenses.

Elder gave one more glance towards the little gathering now moving away from the graveside. He patted the letter in his pocket and his thick lips curled. This would teach Madam Beattie and her henchman Maxwell not to go behind his back in future. He had known nothing of their appointment with the Laird until they failed to keep it.

It was Lady Lindsay who had come into the office and informed them of a diphtheria epidemic and the deaths of several children on the estate, including two children from The Glens of Lochandee.

'Ah, that will account for them missing their appointment with me,' His Lordship announced. Elder had pricked up his ears. 'I thought it was strange. My father had great respect for Mistress Beattie. Mr Shaw considered Maxwell an excellent tenant too.' The deaths explain their absence. 'Write to Mrs Beattie, Elder. Ask her to pass on my condolences to the Maxwells, and to their employee. Explain that I could not delay my return to France but I shall be pleased to restore the original boundaries to The Glens of Lochandee. I shall be damned glad in fact. They seem to be one of the few tenants who are not in arrears with their rent,' he added gloomily. 'See to it without delay.'

'As you wish, your Lordship,' Bert Elder nodded. Inwardly he was fuming. The devil Maxwell had dared to go behind his back. He would pay for this.

He was convinced the Laird would not give a thought to Lochandee, or any of the farms and their tenants, once he returned to France. He would make sure the land would never be restored to The Glens of Lochandee as long as he was Factor. He derived great satisfaction from writing the letter to Alice Beattie, but not in accordance with the Laird's instructions.

'I completely forgot about our appointment with the Laird,' Alice gasped when she opened the letter. 'Oh dear, he is extremely displeased that we wasted his time. He has returned to France. Surely he cannot have heard of our sorrow? Surely he would have understood . . . ? He should have postponed his visit to France and called on all the bereaved families. His father always visited people on the estate when they were in distress — whether they were tenants or cottagers.'

'It seems he's not so compassionate as his father?' Rachel said dully.

'He has no compassion at all! There's not even a mention of condolence. He's more concerned with telling us not to waste his time in future. If we have any business to discuss we must proceed through the same channels as other tenants and make an appointment with his Factor.'

'We know what good that will do us,' Ross muttered cynically, but for once his mind was not on Lochandee. He missed the children more than he had believed possible. He knew Rachel was not sleeping well or eating enough to keep a bird alive. Conan and Bridie were still in the hospital. They had been allowed to visit but only to see Conan through the window and wave to the pallid little boy who was just one in a row of other white-faced sickly children. Seeing the wobbly little chin and his determination not to cry had seemed worse to Ross than not seeing him at all. As for Bridie, she showed no recognition of her mother and Rachel had wept all the way home.

As the days passed Rachel knew she was not alone in her grief. There were several families in the village and parish who had lost children and one family had lost three. She shuddered at the thought of such tragedy.

Eventually the day arrived when Conan and Bridie were allowed to return home. Conan was pale and listless. He was to be kept away from other children until Doctor MacEwan pronounced the epidemic completely over.

Four weeks was a long time in the life of a six-month-old baby and Rachel was heartbroken when Bridie showed no recognition. Her own milk had dried up. Bridie had lost weight and Rachel was desperate to give her nourishment. The nurses had been kind but they were all unfamiliar faces in strange surroundings. Back at Glens of Lochandee, Bridie was too young to understand she was home again — safe, secure and loved.

To her it was just another strange place with more unfamiliar faces. She cried more than she had ever done. It was Alice who constantly cuddled the little girl and re-established the continuity of routine which Bridie had missed. Rachel knew how necessary this was. She knew Alice had more time for sitting down with Bridie in the ancient rocking chair, for singing to her and soothing her. She knew how badly Alice was missing Margaret who had toddled after her so happily. She was grateful for Alice's help and patience, but she could not suppress the fleeting stabs of jealousy.

Her heart ached with sorrow for the loss of Margaret, and guilt because she believed she must have neglected Bridie. If she wakened in the night Rachel nursed her longer than was necessary, finding comfort in the small warm body close to her breast.

'You're spoiling the wee lass,' Ross said more than once. 'I'm loving her. She can't have too much loving.'

* * *

Rachel knew she would never forget Margaret Alice, the little daughter she had borne and loved so well. Like Bill Carr she grasped at her own philosophy to bring her comfort. Remembering Margaret's apparent perfection she wondered if God had deemed her too angelic for the world she would live in and had chosen to spare her the toils of earthly life. When Conan asked where Margaret had gone and why she wasn't coming back she told him she had gone to heaven to live with the angels.

'Is it a nice place to live?'

'Oh yes. Margaret will be happy there. She will not have any more pain.'

'And no awful cough? No horrid medicine?'

'No, she will not have any of those things,' Rachel had answered, and prayed to God she was right.

* * *

Christmas and Hogmanay passed almost unnoticed. There had been two more cases of diphtheria at the beginning of December. One of the children had died. Since then the infection seemed to have faded away and by the end of January life reverted to as near normal as it would ever be for those who had lost children. The Reverend Simms was joined in fervent prayers for better times ahead.

CHAPTER TWENTY-FOUR

As spring came and the young lambs were born Ross wished they had been able to rent the extra land to provide fresh spring grass for the ewes and their offspring. It angered him to see the stretch of land which McNish and Jim Douglas had given up. It lay neglected on the boundary of The Glens of Lochandee. Already there were signs of bracken and reeds and the brambles and gorse would soon spread from the hedges into the fields.

'Surely the Laird cannot know his land is being so shamefully wasted,' Alice said. 'No wonder he's short of money, but he has only himself to blame. His father and grandfather always came to inspect their property from time to time, and they had far more reliable Factors than Mr Elder.'

'It makes me wonder if there will be a future for Conan in farming.' Ross said morosely.

'At least he's doing very well with his lessons, according to Mr Hardie, the headmaster,' Alice remarked. 'You should be proud of him Ross.'

'Rachel is proud enough for two of us.'

'You must admit there is little he misses with such sharp eyes and ears,' Rachel said defensively. She knew Margaret's death had grieved him, as it had herself, but she had a feeling that Ross could not bring himself to express pride in his son. He never praised Conan and it had begun to cause tension between them. But it was the death of Sam Dewar which caused the most serious rift of all.

* * *

On a Saturday morning in August, Rachel received an astonishing letter from Sam Dewar's lawyer.

'Sam has left nearly everything he possessed to Conan!' she gasped.

'To Conan? Why would he do that?' Ross demanded.

'I don't know. According to the copy of his will, which the lawyer has enclosed, Conan was only a few months old when he made it.'

'I expect it was just the whim of a lonely old man.' Ross shrugged. 'I don't suppose he had much to leave to anyone.'

'More than you think. Listen to this. Shortly before he died he had added a request that three hundred pounds should be paid to Meg for looking after him.'

'Three hundred pounds! I'm sure Meg was a good neighbour . . . but even so . . .'

'She was a very good neighbour. But listen! He owned his house and shop and the fields. After his visit here, to Lochandee, he instructed his lawyer to sell them after his death. The proceeds, and the remainder of his savings, are to be put into a Trust for Conan. I am to be the main Trustee, but his lawyer, Mr Finlay, will be my adviser. The money is to be used for Conan's future. A Trustee — whatever that means? Goodness! I can scarcely believe this. The total comes to one thousand, one hundred and eighty-nine pounds, ten shillings and sixpence!'

'One thousand! Pounds? But where did he get all that? And why would he leave it all to a baby? Your baby, Rachel! Why your child?'

'I don't know. The solicitor requires Conan's birth certificate and he has sent some papers for me to sign . . .' She

259

looked up and saw Ross's face flush, but he scowled and his eyes narrowed.

'What is it? Is something wrong?'

'No!' Ross said harshly. 'Oh, no. Why should there be anything wrong? Some old man leaves your son all his worldly goods. Why?' His tone was a mixture of accusation and sarcasm, and Rachel hated it.

Conan, cleaning his clogs in the adjoining scullery, had paid little attention until his father's raised voice startled him. It was so unusual to hear his parents quarrelling. He listened curiously.

'Conan is your son too. Surely you are pleased that he has been so fortunate?'

'My son . . . Mine?' Ross had not consciously intended to form a question.

'What do you mean by that?' Rachel demanded angrily.

'Nothing . . . Except . . . Well why would a man leave everything he possessed to a young child, unless he had a particular feeling of . . . of responsibility? Or . . . or . . .'

'Ross! What are you saying? What are you implying?'

'Nothing.'

'Yes, you are! You surely can't think Sam Dewar had anything to do with . . . with . . .' She stared at Ross, her eyes more green than blue now, and sparking angrily. 'You can't still doubt that Conan is your son? Not after all this time?'

Ross was silent. Pale, angry, guilty. Jealous? He could find no words to express the confusion he felt.

'Is that why you never praise him? He tries so hard to please you — you more than anyone else, because you are his father. Have you ever told him you love him? Have you ever told him you are proud of his achievements at school? No, you have not. I blamed Gertrude Maxwell! I thought she had repressed your natural emotions. Now I know . . .'

'Rachel . . .'

But Rachel was beside herself with anger and indignation. When Ross reached out a placating hand she brushed it furiously aside.

'Just get me his birth certificate.'

'Very well,' Ross muttered stiffly. 'But — I had better warn you . . .' He bit his lip, wishing now that he had explained about the birth certificate long ago. Changing it to show he was the boy's father had not been the simple matter he had anticipated. He had not wanted to upset Rachel just when she was settling in so well at Lochandee. But he ought to have explained later. He knew how it would seem to her now, especially right now, after his stupid outburst. Already he regretted his words, his petty suspicion, his fleeting jealousy. 'It has not been changed. It still bears your maiden name — O'Brian.'

'But you promised!' Rachel's voice rose.

Conan understood little of all this, but he did know the matter was serious enough to make his parents angry, and he was the cause.

Rachel's face was white. Her green eyes flashed.

'After all these years, you do not believe you are Conan's father.' She gritted her teeth. 'You really think Conan is not *your* son? How dare you, Ross? How can you?'

'I did not say that. It was not possible to change the certificate because . . .'

'You have not added your name to his birth certificate,' Rachel hissed. 'That is what you said. There can only be one reason.' Without warning she burst into a storm of weeping. All the old hurt resurfaced. Ross had let her down again.

'It was not like that, Rachel!' Ross reached out for her but she jerked away from him in anger. 'Please, let me explain?' His hand fell helplessly to his side as she dashed out of the kitchen. Why hadn't he told her at the time? He knew how much the birth certificate had mattered to her. As time passed he had forgotten about it. Conan was known to everyone as Maxwell, and that at least was acceptable and legal.

* * *

Rachel felt even worse when she went into Conan's bedroom later that evening. She had heard him tossing and turning restlessly.

261

'Why are you not asleep, Conan?' she asked softly, bending to stroke his wayward hair and kiss his cheek. He considered himself a big boy now and the only time he allowed her to kiss him was when they were alone and he was tucked up in bed.

'Mama . . .' He bit his lip and Rachel wondered if he had been crying. 'Mama, I do belong to Dad, and to you, don't I? He is my father . . . ?'

Rachel caught her breath. 'Yes!' she said. Then more gently, 'Of course you belong to both of us. We love you very much.'

'Does Dad love me as much as he loves Bridie?'

'I'm sure he does,' Rachel assured him. 'Would you like me to read you a story to help you get to sleep?'

'Course not! I can read my own stories now.'

Bridie remained a happy smiling little girl, ever ready for a cuddle and a kiss, unaware of the undercurrents between her parents, but there was a change in Conan as the weeks went by. Rachel knew she was not imagining it. He had lost his mischievous smile and cheeky grin, in fact he rarely smiled at all. He was too thoughtful, too withdrawn for a nine-year-old. He seemed to be brooding over some secret anxiety.

Rachel was not aware that her own tension was equally plain to those closest to her. She did not discuss her concerns over Conan with Ross any more. Alice sensed all was not well but she could neither understand the reason nor bridge the invisible wall which Rachel seemed to have erected between herself and the world.

Ross was at a loss to know how to placate her. She had written to the lawyer enclosing Conan's birth certificate. It hurt her to explain why it bore her maiden name. She did not realise her circumstances had been Sam Dewar's main reason for leaving his house, and later its proceeds, in the care of a young woman he admired and respected. Sam had trusted her to use his legacy in the best interests of her child, even though the boy was no relation to himself.

Even when Sam Dewar's affairs had all been taken care of, Rachel remained subdued and withdrawn. Ross had given up trying to explain why the birth certificate could not be changed, however much he might want it. In his heart he blamed himself. If he had been there when Conan had been registered, if he had been present to claim his son, then the certificate could have borne his name after they married. As it was, the current law allowed no more than a brief addition in the registrar's records. Rachel had refused to listen to any explanations, or even to discuss it. She was convinced he was making excuses.

When Ross took her in his arms at night she no longer responded. He could not arouse her to the passionate lover he had always known. Even worse he missed her as his friend and confidante. They were like polite acquaintances. He knew she was brooding, blaming him, watching his reactions whenever he was with Conan. It made him strained and edgy with his son.

It was nearing the end of the spring term when Rachel met Mr Hardie, the headmaster of the village school. He mentioned his concern for Conan.

'Ever since he returned after the last summer holidays he has seemed unable to concentrate on his lessons as he used to do. He's an intelligent boy. He was so keen to apply himself. A change has come over him. He seems wary, nervous almost. He's less sure of himself and his own ability. He's more ready to pick a fight with other boys. I had such great hopes for Connor. I believe you call him Conan?'

'Yes, yes we do . . .' Rachel answered absently. Her mind was searching for things which might be affecting Conan. It did not occur to her that he had overheard her quarrel with Ross, or that he was too sensitive to be unaware of the tension between them. She could never have guessed that he might blame himself for her own unhappiness.

* * *

Meg was Rachel's confidante. Their weekly letters had often proved a mutual comfort when either of them were anxious.

Rachel had been too hurt by what she considered Ross's rejection of Conan and his mistrust of herself, to confide in anyone, even Meg.

Supposing Conan had sensed his father's rejection? Suddenly all her fears and uncertainties seemed to pour onto the page as the words flowed in a long letter to Meg.

The reply came by return, evidence of Meg's genuine concern.

"I think you and the children should come to visit us at Easter, dearest Rachel," she wrote.

We would love to see you all. The change will do you good and it would make me so happy.

Meg always saw the good side of everybody and she had a most forgiving nature.

Ross was such a loving wee laddie when he was young, but Mother rebuffed him so often. I believe he learned to suppress his feelings at an early age. Don't you think all those years of repression may have become a habit? Even with Conan? I admit he seemed to be different with you — almost as though he had found his soulmate. Perhaps you released the real Ross.

Please, dearest Rachel, try to understand and forgive his complex character. I'm sure there must be an explanation. I know you love him, and I know he loves you. Please try to forgive and understand him. Even husbands and heroes are little boys at heart.

* * *

Alice readily agreed that Rachel should visit her old friend.

'Emmie's proving useful now that she is accepting the death of wee Frances,' she said. 'We shall manage. As a matter of fact I have been concerned for you and Ross recently, my dear.' Alice paused, hoping Rachel would confide in her. Rachel merely withdrew into herself.

Alice shook her grey head. She could not solve other people's problems but she did not like the atmosphere they created in her home. It troubled her, and she knew it affected Conan. She had seen him watching his father with an intensity which puzzled her. They no longer laughed, or even spent time together. Conan was moody, even bordering on sullen, whenever Ross asked him to do anything.

The short holiday at Ardmill with Meg and Peter and the children proved a great success.

'It would have been lovely to see Willie and Ruth and the children,' Rachel said the night before she was due to return to Lochandee.

'Yes, I miss them terribly, but,' Meg chuckled, 'have you noticed how well Polly and Conan have been getting on?'

'I noticed them having long chats. And Rory and Max have been wonderful at entertaining Bridie and making her chuckle. She will miss their company, and Jane and Mary too. Polly seems to be doing really well at school?'

'She is. We were so proud of her last year when she won the scholarship to attend the Academy. She will be able to stay there until she is sixteen and she loves it. She would like to be a teacher herself.'

'You have brought them all up beautifully, Meg,' Rachel said sincerely. 'Mr Hardie had great hopes of Conan but I fear they will all come to nothing.'

* * *

Rachel had been back at Lochandee for nearly a week when Meg's letter arrived.

'I think Polly may have discovered what has been troubling Conan all these months,' she wrote. 'He told her he had overheard you and Ross quarrelling. He did not fully understand what it was about but he has jumped to the conclusion that Ross is not his real father and that he does not want him as a son. I do hope you can reassure him, Rachel. Surely there must be an end to all these uncertainties in our family? I fear my own Mother's influence has been far reaching into all our lives. I thank God many times that Peter has been so patient and loving with me, and with our children. Ruth and Willie have overcome her domination and they seem very happy together. I hope and pray you and Ross will find the strength to resolve your problems and regain your happiness. You have both suffered too much anguish already.'

* * *

Rachel knew Meg was right but somehow she could not bring herself to bridge the gap she had created. She thought there seemed to be little change in Conan's attitude in spite of his holiday but she was wrong. Mr Hardie waylaid her at the village a few weeks later, beaming with satisfaction.

'Conan is our star pupil again. I am almost afraid he has gone to the other extreme he's working so hard. I am pleased you have managed to help him overcome his problems. One day you and his father will have cause to be proud of him, I am sure of it.' He hesitated, then added diffidently. 'Though I do not foresee him wasting his abilities on farming.'

'You think it is a waste of ability to farm, Mr Hardie? To care for the welfare of animals? To tend the crops? To produce food to keep people from starving? You think all these things do not require skill and intelligence? Arithmetic and budgeting? Calculating how many cubic feet of hay we have left or the size of the corn stack, worrying how long it will feed the animals if winter stretches into spring? You think all these things do not need Conan's intelligence?'

'No, no. At least I did not mean to make you angry Mrs Maxwell, or infer that farming was easy . . .'

'It certainly is not!'

'Yes, yes. I-I understand . . . but I simply do not visualise Conan using his talents to farm.'

266

'Well I hope you will not voice your opinion to Mistress Beattie. She has set her heart on Conan following in my husband's footsteps and farming The Glens of Lochandee.'

'Yes,' the schoolmaster sighed. 'Preservation of her beloved land has always been Alice Beattie's first priority. Indeed I fear she is passing on her enthusiasm to your daughter.' He smiled. 'Young as she is Bridie can tell us everything that's going on at the farm. She's far less concerned about reciting her multiplication tables than about the number of chickens which might have hatched now that she has to come to school. But have you talked to Conan yourself recently? He told me he would like to build aeroplanes — even fly one.'

'Ah!' Rachel laughed in relief. 'Surely all small boys want to drive a train? I suppose Conan thinks aeroplanes are something similar. It's just a little boy's day dream.'

'Maybe, Mrs Maxwell.' Mr Hardie sighed. 'Maybe you are right. I am sure you know your own son better than I do.'

This conversation gave Rachel much to think about. She paid more attention to Conan, the books he had begun to read from the local lending library which supplied the school, the way he seized any opportunity to listen to the radio. It was true he performed his tasks around the farm diligently as soon as he returned from school — but did they really interest him?

Although she was only five years old, Bridie already had a calf of her own. She called it Silky Socks because of her smooth red and white hair and dainty feet which looked as though she was wearing four white socks. She fed the calf herself each day. Her two pet lambs had quickly learned to follow her everywhere in the hope of getting a bottle of milk. She would have taken them to bed if Rachel had not been firm. Bridie almost always accompanied them to the milking. Already she knew most of the cows by name. Her pinafores were always filthy long before bedtime but Bridie just tossed her brown curls and wrinkled her little freckled nose. Her wide smile was innocent and would have melted the most stony of hearts.

'Silky Socks doesn't mind if I'm not clean. She knows my two wee lambs couldn't help it.'

* * *

Long before the summer holidays of 1921 had begun the Government announced restrictions on the movement of animals due to an outbreak of foot-and-mouth disease. The very mention of it was enough to fill hearts with fear.

Great preparations had been made to celebrate the Highland Show. The first show had been held in 1822 and the centenary show was to be held in Edinburgh. HRH the Prince of Wales was President of the Society and his attendance was anticipated with enthusiasm and excitement. Large crowds were expected to attend.

When the show officials banned all entries of cattle, sheep and pigs as a precaution against spreading the foot-and-mouth infection there could be no doubting the seriousness of the situation, especially when it was such an auspicious occasion. The Duke himself declared that Edinburgh was weeping in sympathy when the rain came down on the opening day and the cattle and sheep pens lay empty and deserted.

It was every farmer's dread that his precious cattle and sheep would catch the infection, and it was a government regulation that infected herds and flocks must be slaughtered. No one travelled unless the journey was absolutely essential and there were tins of disinfectant at the end of every farm track.

Ross was on edge. A dispute with Jo Scott, a relief postman, upset him even more. He did not like making enemies but Jo was a sullen man when thwarted. Bill Carr had fixed a letter box at the end of their own farm road so no one came in, or out, unnecessarily. Even the pony's feet and the wheels of the trap were thoroughly disinfected after taking the milk to the station each morning. Defiantly Joe was determined to take a shortcut through The Glens of Lochandee and across the field track to the two neighbouring farms further up the hill. He made the return journey via the same route.

'You could spread the disease from one farm to another,' Ross explained patiently, stopping him halfway up the road.

'Ye're making a fuss about nothing!' Joe accused. 'I've never been near any disease.'

'None of us can be sure of that. Anyway it's not much further round by the public road and it's a lot better for cycling,' Ross said.

'I dinna want to go that way.'

'And I'm not taking any chances.' Ross cut the persuasion. He was exasperated and anxious. 'Our Ayrshire cattle are pedigree and far too precious to risk losing them through being careless, or saving five minutes of your time.'

'I've half a mind to give you this in your jaw, y' cheeky bugger!' Jo threatened, holding up his clenched fist before Ross's face. Ross did not flinch. His eyes were cold.

'You can try all the threats you like but no one will cross Glens of Lochandee land until the epidemic is clear. No one.'

Joe Scott glared back angrily. He uttered several oaths but eventually he turned away and went round by the road.

* * *

Billy McLaughlan, their regular postman, would never have tried to cross the fields in such a crisis, but Billy was the most genial and obliging of men. Rachel knew Ross longed for her support and reassurance that he had been right to ban Joe. She remained stubbornly silent. Although she felt happier about Conan since her visit to Meg's she could not bring herself to dispel the coolness which had developed between herself and Ross since their quarrel over Sam Dewar's legacy.

She knew Joe Scott would forget the dispute as soon as things were back to normal but in the interval he would express his displeasure to anyone who would listen, and that would include McNish. Their neighbour was notoriously fond of gossip and a dram or two to go with it. The Factor was known to be a frequent caller in spite of rumours that McNish was still unable to pay his rent, even without the land which was rapidly turning into wilderness.

Days passed. Tension increased. There were reports of an outbreak of foot-and-mouth disease on a farm on the other side of the village of Lochandee. Then suddenly Conan arrived home from school, his eyes wide and distressed.

'They are killing all Mr Price's cows and sheep and burying them in a huge hole,' he announced breathlessly. 'Billy and Jean couldn't come to school. Peter Taylor says the farm on the other side of McNish's have got foot-and-mouth and Patsy Fleming was crying because she says they will kill her pet goat, and . . .'

Bridie had listened to this breathless account in open-mouthed astonishment.

'No!' she yelled loudly. 'You're telling lies, Conan! You are! You are!' She turned tearfully to Rachel. 'They don't kill pets, do they Mama?'

Rachel could not answer. She felt distraught at the news.

'No, oh surely not,' Alice whispered. She buried her face in her hands to hide her dismay. Ross sank down on his haunches and put his hands on Conan's shoulders staring into his troubled young face.

'Tell me exactly what you heard, laddie.'

'Mr Pearson says it's true,' Conan muttered, forgetting he was not supposed to linger at the cycle shop.

'I see . . . And did you remember to dip your clogs on the way home?'

'Course I did!' Conan declared indignantly. Ross nodded, but he looked up at Rachel.

'Do you think it would be a good idea to keep him away from school for a while, until we see how things go?'

'All right.' She laid her arm on Conan's shoulder. 'You can read your books at home. You will soon catch up.'

'Meanwhile I will tell Sandy and Bill. I'll warn them not to go near the boundary fields. If McNish's cattle get the disease that stretch of wild land will be a benefit after all. It will make a barrier between us.'

'Yes,' Alice nodded. 'We must avoid every possible contact from man and beast.' Everyone agreed.

'We shall be all right, Bridie.' Ross summoned a reassuring smile for his small daughter. He hated to see anxiety on such a young and innocent face.

* * *

Time passed slowly. Each day was fraught. There were rumours of more farms affected on the other side of the glen to the north of the village. Still the cattle and sheep at The Glens of Lochandee remained healthy.

'You are a good lad staying at home, Conan,' Ross said. 'It looks as though our precautions are paying off.'

The shadows were lengthening and Alfie had gone for his usual stroll around the animals after the evening meal. Alice always maintained he went to say goodnight to them all before he could go to bed himself. On this particular evening he had not been out long when he came bursting through the door, startling them all. He was gabbling excitedly, jigging his rear end up and down and shaking his wrists.

'Have you been stung, Alfie?' Ross asked.

'Na-aw!' Alfie cackled anxiously. 'Hs-rss.' He beckoned frantically. Ross followed him outside. There was nothing to be seen except a huddle of sheep in the field nearest the farm steading. Alfie hung his head dejectedly.

Alice was quiet for the rest of the evening, but before she went to bed she said anxiously, 'Alfie understands more than we often give him credit for. I'm sure he was trying to tell us something important. I felt it was some kind of warning.'

CHAPTER TWENTY-FIVE

The following morning Ross noticed that Ben and Trust, the two collie dogs were uneasy and he remembered Alfie's strange antics of the previous evening. As soon as he had taken the milk to the station he checked all the sheep and cattle, making sure none had strayed. He even checked the boundary fences and for good measure he climbed the ancient oak tree to get a clearer view.

He stared towards McNish's farm in dismay. There was a heap of freshly dug soil and beside it lay several cattle, their legs pointing skywards.

'Dead! Oh my God, McNish must have got it.' He hurried home to break the news.

'It is a good thing you stopped the postman, Ross,' Alice said. 'We have had no contact with McNish or his premises. We should be safe.'

'I pray so,' Ross breathed fervently.

After the evening milking Ross was making his way across the yard when he saw Alfie waggling towards him. He was doing his peculiar bobbing up motions again as though he was on a horse. A horse! Ross spun round and raced towards the field at the back of the buildings. He was just in time to see Elder on his powerful hunter cantering amongst the sheep. Ross bellowed in fury.

Elder turned in the saddle and gave a mocking salute. Ross ran towards him. Elder gave a sneering laugh.

'I'm the Factor, remember? Just checking up.' He dug in his heels. The big horse galloped towards the boundary fence, clearing it with ease. He rode away over McNish's land towards his yard. Ross could scarcely believe what his eyes were seeing. He felt sick.

Alfie was cackling triumphantly and nodding his head. It was clear now. He had been trying to tell them about Elder yesterday. How many times had the Factor ridden through the infected farm, or other farms in the area, then onto Lochandee land? Why now? He had never come near The Glens of Lochandee since Alfie hit him with the shovel. He had paraded along the boundary fences, inspecting the fields from there. Even a sadist like Elder would not deliberately try to spread the dreaded foot-and-mouth disease. Would he?

That night Ross lay restlessly beside Rachel. He longed to share his anxiety with her and hear her reassurance. These days her polite manner proved a more effective barrier than a stone wall. He kept his anxiety to himself.

Late the following afternoon anxiety drew Ross to the tall oak tree again. His own sheep were grazing peacefully. He stared towards McNish's farm. The cattle were no longer there but the soil was heaped in a mound and men were still shovelling. Ross buried his head in his hands. He prayed the disease would not spread to Glens of Lochandee. His thoughts were melancholy as he perched in the fork of the broad branches, lost in his reflections.

He was just about to stretch his stiff limbs and return to the milking when he saw the horse and rider coming across McNish's field. They were heading straight towards the only fence which presently bordered The Glens of Lochandee. Horse and rider sailed over without effort. At any other time Ross would have admired the magnificent animal but Elder was deliberately heading towards the flock of sheep. He was dropping bits of fleece! Fury boiled in Ross. He could barely contain himself as Elder cantered through the huddling sheep. He rode in a wide arc. Ross judged he must come within a few yards of the tree. With a supreme effort he curbed his anger and waited, preparing to swing from a lower branch.

Elder was near enough for Ross to see his smug expression. He guessed they would soon swerve away from the tree again. He gave a loud 'Halloo-oo' and swung himself from the branch to within feet of the startled horse. The big chestnut reared in fright. Elder yanked cruelly on the reins, striving to keep his seat. Ross 'halloo-ed' again, then again. Fury prevented him enjoying Elder's fear and anger as he catapulted to the ground with a dull thud. Ross felt no pity. He ran towards him and yanked him to his feet by the scruff of his thick neck. He was not a fighting man but his temper was uncontrollable as he looked into the flabby sneering face. Almost of its own volition, his fist clenched and landed with all the force he could muster into Elder's jaw.

'You'll pay for this,' the Factor spat venomously. 'I'll have you out if it's . . .' Ross's fist struck again, at the same time he released his grip on the Factor's collar. His heavy body sank to the ground like a rock. Ross wiped his hands as though they were filthy, picked up his cap from where it had fallen, and strode away. Out of the corner of his eye he saw the horse had jumped back over the fence instinctively and was now cropping grass some distance away. Elder would catch it eventually. He would not explain away his split lip and swollen jaw so easily.

Ross felt no remorse but he was not used to violence and his stomach churned. Elder had deliberately tried to spread the foot-and-mouth disease to The Glens of Lochandee, he was sure of it now. Surely only a man eaten up with evil could do such a thing.

It was some days after Ross's encounter with the Factor when he noticed one of his best milk cows was unwell. He had milked her himself and the piggin had been less full than usual and he stared in sick disbelief. They had taken every possible precaution. In his heart he had not really believed the Factor could carry the disease so easily, even though he had come directly from McNish's infected buildings. Yet here was a cow dribbling saliva like a tap. He called Bill Carr to help him while he opened the animal's mouth. Their eyes met in silent agony at the blisters peeling away, leaving raw tongue.

'Oh, God!' Ross groaned and felt his stomach heave. 'How could I believe we might escape.'

'That's it then, boss?' Bill ventured fearfully. Ross nodded and turned towards the house like a man in a nightmare.

* * *

Try as they might to shield Bridie and Conan from the ensuing horrors it was impossible not to tell the truth. Bridie was inconsolable. She simply could not accept that her beloved Silky Socks had to be killed and buried in a big dark hole. Who could hurt her gentle little lambs?

Amidst the confusion no one noticed Bridie had disappeared. Rachel and Alice searched everywhere in the buildings and lofts, even in the little copse. There was no sign of her, or of her two pet lambs.

Rachel felt panic rising in her but she could see Alice was exhausted and anxious. She insisted she return to the house for a drink of cold water and a rest. So Alice was sitting quietly, despair washing over her as never before, her head bowed. In the silence she thought she heard a baby cry. She listened. Not a baby — a lamb! She stood up, listening intently. She followed the faint sound to the pantry but it was empty. Beyond the pantry a door lead to the old cellar. It was only used at pig killing to cure the bacon and hams on the cold stone slabs. The damp stone steps descended into inky blackness. Bridie never went in there. She hated the darkness and the peculiar smell. She was only five years old. She would have to be desperate to go down there alone. Even so Alice opened the creaking door.

'Bridie,' she called softly. There was no reply but she heard the unmistakable sound of a muffled heart-rending sob. Alice found a candle and matches on the pantry shelf. Carefully she descended the uneven steps. Through the gloom she saw the yellow glitter of eyes as she raised the flickering candle. Bridie's tiny figure was hunched beneath a stone bench in the furthest corner of the cellar. The little girl had an arm around each of the pet lambs, her cheek resting on one soft black head. Tears poured silently down her cheeks and her small shoulders shook with stifled sobs. Not even Alice's gentle coaxing could persuade her to come out.

Eventually it was Conan who came to the rescue. Talking softly, he led Bridie out, hugging her small body tightly against his bony young chest. His hand stroked her long brown curls with gentle fingers as she clung to him, sobbing as though her little heart would break.

Ross knew it was the most difficult task he had ever had when he bent to take the two trusting young lambs to be slaughtered. They had known so little of the joy of living. Please God let those in authority have made the right decisions. Certainly the disease was a dreadful scourge with the affected animals growing more sick by the minute, but he was certain the disease would not have spread without Elder.

Rachel herself had shed more tears than she cared to admit. She felt lost, wrung out and limp, like a piece of old rag. She had done her best to protect Alice from the terrible sight of her cherished Ayrshire cows lying bloated and grotesque beside the huge pit. It was the first time she had seen Alice weep and she felt helpless to offer comfort. What use were words?

Her heart ached for the pain Ross had suffered as he guided his animals to their death, one after the other, each one docile and trusting.

It had been a day none of them would ever forget. Ross was too dispirited to eat by the end of it. He was too tired

and sick at heart to relax, even in sleep. Rachel felt him tossing and turning beside her in the darkness. She put out a
tentative hand, gently, rhythmically she soothed his restless
limbs. She stroked the hard flatness of his stomach, feeling
his muscles tense as her fingers moved lower, soothing and
seducing. He needed her, they needed each other, now as
never before.

'I do love you, Ross,' she whispered. He turned then,
drawing her into his arms, holding her close.

'I need you, Rachel. God, how I need you!' He groaned
and buried his head against the silken warmth of her breast.
She felt his eyelashes damp with the tears he was struggling to
suppress and she stroked his hair gently as she would a child.
Presently he lifted his head and kissed her lips.

'Thank you, Rachel,' he murmured against her cheek,
'Thank you for coming back to me today. I don't think I
could go on without you. You are my life, my love . . .'

'I know, I know . . .' Their loving was tender, their
union slow and beautiful — a shining dream in the darkest
of hours.

There were many nights when the only comfort either
of them could find was in each other's arms. The hollow
silence of the empty sheds, and the bare fields devoid of cattle
and sheep, were constant reminders of the awful fate of their
precious animals. There was little consolation to be had from
the well-cleaned buildings, all of them painstakingly painted
with lime both inside and out.

Alice seemed to shrink into a shadow of her former self.
Rachel understood and did her best to offer comfort and
cheer. She knew many of the cows had been bred down generations of the same families Alice had known as a child. The
famous Ayrshires had been as much a part of Lochandee as
she had herself. Now they were gone — wiped out.

The milk customers which Ross had built up could no
longer be supplied. There was no cream to make butter for
the village customers either, no pig to kill for the winter.
Only the hens and horses had survived. The eggs were all that

was left to eat or to sell to bring in a meagre income and pay the wages of Sandy Kidd, Bill Carr and Beth.

Gone was the rigid routine of twice-daily milking and the awful silence of the byres cast a gloom over everything during the following months. Eventually the Government paid compensation for the compulsory slaughter of the cattle and inspectors decided if and when stock could be replaced.

Alice was dismayed when Ross suggested buying some Friesian cattle. They both knew her own beloved cows could never be replaced and he believed the black and whites would be more productive. Willie and Ruth rarely wrote except at Christmas but they had heard of the Lochandee catastrophe from Meg and wrote to commiserate over the loss of the Lochandee Ayrshires. Willie had mentioned the black and white cows which were replacing many of the dairy short-horn herds around him in Yorkshire. He said the bull calves made better beef cattle than the dainty Ayrshires, and they were excellent milkers. He knew of six well-bred heifers for sale and offered to negotiate on Ross's behalf, and also to supervise loading them on to the train.

'He says the herd is free from tuberculosis and he does not think they have any trouble with contagious abortion,' Ross said, knowing that either disease would mean another disaster if they bought in infected cattle. It was one of his greatest worries. Eventually Alice agreed to compromise and have some of each breed.

The Lochandee Friesians were the first in the area and several farmers came to see them and ask about their performance. Bridie had adopted the first Friesian calf to be born at The Glens of Lochandee. She had named it Star on account of the white mark on its face, but even Ross could see it was not so adorable as Silky Socks had been.

* * *

The following summer Conan came home from school and proudly announced that he had passed the examinations

278

which would allow him to attend Dumfries Academy. He had the cheeriest grin anyone had seen for a long time.

'You will tell Aunt Meg, Mother?' he asked eagerly. 'I promised Polly I would work hard and keep up with her, and I have. I think she will be pleased.'

'I'm sure she will,' Rachel assured him happily. 'We all are.'

'Indeed we are,' Alice added her praises and so did Beth, with considerable teasing about widening the door to get his head inside.

'You've done well, laddie,' Ross said gruffly. 'You will have a long day though, with a three mile cycle ride every morning and evening to catch the bus to Dumfries.'

'I will do Conan's work,' Bridie piped up eagerly. She was seven years old and desperate to learn to milk a cow of her own. She already had her own brood of chicks. Ross smiled fondly. He had never managed to get her another calf as beautiful as her beloved Silky Socks. Bridie was loyal but resilient — even with her pets.

'All in good time, lassie. You'll be a great help to me soon.'

'I shall need a bicycle of my own,' Conan said slowly, thinking over his father's words.

'Don't worry,' Rachel assured him. 'We shall find the money for that.'

'Mr Pearson promised to help me make one for myself if you would buy the frame and wheels and the lights and brakes and things . . . ?' He looked hopefully at his parents.

'Grandfather says Conan would be a great help to him if only he had a bit more time to spend in his workshop after school.' Beth related enthusiastically, unaware that neither Ross nor Rachel knew of Conan's frequent visits to the cycle shop. He was eager to learn and deft with his hands, often performing tasks the old man's stiff fingers found impossible now. Moreover Beth's grandfather enjoyed his company and his enthusiasm.

Conan bit his lip and looked warily from one parent to the other. He loved the smell of grease and oil and working beside the old man but he had the feeling his parents did not approve of anything except farming. He understood as well as anyone that money was short. It had been a lean couple of years since the foot-and-mouth disease with no lambs to sell and no pedigree heifer to take to market. Even now there were still some empty stalls in the byre so there was not as much milk either.

* * *

Changing the breed of the Lochandee cattle was not the only concession to changing times. In the village there was an unusual stir of excitement as large steel towers were being erected on either side of Lochandee village, marching across country from the town of Dumfries. They were to bring electricity to the village and some of the nearby farms were being offered a supply, but only if they would guarantee to use sufficient to make the installation economical to the electricity company.

Surveys were carried out and agreements made with landlords and tenants. The electricity pylons needed land, and later access would be required for their maintenance. Some tenants objected to the ugly pylons and rows of wooden poles. Alice considered them all an unwelcome addition to her beloved glens, even while she acknowledged electricity appeared to be a sign of progress.

'You will have to get permission from the Laird to erect your unsightly structures,' she told the surveyors. 'We are only tenants of the land.'

'Wait until you see the benefits the electricity will bring,' the young man grinned, 'and we do need the co-operation of the tenants as well. We don't want to harm your crops, or your animals, nor do we relish working in a field with a bull beside us. Who farms the land above yours?'

'Mr McNish has one field adjoining ours. The fields which are growing wild are not let.'

'No tenant? You mean they are just left to go back to gorse and bracken?' the young man asked incredulously.

'That's right.'

'What can his Lordship be thinking of? Doesn't he need the rents?'

'Apparently not,' Alice shrugged.

'Well I shall have to get him to sign the forms to give permission.'

* * *

The surveyor never did get the Laird's signature. News of his death reached The Glens of Lochandee with reports that he had been caught up in a riot while visiting a Jewish family in Germany.

The news was greeted with foreboding, amongst villagers and farm tenants alike. There would be death duties to pay and it was common knowledge that the Laird had never replenished the family coffers after the death of his father. Indeed it was rumoured that his extravagant living and the Factor's inefficient management had depleted them still further.

CHAPTER TWENTY-SIX

Six weeks later Alice was surprised when a large car drew into the farmyard. A man in chauffeur's uniform jumped out and opened the door for a slim woman veiled and gowned in black.

'The Laird's widow!' Alice gasped. 'What can she want here? Will you show her into the front sitting room please, Rachel?' Alice was all of a flutter. 'I must wash my face and tidy my hair.'

Rachel led the woman into the house. She did not feel the awe which Alice clearly felt. The woman looked pale and strained.

'We were so very sorry to hear the news of his Lordship's death,' she said sincerely.

'Thank you,' Lady Lindsay nodded. 'You must be Mrs Maxwell?'

'Yes, your Ladyship.'

'I believe your husband is joint tenant with Mistress Beattie? I would like to meet him.'

'I will bring him for you as soon as Mistress Beattie returns. Can I get you some refreshment?'

'Nothing, thank you. Ah, you are Mistress Beattie?' she asked, looking over Rachel's shoulder. 'I am pleased to meet you. I believe you were a close friend of my late father-in-law?'

'We rode together when we were young,' Alice said warily.

'He spoke of you with great affection and respect.'

'Why, thank you, your Ladyship.' Alice flushed, but with embarrassment or pleasure Rachel could not tell.

'He told me you were once as familiar with the farms on the estate as himself and the Factor.'

'Did he really tell you that?' Alice seemed overwhelmed. 'We did ride around most of the estate.' She sighed nostalgically. 'My grandfather often accompanied us, you understand. He taught both of us to ride and care for our ponies. How we loved the countryside, in all its seasons.'

'Unfortunately the estate is not in such a healthy state now. To be frank with you, I do not know what will happen, or what inheritance there will be left for my own young sons. It will take time to settle my husband's affairs.'

'I am so sorry . . .'

'Meanwhile a surveyor from the electricity company came to see me recently. He informed me that the land bordering The Glens of Lochandee is returning to wilderness. I understand Mr McNish and Mr Douglas gave up their lease on those fields some time ago. I believe it has never been re-let. Would you and Mr Maxwell be interested in taking on additional land? The lease can only be a short one at this stage. I realise that makes it a less attractive proposition.'

'I'm sure Ross would be interested. He has been frustrated by the neglect ever since the land became vacant and we were refused the tenancy.'

'Refused?' Lady Lindsay's mouth tightened. 'Another of Mr Elder's incomprehensible decisions no doubt! As though the estate affairs are not bad enough without sheer neglect!' Lady Lindsay said tightly. 'I may as well tell you, my father believes Mr Elder has done more harm than good since he became Factor. He has dismissed him. Until the estate affairs are more in order I must ask you to come to me if you have any problems, or anything you wish to discuss.'

* * *

Ross was elated when heard Lady Lindsay's news. The rent was reasonable to compensate for the neglect and the short period of the lease and they had been promised a longer lease once the estate had been satisfactorily settled. He was relieved to hear there were no plans to sell The Glens of Lochandee, or any of the other farms immediately bordering Valantannoch and the Home Farm. Outlying farms would be sold to pay the death duties and the future of the remaining farms was still undecided.

Ross's jubilation was infectious and when he pulled her triumphantly into his arms later that night Rachel found herself sharing his joy, responding to his passion, revelling in their exultant union. Love and desire flared between them and their tension over Conan's future was set aside. Surely he would appreciate this was all for his benefit one day.

Many months later, when the electricity supply had been connected to Glens of Lochandee, a little red van chugged up the road with the name Harry Mason painted on the side. A cheery faced man hopped out and announced that he was selling electrical appliances.

After a great deal of talking and demonstrating and bargaining Alice resisted the electric irons but she succumbed to the purchase of a Hoover vacuum cleaner for the sum of four pounds, nineteen shillings and sixpence. Beth, who had been agog with excitement, clapped her hands in delight.

'You will never need to lift your carpets at spring cleaning time again,' Harry Mason assured them.

'Well I trust you are telling the truth,' Alice wagged her grey head sternly, 'because that is exactly why I have bought this wonder sweeper of yours, young man. I am getting too old for hanging carpets on the clothes line and spending hours beating the dust out of them every spring.'

'You willna regret it, ma'am. I'll be back in six months and see how you are faring.' He gave Beth an audacious wink and a broad smile creased his leathery face when he saw her blush. 'Maybe I shall be able to sell you a refrigerator to keep your milk and butter cool then.'

'Indeed you will not! The dairy keeps them cool enough. Today's extravagance will be enough to last me a lifetime. Two weeks of a man's wages your magic sweeper has cost me.'

'Well, I am grateful for your custom, Ma'am. Just to show how grateful I will make this young lady a gift of a paper lampshade to shield her bonny eyes from the glare of the electric bulb. If you'll accompany me to my van, Miss . . . ?'

Beth followed willingly. She had known the local men all her life and this stranger brought a frisson of excitement. He might not be the most handsome of young men but he was certainly cheerful.

Harry's red van became a familiar sight at Glens of Lochandee, but it was not because he was selling electrical gadgets to Alice Beattie. He was completely captivated by Beth and, like Conan, became a frequent caller at Mr Pearson's cycle shop. The old man was growing frail and he welcomed Harry's cheery company and his willingness to lend a hand. When Beth had an evening off and on Sunday afternoons they frequently spent their time together at the old man's cottage, or walking by the loch before having tea with him. It was Harry's kindly manner and his patience with her grandfather which made Beth realise Harry was the man she longed for to share the rest of her life.

* * *

A year after his first visit to Glens of Lochandee Beth and Harry Mason were married. It was a quiet wedding but Bridie was terribly excited when Beth asked if she could be her bridesmaid along with Emmie.

They set up house with Mr Pearson until the old man died a few months later. Much to Conan's delight Harry decided to keep on the cycle shop and combine it with small electrical goods and repairs.

Unknown to his parents Conan had called on old Mr Pearson almost every evening on his way home from school.

He missed the old man badly but his interest and enthusiasm quickly earned Harry Mason's respect. The two soon became friends in spite of the difference in their ages.

* * *

When Lady Lindsay made her second visit to Glens of Lochandee the affairs of the estate were far from being settled. She looked even more pale and strained than she had the previous year.

'I know times are bad for farmers as well as landowners,' she said with a note of weariness in her voice, 'but I must raise more money from the rents. They are our only income now, and I am afraid there will be no money for repairs this year.' Ross stared at her.

'But we have never received money for the repairs we have carried out — not since Mr Shaw left.'

'Of course you have,' Lady Lindsay corrected him. 'They are all there in the ledgers and Mr Elder's reports on the dates he carried out his surveys.'

'Surveys!' Ross gave a hollow laugh. 'He never came near to inspect anything and he certainly never paid for repairs.'

'It is true,' Alice nodded her support for Ross.

'Then he must have taken the money for himself!'

'We had heard things were not going well,' Alice said placatingly. 'I believe Ross was half expecting a rent rise and we are used to carrying out our own maintenance.'

'We are,' Ross agreed, 'but I would have liked the estate to extend our byre to make room for more milking cows?'

'It's impossible,' Lady Lindsay answered without hesitation. She rubbed her hand over her brow. 'I am sorry. The farms we have sold have barely covered the death duties.' Then almost under her breath she added, 'If only that were all.'

There was silence. At last Ross ventured,

'Would you give your permission for us to knock the wall out of the barn which adjoins the byre then? We could add extra stalls to milk the cows ourselves. Of course it would mean a shortage of barn storage but . . .'

'Barn storage!' Lady Lindsay echoed. 'There's little else but empty sheds on your neighbour's farm. Mr McNish is giving up at the May term. If you can afford to pay the rent you can lease Nether Lochandee also.' She spoke without much hope of anyone taking her suggestion seriously. She was no fool. Prices were poor for all farm produce. They seemed likely to remain so with the cargo ships of cheap imported foods queuing to be unloaded in all the ports.

'Are you serious?'

'Ross . . .' Alice cautioned.

'I am serious.' She looked at Alice, 'but only if it is what both of you want, and if you can pay the rents,'

'It will not be long before Conan leaves school. That will be another pair of hands to help,' Ross declared happily when Lady Lindsay had departed.

'Conan? He's too young,' Rachel protested.

'Lots of farm lads leave school at thirteen if they are needed to work.'

'But he loves the school. His teachers are expecting him to stay on until he's sixteen.'

'Sixteen! Does he mean to stay at school until he's an old man then?'

'They have important examinations then. He told me his maths teacher keeps suggesting he should go to university.'

'University? Whatever would he go there for? That wouldn't help him to farm.'

Rachel bit her lip, but she made no reply. She was beginning to suspect that Conan would never be happy working on the farm with herself and Ross. The farm and the animals meant everything to them, as they did to Alice. Conan reminded her more and more of her father but his mind was sharper, more enquiring, than her father's and he had a more restless nature too. Young as she was, Bridie was the one who took an interest in everything to do with the animals and the farm.

* * *

The following year Lady Lindsay made another of her annual visits. She congratulated Ross on his progress, but he waited tensely. Rumour had it that the late Laird's debts were even more crippling than the taxes and several more farms were on the market to sell.

'The remainder of the estate is to be settled on my two young sons,' she told them with a faint smile. 'My brother is coming down to stay with us. He will help me run the estate.'

* * *

Two years later Bridie also passed an examination admitting her to Dumfries Academy. Conan, who was four years older, still attended school. The Rector had written to Ross requesting he be allowed to stay on. He worked hard at his studies but he always finished his tasks on the farm. Rachel knew he did not enjoy the work but he did it without complaint and she felt torn between the interests of the two men in her life especially as she had guessed Conan still spent time with Harry Mason learning about his appliances.

She respected Ross, she shared his ambitions and his love of the land, but in her heart she feared his dreams for the future would never be Conan's. Alice had also begun to suspect Conan's heart was not in farming. It grieved them both. They had believed the future of Lochandee would be safe for at least another generation. They all worked hard to make a living from the land — and what else was there? Men all over the country were desperate for work, families hungry for food, children barefooted and ragged. Surely Conan should be happy to have all these things, even though the work was often hard and the weather frustrating.

Conan never mentioned his own ambitions or secret dreams. He had grown more withdrawn, even from herself, Rachel reflected sadly. Once they had been so close, now all she knew were the results of his school work. These were always excellent, especially so in mathematics and science. So it was a big surprise when Bridie came home and announced that he had won a special prize for an essay on the future of the British Empire.

'Of course most of the girls think he's wonderful anyway,' she grinned, 'even without prizes. Sometimes I'm quite proud to claim him as my big brother.'

'And so you should be,' Rachel smiled back at her daughter. Bridie was such a happy girl. She loved everything about the farm and the animals but she seemed popular at school and her own results were surprisingly good. Rachel was proud of both of her children.

'I always regretted not having a brother,' Alice smiled wistfully, 'but I suppose it had its compensations. After all I would probably have had to leave The Glens of Lochandee.'

'Would it have made a difference? Having a brother?' Bridie asked thoughtfully. 'I would hate to leave here. Ever.'

'You will change your mind when you grow up and want to marry,' Rachel smiled, patting her shoulder on her way out to gather the eggs. Bridie stared at her mother's receding back.

'I wouldn't marry a man who wanted to take me away from Lochandee,' she said firmly. 'You didn't, did you, Auntie Alice?'

Bridie was the only one who referred to Alice as "Auntie" and no one knew quite how it had come about but Alice liked it. As the years passed she had grown extremely fond of Bridie. She would never be the exquisitely beautiful child that her elder sister, Margaret Alice, had been. No doubt the years would have changed her angelic beauty of course. Bridie certainly had character and personality. Moreover she was blessed with a kindly nature and infinite patience.

'Would you have married Mr Beattie if he had refused to stay here with you, Auntie Alice?' Bridie persisted.

'Probably not.' Alice's eyes took on a dreamy, distant look. 'But first love . . . So tender and strong and true . . . I might have given life itself had there been any possibility . . .' She was speaking very softly, more to herself than to Bridie. There was silence in the room. Bridie was far too sensitive to pry further. She felt she had shared a rare moment — possibly a confidence not meant for human ears.

It was one of several cherished, half-forgotten memories, shared by Alice as her life advanced. Bridie on the threshold of womanhood was a patient listener. During the winter of 1937, Alice suffered two severe attacks of bronchitis. During her recuperation there was nothing she loved more than to have Bridie read to her in the hour before she settled to sleep, with the flickering flames sending shadows up the bedroom walls and the shaded light of the new electric lamp casting a halo around Bridie's shining dark brown hair.

Conan, on the other hand, alarmed her a little with his youthful enthusiasms and robust criticism of public leaders. The previous year the Olympic Games had been held in Berlin to the glorification of the Nazi regime, but when Jesse Owens had won four gold medals and broken two world records, the Nazi leader, Adolph Hitler, had refused to shake his hand.

'And why?' Conan had stormed indignantly, 'Because he's black. What right has this man Hitler to decide what colour a man's skin should be? Or what religion he should follow?'

'Calm down!' Ross had commanded irritably. 'Whatever a German man chooses to do, it's not our affair. He is no concern of ours.'

'Can you be sure of that, Father? If he gets away with all his ideas he may choose to rule the world.'

'Don't talk nonsense!' Ross snapped. He was often impatient with his son's avid reading of the newspapers.

In Alice's opinion the year had ended even more depressingly than anyone could have foreseen with the abdication of the Prince of Wales for the sake of his beloved Mrs Simpson. Alice had been brought up with the strongest sense of duty. She herself had found the strength to utter that short, but powerful word "no". It was her belief that no woman worth her salt would have allowed a man to give up his title and position — his kingdom.

So as Alice lay recovering during the dark winter days she had plenty of time to reflect on the events of the year which was drawing to a close. The country had a new King and Queen and two young princesses, and the king's elder brother had married Mrs Simpson and gone to live in France. Conan reported scathingly that they had been greeted by the Nazi leaders like long-lost friends, according to an article in one of the daily newspapers.

The Government had a new Prime Minister in the form of Neville Chamberlain. His burden was a heavy one with hungry, angry marchers in Britain, and much unrest abroad.

Conan was eager to join a group of boys training in a junior defence league, but his work on the farm, after school and at weekends permitted little time for such activities. Both Rachel and Ross were adamant in this. Conan knew that it was only his mother's influence which had allowed him to stay on at school after his fourteenth birthday. Later it transpired it was the death of a boy entirely unknown to him which decided Conan's immediate future.

CHAPTER TWENTY-SEVEN

The January morning was crisp and crystal clear. Rachel gazed across the patchwork of fields and hedges which sloped away from the house and steading of The Glens of Lochandee. She loved the familiar scene in all its seasons but on this particular morning she breathed in deeply, filling her lungs with ice cold air, watching like a child as her breath rose in a cloud before her face. Overnight the familiar green and brown world had been transformed into a fairy tale wonderland. Every bough and twig, every pebble and blade of grass had been painted with glistening frost, sparkling in the morning sun as brightly as a thousand diamond tiaras.

'What is so entrancing?' Ross grinned, coming to where she stood, gazing down the glen, to the Solway Firth glinting in the distance, with the purple outline of the Galloway hills beyond. Today they were etched sharply on the canvas of the sky, their outline faintly edged in gold from the morning sun. There were days, sometimes weeks, when the hills across the Firth were not visible at all.

'It's all so beautiful,' Rachel breathed, stretching her arms in a wide embrace. 'No human artist could ever create anything so lovely.'

Ross's face softened. He smiled back, their eyes meeting, holding, sharing the moment.

'Ah, Rachel.' His voice was husky. 'You're still as enthralled by the simple things around us — just as you were the first time we climbed the hill together, back at Windlebrae. Do you remember?'

'Do you think I could forget?' She smiled up at him, the dimple flashing as it always did when she was happy. Automatically their fingers entwined as they had all those years ago. Rachel sighed softly. Even though they argued quite fiercely sometimes, they still loved each other, still had these special moments to treasure and remember. They were more precious than gold or jewels — or a crown and a kingdom.

At midday Alice greeted them with the news that two boys had drowned while skating on the frozen loch.

'Beth telephoned from the village to tell us. She says everyone there is horrified by the tragedy. There is a rumour that one of the boys may be Lady Lindsay's son.'

'Oh no! Surely not.' Rachel's eyes were round with dismay. 'She has had so much grief already.' Stories were rife but it was several days before the identities were confirmed as Lady Lindsay's eldest son and his cousin. Although the boy was heir to the estate, the funeral was private. None of the tenants attended as they had attended the funerals of his father and grandfather.

Some weeks later a stranger came to The Glens of Lochandee. He introduced himself as Allan Maitland, brother of Lady Lindsay.

'My sister is too distraught to visit her tenants in person, but she wanted you to know of her plans as soon as possible.'

'Plans?' Ross tensed.

'I'm afraid the estate will have to be sold.'

'Oh no!' Alice gasped in real distress.

'I fear there is little option. There were still debts to pay following Lord Lindsay's death. The loss of his heir so soon after has dealt a crippling blow. My sister and her younger son will move north to live with my father. The whole estate will be put on the market within six months.'

'Thank you for telling us,' Ross said quietly but his voice was hoarse, his face pale. Suddenly everything he had worked for, all his plans for his family, all his ambitions seemed to have been swept from under his feet as easily as a child's sandcastle before the morning tide.

'There are a few tenants whom my sister valued highly. Had it been possible she would have given you longer notice, even a chance to buy the land gradually. As it is . . .' he shrugged helplessly. 'All those who rent cottages or shops in Lochandee village will be given an opportunity to purchase their own homes, but time is short. We regret there will be few who can take up the offer.'

Before leaving he expressed his sister's bitter regret once more. Ross and Rachel had no doubt he was sincere but it did nothing to alleviate their anxiety. As for Alice, the thought of leaving her beloved Glens of Lochandee at this late stage in her life grieved her sorely.

Her health did not improve. The doctor blamed the effects of the bronchitis but Rachel knew it was more than that. She seemed to have lost the will to live and showed little interest in her surroundings.

'Whatever happens you will always have a home with us,' Rachel assured her gently. 'You have been the best friend Ross and I have ever had — as close as a mother to both of us.'

'Thank you, Rachel dear. I believe that is the nicest compliment anyone has ever paid me.'

'We must hope the new Laird will renew our leases and not demand rents we cannot pay.'

'Yes, we can only hope, and pray.' Alice sighed heavily. 'Everything seems so insecure. The very fireside we sit by is part of the farm. If we cannot farm the land I cannot keep my home either.' She shook her grey head wearily. 'Then there's Sandy Kidd and his family, and Bill Carr and Emmie. They all depend on us for their homes and work . . .'

Ross could not sleep at nights. Part of him felt sick with worry, but there was a wild idea which kept returning to his mind. Eventually he decided he had nothing to lose. He had dealt with the bank in Lockerbie a few times in the past. He made an appointment to see the manager.

Mr Hubert Harrison was short and square in a dark pin-striped suit. This, the pince-nez stuck on the end of his nose, and the big mahogany desk all combined to intimidate Ross. The gloomy ochre walls with their dark oil paintings of previous bank officials did nothing to calm him. He felt he would rather face a bad-tempered bull any day. Animals he could handle, but bank managers were an unknown species to him.

Nothing for it but to take the bull by the horns, he decided. The irony of the thought brought a wry glint to his blue eyes.

'It's a light-hearted matter you wish to discuss, Mr er . . . ugh Maxwell?' Mr Harrison enquired stiffly.

'No Sir!' Ross frowned. 'I would like to buy a farm and I need to borrow money.'

'And how much do you have already.'

'None, Sir.'

'None! Then we need not waste time — yours or mine.'

'B-but I do have stock. Cows and sheep and three pairs of fine Clydesdale horses. They are all paid for. I have ploughed all our money back into the farm, mending fences, ditching, increasing the number of cows, keeping the buildings repaired when the landlord could not afford to do it.'

'All of which makes the farm more valuable to a prospective landlord now, no doubt,' Henderson remarked dryly.

'Why, yes. I suppose it does,' Ross agreed. 'I had not considered that.'

'You have no money in this bank. Do you owe any rent?'

'No, certainly not.'

'No need to be indignant. Most farmers are at least a year behind with their rent. What is the name of the farm?'

'The Glens of Lochandee.'

'Lochandee? But surely the Beatties are tenants there?'

'Mrs Alice Beattie is a joint tenant.'

'You have discussed this with her? I understood she was a woman with good sense, but apparently not.'

'I have not discussed buying the farm with Mrs. Beattie,' Ross admitted, flushing. He felt like a naughty schoolboy who had not done his homework. 'I did not want to add to Mrs Beattie's worries. The debt must be my own. She is not in good health.'

'I see. She would be more worried if she heard the proposition you have put before me. No man in his senses would consider buying a farm at the present time. Certainly no bank would loan you money for such a crazy idea.' He pulled himself to his full height, which barely reached Ross's shoulder. 'Good day to you.'

* * *

Ross was deeply depressed. His last hope was gone. It took two miserable weeks before Rachel could persuade him to confide in her. When he did she was silent with astonishment.

'So you agree with him,' Ross muttered despondently. 'He's a pompous, puffed-up pin-stripe. He needed to sit up straight just to peer over his shiny-topped desk.'

Whatever arguments they had had over Conan, Rachel had always supported him in his work, and in his plans for The Glens of Lochandee.

'I did not say that, Ross. I am just so . . . so surprised. It is true that it would be hard to repay the money — but at least we have always managed to pay the rent on time, and usually find a little to carry out repairs and buy a horse or a couple of cows . . . I need time to . . . to take it in.'

* * *

As she deftly rolled the scone dough and placed the triangles on the girdle the following afternoon, Rachel confided the reason for Ross's depression to Alice. The older woman was sitting by the fire, swaying gently in the old rocking chair. It seemed to be her main pastime these days.

'Buy Lochandee? Ross wanted to buy the farm himself?'

'You do think it's a crazy idea then?' Rachel asked tensely.

'It is a big risk. It would be a huge burden — for both of you. Prices are so low for everything we produce. There would be interest to pay, as well as repaying the loan. If you fell behind with that, the bank would re-possess the farm. Ross could be left with a debt and nothing to show for it — not even a job.'

'But we love The Glens of Lochandee,' Rachel protested brokenly. 'He has worked so hard . . .'

'You have both worked hard.' Alice's voice was gentle. 'I know you have come to love this place as much as I do. My life is drawing to a close now, but you . . . you are young, Rachel, with most of your life before you.'

'It was Conan's future I was thinking of, too. I wondered if I should offer Ross the legacy which Sam Dewar left him. After all it is home to all of us. I am the main trustee. Do you think I should be taking too big a risk with his inheritance?'

'I had forgotten about that!' Alice's gaze was more alert than it had been since the day they heard the estate was to be sold. 'I just don't know . . .' she said slowly. She fell silent and Rachel continued with the baking.

* * *

When Ross and Rachel returned to the house after the milking was finished that evening Alice had the supper ready and the fire blazing merrily. These were tasks she had not attempted since her last illness. There was a glint in her eyes they had not seen for a long time and it cheered them both.

Alice waited until Conan and Bridie had gone to bed and Alfie had returned to the bothy.

'I want to talk to you both,' she said, 'about the future. The future for all of us. The future for Lochandee. Rachel told me you went to see the bank manager, Ross.'

'Yes. He thought I was crazy to think of buying land,' Ross admitted dejectedly. 'I suppose we shall just have to pray someone will buy it and let it out to us again, and hope we can pay the rent he demands.'

'I do not think it was such a crazy idea, if you are both sure it is what you want to do for the rest of your lives. Both of you?'

'It is,' they said in unison — and turned to smile at each other as the words came spontaneously.

'How much did Lady Lindsay's brother say they wanted for the land?'

'Twenty pounds an acre,' Ross answered flatly. 'I suppose you are right, we should be paying it off for the rest of our lives. Maybe I am crazy, as Mr Harrison says.'

'I think you should see my solicitor, Mr Niven,' Alice suggested. 'The trustees for the estate will probably take less, especially for the higher land which was Nether Lochandee. It has been badly neglected. We are sitting tenants too. Mr Niven will know what needs to done. He will offer a price on our behalf. Rachel is willing to put in Conan's legacy so I . . .'

'Well most of it,' Rachel amended, flushing. 'We have not discussed it yet.' She threw Ross an apologetic glance, but she need not have worried. His eyes were shining.

'You would do that?'

'We could put a thousand pounds towards a deposit on the land and leave a hundred and eighty nine pounds in the bank.'

'And I will put in the remainder of my grandmother's legacy. Nine hundred and fifty pounds,' Alice said.

Ross stared at her speechlessly.

'I-we . . . I can't take your money — but I do thank you for the offer of it. It is wonderful to know you have faith in me — both of you,' He turned to Rachel with a beaming smile.

'Well your offer may not be accepted, but at least you will have tried. If you get it, then I insist on putting in my savings too.' She silenced Ross's protest with an imperious

298

wave of her hand. 'Remember Ross, The Glens of Lochandee claimed my heart long ago. The thought of leaving this house was breaking my very spirit. Now you have offered fresh hope — a future to plan. You will still need a substantial loan but there are other banks. Mr Niven will probably recommend you go to Dumfries and he will know which one you should try first. He may even speak on your behalf. I shall write him a letter so that he knows you have all my support.'

* * *

It was the end of the May term. Ross was the jubilant new owner of The Glens of Lochandee. It was true that he now had a bank loan of two thousand five hundred pounds, as well as owing money to Alice, and to Conan's Trust fund. He was not sure how he and Rachel would ever repay it, as well as the interest, but he was determined to try. Mr Niven had been filled with doubts. Ross knew it was only Alice Beattie's staunch recommendation which had persuaded the old solicitor to act for him.

Rachel wrote to Willie and Ruth, as well as to Meg, jubilantly telling them their news. She was dismayed when the replies came. Meg and Willie were filled with doubts, almost bordering on recrimination in Meg's case. It was clear she thought Conan's legacy should not have been put at risk. Peter, on the other hand felt it was a wise investment to secure their home and their livelihood. Ruth reported that her father felt they had done well and he wished them every success.

'It's plain to see it's those who know least about farming who are in favour,' Ross commented gloomily. 'We shall have to work even harder and prove Meg and Willie wrong. Conan must leave school. We shall need his help.'

Ross believed more firmly than ever now that his son's place was on the land, working beside him, acquiring the thousands of bits of knowledge he would need to farm Lochandee, to care for the cattle and sheep, horses, pigs, and crops.

'He has so much to learn,' he declared vehemently, 'and now he will have a future worth working for. What good can it do him staying at school? He had his sixteenth birthday last week. He is a man.'

Rachel bit her lip. She knew Ross was right. If Conan was going to farm The Glens of Lochandee he did have many skills to learn. Somehow she could not imagine him farrowing a pig or drenching a sick cow. He would not even know which of the bottles in the medicine chest to use, much less how to get the cow to swallow it. It was true he could plough a furrow almost as well as Ross himself, even though he lacked practice. She sighed.

'It's his life. We will discuss his future with him. But we must let him make the decision himself.'

Later that evening, before either Rachel or Conan could say a word, Ross was putting forward his firm opinion of where Conan's duty lay. Rachel threw him an angry look. She was amazed when Conan calmly agreed to his father's suggestions. She had never known him to be so amenable regarding anything to do with farming.

Later Rachel found him sitting on a fence looking over the fields, chewing abstractedly on a stem of grass. She could not resist asking,

'Conan . . . are you sure? About leaving school, I mean?' He gave her the steady look and slow smile which reminded her so much of Ross.

'Can you ever be sure about the future, Mother? What did you dream of when you were sixteen?'

Rachel flushed. At sixteen she had been an orphan. She had been dangerously innocent. She had been in love with Ross. She had been cruelly beaten by Gertrude Maxwell. She shivered.

'Life was different when I was your age, Conan.'

'Exactly. Well, I have a feeling that my life is just starting. Mother . . . do you think there will be another war?'

'A war? I do hope not!'

'Anthony Eden resigned as Foreign Secretary because he thought Mr Chamberlain was too eager to please Hitler and Mussolini, didn't he?'

'I don't know. You read far too much about politics. Maybe your father is right. Perhaps it's time you learned about things which will do you some good in life.' Rachel's tone was sharper than she had intended, but Conan did not seem to notice.

'The Government must have paid some heed. They must think war is a possibility or they wouldn't be issuing all the gas masks. And look how much money they are spending on defence, and on building new aerodromes for the Royal Air Force.

'I expect they are just taking precautions.'

'Maybe they know that if the man Hitler can get away with it he would rule the whole of Europe — maybe Britain too.'

'Never. Anyway it's not our business. Do you think you will miss your studies at school?'

'No. I can choose what I want to study now. Decide my own future.'

Rachel would not have felt so reassured if she had known what Conan had in mind.

CHAPTER TWENTY-EIGHT

It was the beginning of September and Conan listened to every radio news broadcast he could manage. Rachel felt he was obsessed with the talk of gas masks and air-raid shelters, Hitler, the Jews being forced to flee for their lives.

Everyone was tense since the increasing threats to Czechoslovakia. The Chancellor of the Exchequer had made it clear that Great Britain and France were devoted to the ideals of democratic liberty and determined to uphold them. People were beginning to interpret this as a threat of war if Hitler went ahead.

Rachel knew that Beth and Harry Mason always saved their newspapers for Conan to read.

'I do wish you would not give them to him, Beth,' Rachel had declared irritably only a week ago. Much to her dismay Beth's face had crumpled and she struggled to hold back her tears.

'Conan thinks it would be a great adventure if there is a war, but my Harry would be one of the first to be called for service. We — we haven't even got to a-a baby yet. I don't want him to leave me. He has already been for retraining. Who would look after the shop?'

'Oh Beth! I'm so sorry. I hadn't thought of that.' Rachel had said no more about the newspapers but she knew Conan cycled down to the village whenever he got the opportunity. Sometimes he stayed to help Harry with his electrical repairs, or with the bicycles, but he nearly always returned with a folded paper tucked inside his waistcoat, or in his jacket pocket.

* * *

On this particular September evening, however, Ross insisted Conan should take the milk cows to one of the top fields which had been part of the neglected Nether Lochandee land. It had been ploughed and re-seeded. They had been rewarded with a fine crop of hay in August and now it had produced an aftermath of fresh grass and clover. It made a valuable feed at the end of summer when the usual pastures were stale and often bare. It gave a much needed boost to the milk yields too.

'Bridie enjoys tending the cows while she is doing her reading for school,' Conan argued.

'She has a lot of written homework to do tonight,' Ross insisted. 'You will have to take them. It's a fresh field and the cows will be greedy. Keep a careful eye on them and don't let them graze too long and eat too much clover. Bring them back to the meadow ready for morning and be sure to fasten the gate properly.'

Conan tucked the latest newspaper up his waistcoat and set off with the herd of milk cows. They ate the fresh grass with evident enjoyment, barely pausing, storing it up to chew again later. They seemed to know their time would be limited and were determined to make the most of it. They are not so stupid as people think, Conan decided with a smile as he settled himself comfortably on the grassy bank with his back against a tree. After about half an hour he stirred himself and made a leisurely inspection of the cows. They scarcely looked up as he moved amongst them. He settled down with his paper again. An advertisement for an Air Training Corps in a village hall about three miles from Lochandee caught his eye. Further down there was an article about the successful response to the government recruitment campaign for anti-aircraft forces. Conan's attention was riveted. The cows were forgotten.

It was the restless mooing, pawing and crowding of the cows which drew his attention. They seemed to be gathering around something at the far edge of the field. He had not realised they had wandered so far away. He jumped up and loped across the grassy pasture, already damp with autumn dew.

His face paled as he drew near the bunch of cattle. Some of them were giving low roars — whether of fear or grief or whatever cows felt for their fellow animals, he did not know. Lying in the midst of the milling throng lay one of their best milk cows, her belly distended like a balloon, her legs almost pointing skyward already. She was groaning in pain and there was no way Conan could get her to her feet.

He broke into a cold sweat. There was only one remedy. He needed to plunge a knife into her abdomen to release the gas and stop the pressure on the cow's heart. He had only a penknife. It was far too short. Besides it had to be plunged in exactly the right spot. He had never seen it done. It was a drastic cure — an absolute last resort.

There was a special knife in the wooden medicine chest at home. It was long and pointed and had a sheath with a lip which stayed in the cow's side to allow the gas to pour out. He began to run across the fields, down the track towards the house. He saw his mother in the vegetable garden and began to call. She did not hear him until he was almost at the farmyard.

'Where's Father?' he panted, bending double with the stitch in his side. 'Cow. Blown up . . .'

'I'll get him.' Rachel wasted no time. She knew by the sight of Conan's white face that it was serious. He did not panic easily.

Conan followed his parents back to the field. He was amazed how fast they could run in an emergency — both of them. He was still trying to catch his breath.

They were too late.

* * *

Ross did not say a word. Conan thought it would have been easier if he had shouted at him, called him names — anything to show the anger and disappointment behind the stern white mask, the clenched jaw. He could not know that Ross had learned to repress his feelings almost from the cradle.

Conan knew how he must feel. He knew every penny was needed to pay the bank. He did not know all the cows in the herd yet, not as Bridie and his parents did, by name, by their performance at milking, by their personalities and conformation — but he did know this was one of the best yielders. It had been bought as a heifer from a famous herd in Ayrshire after the foot-and-mouth epidemic.

Rachel tried to hide her dismay. A cow was a big loss to them at any time but especially now with such a burden of debt hanging over their heads. She shook her head and bit hard on her lower lip. She wanted to weep for Ross, but when she looked at Conan the accusation died from her lips. He looked ready to burst into tears himself as he stared at the lifeless cow. Death was such a final thing.

'We'd better round up the rest and get them down to the meadow,' Ross said flatly. He turned to Rachel. 'I'll walk amongst them for an hour or so, just to make sure there are no more.'

She nodded.

'Tomorrow,' Ross looked steadily at Conan. 'You will bring the buggy and get her out of the field. You'll need to dig a good-sized hole to bury her properly.'

Conan nodded silently. He knew he deserved all the blisters he would get by the time he had finished. If only he had concentrated on the cows. If only he had listened to his father's advice.

'You learn by your mistakes, laddie,' Alice nodded when she heard what had happened.

'I certainly hope he will,' Rachel said sharply. 'That is not the sort of mistake we can afford.'

* * *

Just when war seemed inevitable news came that Mr Chamberlain was to attend a conference with Herr Hitler, and other leaders. It was in the early hours of the morning before an agreement was reached. Alice had listened anxiously to the BBC Home Service and she reported eagerly on what she believed was a successful outcome.

'Hitler has been granted most of his demands but the Czechs were not present to voice any dissent. Mr Chamberlain received a tumultuous welcome on his return from Munich. He appeared with the King and Queen on the balcony at Buckingham Palace. "*I believe it is peace for our time*" he declared. He informed the House of Commons that the Anglo-German accord had brought peace with honour.'

Alice repeated Mr Chamberlain's words over and over, so great was her relief.

When Conan dared to question how the Czechs must feel, knowing that part of their country had been handed over to Hitler, she chided him.

'You are too sceptical for one so young.'

* * *

A month later he reminded Alice.

'I was not the only one who had doubts about the peace accord with Germany.'

'You are too smart for your own good,' Rachel told Conan irritably. She had an uneasy feeling that Conan, despite his youth, had a better idea of the undercurrents of politics than any of them, wrapped up as they were in their own problems of work, work and more work, with the worry of paying their debts.

In spite of his shock and remorse for losing one of their best cows Conan had not forgotten the announcement he had read about the Air Training Corps in a nearby village.

As the days grew shorter the evening work grew less. The meetings were within cycling distance. He made up his mind to join the group of other young men who met each week.

Bridie had a school friend named Fiona Sinclair from the same village and she soon discovered the reason for his weekly cycle ride in the dark. It troubled her that Conan had not confided in their parents but she kept his secret.

* * *

When news began to filter through about the dreadful atrocities which had occurred to Jewish men, women and children throughout a long night in November, Conan's feelings got the better of him.

'There will be a war! Britain will have to fight for the freedom of ordinary men and women, and I shall fight too,' he declared in an unexpected outburst.

'Conan! You are just a boy . . .' Rachel began.

'No! No, I am not *just a boy*. I have been going to meetings of the Air Training Corps. If our politicians have the guts to stand up for the principals of freedom and honour, then I must play my part too, as soon as they will take me! I mean to be ready.'

'You have been going to meetings?' Ross echoed sharply. 'You mean to tell me you have not been spending every Wednesday evening helping Harry Mason with his repairs as we thought?'

'I did not tell you that,' Conan defended himself, but his colour had risen. He looked like a guilty child to Rachel's eyes. 'You assumed I went to Harry's,' he mumbled. 'As a matter of fact one of Sandy's sons goes too.'

'Our Sandy? Sandy Kidd?' Ross looked incredulous. 'I thought young Willie was working over the other side of Lochandee.'

'He's working on a farm there, but he cycles to the meetings. We all do.'

'Sandy never mentioned it. Does he know?' Rachel asked.

'I don't know,' Conan shrugged. 'I expect Willie will tell him when he's ready,' he added warningly.

* * *

Rachel could not help worrying and nothing Ross could say could comfort her. Tension mounted.

'It's always Conan!' Ross raged one evening. 'He has always come between us.'

'You should be concerned about him too. He's learning about fighting a war. A war, for goodness sake — not a children's tea party. He's your son too!'

'Well, it doesn't feel that way!' Ross stormed and took himself off to look around the cows. The byre was often the most peaceful place he could find in the evenings. He loved the warmth, the pungent smell, cows contentedly chewing their cud, the odd grunt and snuffle as they settled down for the night in their stalls. He was proud of the herd he was gradually rebuilding. He loved the farm, the land, the whole area around Lochandee. It was his life. He could not understand how a son of his could want anything more.

Rachel hated quarrels. She felt strained and tense. She spoke in haste but Ross did not understand how she felt about Conan. He was more worried about repaying the debt he owed to the bank. Prices were not improving in spite of the fledgling marketing boards which now organised the sale of the milk.

* * *

It was a long winter at Lochandee and things did not improve when spring came. There were increasing fears that war was inevitable. As many had predicted, Hitler had not kept to the peace agreement. In Britain the Territorial Army was to be doubled. Drill halls were being built all over the country for training. Plans were announced for evacuation of children from the cities to the country. Men over twenty were called into the forces. A register of all younger men was being compiled. Everyone would have a job to do. Beth grew more and more tense and frustrated. She longed for a baby and she hated the thought of Harry going off for training. 'But you will not need to go away, Conan,' Rachel said when announcements were made listing essential workers. 'Miners are needed at home to produce enough coal for the factories to build the ships and aircraft and weapons. Farmers are exempt too, now that the Government wants us to produce as much food as we can. They are afraid the Germans will try to sink our ships and starve us into submission if we cannot get supplies.'

Conan tightened his lips and shook his head, but he made no reply.

'Your mother is right!' Ross told him sharply. 'See here,' he waved a newspaper at his son. 'We produce less than a third of our own supplies. An army of hungry men will not be fit to fight! Can't you see that? The Government are urging us to plough up grassland and sow grain instead. They are even giving two pounds an acre to help us do it. Suddenly they are desperate for home-produced supplies, but it will not be a case of supply and demand for farmers. They are setting up a ministry to control supplies of food and prices.'

* * *

At the end of May Conan celebrated his seventeenth birthday and wished he was twenty. Harry Mason had to do more training and was forced to be away from his little shop more often than he could afford. Conan helped whenever he could but Ross was ploughing more of the neglected land he had acquired with Nether Lochandee and no one had much free time.

Some of the higher, wetter land would never be fit to plough but that was all the more reason to make the best of the fields nearer the farmyard. All the pastures he had brought into the Lochandee rotation had grown better grass and the animals were thriving on it. He was not so happy about growing large areas of corn though. It was never easy to gather in the harvest with the notoriously wet climate of south-west Scotland but if the Government brought in the ruling he would be forced to grow corn whether it was practical or not.

* * *

All through the hot summer days tempers were frayed. Everywhere people were tense.

Sandy Kidd's elder son, Frank, returned to Lochandee to work for Ross. Unlike his younger brother Willie, he did not enjoy living in a bothy away from home, though he loved his work on the land, especially with the horses.

'I shall have to take care,' Bill Carr chuckled, 'or young Frank will be taking over both my job with horses, and my daughter.' Emmie blushed furiously and Frank glanced at her shyly from under the peak of his flat cap. Ross and Sandy laughed. Alfie joined in with his usual cackle, though he had no idea why they were all smiling. There was no doubt the two young people had got on well together since Frank returned to work at Lochandee even though Emmie was a couple of years older.

* * *

There was little cause for laughter a few weeks later. It was the first Sunday in September. The village church had been well-filled for the morning service, as it usually was these days. Even the least devout seemed to have an urge to attend and join in the prayers for peace. The minister's sermon was longer than usual, his prayers too. The congregation grew restless. Most of them were ready for their Sunday dinners.

They had almost finished singing the last hymn when the Beadle entered through the vestry door, his face pale and stern. He handed the minister a folded note and retired to his place at the back of the church.

As soon as the last notes of the hymn died away the minister read out the message.

'We are now at war,' he read gravely. 'The Prime Minister has declared the Country is at war with Germany. Let us pray for our King and Country.'

A few hours later their President made the same declaration on behalf of France.

* * *

It was a shock when an official letter arrived requiring Alfie to attend for an interview and medical examination in readiness for joining the army. Alfie had no idea what it all meant since he could neither read nor write and he had rarely left the farm. Never in his life had he been further than the blacksmith's in the village. Rachel wrote a letter explaining Alfie's mental condition but the officials were adamant that he must attend.

Ross decided he must take him in the car, and if possible accompany him into the interview but this was not permitted. Long before the officials had finished their questions poor Alfie had messed his pants, wet himself and was sick over the wooden table at which two men sat filling in forms. Ross could hear Alfie getting more and more hysterical and he could imagine his long gangly limbs flailing everywhere. He could sit still no longer and he jumped from his chair. He was on his way to the door when it was flung open and two burly fellows almost carried Alfie out bodily.

'We did tell you he was not suitable for army training,' Ross protested in annoyance. Alfie's distress upset him dreadfully.

'It's our job to check for ourselves, Mr Maxwell,' one of the officials told him curtly. 'We receive all manner of excuses.'

'But Alfie is in a reserved occupation, in addition to his condition . . .'

'Ah, we have many men who would like to claim they are in essential work. It's just an excuse for most of them and essential workers will be cut to the minimum. The Government are encouraging women and girls to fill the places of men on the land.'

'But there is a lot of work which women cannot do!'

'Then the few men left will need to do the heavy work and leave the rest to the women. You will need to reorganise, Mr Maxwell. Good day to you.'

Frank Kidd was not so lucky. He celebrated his twentieth birthday in the middle of October. He was called for his medical and drafted to the army. His brother, Willie was eighteen the following month and immediately volunteered for the RAF and was accepted.

'Our time in the Air Training Corps helped me get in,' he told Conan triumphantly, but his parents were devastated to find that both their sons were leaving the glens and going to war.

During the winter Conan did the work he was asked to do but it was clear to everyone that his thoughts were on other things. Beth was angry and frustrated, tearful and tense when Harry was away. Conan helped her with the bicycle repairs as much as he could but they both knew she would not be able to keep it going without Harry.

It was a Saturday morning at the end of March when Conan waylaid Emmie on her way back to her cottage after finishing the milking.

'I'm going off on my bike as soon as I've finished here, Emmie. Will you go across to the house about half past eleven and tell mother I shall not be back for dinner. I'll be home in time for milking.'

'Why can't you tell . . . Oh no, Conan! You're going to volunteer! That's why you don't want them to know where you're heading, isn't it? Isn't it?'

Conan raised one eyebrow in the quizzical way he had and gave a wry grimace.

'Don't go, Conan,' Emmie pleaded. 'Not you as well. Please don't volunteer. They'll send for you soon enough if they need you.'

'I must go, Emmie. I must . . .'

'Are you so keen to kill people?' Emmie demanded harshly, but her dark eyes were glinting with tears.

'Kill people!' Conan was startled.

'Yes kill! That's what war is all about. Killing people on the other side. Some of them are innocent men and women and children . . .'

'Is that what Frank tells you when he writes?' Conan asked uncertainly.

'Frank hates the war. He hates being away from Lochandee and he hates all the things soldiers have to do. I wish he could have had the chance to stay at home.'

'Aye . . .' Conan bit his lip. 'Well I'd still like to see what they have to say. Maybe the RAF will not be as bad as the Army — if they'll have me that is. You'll tell Mother . . . please Emmie?'

'All right,' Emmie agreed resignedly, 'but I still think you're crazy to volunteer.'

Emmie's outburst gave Conan much to think about as he peddled swiftly along the narrow country roads. There were primroses blooming along the grassy banks and some of the hedges were bursting into leaf — fresh and green. Spring was in the air. In his heart Conan did not really want to leave Lochandee, but he felt compelled by some inner conviction. Even so, if there were jobs for him in the RAF where he did not have to kill people he might prefer them, if they gave him a choice.

At half past eleven Emmie went nervously across to the house with Conan's message.

'Where has he gone?' Rachel asked distractedly.

'He . . . he didn't say.'

'Oh, well I don't suppose he'll starve. Come and say hello to Beth.'

'Beth's here? Is the shop shut today?'

'I shall have to give up the shop until the war is over,' Beth said wearily, coming to join them in the pale spring sunshine. 'I hate Harry being away. I don't even have his baby to nurse or to — to . . .'

'Hush Beth, don't cry. Don't upset yourself,' Rachel urged. She turned to Emmie. 'Beth is wondering if we have any work for her here.'

'Any work? More than you'll want, I'll bet.' Emmie grinned at Beth, trying to coax a smile in return.

'I think Ross will be pleased to have you back instead of a land girl, especially one from the city.'

'I hear some of them are quite good,' Beth summoned a wan smile, 'but our braw blacksmith did not say what they were good at!'

'Surely he doesn't still have a roving eye!' Rachel exclaimed. 'He's too old.'

'Are they ever too old?' Beth grimaced wryly, thinking of some of the stories Harry had told her about his fellow soldiers.

Harry Mason came home on leave with a forty-eight hour pass. At his request Conan cycled down to the village to see him.

'I have not told Beth yet,' he confided, 'but we are being drafted abroad. Don't know where, so don't ask. I do know Beth will be upset so I'm putting it off. I want to make the most of our time together. That's why I want to beg a favour?'

'Beg away then,' Conan grinned.

'Would you help Beth sort out the remains of my stock, sell off anything you can?'

'Of course I'll do that,' Conan promised, 'If Father will lend me the car I will take the rest to that shop in Annan. They will surely give you something for the spare parts?'

'That's a great idea! I'll pay for the petrol. One and ninepence a gallon it is now, I believe, and getting scarce. I'm glad we sold the van.'

'I'd better get started as soon as you leave, in case I get my own call-up papers.'

'Aye,' Harry sighed. 'I heard you'd volunteered, you silly bugger!' he punched Conan playfully on the shoulder. 'I'd give anything to stay here with Beth and rear a family, but it's not all bad. Your parents will get an awful shock though,' Harry added gravely. 'I think you should warn them.'

'No,' Conan shook his head emphatically. 'It will be bad enough when the time comes. Father will accuse me of deserting the glens and the family, wasting the opportunities he's given me. Mother will be upset because I'm going away and may never come back. They only ever quarrel about me. Bridie is so soft-hearted, even about her chickens, so I expect she will be in tears. I'm telling you, Harry, I'm dreading it. If I could just disappear I would.'

'No! You can't leave without a proper goodbye. That would be the coward's way — and I know you're no coward, lad. Anyway I'm relieved to know you'll help Beth sort things out, and I'm glad she's going back to work at Lochandee. It will be a lot better for her than working in the munitions factory they're building down near Annan.'

Harry's brief leave was over all too soon and Beth was glad to throw herself into clearing out the shop. She missed him terribly. She sensed he was being sent to some sort of dangerous or secret posting this time. He had warned her she might not hear from him so regularly.

'As soon as I can let you have a proper address I will, but meanwhile they'll forward my letters on to me, so be sure and let me know if there's any news . . . ?'

'I will,' Beth promised. 'You know I will, but I miss you so much, Harry. It makes me . . . Oh I don't know — frustrated and restless and . . . I just wish you hadn't to leave me.'

Beth knew Harry longed for a baby as much as she did but a fortnight after his departure she was plunged into despair again, in spite of the passion and desperation of their last night together. She was miserable and depressed and she could not bear to tell him yet. She would wait until he sent his proper address in case the letters were censored. It made her feel inhibited.

CHAPTER TWENTY-NINE

'Cheer up, Beth,' Conan urged, 'Harry will be back before you know it.' It was late on a Saturday evening. They had finally cleared out the remains of the stock and swept the dusty floor and shelves for the last time. They were both weary and dirty with dust and oil, but Conan was relieved they had completed the clearing out before his call-up papers came.

The empty echoes of the shop seemed to depress Beth more than ever. It saddened Conan to see her so down in spirits. He had known her all his life. They had almost grown up together and there had always been affection between them. His face reddened as he remembered some of his teenage fantasies. Since she married Harry Mason and moved back to the village he felt almost as much at home in their house as he did in his own.

'I could die for a cup of tea,' he said now, thinking the age-old brew might comfort Beth. 'I'll finish off in here if you go through and poke up the fire and get the kettle boiling.'

'All right. I feel filthy though. I think we could both do with a good wash before we eat. I expect the water in the boiler will still be warm. The fire has been lit most of the day. I shall have to be more economical with the coal in future, I suppose.' She sighed heavily.

'Right,' Conan nodded absently.

'Is something bothering you?' Beth asked on her way through to the main part of the cottage. 'You're not regretting volunteering, are you?'

'Oh no. I think I'm looking forward to some of the new experiences. Most of the lads in the ATC seemed to have . . . well you know . . . been with a woman. Even the ones who weren't married seem to know . . . What it's all about.'

'Oh, Conan! Most of the girls in Lochandee fall over themselves just to get a smile from you. You could have any one of them for a girlfriend.'

'Och, they're just schoolgirls most of them.'

'Oh yes? It's not that long since you left school, *old man*!' Beth teased and went off to put the kettle on, chuckling as she went. Conan smiled to himself. At least Beth had cheered up now.

Minutes later she was back with a block of soap and a clean enamel pail half full of warm water.

'There's plenty of warm water. I'm going to wash my hair while the kettle boils. I thought you might like to wash? I never realised we had so much dust in here.'

'Thanks Beth. I'll just finish sweeping up the pile of dust and shavings.'

Conan took his time and then he stood the pail of warm water on the old workbench. On impulse he stripped off his shirt and dipped his head in the pail, working up a lather with the soap and washing his head and arms. It felt wonderful to be clean again and he dashed out to the back yard to rinse himself off under the pump. The water was cold and invigorating. Beth had forgotten to give him a towel. Shaking his head like a dog out of a river he laughed and hurried through the back door of the cottage, droplets glistening on his ginger-blond lashes and on his broad shoulders.

The back door opened straight into the small scullery and Beth was bent over the stone sink rinsing her hair. She jerked upright, startled by his sudden entry. Conan skidded to a halt, his eyes widening. Beth was stripped to the waist.

'I-I'm s-sorry,' he stammered. 'You didn't leave me a towel.'

Swiftly Beth seized her own towel and pulled it around her shoulders.

'I forgot about a towel,' she apologised, already recovering from the shock of his intrusion, though her skimpy towel barely covered the fullness of her breasts and her dark hair was dripping everywhere. Conan could not take his eyes off her.

'You're beautiful,' he breathed unsteadily. 'Really beautiful.'

'You're not a bad hunk of man yourself,' Beth told him wryly, surveying the breadth of his shoulders still glistening with water. His chest was lean and muscular, not an ounce of spare flesh on him. She pulled herself together. 'And I'm old enough to be your mother, so I can't be that beautiful,' she muttered in an effort to draw Conan out of his enchanted trance, but there was a traitorous desire clenching her own stomach. It was clear he had never seen a half-naked woman before.

'You're barely twelve years older than I am . . . You're a real woman . . .'

'Pass me another towel, please, to rub my hair dry. They're over there on the clothes horse.'

Conan reached for the towel.

'I'll rub it for you.' He turned her towards him. He was more than a head taller than Beth and he rubbed her head gently. She could see the rapid beating of his heart close to her face as he towelled her hair.

Beth loved Harry deeply. She knew he was the best thing that had ever happened to her, but that did not prevent the surge of longing which shuddered through her. She was missing her husband, yearning for his arms around her. She was barely aware that Conan had stopped drying her hair and was looking down at her. The towel had slipped a little from her shoulders. Slowly, almost reverently, Conan touched the rounded fullness of her breast. His fingers moved into a stroking caress. Beth caught her breath, feeling a rush of desire as primitive as the wildest jungle animal.

'Let me, Beth?' Conan whispered hoarsely. 'Please . . . ?'

Their eyes met. Beth saw the raw desire in his, and with it a faint uncertainty. Her heart filled with tenderness, but her body responded with a passion beyond her wildest imaginings.

'It is so wrong!' she muttered helplessly. Her arms closed tightly round his naked torso. She revelled in the hard, lean strength of him. He picked her up as easily as if she was a child, his gaze holding hers, waiting. She closed her eyes briefly. Opened them. Looked deeply into his.

'The bedroom is across the passage.'

Conan pushed the door open with his toe. He set Beth on the bed as gently as if she had been made of the most fragile porcelain. She felt cherished. His youthful adoration was totally at odds with the manly desire which could no longer be hidden. Beth was filled with a confusing tumult of emotions. She did not understand herself. Afterwards she might hate herself, but for now she wanted this body of a fair young God as much as he wanted her.

* * *

Later they lay side by side on the bed. Conan raised himself on one elbow and looked down into Beth's face. He smiled. It was a slow, attractive smile.

'Thank you, Beth,' he said softly. 'Thank you from the bottom of my heart. You have taught me more than you'll ever know.'

'God, Conan, you've nothing to learn! You'll break a lot of hearts I reckon.' Beth reached for a blouse from a nearby chair and pulled it on. 'I feel a bit less of a wanton woman when I'm covered up.'

'You're not a wanton woman,' Conan smiled, but he got up from the bed and pulled on his trousers. 'There, we are both respectable again.'

'Yes . . .' Beth said doubtfully. 'Conan . . .' she bit her lip frowning slightly.

'What is it Beth?'

'I-I should not have let you . . . I'm not really a wicked woman you know . . .'

'Oh, Beth, I know that!' Conan laughed softly.

'I love Harry. I miss him terribly. I . . . I think that's why, why I enjoyed it so much with you tonight. I-I feel so frustrated without him.'

'Ah, yes, Harry . . .' Conan looked grave. 'I cheated on Harry tonight, and he has been such a good friend to me too. I'm sorry about that — but it's the only thing I'm sorry about,' he added seriously. 'You'll not tell him, Beth, will you?'

'No! Never! He would be terribly hurt.'

'Yes,' Conan nodded, relieved. 'It's our secret then.'

'You . . . you'll not get drunk and . . . and boast about your conquests, Conan, will you . . . ?' Beth asked biting her lip.

'Conquest? Beth you're not a conquest. You've given me the greatest gift anyone could give. You were so patient . . .'

'I didn't need patience! Come to think of it, I didn't need anything. You're a natural lover boy, Conan Maxwell. I just hope you will not be too free with your charms though — for your own sake,' she added seriously. 'You wouldn't be the first attractive man to be trapped into marriage by an unscrupulous hussy who tells you she is expecting your child. And then there's these diseases some women pass on . . .'

'I can afford to be choosy now,' Conan said, equally serious. 'I can promise you I shall not take any woman if I cannot respect her as I respect you, Beth.'

'Thank you, Conan, you make me feel a bit better about deceiving Harry.'

'I don't know about this thing called love though.'

'You will when you experience it!' Beth assured him softly. 'And it's a whole lot more than sex, I can tell you.'

'Is it?' Conan asked sceptically, thinking of the conversations of some of the men he had overheard.

'Oh, there has to be desire and passion — of course there has. But to spend the rest of your life with a person . . . It — it's like meeting someone with the mirror-image of your own soul, sharing your thoughts and feelings and interests. Not that you can expect to agree all of the time about everything. In fact that would make life a bit dull I reckon, and the making up is fun.' She chuckled. 'But you have to be comfortable together . . . You'll know when you fall in love.'

'I'll take your word for that. You and Harry always seem happy. Mother and Father must love each other . . .'

'They do, believe me,' Beth assured him. 'They've been good friends to me. I'd hate them to think I had betrayed their trust and seduced their son. You promise you'll never tell a living soul about what happened between us tonight, Conan?'

'I promise. See,' he reached for the Bible laying on the chest of drawers beside the bed, and laid his hand on it. 'As God is my witness I shall never mention what happened tonight to anyone, unless it's at your request.'

'Thank you.' Beth smiled and put her hand on top of his where it lay on the Bible. 'I think we shall always be friends, Conan.'

'Of course we shall.' He leaned forward and kissed her cheek. 'Good night, Beth.'

'You'll take care cycling home? It's dark outside. There's been a lot of accidents since the blackout.'

'I'll be careful.'

* * *

On Monday morning the postman brought the usual weekly letter from Meg, but it was much longer than it had been recently.

'Oh no!' Rachel gasped. 'The twins are going abroad to nurse. Peter will be upset. They have done so well with their training. What a blessing Polly took up teaching. At least she will be staying in Glasgow and she does enjoy it.'

'Yes,' Conan nodded. 'I remember it was always what she wanted to do. I imagine she'll be good at it. But somebody has to nurse the wounded soldiers. I wonder whether Jane and Mary will be sent to the same hospital?'

'No. Meg says Mary will be staying in London for a while to do some special training. Jane is going to France straight away.'

'Who is your other letter from?' Ross asked, looking up from his own letters.

'Ruth. She says wee Josh has passed his medical for the Army but their own doctor wrote a letter to the authorities explaining that Willie was suffering from a stomach complaint and he needs Josh at home to run the farm.'

'I expect they would have let him off anyway,' Ross nodded. 'After all he is in a reserved occupation and the Government are crying out for food since the German U-boats started attacking any and every cargo ship they see.'

'Even for us the rationing takes a lot of getting used to, especially now the Government are controlling the number of pigs we can kill and what we do with the eggs and milk and butter.' Neither of them noticed how Conan's face had paled as he rose from the breakfast table and went outside to get on with his work.

Damn cousin Josh! he thought. He was staying at home and his father would be even more angry when his own call-up papers came.

A couple of days later, shortly before his eighteenth birthday, Conan received the expected letter from the Royal Air Force. Later that evening he broke the news to Bridie.

'You volunteered?' Her eyes were round with shock. 'You go so soon . . .' The tears Conan dreaded made her eyes luminous as she struggled to hold them back. 'What will Mother say . . .'

'I'll tell them both, but not until I'm ready. I want you to do me a favour, Bridie. Will you call in on Beth on your way home from school tomorrow afternoon? Tell her I leave Lochandee the day after tomorrow. You'll not forget?'

When Bridie called at Beth's cottage she found her in the cleared front workshop. She was painting the walls with yellow distemper. The floor had already been scrubbed twice and all the shelves and the old workbench had gone.

'Goodness it doesn't look like the shop at all!' Bride exclaimed wandering around. It seems so much bigger. Lighter too.' She looked through the door where Mr Pearson had once kept his papers and special small tools, an armchair and a small table. 'I always thought this was a sort of cupboard but it's quite big now it's empty.'

'Aye,' Beth sighed and wiped a weary arm across her brow. She had worked really hard since the evening she had spent with Conan. She knew at least part of the thrill had been due to forbidden fruits. Conan was a handsome lad and he was strong and virile, but it was not something either of them would repeat, or wish to. She had thrown herself into the task of cleaning and decorating the shop end of the cottage hoping to banish the twinges of guilt she felt whenever she thought of Harry. He did not deserve an unfaithful wife, and him away fighting for his country.

'You've painted the ceilings white. What are you going to put in it, Beth?'

'Yes, I thought I might try making a pattern with a sponge and green distemper on the walls. I've volunteered to take in some evacuees.'

'Evacuees? But I thought most of them went back home again.'

'I know, but they are only sending families who want to be evacuated this time. I'm having a mother and two young children. Their father is in the Royal Navy. I want it to look as nice and as pretty as I can make it for them. It must be awful having to leave everything behind.'

'Yes.' Bridie remembered the reason for her visit. 'Conan is going to the Royal Air Force.' Her voice trembled. 'He l-leaves tomorrow.'

'Ah, I see. He has got his papers then?' Beth nodded thoughtfully.

'You knew!' Bridie's eyes widened. 'You knew he had volunteered?'

'Y-yes. I promised to go up to the farm whenever he got word to leave. Your parents will need all the help they can get. I thought it was a good time for me to start work again — try to replace him a wee bit, maybe comfort your Mother . . .'

'Oh, Beth!' Bridie suddenly flung herself into Beth's arms and wept. 'You're so good to us. You must be missing Harry terribly. War is a dreadful thing!'

'Hey, let me put my brush down, Bridie, or you'll be having yellow streaks in your hair!'

Bridie strove for control and brushed away her tears with the back of her hand.

'I wish Mother would let me leave school now that I'm fourteen. I could help such a lot. They say the new land girls all wear breeches and they are learning to plough and do all the things the men usually do.'

'Aye,' Beth sighed, 'We shall all have to learn to do things we never thought possible if this war goes on.' She frowned. 'I just wish Harry would write and tell me where he is. I know he has been sent abroad but I don't know where. I've only had one short letter and it was forwarded on from a central office in England.'

* * *

The moment Conan had dreaded arrived. He had already arranged to leave his cycle at one of the cottages at the cross-roads. Bridie had promised to get Fiona Sinclair to ride it halfway to the village after school.

'There's no need for you to waste petrol giving me a lift in the car, Mother,' he insisted. Now that the time had come to actually leave Lochandee and all his friends and family he was half-afraid he might break down himself. There was no way he could bear his mother's tears on the journey to the station.

It had been hard enough saying goodbye to Alice Beattie. She had wrung her hands over and over again in her distress. For the first time Conan realised how old and frail she had become.

'They have made Mr Winston Churchill the Prime Minister,' her voice quavered, 'but have they done it in time? Nothing to offer, he says, except "*blood, toil, tears and sweat*" . . .' She seemed so sure she would never see him again and the thought upset Conan more than he had realised. 'May God go with you, laddie,' she had whispered huskily. He had hugged her thin shoulders and left the room swiftly before she saw the tears glinting in his own eyes. How much worse it was going to be saying goodbye to his parents.

Rachel understood. She felt as though her own heart was breaking but she was not alone. Every day thousands of women must feel the same agony and she was determined to make the parting as easy for him as possible. She must be cheerful, she must hold back the tears — at least until he was out of the house.

If only Ross would let him go without making a scene. She had seen the utter shock in his face when Conan broke the news that he would be leaving today. She knew Ross had convinced himself that his only son accepted the demands of farming Lochandee. She had known better. She had sensed the preoccupation in Conan, the intensity in his eyes when there were reports of another ship sunk and lives lost, or another aircraft missing. She had known he would not be content to let the war go on without him.

So she hugged Conan tightly, promised they would all write often, and hoped he would write whenever he could. His face was pale and strained.

'Don't come outside, Mother,' he pleaded huskily.

'But your father . . .'

'He's waiting to say — to say goodbye.'

Rachel nodded dumbly. She felt the tension in him. Then he was gone, round the corner of the house, into the yard, out of her sight. She clenched her hands tightly but she could not stand still. One final wave, a last glimpse of the child she had reared to manhood. She ran to the corner of house and stopped short seeing Conan and Ross facing each other. How alike they were — one older and broader, but handsome still, the other with the same direct gaze, the erect shoulders, square and strong, but still so slim. They were not quarrelling and she saw Conan's wavering smile before he half turned. She guessed he was holding onto his emotions with an iron will.

Rachel watched in astonishment as Ross pulled Conan into his arms in a fierce hug. She saw the tears spill from Ross's eyes — Ross who never showed emotion in front of his children or friends.

'My son.' He had his eyes screwed tightly shut. 'My son . . . I am proud of you.' Another hug. 'God keep you safe . . .' Rachel did not wait for more. She could not see Conan's face, or read the words on his lips, but her heart was full. She was so thankful that the two men she loved were parting with affection and respect.

It was some minutes before she heard Ross's booted feet approaching the house. She guessed he had needed time to compose himself but as soon as she saw him she flung herself into his arms and her own pent-up emotions overflowed like a river in flood.

'Hush, Rachel,' Ross soothed huskily, stroking her hair as though she were a child, patting her shoulder. 'You were very brave . . .' He laid his cheek against the softness of her hair 'Braver than I was, I fear,' he murmured sadly. 'So many things I should have said. My only son, and I have let him go . . . never told him how dear he is . . .'

Rachel controlled her sobs with an effort as she heard the anguish in Ross's voice and felt him holding her tightly, his cheek against her hair, his breath soft and warm against her temple. She burrowed her arms beneath his jacket and hugged him, pressing her head against the hardness of his chest, feeling the imprint of his waistcoat buttons against her face.

'I do love you, Ross.' Her voice was low and tremulous but he heard.

'I know,' he murmured huskily. 'I love you too. In fact I don't know how I could manage without you . . .' His arms tightened and she felt him shudder against her.

'You will not have to. I'm not going anywhere.'

'Thank God for that! It's only now that I truly understand how cruel this war is to all the thousands of families that are split apart . . . husbands and wives, parents and children . . .' His arms clenched. It was not like Ross to be so emotional, or at least he rarely let his feelings show. 'Let's go upstairs . . . ?' he whispered.

'Now?' Rachel leaned back in his arms, staring up into his face. 'In the middle of the day . . . ?' She was incredulous. It was just the comfort and loving she needed to get her through the rest of the day. 'How did you know . . . ?' she whispered, 'that I need you to love me?'

'Because I need loving too . . .' Ross bent to unlace his boots.

* * *

The rest of the day passed in a haze of joy and sorrow for Rachel. Ross had made her feel like a young desirable girl again. Together they had found comfort, but they had more, so very much more in the exultant triumph, the ultimate fulfilment. All the tensions and arguments evaporated. They were united in their love for each other. Whatever happened in the future, so long as they had each other, surely they could endure and survive.

Just after midday Beth cycled up the road to The Glens of Lochandee.

'I thought you might be ready for another pair of hands,' she greeted Rachel, but her smile was wan.

'Oh Beth, we do need all the help we can get, especially now Conan has gone. But . . .' Rachel looked at her more closely. 'you are looking pale and tired. Are you all right? Harry . . . ?'

'I'm fine. I've been working extra hard to get the cottage ready for the arrival of my evacuee family. If I only knew where Harry is. I feel here . . .' she clasped a hand to her heart, that he is in danger somewhere.' Her voice trembled but she pulled herself together and took a deep breath.

CHAPTER THIRTY

The new Government under Winston Churchill, with Clement Attlee as deputy Prime Minister, made sweeping changes. They worked for the good of the Country and made an effort to gain support from all quarters, including that of Ernest Bevin, the trade union leader, and Lord Beaverbrook, the newspaper owner. New measures gave the Government unlimited authority over every person and all property.

'Even the banks!' Ross read in alarm. 'I hope Mr Reid will not withdraw our loan. Even with Beth's help I don't know how we are going to manage the work with all the extra ploughing the War Agricultural Committee is demanding.'

'We'll get through. Bridie is a great help. She keeps pestering me to let her leave school. We shall have more eggs than ever before with all the broody hens we have sitting on eggs. That's one advantage about the government controls, they guarantee to take all we can produce. Now that the eggs are collected and sent to a central packing station we know we shall be paid for them — so long as we don't surrender to the Germans.'

'Only God will help us if it comes to that,' Ross shuddered. He reached for Rachel's hand. 'You're a great support to me.' His gaze held hers and there was a world of love and desire in his blue eyes. He had been so gentle and attentive since Conan went away. Rachel suspected he was missing their son as much as she was, but it was wonderful to find comfort in each other, talking together, walking together — almost as they had been when they were young lovers at Windlebrae. Poor Beth didn't even have that consolation.

'I reckon the hens should make enough money to pay the wages and everything we need in the house, or at least everything we are allowed to buy with all the rationing,' Rachel said.

'If anyone does manage to make a profit the Government have the power to charge a hundred per cent tax now — but I suppose we are better to pay towards our own freedom than be taken over by a dictator like Hitler.'

'We would all be slaves, if that happened, and lucky if we got enough food and a coat for our backs.'

'Yes,' Ross sighed. 'I should never have opposed Conan as I did. He understood what was going on better than we did. Where would the Country be without young men like him?'

* * *

It was the middle of June before Beth received the longed for letter direct from Harry and she peddled up the road to Lochandee as though she had wings, so great was her joy and relief.

'He says he is one of the lucky ones!' she told Rachel breathlessly. 'He does not give many details, but at least it sounds more like my Harry. He says he was rescued from Dunkirk on a little fishing boat. He was plucked from the enemy just in time. A lot of his comrades have not been so lucky.' Beth wiped tears from her cheeks with the back of her hand. 'I'm so relieved he's safe. I just knew he was in danger. His letters never seemed to reply to any of the things I asked him, or told him. I knew mine were going to a central address somewhere and I couldn't write a proper letter when I knew some strange man might be censoring it.'

'I expect Harry felt the same,' Rachel comforted her. 'and I suppose there would be lots of delays. Now you can tell him how much you miss him. Does he know his cottage has been taken over by evacuees?'

'No, not yet. I've such a lot of things to tell him. I think he will like Carol, though. She's fitting into the village very well and she keeps the cottage clean and tidy and does all the washing and ironing while I am here at Lochandee. She says keeping busy helps to take her mind off John, her husband. The wee girls are lovely . . .' Beth added wistfully. She bit her lip and turned away.

She had not told Harry that she had failed again, even after his last leave with all the passionate urgency of their lovemaking. Suddenly she stopped in the middle of the yard. Her hand flew to her mouth. Her monthly rhythms were always so regular. Could the anxiety over Harry have altered them? Certainly she had felt lethargic and tired, but then she had been so worried. Worry affected things, didn't it? She frowned making mental calculations, but there was no doubt she was overdue. It was only a week. It would probably all sort itself out now that her mind was easier. Even so some instinct prevented Beth from mentioning babies when she wrote a long and loving letter to Harry.

Two weeks later Beth was convinced she must be expecting a child. Her face was pale, her mind wild with worry. The child was not Harry's! However much her heart and mind willed it, she knew the baby could not be her husband's.

Another week, another letter, the same question came from Harry.

Beth knew for certain now that she was carrying Conan Maxwell's child.

That evening when Carol and her two children had settled for the night Beth sat down with her pen and writing pad at the kitchen table. She chewed her pen so hard the end came off in her mouth. She clenched her fingers.

'Please God, help me do the right thing!' she prayed silently. She couldn't bear to hurt Harry. She loved him and he loved her. He did not deserve to be betrayed. Suddenly her mind was crystal clear. She would tell him they were expecting a baby at last. No one need ever know the child was not his. No one ever would. The secret was hers, and hers alone.

'After so many disappointments I had to be sure before I told you . . .' she wrote. 'I have not been to the doctor, but I know.'

Harry's letter came back by return. He was jubilant. He had asked for leave. He might only get twenty-four hours but he would come if he had to walk all the way.

In fact Harry got thirty-six hours leave and Beth knew beyond doubt she had done right to keep her secret. He declared himself the happiest man on earth. As she lay in his arms, satiated by love and talk she murmured,

'You know, Harry, I can't help wondering whether Mrs Maxwell might be expecting a baby again . . .'

'Mrs Maxwell!' Harry laughed. 'She can't be! Can she? I mean she has a grownup son. Bridie must be fourteen or fifteen . . .'

'I know. But she can't be more than about thirty-eight. She's very pretty.'

'Not as pretty as my wife.' Harry grinned and hugged her close.

'Och, I know what you are wanting Harry Mason. But seriously, Mrs Maxwell is usually so strong and healthy. If she's not expecting a baby it must be something serious because she's sick every morning. She's been like that for at least two weeks, maybe more.'

'Well . . . well. Better to be a late baby than an illness,' Harry mused. But nothing could wipe away the huge grin he had worn since he had heard their own good news.

* * *

Rachel did not believe she could be expecting another child, in spite of the passionate loving she and Ross had indulged in since Conan's departure. Common sense told her that it was possible. She had been seventeen when Conan was born. Then, as now, the awful nausea had started almost immediately.

'You must see the doctor,' Ross urged anxiously. 'Suppose it's something else. You were never so ill with Margaret and Bridie.'

Reluctantly, Rachel visited Doctor MacEwan. He confirmed her suspicions and advised her to take more rest.

'Rest! Doctor there's no time to rest with the young men away at the war.'

'I thought you had one of those machines for milking cows now at Lochandee?'

'We do, but someone still has to put the machines on and off the cows and empty the buckets and carry the milk to the dairy. Besides there are so many other things to do besides the milking. The turnip hoeing will be starting soon and the sheep are ready to be sheared . . .'

'And then it will be hay time, corn harvest, potatoes. I know, I know! There's little time between farming seasons. But for the sake of your health, especially at your age, you must try to rest. How is Mrs Beattie?'

'Not very well. Her lips are so blue. Some days it's quite alarming.'

'She knows her heart is not so good. She does not fear death. She seems more concerned for the future of The Glens of Lochandee, since young Conan went away.'

'Yes,' Rachel sighed. 'We try to reassure her. Bridie loves Lochandee as much as anyone. She pesters me to let her leave school and work as a land girl.'

'Well if your own health is at stake you might be wise to consider her suggestion. Alternatively there's a rumour that prisoners of war are to be billeted near Lockerbie. Some of them are German and Italian men who have been resident in Britain. I believe they are to be allocated to farms under supervision. I should think you have enough land to qualify for extra help. Ask your husband to consider it.'

'I will,' Rachel nodded thoughtfully.

'By the way, Mrs Maxwell, my wife is hoping to get a little concert organised for the winter. Just an effort to bring some cheer to the village, you understand.'

'Well, we could all do with that I suppose, but it will be hard to think of Christmas for families where the head of the house is away. It must be terrible for those who have lost their husbands . . .' And sons, Rachel added silently, thinking of Conan, praying he was safe, as she did a hundred times a day.

'Yes indeed. If the concert raises any money my wife thought it might be used to buy gifts for the children in the parish who have lost their fathers. We have four families already. We wondered if your husband would play the fiddle. My wife's hoping to persuade Bridie to sing. She has a delightful voice. I have admired it often in church.'

'Why, thank you, Doctor MacEwan.' Rachel flushed with pride. 'I'm sure Ross will help. I shall leave it to Mrs MacEwan to persuade Bridie though. She has never sung in public.'

* * *

As the weeks turned to months Rachel's nausea never completely cleared as she had expected it would. She felt her cravings always seemed to be for the things which were rationed or unobtainable. Beth, on the other hand, blossomed with good health and happiness. Rachel was delighted for her, but her condition meant she too would be unable to carry out the heavier work. So Bridie got her wish to finish school at the end of the summer term.

Alice Beattie took Bridie's hand between her own two wrinkled ones and smiled warmly.

'I'm glad you're coming home to The Glens of Lochandee — just as I did, Bridie. I know how much you love it, lassie. You'll not regret it.' A few days later she wrote a letter to her lawyer, adding a codicil to her will.

* * *

Conan had made two short visits home but at the beginning of November he wrote to ask if the rations would stretch to three of his fellow airmen.

Mark comes from Derbyshire. He is a pilot but he was studying Accountancy at university. Recently his twin brother died when his plane was shot down over the Channel. George is from London. Their house was bombed and both of his parents were killed. If you can feed us all I'm sure a brief spell in our peaceful glens would help them.

You already know about Nick, the friend I mentioned when I wrote to Beth. He is a flight engineer, like me now. We trained together and if we both come through this awful war, we have vowed to set up a garage. We shall have to start small but someday I plan to have buses and take people for holidays. Can you believe that some of the lads have never seen a newborn lamb, or a sprig of heather, or heard the cuckoo call?

Now I must end because it's time for tea. Sunday tea is the best meal of the week — a thick slice of cold ham with pickles, and bread with a scraping of butter. At least we can see what it is we are eating. They don't mix it up with other things on Sundays.

There were a few more lines hoping they were all well, but Rachel's heart sank. She knew by Ross's silence that he had received a blow when Conan mentioned his dream of setting up in a garage. She guessed he had never given up hope that he would return home and take over the farm. Strangely, Alice seemed quite serene and untroubled by Conan's plans for the future.

* * *

After two postponements, Conan finally confirmed that he and his friends were to get three days leave at the beginning of December. Harry Mason and two other men from the parish were also on leave for the Saturday and Sunday. Mrs MacEwan promptly decided the concert should be brought forward by one week for the benefit of the young servicemen.

A hectic week of practices and hasty dress rehearsals ensued. No one believed the concert would be ready in time, but young women and old men joined together to put up the makeshift stage in the village hall. The two schoolteachers had drilled their pupils in a short sketch and begged or borrowed blackout materials and old clothes to improvise costumes. There was to be a clown but his identity had been kept a strict secret. It did not occur to any of the villagers that it might be a woman dressed as a clown — least of all the minister's wife.

'We'll show that man Hitler that all the rationing and clothing coupons in the world will not crush the spirit of the folks of Lochandee village,' Mrs MacEwan declared after the final dress rehearsal.

Bridie was dreadfully nervous. The arrival of Conan and his friends made her feel even worse, they all looked so handsome in their uniforms.

'Ah, so quiet it is,' Nick Jones reflected dreamily, staring up at the starry sky. 'It is my own Welsh valley it brings to my thoughts tonight.'

'But more beautiful, of course,' Conan teased and received a playful thump on the shoulder. The other two airmen were quiet. George Green was a city dweller. He had never known such peace.

'Have you ever heard of silence keeping you awake?' he ventured. 'I know it must sound strange, but I couldn't get to sleep last night. I thought I must have died and gone to heaven.'

* * *

There was no drone of aircraft, no sirens, no drunken airmen, no clash of morning milk bottles — nothing!'

'Peace.' Mark nodded. He was missing his brother dreadfully. He could have done with half a lifetime, here in the gentle glens. Bobby would have loved it too. The two of them had spent most of their school holidays roaming the Derbyshire moors. Once they had gone to some caves with a party of older men but neither of them had liked being underground.

* * *

There was no doubting the warmth of the welcome for all of them when they arrived at the village hall. An elderly woman with a hooded torch showed them the way up the uneven path, ushering them swiftly into the dimly lit hall with its heavily shuttered windows. Rows of wooden forms had been set out facing the small stage.

Conan and his friends joined Harry and the other two men in uniform. By mutual consent they preferred to forget about the war, for one evening at least.

Bridie felt her voice would never carry to the back where the uniformed group had gathered. Her throat and mouth felt like sandpaper, dry with nerves. Her first song was "Somewhere Over the Rainbow" and it was an ordeal Bridie felt she would never forget as long as she lived. Amazingly there was a spontaneous burst of applause. Then from the back of the hall came the very Welsh voice,

'Wonderful! Even the girls in our valleys cannot sing better!'

Bridie doubted if he was speaking the truth but she sent a silent prayer of thanks for Nick's boost to her confidence. She sang the "Isle of Capri" with almost as much gusto as Gracie Fields herself.

Ross had selected his own music with some care. The minister's wife was to accompany him on the piano and they had managed a few practices. He avoided the jigs and reels since there was no room for dancing tonight. The audience seemed to enjoy participating and there were several requests until the minister had to stand up and remind the audience there was still a second half of the concert to follow.

'Maybe we shall persuade Mr Maxwell and his daughter to give us a concert every month since they are so popular.' He beamed when this was greeted with loud cheers of approval. Rachel, sitting near the back with Beth, felt her cheeks glow with pride.

Mrs MacEwan had planned the program specially to have Bridie as the finale in the second half. Ross too had chosen quieter, more nostalgic lullabies. But it was Bridie's clear young voice which brought a lump to many throats as she sang 'We'll Meet Again.'

'She sings that so — so beautifully,' Beth whispered huskily, her mind on Harry. She hated saying goodbye.

'She has her father's ear for music,' Rachel nodded proudly.

But it was the pure sweet notes of "Home Sweet Home" which caused more than one tear to fall.

Then spontaneously the young airmen were drawn forward by the rest of the audience as they all clasped hands for a rousing chorus of Auld Lang Syne.

* * *

All too soon it was morning again and time for Conan and his friends to leave The Glens of Lochandee. They were sincere in their praise of Scottish hospitality in spite of the rationing.

'I hope you will all come back to see us,' Rachel told them warmly. 'You will be very welcome, even if Conan is not free to come with you.'

'It is kind you are!' Nick Jones exclaimed in his lilting voice. His eyes moved to Bridie, 'I shall be accepting for sure.' He smiled and kissed Bridie on both cheeks. 'Will you write to me?' he asked.

'And to me?' George and Mark echoed in unison.

'It's true we all love getting letters,' Conan nodded at her.

'Aah Conan is boasting to us always about the long letters you write to him, telling him about your lovely Glens of Lochandee,' Nick said.

'Well he's not very good at writing back!' Bridie exclaimed. 'I didn't even know you appreciated my efforts, big brother.'

'Oh, I do, indeed I do, Bridie.' Conan sounded more serious than she had ever heard him. 'You'll be sure to tell me as soon as . . .' he looked to where his mother was talking to Mark. 'As soon as I get a wee brother or sister, and that Mother is all right? Who would ever have thought . . . ?' He raised his eyebrows. Bridie grinned at him.

'I think it's wonderful! They must be still in love after all these years.'

'Och, you old romantic!' Conan teased.

'And what is being wrong with good old romance?' Nick winked at Bridie, bringing a blush to her rosy cheeks. 'It makes me feel I could be killing old Jerry with my two bare hands for the sake of your lovely sister, and her friends of course.'

'Oh of course,' Conan mocked. 'You need to watch old Nick, Bridie. But Mother and Father are not the only ones. I believe Harry is thrilled to pieces because he is going to be a father?'

'I know,' Bridie smiled. 'I'm glad for them. Beth has wanted a baby of her own for ages. She told me.'

All too soon the chatter had to end. Goodbyes were said.

'You're a lucky fellow, Conan,' Nick Jones sighed wistfully. 'I don't think I could have torn myself away from all that — not when you had a good enough reason to stay — family and friends, the valleys and lakes . . .'

'Glens and lochs,' Conan grinned, 'at least that's what we call them in Scotland.'

'Whatever you call them, it's beautiful countryside, warm-hearted people — and a lovely sister.'

'I reckon it's a good job we are taking this philanderer away with us,' George teased.

'I'm glad you asked me to come with you, Conan,' Mark said quietly. 'Thanks.'

'We are pleased you agreed to come.'

'Your mother told me you had another sister?'

'Yes. She died when she was young, but I don't think Mother ever forgets.'

'No. Yet life goes on.' He sighed. 'Yes, I'm very glad I came.'

* * *

Christmas was a subdued affair everywhere in spite of the extra rations of four ounces of sugar and two ounces of tea. Women had done their best to save up coupons and improvise as much as they could, but everyone was aware of the serious threat of invasion and the devastation and suffering caused by the bombs.

Rachel was far from well. Doctor MacEwan warned her to rest her swollen legs as much as possible. There was still no word of the prisoners of war coming out to help. Beth only went home at weekends now to save the bicycle ride from the village. She had kept in remarkably good health and still helped Bridie with the milking and the hens. Ross forbade her to attempt any of the heavier tasks.

* * *

At the end of January they were all taken by surprise when Rachel announced in the middle of the Monday morning washing,

'I think the baby is coming! It isn't due for at least another three weeks by my reckoning . . .' She broke off, with a gasp, doubling up as pain enveloped her.

'Get your father, Bridie!' Beth called in panic. 'Bed . . . you must go to bed . . .'

* * *

Doctor MacEwan arrived in person in response to Ross's garbled telephone call.

'Mrs Warner, the new midwife, is on her way.'

Three hours later Doctor MacEwan informed Ross that he had another son.

'He's a mite early, and a bit on the small side — just over five pounds. But with careful nursing and plenty of warmth, he should survive. The midwife thinks he will be a bit slow to feed at first. I leave these things to the womenfolk. They have more experience about such matters than we men.'

'But Rachel? My wife, is she all right? Can I see her now?' Ross demanded tensely.

'You'll be able to see her shortly. To tell the truth I think it's for the best that the baby is as impatient as his father . . .' He quirked his bushy eyebrows humorously, but Ross was too anxious about Rachel to notice. 'I'm serious, Mr Maxwell. It is fortunate the baby is early. Another month and your wife's health could have suffered badly. You will have to give her time and be patient. Your son will need some extra care.'

'He's so small!' Rachel lamented tearfully the following day. 'Do you think we should ask the minister to come and christen him?'

'Doctor MacEwan seemed to think he would be all right,' Ross tried to reassure her. He was far more concerned for her own health in spite of her protestations that she was fine. He consulted the midwife, a homely little woman called Amy Warner.

'I'm well pleased with your son, Mr Maxwell. He is feeding better than I expected. But, if it would put your wife's mind at rest, I see no harm in asking the minister to christen the wee fellow. Have you chosen a name yet?'

'Name? Why no, we have not discussed that.'

'Well,' Amy chuckled, 'You had better go and talk with Mrs Maxwell first then. Don't worry if she's a bit tearful. It was a short labour but not an easy one.'

Rachel decided they should ask Alice to choose the baby's name. Alice was overwhelmed.

'What about calling him Ewan — after the doctor? He's a good man. Ewan Alistair perhaps? My own name was McAllister. Would you consider that?'

Rachel and Ross approved her choice. When he was three days old Rachel was allowed downstairs to Alice's room for half an hour. There the minister blessed them all and carried out the christening of Ewan Alistair Maxwell. Bridie was his godmother and she could not have been more proud of him if she had created him herself.

It was over three weeks later before Beth's baby was born. It was a prolonged and difficult labour.

'It would have been better if the wee mite had come when it was due,' Doctor MacEwan muttered exhaustedly. Amy Warner felt the baby was far too big for Beth's small frame. She had realised from the beginning she was going to have problems. She had sent a note across to the Doctor's house to warn him, but it was the following evening before his help was required. He gave Beth chloroform while he used forceps to help her baby into the world.

When Beth saw the tiny face with its purple wounds and the misshapen head she wept bitterly. Amy Warner tried to reassure her that the marks would fade and the little girl would grow up as pretty as her mother but Beth would not be consoled. She longed for Harry — and yet she did not want him to know what a mess she had made of their longed for child.

In the end it was Bridie, with all the wisdom and tact of a woman twice her age who wrote to Harry. She had asked Amy Warner to tell her the truth.

'I am telling the truth lassie,' Amy Warner assured her in all sincerity. 'I've seen babies much worse injured than this wee mite. Doctor MacEwan is a patient man and he has a lot of skill. In three months you will scarcely know the baby had such a difficult passage into the world. If I were you I would just tell the father he has a fine baby girl or he'll imagine all manner of things and he'll worry needlessly. Tell him his wife will write as soon as she has regained her strength, but she wanted him to know straight away.'

Bridie nodded and wrote Harry the nicest letter of congratulations she could think of. Although she was unaware of it she had a delightful way with words. Harry carried her letter next to his heart until it fell to shreds.

'You've made me the happiest man on earth, even with all the problems of army life,' he wrote in a short letter of acknowledgement. 'I'm longing to be back home with Beth. I can't thank you enough, Bridie.'

Lucy was six weeks old when Harry first saw her on a fleeting forty-eight hour visit. He thought she was perfect. When he understood the reason for her tiny head still being a little lopsided his concern was all for Beth.

'I do believe she's going to look like my mother,' he said happily. 'At least she has the same colour eyes — a sort of bluish green.'

'I think all baby's eyes are blue at first,' Beth said uncertainly.

'I don't know and I don't care.' Harry chuckled, watching the rosebud mouth searching for food. 'I think she's just wonderful and so are you. I've got the two best girls in all the world.'

After his visit Beth's health and spirits improved rapidly. She had been unaware of having any apprehension or depression, but suddenly a weight seemed to have lifted. She would do everything in her power to make things work out for her little family. She wished with all her heart that Harry had been Lucy's real father, but she had no regrets about her daughter's birth when she saw the happiness on Harry's face as he cradled her in his arms.

* * *

It was the middle of April and spring was in the air. Bridie loved all the seasons and everything about her life at Lochandee. She loved writing letters and keeping her diary. She loved reading too, but she had no regrets about leaving school to spend her time on the farm. Each evening before Alice settled for the night she looked forward to hearing Bridie's lively account of the happenings of the day. Sometimes it would be an unexpected brood of chicks, a new calf or a stubborn ewe.

On this particular evening Bridie had helped three tiny lambs into the world and they were all alive and well. She was bursting with pride and satisfaction.

'Father says I'm better at helping the ewes to lamb than he is because my hands are smaller, especially now that I'm getting to know how to deal with all the little complications.' Alice smiled fondly at the sparkling eyes and glowing skin. She leaned forward and took Bridie's hand in hers.

'I know now I need not worry about the future of The Glens of Lochandee, Bridie. It will be as safe in your hands as it ever was in mine. I'm truly thankful.' She smiled serenely and her eyelids drooped.

'I will leave you to rest now,' Bridie murmured softly.

'Goodnight, my dear . . .'

A little smile curved Alice's lips as she thought of other springs, of lambs at play, of sunshine and showers in her beloved Glens of Lochandee. With a sigh of contentment she closed her eyes for the last time.

CHAPTER THIRTY-ONE

Ross and Rachel knew they had lost one of the best friends they would ever have in Alice Beattie. She had possessed a rare combination of wisdom and compassion. Her quiet dignity had earned respect from almost all who knew her.

Her death was the first real loss Bridie had experienced and her heart was filled with genuine sorrow. Conan's friend, George Green, had been killed soon after his visit to Lochandee and Bridie had been shocked at the thought of a young life cut cruelly short, but she had not known George well. He had not been a daily part of her life since the day she was born, as Alice had.

She continued to exchange letters with Conan and his two remaining friends but it was Mark who seemed to understand how much she missed Alice Beattie, perhaps because he had suffered an even greater loss with the death of his twin brother. His letters were sensitive and kind. Nick apologised for his inadequacy as a letter writer and Bridie understood he did not find it easy to put his sympathy into words.

'Bridie seems to have grown into a woman so quickly,' Rachel sighed. Ross agreed, but he was proud of Bridie and the knowledge she was acquiring about the running of The Glens of Lochandee.

'We are living in troubled times. Death seems to be all around us, but Bridie will cope. She has your spirit, Rachel. I remember your dignity and courage at your father's funeral, and I knew how close you had been to each other.'

'We all learn from life's experiences I suppose, but I must admit I have missed Alice even more than I expected. She was more than a friend to us.'

'So have I.' Then Ross smiled remembering fondly. 'Even at the end she left me good advice in her letter. She wanted to explain why she had left her share of the land and stock to Bridie.'

'Yes, that was a surprise. She left me quite a nice little nest egg, as well as her jewellery and other treasures. I certainly didn't expect anything. I suppose we can't blame her Canadian cousins for being so angry and trying to contest her will. It was kind of old Mr Niven to come and tell us how much she had appreciated our help and friendship. I know he was her solicitor but I would have hated him to think we had only cared for her to get her money.'

'He said she would have had neither money nor home if she had depended on her cousins.' Ross looked serious. 'It was a nasty letter they wrote. Perhaps Alice expected something like that when she instructed Mr Niven to deal with them. I doubt if I shall be able to follow all her advice though.'

'I expect you will. I think she knew all of us better than we knew ourselves. She was right about you.' Rachel chuckled, giving him a playful punch. 'You are ambitious, and you do think women cannot make decisions as well as men.'

'I wasn't aware of feeling that way. I thought I was protecting and caring for my women.' Ross put on a pretence of hurt.

'Of course you do care for us,' Rachel gave him an affectionate hug. 'It's just sometimes you forget we have minds of our own?'

'O-oh no!' Ross chuckled. 'I'm never allowed to forget that! I was pleased to know Alice had faith in me though.'

'Her faith was justified. We are making better progress at paying off the loan than we ever expected. Prices may not be high but at least we know we can sell everything we produce during this hateful war. Are you going to buy a tractor to do the ploughing, or were you just teasing Bill Carr?'

'I'm seriously considering it.' Ross chewed his lip thoughtfully. 'The Government are demanding that we plough more and more land to grow corn. I can't see how we can manage to get enough acres cultivated without more men and horses, and neither are available. Then there is the sowing and the harvest. Conan thinks he can teach Bridie to drive the tractor.'

'If he can get enough leave,' Rachel reminded him. 'Nick and Mark have promised to spend their next leave here too. They are all eager to help if they can.'

* * *

As it happened, it was only Nick who managed to spend a precious week of his leave with them, and that was only because he had been slightly injured. None of them discussed their work. It was strictly forbidden in case any information fell into enemy hands.

Rachel knew that Mark and Conan had been due for leave. They nearly always flew together but she couldn't help worrying. She always wondered if they were being sent on a particularly dangerous mission, although she considered they were all dangerous since the reality of war had been brought so close to home. Shortly after Alice's death, a bomb had been dropped on the little town of Gretna. Since then her heart quailed whenever she heard aeroplanes, knowing they were intent on destruction somewhere. In spite of reporting restrictions news filtered through of the devastation of Clydebank as well as other ports and cities.

Nick was no expert at cultivating the land but he understood machines. Amidst a lot of laughter and cheerful banter he and Bridie mastered the art of starting up the new Fordson tractor and manoeuvring it around the farm. Bridie was determined to learn to plough with it. Despite a lot of teasing about her wobbly furrows, she got the soil turned over a great deal faster than Bill Carr could plough with the horses.

In January two members of the War Agricultural Committee came to The Glens of Lochandee. Ross greeted them curtly.

'I know it is your job to inspect the farms and to see whether we can produce more. Well I'm telling you now we are ploughing as much as humanly possible with the labour I have left.'

'We have not come to inspect The Glens of Lochandee, Mr Maxwell,' the tall man explained. He introduced himself as Mr Silverman. 'This is Brigadier Crossley. We are here to ask you to join the Committee. Your name has been proposed by several farmers in the area. Your views and farming practices are well known and respected.'

'Why — why thank you.' Ross was taken aback. He frowned. 'But I am not at all sure I would like to join you, gentlemen. As I see it, inspecting neighbouring farmers, telling them what they must do . . .' He shook his head. 'No, that is not my line.'

'We are only asking you to advise them, Mr Maxwell.'

'It is for the good of the country after all.' The Brigadier lowered his voice and looked around him, even though they were inside the house. 'It is essential to get every ounce of food we can grow if we are to feed our own people. The German U-boats are destroying hundreds of tons of food, even though our ships are travelling in convoy. The situation is far more serious than we would wish the general public to realise.'

'But we are all doing our best,' Ross protested.

'You may be, Mr Maxwell, but not every farmer is. As a matter of fact there is one particular farm we would like you to supervise. It is only a few miles from here, nearer Lockerbie. The owner is an old friend of mine, Brigadier Jamieson. His late wife left him two farms and a large house. He sold one of the farms some time ago but he has about twenty-five acres of park land around his own house, as well as sixty acres of woodland, and the farm of Wester Rullion. The tenants there had one son. He was lost at Dunkirk and they have no heart to carry on. They exist with a few animals in the fields closest to the house. They don't want to leave their home, but they don't want to farm. The Brigadier considers they have made the supreme sacrifice already with the death of their son so he is refusing to evict them.'

'Evict them! I should think not,' Ross exclaimed.

'We don't want that either,' Mr Silverman said mildly, 'but we do need to get every acre of land into full production and it is a good farm going to waste. We hoped you would consider talking to the Forsters at least. If they refuse to move out, then they must let us cultivate the land. The farm is almost two hundred and twenty acres. We could supply a tractor and a driver, as well as some of the other machinery, if you would agree to supervise the work and get the land back into cultivation.'

Ross was silent, considering. He bit his lip.

'If the place needs a lot of attention I should need to leave the running of my own farm to my wife and daughter during my absence. Bridie is only seventeen.'

'Amazing what our women are doing for the war effort. Amazing!' the Brigadier puffed out his chest. Ross guessed he must be in his sixties and wishing he was still commanding his men.

'Give me a few days to consider,' Ross said. 'I will drive over to see the Forsters.'

'Ah yes . . . well we could maybe get you a few extra gallons of petrol to help with the travelling.' Ross knew they were assuming he would take on the job. They regarded it as his duty but he could not contemplate the prospect with any enthusiasm. He knew some farmers felt they had been hounded by the War Ag. as the organisation was called locally.

* * *

Bridie recounted all the events that happened at The Glens of Lochandee and in the village when she wrote to Conan, so the visit from the "War Ag. Men" also had a mention. Conan was a good letter writer himself when he put his mind to it but his letters were short and Bridie sensed he was either very tired or preoccupied with other things.

Nick, on the other hand, always wrote scrappy notes, but Bridie had learned that he really did appreciate her own efforts. She had tried to thank him for giving up his leave to teach her to drive the tractor.

'Just keep writing me letters, Bridie. That's all I ask — at least for now.' He gave her one of his wicked winks. 'You know by now I am not much at writing letters myself, but I really look forward to receiving yours. You give us all a breath of the outside world and remind us what we are fighting for when we get a bit down.'

'I can't imagine you ever getting down in spirits, Nick.'

'I'm afraid I do, sometimes. When a plane has been shot down and you know you've lost a bunch of good mates. Things like that. So you see your letters are refreshing, and appreciated. Don't ever forget that, even if I don't write much in reply.'

'Conan says you are not supposed to write about your work.'

'No. We can't be too careful. It's surprising where the Germans have their spies. Does Mark write to you?'

'Oh yes. He wrote some lovely letters after Aunt Alice died. He really seemed to understand how much I missed her, even though she was not really my aunt, or a proper relation.'

'Mark misses his brother badly. I never had a brother or a sister, so I suppose I don't really understand. Some of Mark's crew think he places less value on his own life now.'

'Conan says he is very brave,' Bridie said uncertainly. 'He thinks he will get a medal when the war is over.'

'Mark is brave all right, but the rest of his crew depend on Conan to be a steadying influence. He's a good flight engineer you know. I know it's not what your father wants him to do, but if we both come through safely we do plan to go ahead and set up a garage.'

'I know.' Bridie was silent for a while, then, 'Where? I mean where would you like to have a garage? Would you want to live in Wales?'

'Not really. I've nothing to keep me there now.'

'But your mother?'

'My parents married when they were young. They were childhood sweethearts, I suppose you would say. They had resigned themselves to being childless and I suspect they were happy and complete just the two of them. Then I came along when my mother was forty-one.'

'That must have been a surprise.'

'More of a shock I think.' Nick gave a wry grimace. Underneath the usual banter Bridie thought she detected a little sadness.

'Conan told us your father died last year.'

'Yes, he had a small engineering business but everything had been turned over to the war effort and I suspect he was working too hard. My mother missed him dreadfully. She — she died three weeks later.'

'Oh Nick! I'm so sorry. Conan never told me that.'

'He didn't know. I-she just went out one night — walking. It was very wet. They often walked by the river — my mother and father — it was their favourite place. I don't know whether she slipped or — or whether she went in. She drowned anyway.' He swallowed hard. 'I don't know why I'm telling you all this, Bridie. I've never told anyone else.'

'Then I'm honoured, and I'm glad you did tell me. We all need friends to share our troubles.'

'And you're a real pal, Bridie. I appreciate it.' He gave her a warm hug and kissed her cheek. After that Bridie made a real effort when she was writing to Nick. She realised he found it easier to talk than to write.

* * *

Rachel understood why Ross did not relish the prospect of visiting the Forsters.

'I'll come with you and wait in the car, if you like?' she offered. She was secretly afraid they might attack Ross with a pitchfork, or even a rifle, if they resented his interference.

The farm steading at Wester Rullion was muddy and neglected with broken hinges on doors, slates sliding off the roof, walls crumbling for want of repair, manure piled high in one of the stockyards. She watched as Ross knocked at the door with its peeling paint. It was opened a crack and a woman peered out. Rachel watched intently as he tried to explain his business but a tap on the car window distracted her attention. She wound it down to speak to the elderly man.

'Are ye lost?' he asked.

'Er . . . no, I don't think so. My — my husband wanted to speak to a Mr Forster . . . ?' She looked over towards the house.

'That's me then. What does he want? We don't have visitors. Not since . . .' He frowned fiercely. 'Not since our laddie went.'

'My son is in the forces,' Rachel said gently. 'Every morning and every night I pray he is still safe. War is an awful thing.'

The man looked at her keenly. 'Aye,' he muttered gruffly. 'Aye. Ye'd better come wi' me then.' He led her towards the house and introduced her to his wife. Seeing her husband, and another woman, seemed to reassure Mrs Forster and she opened the door wider and bid them enter. There were photographs everywhere of their son in all stages of his life from a little boy in frocks to a handsome young man in army uniform.

'I'm glad you came too,' Ross said afterwards. 'I got the feeling they were almost pleased to see us, but they would never have welcomed me on my own.'

'I think it helped when they knew we understood about their son.' Rachel sighed. 'It must be awful . . .'

'Don't think about it,' Ross said softly and patted her hands where they lay clenched tightly in her lap. 'Conan will come back safely, I'm sure he will.'

'Will you be very angry if he doesn't want to farm The Glens of Lochandee, Ross?'

'Not any more. I shall just be thankful when the war is over and he's back safely, whatever he decides to do with the rest of his life.'

'I'm glad, especially when we have Bridie and Ewan as well.'

'We're very lucky. We still have each other.' Ross gave her a sideways smile. He's still as attractive as ever, she thought with a lift of her heart.

'Bridie is amazing. I never believed a girl could tackle the work she does. Even Sandy admits she's better at ploughing with the tractor than any of us, now she has learned how to handle it. She's certainly better at helping the ewes to lamb and rearing the calves.'

'A-ah!' Rachel laughed merrily. 'You should never underestimate a woman, Ross.'

'No, so it would seem. Mrs MacDonald once said the same thing. She was referring to Alice Beattie.'

* * *

Conan and Nick were spending their leave together at Lochandee in the late summer of 1943. It was harvest time so Bridie persuaded them to help her load the carts with sheaves of corn at Nether Rullion. The Forsters had agreed to most of their land being cultivated on condition Ross took charge. They were content to be left with three small fields closest to the steading, enough to grow a bit of hay and grazing for their three cows, the hens and a couple of sows.

Rachel had packed them a picnic for their midday break and the three of them propped themselves against a pile of sheaves to relax and enjoy the sunshine.

'You know, Conan,' Bridie reflected between mouthfuls of bread and cheese, 'if you still want to have a garage and buses, you should ask Father if he could buy a bit of land from Brigadier Jamieson. The small field at the bottom of this one borders the main road into Lockerbie. It would be an ideal spot for catching passing trade.' Conan looked at her sharply.

'That can't be the main road to Lockerbie, is it?'

'It is. When I am on top of the load of corn I can see vehicles going into the town. A string of those army lorries went up yesterday, and one day when I was here, a convoy of tanks went along.'

'I'll go and take a look as soon as I've eaten this. You coming, Nick?'

'No thanks,' Nick answered drowsily. 'I'm gathering my strength to keep up with this slave-driver you call your sister.' He gave Bridie a teasing glance. Conan shrugged and loped away down the slope. Bridie bunched a fist and aimed it at Nick. He caught it and held it in his hands, gently unfolding each finger in turn. Almost caressing them.

'What neat capable hands you have, Bridie.' He sighed. 'I really do look forward to your letters every week you know.'

'Mmm,' she leaned back against the stooks, her free hand behind her head, her face, with its faint dusting of freckles, raised to the September sun. She gave him a teasing sideways smile. 'Yours are improving a little. I'm beginning to feel I know you quite well.'

'You are?' He seemed pleased as he turned towards her, cradling her hand against his chest as he looked down into her face. Their eyes met, and held. Slowly, his eyes never leaving hers, he bent closer. His lips found hers in a gentle kiss. There was a question in his grey eyes as he raised his head.

'Mmm . . . I liked it,' Bridie murmured ingenuously.

'Oh, Bridie!' he gave a low laugh, his eyes alight. 'Are you always so — so honest and straightforward?'

'Always,' she nodded solemnly, but her blue eyes were sparkling.

'You're precious! Most women flirt outrageously and go all coquettish if a man so much as smiles their way.'

'You've known a lot then?'

'A lot of what?' He looked puzzled.

'Women of course.'

'I don't go around kissing them if that's what you mean — or anything else for that matter.' His voice dropped, 'But, since we are being honest with each other, I confess to liking our first kiss so much I'd quite like another . . . ?' This time the look in his eyes brought the colour to Bridie's cheeks. She was neither experienced nor sophisticated in such matters and her heart beat an excited tattoo. Nick's kiss was a sweet, lingering exploration as he slipped his arm around her, holding her closer.

'What's this then?' Conan's voice startled them. 'Is that why you sent me off to view the road, Bridie Maxwell?'

'No! It is not!' Her cheeks were burning. She wished Conan had not returned so soon, but perhaps it was just as well he had. Nick gave her a deliberate wink then turned to look up at Conan.

'Well?'

'Well what?'

'Did you approve of the site?'

'Not the sight I've just witnessed. I hope you're not taking advantage of my young sister, Nick?' Conan's tone was half joking, but his eyes were serious.

'Conan! It is far too much respect I have for Bridie. You should be knowing I would never take advantage of her.' Nick's Welsh accent was more apparent. Although his voice was low there was anger in it too.

'Yes,' Conan nodded ruefully. 'Yes I do, old boy. But there's not many of the fellows I'd trust with her.'

'Hey, I'm present, you know. And you needn't worry, big brother. I may have led a sheltered existence but I'm not exactly stupid, you know.'

'I do know. Far from it. It's just that I always think of you as just a kid.'

'For goodness sake, Conan, I'm eighteen.'

* * *

All too soon their leave was over and the rest of the harvest seemed to drag on interminably. Normally Bridie enjoyed every season in its turn but there really was far too much to do and not enough labour to do it well. Inside she was restless. Nick's kiss had awakened a tumult of emotions in her — and it was not just his kiss either, nor even the touch of his hands. It was the look in his eyes — full of questions, full of promises too? She was not sure. He had made her feel all of a-tremble inside, and now he had gone. She was filled with a yearning she had never known before.

'I can't wait for this war to be over,' Nick had written in his first letter after he had returned to base. My sentiments exactly, Bridie had echoed silently.

* * *

No amount of wishing could bring the dreadful war to an end. Winter came and spring followed with stricter rationing than ever. Every scrap of iron from garden gates and fences had long since been removed and taken to the factories for making into weapons. Conan came on brief spells of leave, often bringing Nick with him. At the very end of May he arrived very late in the evening, accompanied by Mark instead. Bridie hid her disappointment. She liked Mark, and he still wrote the best letters, but he was not Nick.

'I don't like to see Conan so tense,' Rachel said as she snuggled into Ross's embrace in the big bed. Ewan still slept in his crib in their bedroom. Although he was a sturdy two-year-old he was Rachel's baby and she felt it was safer to have him near when the aeroplanes droned through the night skies. He had boundless energy but he slept soundly and rarely disturbed them.

'It's enough to make any man tense flying into danger so often, never knowing whether you will return, be killed, or be taken prisoner.' Ross held her closer, knowing she needed comfort. There would always be a special bond between her and Conan but he was no longer jealous. Indeed his own heart ached every time he watched his eldest son going back to base. 'He looks so much older than his twenty-two years. Older and far too tired this time.'

'Mark looks even worse I thought. If this war goes on much longer I think he will be heading for a breakdown of some sort.'

'I'm sure you'll see to it that they get some good wholesome food, if nothing else, dear Rachel.' Ross stifled a yawn. There were never enough hours in the day for all he needed to do.

Conan would never admit to his parents that he was finding life a strain but he talked to Bridie.

'There was a rumour going around the base just as we left. Some of the British and Allied airmen are supposed to have made their escape from one of the German prisoner-of-war camps.'

'Could it be more than a rumour?'

'It is supposed to be impossible to escape from the camp they were in. A group of them had made a tunnel — or so the story goes. If they did, it must have taken forever.' He passed a hand over his brow as though the thought of it wearied him. 'A worse rumour is that a number of them were — were shot. Shot in cold blood, so near to being free. God, war is a cruel thing.' Bridie heard the tremor in his voice. She dared not look at him. There were tears in her own eyes and in Conan's too.

'Is there no end in sight?' she asked huskily.

'The generals and politicians keep trying new strategies. We never know where we are going, or what our target will be until just before take-off. It's just as well — it doesn't do to think too much. It's impossible not to sometimes, though, especially when you know there will be innocent women and children dying down below us. This war isn't their fault, any more than young Ewan is to blame. They are ordinary families, human beings, just like us.' There was a break in his voice.

It was the first time Bridie had heard him sound so depressed. Usually he and Nick laughed and joked, and showed only cheerful faces.

'Will you and Nick get any leave to help us with the harvest this year?' she asked, trying to turn Conan's thoughts to brighter things.

'I doubt it. Sometimes all leave is cancelled at short notice when there is a big raid on. Nick needed to make a visit to Wales this time. Something to do with his father's business and the Government taking over the firm now it has to be wound up legally. Nick thinks he will come out of it pretty well financially. His only fear is that he might not survive to enjoy it with the lady of his choice.' He gave Bridie a teasing glance. She shivered at the thought of Nick never coming back, but she couldn't help blushing at the look in Conan's eye. Nick had never made any promises and she could only guess at his feelings.

Over their evening meal it was Rachel who asked if there was no end in sight to war. Conan and Mark exchanged glances and shrugged noncommittally.

'The Germans have a new weapon,' Mark said. 'It's called a doodle-bug. They have no pilots and when the fuel is done they explode. They've done a lot of damage already.'

'The Government are going to erect prefabricated houses for the people who have lost their homes,' Conan said. 'The car factories are supposed to manufacture them in kits and it only takes a few men to put them up.'

Ross could see they were both avoiding talk of their own activities. He encouraged them to tell Rachel about the houses, hoping it would distract her.

'They're steel-built and single-storey but they have two bedrooms and a living room, as well as a bathroom and a lavatory,' Conan said, flashing his father a grateful glance.

'Don't forget the kitchen,' Mark prompted. 'It has a washbasin and a copper as well as a cooking stove and refrigerator, and a small table which folds down to save space.'

'What news have you of Wester Rullion?' Conan asked, changing the subject completely. 'Bridie said the Brigadier wanted you to buy it. Is he still planning to go off to Canada to live with his daughter?'

'He is but we can't afford to buy Nether Rullion while we're still paying the bank loan, though we should clear that debt in a couple of years if the demand for home-grown food continues.'

'I'm sure home-produced food will be needed for years. The war has caused so much devastation everywhere,' Mark said quietly.

'Well the Brigadier has drawn up a seven-year tenancy agreement for us so we've been lucky with that. The Forsters will continue renting their own bit of land and the house so they are content with the arrangement too.'

Conan bit his lip and eyed his father uncertainly. Rachel saw, and read his mind as she often had in the past. She reached over and patted his hand.

'Don't worry Conan. We're not taking the tenancy because we expect you to farm it.'

'Your mother's right,' Ross agreed. 'Just come home safely. As a matter of fact I told the Brigadier you want to build a garage and set yourself up with a bus or two. He is quite willing to sell you the few acres near the main road if you decide it's right for you and Nick.'

'I shall have to earn some money first,' Conan grinned ruefully.

'We're setting aside the legacy Sam Dewar left for you so you will have a bit of capital to start up.'

Conan's eyes lit up.

'That's the best news I've heard in — in . . .'

'Since the war started,' Mark finished for him glumly.

'Yes,' Conan nodded. 'Nick has money from the sale of his father's engineering business so we . . .' He broke off at the sight of Mark's expression. 'I'm sorry, Mark. I shouldn't be going on about my future, not when you've lost . . .'

'Life has to go on,' Mark said quickly. 'I've made up my mind to take a course in making and restoring fine furniture. That's my father's business.' He looked at Rachel. 'It will please him when I tell him I intend to carry on. It has been in the family for three generations already.'

'Then I'm sure your parents will be delighted,' Rachel told him warmly.

* * *

The two young men left Lochandee at dawn on the first of June to travel back to their base.

"The trains were crowded and we missed our connection at Birmingham," Conan wrote. He always let Rachel know they had got back to base safely. Bridie knew it made their mother happy but Conan had confided it was just as well she did not know when they were flying or she would never sleep at all.

* * *

Less than a week later the Allied troops made a surprise landing in France. Rachel prayed this marked the ending of the war and the return of all the men. She hoped in vain.

Although there were reports that Normandy had been liberated, plans were being made to evacuate more children out of London. The Germans had no intention of surrendering and their flying bombs were lethal and came without warning.

In September Conan came home on twenty-four hours leave. He told no one of his orders but Bridie sensed the tension in him and gleaned enough to hope the war would be over if the next operation was successful. She prayed fervently.

Even prayers were to no avail. The Allied soldiers failed to take a vital bridge and many of the paratroopers were taken prisoner. The German forces were putting up strong resistance in spite of reports that the Allies were supposed to be pushing the frontiers further out every day.

"All the men and women in the Lochandee Home Guard, and in Lockerbie too, have been told they can hung up their uniforms," Rachel wrote in her weekly letter. *"Surely the end of the war must be in*

sight now? Will you be home for Christmas? Would Nick like to spend it with us? He will be very welcome."

* * *

The war was not over and neither Conan nor Nick was able to spend Christmas at Glens of Lochandee, but Bridie was not the only one who was disappointed.

'I was really looking forward to Harry being home to play Santa Claus,' Beth told Bridie. 'Lucy is almost three and Harry has missed so much of her young life.'

'At least we know they are still alive,' Bridie tried to comfort her. 'It said on the radio that Colonel Glen Miller and two of his friends are missing somewhere over the Channel. There is no trace of their aeroplane.'

Beth, who never swore, suddenly burst into tears and sobbed.

'This bloody war! It seems to have gone on forever. Why do good men have to die so cruelly?'

Neither Rachel nor Bridie could answer. They both felt more like weeping with her, but for them worse was to follow.

CHAPTER THIRTY-TWO

It was February with the usual dark and dreary weather so Conan's cheerful letter was doubly welcome to them all.

We have just returned from another successful mission. As usual the padre was waiting to greet us with a cup of hot sweet tea and the bottle of brandy in his hand. I swear it is like nectar from the Gods after six hours of . . .

The next two words had been scored out and replaced by "up there" and the letter continued:

It has become a sort of ritual. The padre always asks "with or without?". Even after the most exhausting trip there is always one of the lads who chants "WITHOUT, Padre! Without TEA, if you please."

We are beginning to feel there must be an end in sight. The atmosphere at the base is lighter and more cheerful, though we have no real news to make us feel this way.

The food is no more plentiful though, but we should not grumble. We are privileged. Cookie still manages to scrape up an egg, as well as bacon, for our return meal. I expect you find it difficult to believe eggs are scarce as gold, when your hens run around the yard, trying to hide five or six eggs in strange nooks and crannies. We always swear we can smell the bacon frying as soon as we cross the Channel on the way back.

Of course nothing tastes as good as your cooking, Mother. Nick and I can't wait for the end of all this so that we can get on with building up a business and a garage together.

I am enclosing a letter for Bridie. Give Ewan a hug from me.

Love to you and Father.
Conan.

Only three days later Ross and Rachel received the news which they had dreaded since Conan first left Lochandee to join the RAF. They had dared to think Germany must surrender soon. They had begun to believe Conan would come through the war unscathed. The shock was worse because it was unexpected.

'I don't believe it!' Rachel whispered hoarsely. 'How can he be missing? How can his plane just disappear? How can he . . .' Her voice had risen hysterically. Bridie watched as her father drew her mother tenderly into his arms, holding her close, murmuring, soothing. His own face was white and strained. Bridie crept silently out into the cold February day, unaware that her own face was even whiter than her father's.

'Lord, lassie! What ails ye?' Sandy Kidd asked in alarm as he met her crossing the yard on her way to the calf house. Bridie always sought solace among her beloved animals.

'It's Conan. Father has just had word . . .' She gulped hard on the knot in her throat. 'He has been reported missing. Their plane was seen by one of the other pilots — spiralling out of control. They were behind enemy lines . . .'

'But he might have survived? Surely to God he might have — have . . . ?' Sandy stared at Bridie in dismay. So far both his own sons were safe. But who knew the day or the hour?

It was several days before Ross and Rachel heard more details. The deaths of the pilot, Mark Murray, and another member of the crew had been confirmed. The plane had burst into flames on impact. The official view was that the other members of the crew had possibly been injured, or even killed, before the plane went out of control and had burned with the plane.

This seemed to Rachel to be the worst of all possibilities. Conan's body had not been found, nor even his identity disk. There was nothing left of her beloved son.

She did not weep. She could not accept it. She could not eat. She could not sleep. When Ross did his best to comfort her she turned away. One morning when she was exhausted from lack of sleep she accused him of not caring, of never loving Conan as she had done.

In her heart Rachel knew she was being unreasonable and unfair but she seemed incapable of sensible thought. She railed against the world. She believed the world was against her. She refused to go to church. She could not bring herself to meet, or speak to, the Reverend Simms.

Ross was worried, but he was hurting too. He felt a gulf was opening up between himself and Rachel, a worse gulf than ever before. He began to feel she was blaming him for Conan's death. She was losing weight and had no energy. Ewan clung tearfully to Bridie for consolation, sensing his mother had no interest in him.

Even Beth's sympathy was repulsed. She still had Harry, so why did Conan have to die?

Nick was missing Conan too. They had been friends since they began their training as flight engineers. Bridie longed to see him, to talk with him, to ask him if he had seen Conan's plane go down. She wanted him to hold her close and tell her the world would come right one day. She knew her own letters were stilted and subdued.

"Dearest Bridie," Nick wrote at last.

I long to visit you and your parents. I can offer nothing in the way of comfort, I know that, but I am missing Conan

too. Do you think it would be in order for me to spend a
night at Lochandee?

Conan knew how deeply I care for you. He would not
have wished to keep us apart. He would have wished us to
be happy together.

Please tell me what I must do, for your sake, and for
your parents.

Ever yours. Nick.

Bridie showed the letter to her father. Her face was troubled.

'Do you think it would upset Mother more than ever if Nick came to see us?'

'I don't know, lassie. I really don't know anything anymore.' He drew a weary hand across his brow. There were dark rings beneath his eyes and for the first time Bridie realised how much thinner, how gaunt his face had become. He frowned. 'I don't think anything can make your mother feel much worse than she does already. If only she could grieve and find a release for the tension. She simply cannot accept that Conan is — is dead. Just you tell Nick whatever you think best.'

Bridie consulted Beth.

'It might help your mother if she talked to Nick. I think he's sensitive and caring underneath his banter. Maybe he could tell her things or she might ask him questions. After all, he was one of the last people to see Conan.'

Bridie followed Beth's advice and asked Nick to visit but it was the middle of March before he arrived at The Glens of Lochandee.

Although Bridie had told her mother Nick was coming, she wondered whether the news had registered. Rachel had nodded listlessly and made no comment.

When Nick entered the kitchen in his RAF uniform Rachel stared at him as though he was an apparition. Disconcerted Nick looked back at her. Then to Bridie's and

Ross's amazement Rachel held out her arms and hugged Nick. Her face crumpled and slow tears began to trickle down her cheeks.

'I-I'm so sorry, Nick.' Her voice shook. 'You were a good friend, I know. I-I just can't believe Conan is dead.' She gave a hiccupping sob. 'You must miss him t-too.' She drew away and wiped her cheeks with the back of her hand but the tears would not stop. She looked across the kitchen to Ross, her eyes drowning in tears. He moved to her side and took her his arms, thankful that the healing tears had come at last. She clung to him like a lost and helpless child.

Over her head Bridie met her father's eyes. She nodded. Taking Nick's hand she lead him out of the kitchen.

'At least they have each other,' he said huskily, 'but I'm sorry if the sight of me in uniform has upset your mother even more, Bridie. Do you think it would be better if I stayed in the village tonight? At Beth's maybe?'

'No! No, don't do that. You may have helped Mother more than we know. Besides . . . I need you too, Nick. I've been longing to talk to you.'

He smiled then and for a moment he looked boyish and happy.

'You don't know how much that means to me, Bridie. You are all I have left now. The only person in the world who really matters to me. I have not dared to think about the future since Conan . . .' He frowned. 'I can't say died. He was so vital and full of life and plans. I can't think of him as dead. I suppose I'm like your mother, I need proof before I can believe it.'

'Did — did you see his plane go down?'

'No. Only one member of another crew saw it spiralling out of control. I've questioned them and questioned them until they're sick of me.' He pulled Bridie into his arms and kissed her hungrily. 'I can't help hoping he may have bailed out,' he whispered against her cheek. She leaned back to peer into his face.

'Is that possible?' she asked eagerly.

'It would be cruel to raise false hopes for anyone, — especially your mother, but it is the one hope I have left. They were behind enemy lines when the plane went down. Surely it would be better to be taken prisoner and have some hope of surviving?'

'I-I don't know? I suppose so. Life is very precious.'

'You are more precious to me than life itself,' Nick said seriously. Gently he drew her back into his arms. He kissed her with reverence, but she felt the tension, the passion, in him.

'The war must be over soon. The Russians are closing in on one side and the Allies on the other. All the surrounding countries have declared war on Germany during the past weeks — Turkey, Egypt, Syria and Saudi Arabia. Hitler cannot have many friends left.'

'And yet he hangs on still, people are dying still. War is a dreadful thing.'

'I know, but Bridie, we must all hope for a future — as Conan did. Do you think, when the time is right, your father would speak to the Brigadier's lawyer about the plot of land for the garage? Conan talked about it a lot and that's where we had decided to set up in business. I can afford to buy the site and set up in a small way. I realise it may take some time to get established, especially on my own.' He hesitated, looking down earnestly into Bridie's face. 'Oh God, I love you Bridie.' He hugged her closer and buried his face in her curly hair. I know I've no right to ask you yet when I've nothing to offer a wife, but will you wait for me, Bridie? I will work hard, I promise and . . .'

'Oh, Nick . . .' Bridie's voice was husky. 'I love you. You must know I will wait for you for ever, if that's how long it takes.'

Nick's eyes shone as though a light had been lit behind them.

'Do you really mean it? It will not take for ever — not now that I have such a prize awaiting me.' He bent his head. This time his kiss was full of passion and Bridie revelled at the desire he could not hide.

'It seems wrong to be so happy when Conan is not here,' he whispered against her cheek, 'but I'm sure he would never have begrudged us our happiness.'

'I know . . . he would not.'

* * *

Nick's visit passed all too quickly but he insisted on accompanying them to church before he left, even though it meant missing his Sunday dinner in order to catch his train.

'Then we must make up a food parcel for you to take back, and some sandwiches to eat on the train,' Rachel insisted. 'Bridie will do that, won't you dear?'

'Of course I will.'

Rachel still could not accept Conan's death but there was a new calm about her and for the first time she accompanied them to church. Nick stood close beside Bridie and their voices rose in perfect harmony as they sang the words of the hymn, "Count Your Many Blessings".

'I didn't know you had such a good voice, Nick,' Ross said afterwards. 'You and Bridie are well-matched for a duet.'

'Thank you, sir,' Nick acknowledged but his smile was for Bridie. As they paused outside the church, Bridie and Ross both moved closer to Rachel, instinctively protecting. They need not have worried. The local people were unfailingly kind and welcomed her back with warmth. No one offered sympathy but they told her they were remembering her and her family in their prayers instead.

'Thank you for coming, Nick,' Rachel said sincerely as they parted, 'You have helped me to get things in perspective — well almost,' she added sadly.

* * *

It was the middle of April when the Allied troops liberated the concentration camp of Bergen-Belsen and other prisoners were liberated in the following days, but it soon became clear that the conditions in the camps had been unspeakably cruel. Mr Churchill declared that words could not express the horror.

Bridie shuddered when she read the announcement. Deep in her heart she had clung to the hope that Conan may have survived as a prisoner-of-war, but perhaps it was not a fate to wish on anyone.

* * *

It was nearly midnight on the last Thursday in April when Ross and Rachel were wakened by an insistent knocking on the back door which was just below their bedroom window. The door was never locked and Bill, Sandy or Alfie would have entered and shouted up the stairs.

'Maybe the mare is foaling,' Ross muttered sleepily but she was fine at bedtime. He padded barefoot to the window and pushed up the bottom sash.

'Nick! Is it really you? Were we expecting you?'

'Tell him to go in to the kitchen,' Rachel said. 'I'll get dressed and poke up the fire. I-I can there be anything wrong?'

Bridie heard the commotion but not the cause. She ran downstairs in her nightgown to see what was wrong. She could hardly believe her eyes when she saw Nick bending over the kitchen fire, coaxing it back to life. He turned at the sound of her voice and caught her in his arms, lifting her off her feet. Even in those few seconds he had time to register the pliant softness of her body beneath his hands and he kissed her with longing. When he raised his head it was to see Ross and Rachel standing in the kitchen door regarding them with a mixture of bewilderment and amusement.

'I-I'm sorry. Maybe I should not have come so impulsively,' Nick stammered, 'b-but I think there may be a glimmer of hope for Conan. Just a — a glimmer . . .' he added anxiously.

'But enough to bring you all this way, laddie,' Ross breathed incredulously. 'Tell us whatever you know.'

'Yes, please . . .' Rachel's face was white.

'There has been word from two of the crew who were with him when the plane came down. I don't know the full story yet but apparently they all bailed out except the pilot — that was Mark — and a fellow called Jim Rudd. Conan landed near the other two but he had sprained both ankles — rather badly, they thought. They helped him find shelter in a nearby wood. Conan insisted they should go on without him. He knew he would hold them up. They made their way through the wood and were given refuge in a small farmhouse. They told the occupants where they had left Conan and the owner promised other members of his group would search for him.'

They were given food and a change of clothes and directions. Five days later they were picked up by the Germans. They have just been freed. According to the men who questioned them they think Conan may have been rescued, but he would be unable to travel. His rescuers would be taking a big risk if they gave him shelter, but apparently many of them are just as much heroes as those at the front.' Nick looked from one to the other. 'I-I know it's nothing definite but . . . I just had to come and tell you. I must return tomorrow but . . .'

'Oh Nick, you have brought us hope . . .' Rachel's voice shook and she sank onto a stool as though her legs were too weak to hold her up.

'I-I thought you might be able to make more enquiries through the official channels. I believe some of the remote villages may not get the news of the Allied advances very quickly. And it depends how badly injured Conan was, I suppose.'

'We'll get onto the War Office first thing in the morning,' Ross said. 'We can't thank you enough for coming all this way to tell us, laddie.' Nick smiled and sank onto a chair himself, suddenly realising he was exhausted.

'I'll make some tea and a sandwich as soon as the kettle boils,' Bridie offered, 'but I'd better get dressed first.'

'Yes, dear, you had.' Rachel gave her a tremulous smile. 'I'm sure you will look after Nick. Your bed is already made up, Nick. We keep it ready for you.'

* * *

Rachel's joy knew no bounds when they received official confirmation that Conan was alive and well. A few days later she received a short letter from Conan himself. Then Bridie received a letter from Nick to say he had been granted special leave to accompany Conan back to Glens of Lochandee.

> *If your parents can find enough coupons for petrol we would appreciate being met at the station. Conan still has a painful limp where the ligaments were torn. They were damaged worse when he had to drag himself further into the wood, to avoid being captured. The doctors say he will need some treatment but he should be perfectly fit within a year.*
>
> *He is being demobbed immediately, along with his civvy suit and all of a hundred pounds for his services. Still what is money when a man has nearly lost the most precious gift of all.*
>
> *I can't tell you how much I am looking forward to being a free man again, Bridie, my dearest love.*

* * *

It was the thirteenth of May when Conan sat beside the radio in the familiar kitchen at Glens of Lochandee and listened to Big Ben chiming three o'clock. Then Winston Churchill made the anticipated announcement that there would be peace in Europe from midnight.

Across the white-scrubbed kitchen table Ross and Rachel clasped each other's hands.

'We have so much to be thankful for.' Rachel said with a tremulously smile. 'Peace at last.'

'Well nearly,' Conan said. 'We still have to conquer the Japanese, remember. Nick is not demobbed yet, and neither are Harry Mason and Frank Kidd.'

'It may not be too long,' Nick said with a rueful smile at Bridie. 'Then we can get on with building a garage — and other things . . .'

'Other things being more important no doubt,' Conan grinned. 'Are you two going down to join the celebrations in the village?'

'We are. We mean to make the most of these few precious days, don't we Bridie?'

'We do, and without big brother watching, if we're lucky.' They grinned at Conan. Rachel and Ross looked up contentedly.

'Yes, you two enjoy the dancing and singing. It will be a wild night in Lochandee tonight.'

* * *

Later, in the privacy of their own big bed Rachel snuggled into Ross's arms.

'It's lovely to have Conan safely home again, and to see Nick and Bridie so happy, and Ewan whooping with glee at all the extra attention,' Ross said, 'but I'm glad we are on our own together at last. I do not feel too old to celebrate.'

'Mmm, neither do I,' Rachel chuckled. 'And we have more to celebrate than most. We still have each other, and our family is complete again. We have even managed to pay off the loan. It's wonderful to know The Glens of Lochandee really is our home from now on. We have Nether Rullion to rent and a small son who's determined to be a farmer. Most of all we have good health to work, and peace and security. We are truly blessed. What more could we want . . .'

'Right now I can think of only one thing, my love.' Ross's hand moved gently feeling Rachel's instant response as they came together in perfect harmony.

THE END

THE JOFFE BOOKS STORY

We began in 2014 when Jasper agreed to publish his mum's much-rejected romance novel and it became a bestseller.

Since then we've grown into the largest independent publisher in the UK. We're extremely proud to publish some of the very best writers in the world, including Joy Ellis, Faith Martin, Caro Ramsay, Helen Forrester, Simon Brett and Robert Goddard. Everyone at Joffe Books loves reading and we never forget that it all begins with the magic of an author telling a story.

We are proud to publish talented first-time authors, as well as established writers whose books we love introducing to a new generation of readers.

We have been shortlisted for Independent Publisher of the Year at the British Book Awards three times, in 2020, 2021 and 2022, and for the Diversity and Inclusivity Award at the Independent Publishing Awards in 2022.

We built this company with your help, and we love to hear from you, so please email us about absolutely anything bookish at feedback@joffebooks.com

If you want to receive free books every Friday and hear about all our new releases, join our mailing list: www.joffebooks.com/contact

And when you tell your friends about us, just remember: it's pronounced Joffe as in coffee or toffee!

Made in United States
Troutdale, OR
07/02/2023

10912183R00228